WRITERS REPUBLIC

DELSAR

THE CHAMPION & THE HERO

A.D. Morway

WRITERS REPUBLIC L.L.C.
515 Summit Ave. Unit R1
Union City, NJ 07087, USA

Website: *www.writersrepublic.com*
Hotline: *1-877-656-6838*
Email: *info@writersrepublic.com*

Ordering Information:
Quantity sales. Special discounts are available on quantity purchases by corporations, associations, and others. For details, contact the publisher at the address above.

Library of Congress Control Number:		2021935400
ISBN-13:	978-1-63728-082-9	[Paperback Edition]
	978-1-63728-083-6	[Hardback Edition]
	978-1-63728-084-3	[Digital Edition]

Rev. date: 03/18/21

CHAPTER 1

THE OUTCAST

"There are people in this world that don't know how to truly smile. Promise me you will help them as you have helped me."

Those were Sariah's last words to her son, seven years ago. It was her final request. Delsar vowed to give his all in helping people find happiness. Her words defined him. It was what she said that inspired the life and salvation of so many others. Who knew a simple smile would be such a powerful tool?

"Thank you, Mr. Guard." A very small and very dirty boy hugged Delsar, who had knelt to the boy's height. He had been buried in dirt all night and it was Delsar who had found him. One of the many tunnels little Lloyd had dug collapsed and covered him up to his neck. His parents spent all night looking for him, as did many of the townspeople.

Delsar showed up in town about an hour ago. He was traveling back to the capital after a very successful mission with a few of his colleagues. Many considered using the King's Guard to locate a missing child a waste of their potential, but not Delsar. With the Queen's blessing, he deployed his entire team of twelve to sweep the area in search of the child. It just so happened that it was Delsar who located the boy behind an abandoned barn and dug him out.

Even though the boy was now rescued, he still trembled, unable to find the courage to look into Delsar's eyes.

Delsar wiped the boy's tears away and gave him a gentle smile.

"If you won't smile, who will?" It was a quote he got from his mother, so many years ago.

Little Lloyd finally looked up at him, returning Delsar's smile. This turned Delsar's gentle smile into a huge grin. Seeing someone smile meant he was fulfilling his promise to his mother. Lloyd started to laugh, a tension-releasing giggle of jettisoned anxiety. Delsar couldn't help but laugh with him.

"Over there!" Someone from the town heard the laughter and alerted the others of their location. The man suddenly realized who had found the boy. "The Queen's Champion!" He dropped to one knee and bowed his head.

Delsar stood up next to the boy and approached the man. "That isn't necessary," he told him. "And please, just call me Arviakyss."

After his mother died, Delsar had decided to take on a less generic name. That way, when people heard it, they knew that hope had arrived. He's not just known as the Queen's Champion. Because he always thought of others first, even simple peasants and missing children, he was ofttimes called the People's Champion.

The man stood back up. "It is truly an honor to have you in our town."

"Never mind me. Let's find his parents." Arviakyss was used to people being awestruck by his presence. He never wanted to be popular or venerated, but it happened. He was often told, usually by the other guards, that he was unnecessarily humble, but he did not see it like that. To him, he was doing what was right, like so many others. Why should he get praised more than those who tried as hard as him?

"Lloyd!" It was the boy's mother. She caught a glimpse of them emerging from behind the abandoned barn.

"Mom!" The two of them squeezed each other as if they would never let go.

She turned her head, still resting on his. "Thank you, Arviakyss. What can we ever do to repay you?"

"Please, your smile is all I desire," he replied.

With that, she and her son gave him very thankful smiles, cueing Arviakyss that his job was done.

That was nearly six years ago. One week before the Queen's murder. The murder that the kingdom accuses him of committing. All the smiles that took him years to create have turned into resentment and fear

2

overnight. The love he had formed with the people was replaced with hate. Now everyone calls him the Queen's Murderer. Since he was no longer the Champion he had worked so hard to become, he took back his old name, Delsar, and never went anywhere near the capital now.

The "Outcast" is what he is known as out here. No one knows that this outcast was once the Champion, Arviakyss.

It's better this way. Delsar remembers how the people he cared about, his country, turned on him over a lie. All because it was told louder than the truth. That's all it takes to have your life ruined. What is the point of helping people smile, anyway? Smiling is just a reaction to being happy, and happiness is only temporary. Delsar knows this first-hand.

His time of happiness has already passed him by. Making people happy is a waste of time. Now he only helps those that can afford him and, even then, he makes sure the people he helps aren't happy after.

"But sir, we can't afford that," says the frail mayor. "You said one hundred gold would be enough. We don't have one hundred fifty."

"And you said it was just a simple cave troll. Next time, get your facts straight, and then I won't have to adjust my price." Delsar has his finger pressed against the man's chest.

"Everyone has already given all they have. One hundred fifty is impossible," pleads the mayor.

"That's not my problem. It's yours," Delsar states. "Speaking of problems, it almost looks as if you no longer have any trolls around to ruin your day. Coming up with fifty more gold is definitely the problem I would rather have. Wouldn't you?"

"I'll come up with something." The mayor runs off, looking rather panicked. He runs through the town, trying to come up with fifty more gold. He returns with only twenty-nine more pieces. "This is every coin we have. We have nothing left."

Delsar snatches the pouch from the Mayor. "Fine! I'll take this."

"Oh, thank you, sir," says the mayor. "You are very kind." A hesitant smile appears on his face.

Delsar hates making people smile. Happiness is fake. Just a small distraction to hide you from reality. "I'll be back to collect the rest. Make sure you have it ready for me or I'll have to take something a bit more precious from you as payment." He's probably never going to return for

3

what he's owed, but he's sure just saying that will crush the mayor's joy. He's not here to make people happy. He's here to make money.

"Of course. Anything you need!" The mayor's smile doesn't leave. "We'll have the money waiting for you when you return."

He's still smiling? Whatever. His temporary joy will leave him with disappointment when he gets smacked by reality.

"Newville thanks you!" exclaims the Mayor.

Newville? What a lame name.

"If there is anything else you need, let us know."

"There is one thing," says Delsar. "Do you know where the nearest tavern is?"

"We don't have anything like that built yet," responds the mayor. "Our sister town in the east should have what you are looking for. Eskor is about ten miles down the eastern road."

"Good. I'm leaving now. Bye." Delsar doesn't care if his "goodbyes" seem blunt.

As he turns to leave, the mayor gives him a more formal farewell. "It was an honor to have you defend us. You are a hero to us. Thank you."

Delsar leaves without looking back. His heart floods with sorrow and darkness. *A hero? Really? His money did the saving. That's what the mayor should be thanking.*

#

It was a three-hour walk to the next town. "Welcome to Eskor," the sign reads, a much better name than Newville. The sun is well past the treeline by now, but people still bustle about. Finding a tavern should be relatively easy. All Delsar needs to do is ask someone. That, however, is not how he likes to do things. He'd rather struggle for an hour than have any unnecessary interaction with people.

Rina's Food and Inn. Perhaps not the highest quality tavern in town, but it's the first one he's found. Upon entering, Delsar encounters a very energetic atmosphere. There is a dartboard with players yelling whether they score or not. The waitress is shouting orders despite being feet away from the kitchen. There is even a band performing in the corner, two people, with a small crowd gathered around them. This is the kind of atmosphere he likes to avoid but as long as he's quick about this and avoids any of the tenants, it shouldn't ruin his evening of solitude.

He walks straight to the counter where the barkeeper greets him immediately. "Hello, friend! My name is Pailess. What can I do you for?"

"I just need food and a room," Delsar replies.

"You're in the right place. This is *Rina's Food and Inn*. It's the best place in town!" The barkeeper smiles joyfully but Delsar returns it with a cold stare.

"Just give me today's special."

"Hey, Mungie! One Rina Special!" Pailess shouts over his shoulder. "That's three silver for the room and because you are boarding with us, the meal is only one extra silver."

"Deliver that to my room," instructs Delsar.

"We don't typically deliver the meals to the rooms."

Delsar slides him a gold piece. "Keep the change."

"But because you're our paying customer, we will bring it to you." He waits a moment for some sort of 'thank you' or even just a response but Delsar doesn't give him any. "Right then! Here's your key. Your room will be up the stairs and the third on the right." He hands Delsar the key which he snatches. "What do you want for a drink?"

"Water," says Delsar. Anything with flavor would give Delsar some form of enjoyment. Enjoyment that will only last until the drink is gone. He turns and says nothing else after demanding water as his liquid of choice. The stairs are clearly marked so he walks that way.

"Enjoy your stay," says the overly happy bartender. At least, he's overly happy to Delsar.

Whether it's paranoia or a simple case of muscle memory, Delsar clears his given room with his sword drawn. The dresser on his left and the chair on his right seem fine. No one would be able to conceal themselves behind the desk in the back right. That just leaves the bed to the left of the window. He quickly peeks underneath it before finally sheathing his sword. He removes his bow from his back and unbuckles his belt, which carries his sheath and his quiver, laying them both by the bed. The kite shield, which he wears on his back as armor, he also removes and rests it on his lap as he sits on the bed. He begins inspecting his favorite possession.

During his fight with the troll in Newville, he had taken a club strike from the monster that cracked against his back. He trusts his shield more than anyone or anything else. It is something that will always have his back and never turn from him because of a lie or jealousy. Upon inspection, he spies a bit of caving near the left side, among the previous dents and scratches. This one is definitely new. The straps and integrity of the shield all seem to be okay. Satisfied, he places the shield with his bow and belt.

He pulls off his hooded, black cloak and checks his satchel. Everything seems to be there. He places the satchel next to his pillow, both for safekeeping and the fact that he carries a knife for protection inside. Lifting up his shirt and wincing from pain, he inspects the bruising to his ribs from the troll strike. A couple of his ribs are surely broken. "Good thing I had you," he says to his shield.

Unfortunately for Delsar, there really isn't anything he can do about his broken ribs other than making sure he doesn't sleep on his left side, tonight. This is nothing new for him. He'd broken his ribs several times before. The only other bones he had broken had been in his hand.

There is a knock on his door. Delsar grabs his shield and holds it up to the bridge of his nose, covering his body down to his midthighs. He walks over to the door and opens it a crack.

"I've got your food, sweetie," says the waitress, holding a tray with a plate and a glass.

That was fast. Delsar wasn't expecting the food for at least another few minutes. He opens the door and peeks around the corner before placing his shield down by the door.

"It's just me," she intones.

Delsar grabs the food from her and flips her a gold coin.

"What's this for?"

"For not bothering me the rest of my stay." Blunt, sure, but blunt is what he likes.

"Speaking of not wanting to be disturbed, there is a young woman downstairs looking for you."

Delsar rolls his eyes, purposely sharing his annoyance with the waitress.

"She said she's been looking for you for quite a while," says the waitress, completely ignoring Delsar's annoyance. "You are the Outcast, right?"

"So what if I am?"

"Well, she's looking for you." Now it is the waitress who seems annoyed. "Pailess recognized you, so I know that you are."

"Then what does she want?"

"She told Pailess that she needs to talk to you."

Delsar lets out an exasperated sigh.

"I'll tell her you're not available," she says.

"No, it's fine. It's probably some job offer." Delsar grabs his shield with one hand and flips it over his back. He places his tray on his bed and straps his belt around his waist. "Let's go," he says to the waitress. "Take me to her."

She ushers him through the hall and down the stairs. "I'm Brianna, by the way."

Delsar doesn't respond because he doesn't care. He can tell that his silence is bothering her.

"There she is, in the corner." She points at someone sitting alone. She looks more like a girl than a young woman.

He approaches the table but stays a few feet back, studying for any possible threat. He scans her up and down. Delsar is only twenty-two, so most people he gets hired by are older than him. However, he's sure she's only seventeen or eighteen. You'd be forgiven for mistaking her hair for brown in bad lighting; however, in the chandelier light, it definitely looks mahogany or a rusty red. She wears a frilled, pink top with a drawstring at its crest and a long, checkered-brown skirt with leather boots to finish her look. All of which are ragged and in serious need of washing.

"I can see you," she says. "You may as well just sit down."

Delsar is pretty sure she isn't a threat. "Very well." He slides into the bench across from her and is just about to get into business.

"My name is Elidria," she says, stopping Delsar from starting the conversation. "But you may call me Eldra. Pretty much everyone does."

Delsar holds up his hand. "I don't care about your nicknames. If you have a job for me, spill it. And know this, I am very expensive."

Elidria scowls a moment but then continues. "I come from a small village in the west called Bihnor. It's right on the coast. A group of mercenaries invaded us and just started shooting everyone. Innocent people. My friends and my family." She tapers off a bit, definitely thinking about it.

"A random group of mercenaries randomly decide to attack a random village that most people have probably never heard of?"

Elidria snaps back from her memories. "I guess so. I don't know why they came."

"This is a job for the Guard, not me."

"But that's just it. They got ordered away just a week before the attack and now they won't return. I've told some, but no one believes me."

"No kidding. Who would be stupid enough to have the Guard removed from our borders? As far as I'm concerned, no one would."

"But someone did, and now I think everyone I know might be dead." She gives him a very sincere look. "Please, Delsar, I need your help."

"Revenge?" he asks.

"To rescue anyone who might still be alive. Please," she says again, looking as if she will break into tears at any moment.

"No." It was like a jab in the stomach.

"But—" she starts.

"I said no. Your story seems a bit crazy, and if it is true, there's no way I can stop a group of mercenaries on my own. This is not the kind of thing I do. If a half-dragon starts terrorizing your neighborhood, you come back and you let me know."

"I plan to fight, too," Elidria states with a very serious face.

Delsar scoffs. "You? Really?"

"And what's wrong with that? It's my home."

"You're too small and frankly, too young."

Elidria stands up and slams her hands on the table. "I'm almost twenty and I heard that you always used your wits and speed to defeat your foes!" Elidria brings her hands to her mouth, realizing immediately the mistake she made.

Delsar thought she was referring to the Outcast until she reacted the way she did. That's when he realized she meant Arviakyss. He exits the booth and grabs her wrist. "Come with me," he says without giving her an option.

"Wait!" she demands, pulling against him, though she can't break free. "Where are you taking me?"

"Don't speak," he instructs without looking back. He guides and pushes her into his room, slamming the door behind them. "Who sent you?" he demands.

Elidria straightens her sleeve as she answers. "My father did."

"And who is your father?"

"Aldameer." She looks directly at Delsar. "Listen, you can't just grab people and drag them around like that."

Delsar doesn't acknowledge her second statement. "And how do you know who I am?"

"My village specializes in making dyes for paints and clothing. Specifically, the color blue. It's one of the perks of living near the ocean."

"I don't care." Delsar gives her a stern look.

"This is all part of how I know."

"No, it's useless information."

"The *Queen*," she emphasizes as she continues, "always ordered the dyes from us. My father hand-delivered them to her. He used to see you with her. So he must have seen you recently and recognized you."

"He must have?"

"Well, he didn't tell me how he knew. He just told me."

"And you trust your father?"

"Of course I do. Don't you trust yours?"

"I don't trust anyone, especially you right now," he says, poking his finger into her collar.

She pushes it away. "Well, that's stupid. Everyone needs someone they can trust."

Delsar begins grabbing the rest of his stuff and securing it. Elidria watches him but says nothing. As he walks past her, towards his door, he stops. "Who else knows who I am?"

"Does it even matter what I say? You don't trust me, remember?" She crosses her arms and he shakes his head as he walks on. She watches him leave the room and disappear down the hall. "Wait!" she shouts running after him. She catches up to him on the stairs and taps his arm. He gives her no mind and continues down. "I love my village and my family," she tells him. "I will do whatever I can to save them. Right now I know that means recruiting you. If I fail, they will all die! Don't you have anyone you love?"

"Buzz off!" Delsar spins around and pushes her down. She hits the floor in a sitting position, hard enough to jar her, but not hard enough to bruise any bones. Most would be embarrassed by all the turned eyes suddenly judging them, but Delsar doesn't care. "I don't know who you are or even how you managed to track me. What I do know is that when I leave this bar, you will never find me again. I invite you to try," he says, pointing his finger directly at her.

Tears begin to drip down Elidria's face as she sits on the floor. "Do you not care about the innocent? They have done nothing wrong!"

Delsar turns away and starts walking for the exit. "No one cares who's innocent and who's not anymore. I don't need you and I don't need your *job*."

Someone grabs Delsar by the shoulder, but Delsar quickly puts the man into a wrist lock and brings him to a knee. "Don't touch me," he says to the aghast man before pushing him away.

"I care," Elidria says, standing back up. "I care for both."

"And you'll die caring!" Delsar pushes through the exit door and bumps into two guards trying to enter. "Sorry troopers. My humblest apologies." Delsar gives a courteous bow and stands aside to let the guards pass.

"Just watch where you're going next time," one guard replies as he walks in.

The other starts to follow but quickly stops after passing Delsar. "Well if it isn't the Queen's Champion? You're under arrest."

"Shame on you for sending a girl by herself," says Delsar, drawing his sword.

The guards look somewhat confused by his comment but don't respond to it. "Don't make this difficult on yourself. Just come peacefully."

"I know about the 'Kill on Sight' order. I think I'll take my chances." The guards are between him and the tavern which means he can make a break for it. The armor a guard wears is heavy. They would never catch him. However, all guards are also equipped with a mini crossbow. He will only need to avoid two shots before he can get away. With his shield on his back, it definitely seems possible.

Time's up. The first guard lunges at him with his sword drawn. Delsar parries the strike and tries to counter with a slash to the guard's shoulder. That attack fails when it gets blocked by the other guard, defending his partner. The King's Guard are supposed to be the best. A two-on-one is going to be difficult with crossbows involved. Typically, Delsar would use his mobility in a situation like this, to get around and isolate. If he tries anything like that, they may just shoot him.

Both guards attack, this time, simultaneously. One strike is again about shoulder height while the other comes low and from the opposite direction. Delsar turns his back towards the higher attack, placing all his faith in his shield, while also stabbing his sword into the ground. One attack slides off his shield while the other clashes with his sword. The instant both swords connect, Delsar sends his knee into the face of the lower guard, sending him backward.

Realizing he's not getting through the shield, the other guard strikes again, this time low. Delsar jumps around his sword, again letting the blades clash, before stepping on the guard's hilt, pinning it to the ground, and using his knee, yet again, driving it into the guard's face. Bones crunch and crack this time. Likely not Delsar's knee.

Delsar whips back around to check on the first guard. A crossbow shakes in the guard's hand but it is pointed at Delsar nonetheless. Before he can react, two arms grab for the crossbow, sending the bolt way off target. Elidria struggles with the guard for a moment but is quickly overpowered.

"You brat!" The guard grabs her hair with his other hand and yanks her away from his crossbow.

Elidria shrieks as her neck is wrenched awkwardly.

Delsar reacts immediately. He pulls his sword from the ground and charges the guard. Spinning counterclockwise, he strikes the guard in his side, creating a huge crunch as the armor bends and caves from the impact. The guard cries out in pain from his ribs snapping under the pressure. Delsar quickly silences him, sending the palm of his hand into the guard's face. He hits the same bloodied location his knee struck moments before.

The guard falls flat and doesn't move. Delsar spins around and locates the other guard, also lying on his back, unconscious. Delsar takes a couple deep breaths and faces Elidria. If this really was a trap that she was a part of, why would she foil it? That guard had him dead to rights.

As if she could read his mind, she says, "I'm not your enemy." She holds out her hand which Delsar grabs, pulling her to her feet.

"You know why they want me dead, don't you?" he asks her.

"What people believe doesn't make it true."

"But it doesn't mean it's not," says Delsar.

"My father said you didn't kill the Queen. I believe what he said is true," she tells him.

"Unfortunately for you, what's true really doesn't matter," he says. "People will believe whatever they hear first. They act upon those beliefs. Whether I'm innocent or not, I will always be hated."

"I don't hate you and I don't believe the first thing I hear."

"Well the sheep do and most people are just that."

"You don't need people to believe you to do what's right."

"Just stop." Delsar holds his hand up and then pinches the bridge of his nose. "If you want me, I'm one hundred gold a day and another five hundred on arrival. If I decide it's impossible and I walk, I still get payment for every day prior. If I do complete your suicide mission, it's another one thousand gold. Got it?"

Elidria is taken aback and tries to process what Delsar just said. "Wait, what?"

"I'm taking the job, Elidria. Can you afford me or not?"

"I think so. The Queen would buy our dyes for a high price. Our treasury should have plenty."

"Then are we agreed?" Delsar asks, holding out his hand.

Elidria looks at it. Tears begin running down her cheeks. She nods her head a few times. "Yes," she says, letting out a stress-relieving laugh. "I agree." She takes his hand and shakes it.

"Then come with me." Delsar sheaths his sword and begins walking back towards Newville. "We have to put as much distance as we can between us and this place before those guards wake back up."

"What do you need of me?" she asks him.

"Just do as I say and what's obvious. Anything else is a waste of time."

"Obvious?" Elidria jogs up next to Delsar. "Do you know where you're going?"

"West."

"Even I know that. Do you know how far Bihnor is from here?"

"Nope."

"Four weeks," she says, sticking her finger up.

Delsar stops and looks at her. "Your village was attacked a month ago?"

She brings her finger to her chin. "I think it's been a month."

"Elidria, if by the time we get there is two months after the attack, no one will be left."

"Don't," says Elidria. "Let me worry about that. I'm paying you just to look. That's what you said."

Delsar starts walking westward again. "Newville should have a horse and carriage we can acquire. That will speed things up."

"Call me Eldra," she instructs. "Everyone else does."

"I'm not calling you something unprofessional."

"'Just do what's obvious.' I'm pretty sure that's what you said. Eldra is easier and quicker to say than Elidria. Does it not make sense?"

"That's *not* obvious and I will *not* call you Eldra because we are *not* friends," he says. "The extra syllables will *not* bother me, *nor* will they get me killed."

"Your loss."

They walk for about two hours before Delsar finally decides they are far enough to put up camp. He sets up a fire and then uses two blankets to make a roof and a floor for sleeping. He pulls some dried meat from his satchel and sits on a log by the fire.

"Didn't you already have supper," Elidria asks him, sitting on the other end of the log.

"Your interruption made sure I didn't," he says, annoyed that she is even talking to him.

"You got that fire going pretty quickly."

"Listen," Delsar starts. "If you wish to talk, make it relevant to the mission. I don't want to talk about how quickly I got the fire going."

Elidria huffs but doesn't quite get discouraged. "If I remember, my father said the mercenaries called themselves the Darkened Wanderers."

Delsar coughs, almost choking on the dried meat. "Impossible," he says, spitting bits of food as he speaks.

"How so?"

Delsar swallows properly and explains. "I defeated them almost seven years ago. The Queen sentenced them to life. It can't be them."

"Perhaps I'm mistaken then," she says, shrugging her shoulders. "It was over a month ago and he only said it once. But you know, if they aren't dead, it could still be them."

"So what if it is them?"

"You said you defeated them. That means you can do it again."

"I had a partner and well-trained guards who followed me into battle. You seem to think all those stories about me I did alone."

"We can recruit others then," she says very confidently.

Delsar gives her an annoyed look. "No."

"But you said you always had others."

"I didn't say I couldn't do it. If people you hire find out who I am, it will make things even harder. I will do this alone." He puts his meat away and stands up. "It's time you get to sleep."

"I'm not a kid, Delsar. I don't need you telling me when to go to bed." Out of everything Delsar had said thus far, that seems to be what annoyed her the most.

"Elidria, just do what's asked," says Delsar. "That's how we will get there quickly and how we will survive." Delsar points at the blankets he set up.

Elidria walks over to the structure and inspects it. "This doesn't look big enough for both of us."

"It's not. I watch. You sleep."

"You're going to watch me sleep?" she asks.

"What?" Delsar exclaims. "No. I'm going to keep watch."

She smiles as she lays down. "You really need to lighten up."

"And you need to realize what we are about to get into. Your family and friends are likely all dead and yet you joke with a stranger. Do you not mourn for those you've lost?"

Elidria scowls. Her eyes start to water a bit. "How I mourn is none of your business and believe me when I say that I have already experienced plenty." She wraps the blanket around herself and rolls over.

"Four weeks of this?" says Delsar, under his breath.

"Goodnight, Delsar," she says, hearing what he said. She lays there thinking the same thing. *We need the Queen's Champion, not this jerk. What am I supposed to do with him?* She closes her eyes and lets her tears flow across her face.

CHAPTER 2

THE EMPLOYERS

6 Years Ago...

"Ha! I found another one!"

"You know, it's not even impressive anymore," replies Galia. She and Elidria have been out collecting snails for their dye exports all morning. Or at least, since the tide started to go back out. The two hundred feet of flat terrain is perfect for finding these surprisingly valuable creatures.

"I beg to differ," says Elidria. "I think it is very impressive that we keep finding them. Think about it. The more we find, the less there are."

"I guess, but now I'm just expecting to find more."

Elidria jumps over a tidepool and sits down on a rock in the middle of it. "Dad was supposed to be back days ago."

Galia steps into the tidepool and snatches another snail before sitting down next to her friend. She doesn't need eyes to see that Elidria is anxious. "If I know uncle Aldameer, which I do, he found some nice, old lady that needs help getting home. He's probably helping someone."

She's right. It is something Elidria's father would do. He's probably not doing that exact thing, but she does get the point. "I suppose, but I can't stop worrying about him."

"Are you worried about him, or are you worried about being alone?"

"You don't know what it's like!" Elidria snaps. She covers her mouth with her hands. "I'm so sorry. I didn't mean to."

Galia smiles. "It's all right. Maybe I was being a bit insensitive. I really don't know what you've been through."

"It's no excuse for me to snap at you."

"I'm already over it. If it makes you feel better, I'm sure your dad knows what day it is. That's probably why he's running late," Galia assures.

"Not in the state *he's* in."

Galia rolls her eyes and puts an arm around Elidria. "You know he's trying his best and he loves you more than anything."

"Yeah. I guess I do."

"Then stop worrying." Galia and Elidria have been friends for as long as either of them can remember. Their parents were friends before they were born, so it does make sense that their kids would become friends too. "This haul is plenty," Galia says, looking in her sack. "Let's head back."

Elidria obliges with just a simple nod. She lugs her own sack of snails over her shoulder and hops off the rock. She looks toward the cliff that leads back up to their village. "We didn't even have to go very far today."

"Nope."

The girls begin their very short walk back. Elidria remains very silent, which does concern Galia a bit. They reach the cliff face before Galia finally breaks the silence. "I'll head up and you load the basket."

"But it's my turn to pull it up."

"Don't fret. Either way works for me."

"I know you're trying to think of something to cheer me up," says Elidria.

"So you admit you're down?"

"I'd be lying if I said I wasn't." Elidria shakes her head. "Just climb to the top. I kind of just want to get lost in my thoughts."

Galia places her sack in the basket and begins her climb up the very narrow staircase that was carved up the side of the cliff. She stops and looks back at Elidria. "How about instead of thinking of all the bad reasons your father is late, you think of all the good reasons."

"It's not that easy anymore." Elidria places her sack with Galia's and unstraps the basket from the rock. "It's all set."

Galia resumes her climb up the cliff. After she disappears from Elidria's sight, the basket begins its own thirty-foot ascent up the cliff by a pulley system. The basket also disappears at the top before reappearing and descending back down. Elidria grabs the empty basket and straps it back on the rock. She then begins her own climb. A climb that many would be afraid to scale. However, for the people of Bihnor, this is just an everyday event.

An arm reaches down to help like it always does. She grabs it but this one is much more firm than Galia's. It pulls her up and immediately embraces her. Elidria knows exactly who it is. "Dad," she says as she buries her head in his arms.

"Oh?" exclaims the surprised Aldameer. He strokes her hair gently, just the way she likes it. "Hey, Elly. I wasn't quite expecting this affection from a simple return."

Elidria looks up at him. A bright smile lifts his rugged features. His eyes shine the way they always do when he's happy. "After what happened, I was kind of worried about you and let my thoughts get to me," she tells him.

Aldameer places his hand on her shoulder. "It was an accident. Some things you have to let go. I'm back now so focus on today." Aldameer looks over at the haul the two girls acquired. "That's a lot of snails in one go. Very impressive."

"And it's not even lunch," adds Elidria.

"No, it really isn't." Aldameer tries his best to smother his smile but just can't.

"What's going on?" Elidria asks him.

He starts to grin. "Yeah, I'm not very good at hiding things. I too have a haul. It took me a bit longer but I think it was worth it."

"What could *you* be hauling?"

"Well, it is your birthday so I figured I'd get you something really special."

"Fourteen isn't a special age," says Elidria.

"Every birthday is special." Aldameer looks over at Galia. "Could you take care of the snails for us?"

"I can handle them," she says with confidence.

"And please bring your family over for dinner."

"Sure thing. Happy birthday, Eldra." Galia gives a wave and carries the two sacks of snails away.

"So?" Elidria is absolutely beaming.

"Right. It's back at the house." Aldameer leads his daughter to the house that they call their own. He opens the door to let her enter first. "Happy birthday," he says as she walks in.

Elidria freezes and tears begin filling her eyes. She tries to speak but her words won't come. She begins to laugh as she brings one hand to her mouth.

"Elidria, my dearest princess," says the smiling Arlayna, arms opened wide.

Elidria laughs again and rushes in for a hug. "Mom. I don't believe it."

Arlayna kisses her daughter's forehead. "Your father found and saved me."

Elidria notices one of her hands is completely wrapped in a bandage. She releases her mother and takes her bandaged hand. Her head spins. She looks into her mother's eyes and tries her best to say more. Nothing she can think of seems adequate. She had already lost and mourned for her mother. How is she right here in front of her? Is this even real? She reaches out a hand and strokes her arm, gently, as if too much pressure might cause her to crumble and fade away. Working up the courage, she whispers, "I thought you were dead. I'm sorry."

"No. Don't apologize for something like that."

Aldameer approaches the two women. "May I?" he asks.

With her other hand, Arlayna pulls her husband in and Elidria snuggles back in as well. "I love you both very much," Arlayna tells them.

"Mom, I-I really don't know what to say."

"Then just cherish this moment."

"Wake up." Delsar crouches above Elidria. He used a hushed tone and shakes her shoulder to wake her up.

Elidria grumbles as she wakes up. Delsar quickly presses his hand against her mouth. She lets out a quick, muffled scream before remembering where she is.

Delsar points through the trees and that's when she notices the troll a mere thirty feet from where she lies. It doesn't seem like the troll has noticed them, but why is there a random troll in the woods? Delsar, with one hand still on Elidria's mouth, pulls a dagger from his satchel.

Elidria gasps. Delsar flips it over and tries to hand it to her. She looks at it for a moment before taking it from him. Delsar gestures her to stay then darts into the woods with Elf-like agility. Elidria's heavy breathing is louder than Delsar's footfalls.

Is Delsar going to fight this monster himself? Elidria puzzles a bit in her head. *Where does he get his energy?* Elidria stands as quietly as she can. She reaches for her bag but is interrupted by a sharp pain in her foot. She clenches her fist to her mouth and squeezes her eyes shut. *What did I just do?* Elidria looks down and sees the knife lying at her feet with a dab of blood on the tip. *The knife! He just gave it to me!* It appears she had subconsciously released the knife and it poked through her boot before bouncing out. She's lucky she went to bed both exhausted and upset last night. Otherwise, she may have remembered to take them off.

The troll lets out some sort of cry and starts charging toward Elidria. *Oh no! Did I scream when I dropped the knife?* Elidria steps back and trips over the blanket lying at her feet. She stumbles back and falls through the makeshift tent. She turns over on her hands and knees and reaches for the knife. It's not there. She must have kicked it somewhere when she tripped. Her heart pounds as she feels her panic mounting. She clambers to her feet but gets tripped up again by the blanket that is now wrapped around her legs. She lands hard on her elbows but quickly kicks the blanket from her legs and scrambles to the nearest tree.

She throws her hands up and screams as the log they used as a bench last night slams into the tree. Rotten wood and dirt fly from the troll's new club, sending debris straight into her face. With the surge of adrenaline, her morning drowsiness has passed; however, her moment of clarity disappears with the dirt and wood that has just plastered her eyes. She squints one eye open and starts to run. She trips again over something but she doesn't go down. With a quick balance adjustment, she takes off in a full sprint. She is determined to not let anything stop her this time.

Her determination does not get her very far. A branch whacks against her face, which doesn't stop her, but it does shift her weight back. She tries to catch herself but one of her feet hits a divot, sending her tumbling head-over-heels. She comes to a stop, flat on her back. A huge shadow looms over her. She knows it's the troll, even if she can't see clearly. The beast raises its log above its head for what will likely be a killing strike. In one last desperate attempt, Elidria lets out the loudest scream she can possibly conjure. The troll hesitates for just one moment. One crucial moment.

The troll lets out an agonized cry as Delsar drives his sword across both its heels. The troll falls to one knee and drops the log upon its own head. With the troll now at a more manageable height, Delsar continues his motion with a finishing strike aimed at the troll's neck. His blade doesn't hit its mark. Instead, the enraged troll flails its body to face Delsar. It leads with its backhand which Delsar catches with his blade. The sword stabs through its hand but doesn't stop it. The hand crashes into Delsar, sending him tumbling back. The troll howls in pain from the sword now protruding from the back of its hand. The troll grabs the sword and rips it out, causing even more damage.

"Hey!" shouts Elidria.

The troll turns back around only to be greeted by a handful of dirt to the face.

"How do *you* like it?"

Delsar takes advantage of Elidria's distraction and grabs two arrows from his quiver. He jumps on the back of the troll and tries to stab them into its flesh. One arrow snaps harmlessly while the other barely sticks in. The troll's skin proves too tough for such an attack. "The sword!" yells Delsar as the troll reaches back and grabs him by the cloak. He attempts to squirm out of his cloak but is unsuccessful because of his shield strapped to his back.

The troll grabs Delsar's legs with its bloodied hand and his right arm with the other. It tries to rip Delsar apart.

Elidria yells as she swings Delsar's sword against the troll's back. It bounces off.

The troll, now even more furious, tosses Delsar against a tree and focuses on Elidria. She swings again with no more success. She catches the arm with the injured hand and leaves a mere scratch. The troll kicks at her but she steps far enough away to avoid the full force. The glancing blow still knocks her on her rear. She instinctively drops the sword to catch herself with both arms to her side. The troll starts to run at Elidria but an arrow bounces off the back of its head. The troll is distracted by

DELSAR

this new development and turns toward the shooter, screaming as loud as it can. With that, Delsar fires another arrow straight into the mouth of the troll, causing it to emit a horrible choking noise before falling forward, flat on its face.

Elidria scrambles back to her feet and grabs the sword. She runs well around the troll and tries to hand the sword to Delsar who just sits there against the tree. "Take your sword!" she commands.

"It's dead," Delsar replies.

Elidria, not completely convinced, carefully walks toward the troll, sword in hand. She pokes its head a little and then again at its neck. Satisfied, she returns to Delsar's side. "It's dead," she confidently states, resting the blade on her shoulder and placing her hand on her hip.

Delsar begins to grimace and tear up.

"Are you okay?" Elidria asks thoughtfully.

Delsar, wincing from pain, replies, "Of course not. It's clear to me that this agreement will not work. You have no combat sense and I'm not going to babysit you all the way to Bihnor."

"Now wait a minute!" Elidria starts. "I'm the one who made an opening for you."

"You're also the one that alerted it to our presence with your uncalled-for squeak."

"I dropped the knife on my foot."

"That's exactly what I'm talking about," he says. "You're useless and a burden."

Elidria tries her best to fight back her own tears. "Then teach me how to fight. Then you can have a partner with you like when you defeated the Wanderers last time. You won't have to save Bihnor alone."

"You don't get it. I'm not saving Bihnor at all. I'm out."

"I'll fight harder than anyone," she pleads.

"Then you'll die quicker than anyone. You're still too small," he tells her like he told her yesterday.

"A sword will still cut."

"What's going to happen when you don't have a sword? When you get punched in the face by a man twice your size?" Delsar asks.

"I'll punch back," she answers.

"You'll be dead! You *will* go down and you *won't* get back up."

21

"But I will, and I won't stop fighting," she says, still very much determined.

"Let's pretend you don't go down, where would you punch back?"

"His face."

"You just broke your hand."

"What?"

"Someone's skull is a whole lot stronger than the little bones in your fist," Delsar explains.

"Then what is the right way?" she questions.

"If you hit someone's face, you should use the heel of your palm."

Elidria extends the palm of her hand toward Delsar. "Look," she says. "You just taught me."

Delsar looks away, putting no effort into hiding his annoyance.

"You have nothing to lose," she continues. "You still know where you're going, you're still getting paid, you won't need to find another job for at *least* a month, and you'll have someone who can watch your back."

"My shield has my back," he states.

"It did a fine job pinning you in your cloak. Don't think I didn't notice."

Delsar rolls his eyes. He reaches into his satchel and pulls out a canteen. "Here," he says, handing it to Elidria.

"What's this for? I have my own."

"Then you can use yours to clean your eyes out."

Elidria's eyes shut tight with Delsar's reminder. She doesn't understand how she forgot in the first place. She feels around her waist, but her canteen was left by the blankets.

"Just take mine," he says, taking her hand and pressing his into her palm.

"Thanks." She pours the water in her eyes and gives a few blinks to let her eyelids do what they were designed to do. Her right eye is still a bit blurry and aggravated but her left feels fine. "So, Delsar?"

"What?"

"Why do you think there was a troll in the woods?" she questions.

"No idea. I killed one yesterday in Newville and paid no mind. To encounter another one just a few miles from the last cannot be a coincidence."

"Do you think we should look into it?"

"No," replies Delsar. "Our priority needs to be getting to Bihnor and," Delsar closes his eyes before speaking quickly and under his breath, "training you."

Elidria lights up. "Really?"

"Tactically, it makes sense. And we are *not* partners." Delsar gives her a stern look and points directly at her face.

Elidria bites her bottom lip.

"Don't make me regret it," he adds.

"I won't."

"Then help me up." Delsar reaches his hand up and Elidria grabs it. She nearly falls forward pulling him up. Delsar grimaces as he stands. "You need some more meat on your bones."

Elidria ignores the comment. "What happened? Where did you get hurt?" she asks, genuinely concerned.

Delsar places his hand on his side and winces. "I hit the same ribs I broke yesterday."

"So that's why you were crying."

Delsar gives Elidria a look.

"There's nothing wrong with that," she says, crossing her arms and sticking her nose up. "I cry all the time."

"Just grab our things," Delsar instructs. "I'd like to get to Newville before breakfast."

"How far is it?" she asks.

"Maybe four miles."

"So we traveled six last night?"

"Yeah."

"Then it should take less than ninety minutes!" exclaims the excited Elidria, slamming her fist in her palm.

"Yeah, sure."

It doesn't take them ninety minutes. At Delsar's slow, agonizing pace, it takes them just under three hours.

Upon entering the town, someone sees them and retreats the other way.

"What has him spooked?" Elidria asks Delsar.

"I told them yesterday that I would return for the money they owe me or that I would take something more precious from them."

Elidria stomps her foot and brings her fists to her hips. "Why would you say something like that?"

"To keep them in line."

"You sound like a dictator."

"If people think I've gone soft, they'll start taking advantage of me. My job is tough and dangerous. That makes it expensive work. If they don't have the funds, I'll take something that I deem fit."

"You used to do this sort of stuff for free and from the kindness of your heart," Elidria states, still a bit appalled.

"Wrong. I used to get paid very well by the Queen. In fact, more than I get paid now."

A figure is running toward them, too far away to make out who it is, but Delsar thinks he knows.

The Mayor of Newville.

"Outcast!" yells the Mayor, and soon he is upon them. "And Miss Eldra," he says, bowing. "I see your search was a success."

"Thanks to your help, Mr. Mayor," says Elidria.

The Mayor looks at Delsar. "I'm sorry but we don't have the funds ready. We're still cleaning up from yesterday."

"That's fine. We'll just take something else off your hands."

Elidria quickly jabs Delsar in his side.

Delsar grunts and grabs her wrist with force. "No! We are not making this a thing." He stares directly into her eyes.

Elidria suddenly remembers his broken ribs and bites her lip. "Sorry," she mouths.

Delsar turns back to the Mayor, wrist still in hand. "We need a carriage."

Elidria rips her wrist from his grasp.

"We do have an extra carriage but I can't just give it away," says the Mayor.

"I'll buy it for one hundred fifty gold." Delsar pulls the exact pouch that was used for yesterday's transaction. "I give this to you and all debts are paid. You owe me nothing."

The Mayor's eyes light up. "We will owe you nothing?"

"I'm not saying it again. You clearly heard me."

"Then it makes sense that you will need a horse to pull it." The Mayor brings his hand to his chin, eyeing Delsar with a faint smile and a peculiar glint in his eye. The man made a quick turnaround from the grateful, gushing mayor he had been yesterday. Clearly, he thinks this relationship is changing.

Delsar squints his eyes, trying to figure out the Mayor's play. "So what if I want a horse. One hundred fifty gold is very fair for both a horse and a carriage. I'm sure that won't be a problem for you."

"We need our horses to help with construction. I'm afraid buying one will have to cost you more than you're used to."

"How much more?" Delsar asks.

"Three hundred."

"For a horse and carriage? Not happening."

"No," says the Mayor, "three hundred for the horse. The carriage is one-fifty by itself."

"Are you out of your mind?" Delsar exclaims. "I could get both for one hundred in the capital!"

"But you're not *in* the capital. If you need transportation, I have it."

"Fat chance!"

"Then you must not have the funds. Perhaps I could take something else a bit more precious off of you. That sword and maybe that shield look like they are worth something."

Delsar's jaw drops for a moment. He storms up to the Mayor and jams his finger into his chest. "You listen here you little punk!" Spit flies from his mouth. "Who's going to stop me from just taking what I want and leaving you with nothing? You?"

The Mayor's confidence suddenly leaves him.

"Wait a minute, Delsar." Elidria steps in and tries to part the two men but neither of them budge to her pushing. "This is an expense that I am willing to pay." She shimmies herself between the men and this time Delsar steps back when she pushes him. "I have three hundred on me right now," she tells Delsar.

"You just so happen to have three hundred golden coins?"

"That's what she said," the Mayor cuts in. "You clearly heard it."

Delsar points his finger past Elidria and at the man. "You—"

Elidria screams and stops Delsar from continuing. She receives confused looks from both men. "It worked against the troll so I thought I'd try it on you."

"Don't compare me to a troll," Delsar says.

"You did stop."

"Fine." Delsar rolls his eyes. "You want to be the boss? You handle this spineless filth."

Elidria scrunches her nose. "I will, so you stop talking." She turns to face the Mayor and gives him a head-tilted smile. "Don't mind him. He's new. I just hired him yesterday so he's still figuring some things out." She lowers her voice and leans in. "He also just broke his ribs and that makes him a bit cranky. I'm learning some things too."

"I understand," the Mayor whispers back. "I, too, hired him just yesterday."

"So what did you do?" she asks.

"It wasn't easy. You have to stay firm with him," the Mayor explains.

"I hear that." Elidria reaches into her bag and pulls out three pouches. "Here's the money for the horse. Delsar can give you the money for the carriage. Then neither of you owe each other anything. Right, Delsar?" she asks loudly.

"Fine." He hands her the pouch which she gives to the Mayor.

"This is the agreed amount. I'll go fetch you a horse." The Mayor runs off.

"It had better be a strong one for that price!" Delsar yells after him.

"Delsar," Elidria starts, "you *do* work for me now. If there is an expense, I *will* cover it. There's no reason to get rash. As crazy as it might seem to you, he *is* a human being, just like you."

"He's nothing like me."

"You're right. I'm not sure where I was going with that, but you do need to be nicer."

"I work for you but I do *not* have to act like you. Got it?"

Elidria gives him no answer.

The Mayor returns with a tall, rugged horse. "This is a horse well worth the price," he says.

"I doubt you would have given me such a healthy horse if I was the one paying for it," Delsar states.

Elidria motions as if she's going to elbow him in the side again, but she doesn't.

Delsar hesitates before stepping forward to take the horse.

"Pardon your manners," says the Mayor. "The girl paid for it."

"That's all right," says Elidria, "he *does* work for me. Delsar, go fetch the horse."

Delsar snatches the lead rope from the Mayor's hands.

"The carriage is out behind the stables. You do remember where they are, don't you?"

"Of course I do." Delsar walks in the direction he remembers the stables are.

"It was a pleasure doing business with you," waves the Mayor. "Good luck on your endeavors and I hope to never see you again."

"Look who has a ton of confidence now that he doesn't owe me anything." Delsar continues to grumble as he walks away.

"Does our payment cover food for the horse?" Elidria asks.

"For you, absolutely." The Mayor looks at Elidria and places his hand on her shoulder. His smile disappears. "I'm not sure what your business with him is, Miss Eldra, but please be careful. He seems to be very short-tempered and I'd hate for you to get hurt because of him."

"I appreciate your concern," she tells him, "but I don't think I'm the one who needs saving." She watches him disappear with the horse around a building. *Him first. Then my village.*

CHAPTER 3

THE MASTER

8 Years Ago...

"That rash looks really bad. That's just from wearing them?"

"Yeah. They are *really* tight. Do you mind?" Arviakyss extends his left arm toward his master.

Galius stops inspecting his apprentice's raw wrist and grabs the bracer on his other arm. "This is the second resize you've needed in the last six months," he says as he unstraps the bracer.

Arviakyss gives Galius a faint smile. "I am a growing boy."

"You're the youngest apprentice *I've* ever had. That's for sure." Galius examines Arviakyss' other wrist. A near-identical rash is on both arms. "I hope you won't need another refitting before your graduation."

"Perhaps if you stop feeding me." Arviakyss looks at the back of his arms. "Do you think we could order padding on the next ones?"

"They already have padding."

"I don't mean just the leather lining. I mean wool or something between the leather and the metal. Kind of like a pillow. That would make them more comfortable and would help cushion any blows I take."

Galius can tell his apprentice is being serious. "If being a guard doesn't work out, perhaps inventing or blacksmithing will be a good fallback." He chuckles.

"Well, Master?" Arviakyss asks again.

Galius lets out a huge, girthy laugh. "I'll add that to the request form. We will have to upsize your order to make room for the extra padding."

Arviakyss pulls out a piece of paper and hands it to Galius. "I already took that into account."

"You're on top of things, as usual," Galius says. "It makes me wonder why you have to wait until you're fifteen to get sworn in. You're more prepared than I was when I graduated, and I was an apprentice for six years."

Galius had apprenticed four others before Arviakyss. The relationships he had with his other trainees were serious. The same kind of discipline they would have gotten in the army. Arviakyss needed no such treatment. He never needed to hear things more than once. In fact, some things he never needed to hear at all. He seemed attuned to common sense, which is what keeps you alive in battle. Even in combat, he always followed instructions and pushed on, despite challenging circumstances. The relationship they formed is more like an uncle and his nephew than anything else.

"The padding isn't anything new," says Arviakyss. "I read that the army has certain armor designed for colder climates. I figured, why only use that stuff in the cold?"

"Then I suppose you won't be getting any royalties for your idea."

Galius, as usual, spoke calmly to Arviakyss. It always surprised Arviakyss on the rare occasion Galius would raise his voice. He would only do so as needed, but it would still throw Arviakyss. Galius only yelled at him, directly, once or twice. The first time was back when they were assigned to each other. Galius assumed Arviakyss was going to be like all his prior apprentices. That yelling would help get his teachings and the horror that may await in battle to stick in their brains.

"I'm going to miss you, son," he tells him.

"I'm not graduating for another month. Besides, we may still work together from time-to-time. You'll have to introduce me to your next apprentice."

"I'm growing old and I'm never home," says Galius. "I'm transferring as a simple town guard where my family lives. It's not hanging up my cape but I likely won't be seeing any more action."

There is a pause in their conversation. Arviakyss' ever-present, subtle smile fades into realization. He passes a hand over his eyes as tears form in the corners.

"Oh, come now," says Galius, "it's not like I'm dying. You can always visit when you have leave. What's that line you said your mother gave you? 'If you won't smile, who will?'"

"That doesn't apply here," says Arviakyss. "You're smiling so the answer is 'you.' It's best to use that line *after* you've saved someone."

"Why do I feel like you've told me that before?"

"It's because I have, on multiple occasions."

Galius lets out another one of his girthy laughs. "I guess I really am getting old."

"You are old enough to be my grandfather."

"And you still squeak when you get excited."

Arviakyss begins to smile again. He really only stops for a few moments at a time. For every wrong in the world, there are a dozen new opportunities to make it right. He looks forward to making that right.

"I'll get your order to the blacksmith. Make sure you wrap your wrists in a wet rag," Galius instructs as Arviakyss begins to pull a rag and canteen from his pack. Galius lets another chuckle escape. "Why do I bother? I'll be back in a few." With that, Galius exits the abandoned briefing room. *That boy is truly something special.*

"No, Elidria. Pull your hand up towards yourself." Delsar has his hand clenched around one of her wrists. The first thing he has decided to teach her is how not to be overpowered by a simple wrist grab. "If you do it your way, you'll be pulling against four fingers. My way you only have to escape the thumb like you did in Newville."

"Like this?" Elidria pulls with all her might. The grip breaks much easier than she was expecting, causing her to whack herself in the nose with the same hand that was just restrained. She lets out a cross between a gasp and a cry, resulting in a sound that more resembles a squeaking.

"Yes," says Delsar. "Just like that." He appears as if he didn't even notice her punching herself in the face.

Elidria places her hand over her nose. A smell of cartilage emanates from the back of her nose. "What if they use two hands?" She sounds like she's suffering from a serious allergy attack.

"If someone is dumb enough to use both their hands to grab just one of yours, you beat his face with the other."

"With my palm," Elidria states.

"Yes. Another thing you can do is exactly what you did to escape one hand except now you can use two." Delsar grabs her hand again and pulls it down. He reinforces his grip with his other hand. "Now grab your hand and pull it away against my thumbs. Also," he adds, "pivot away so that you *don't* whack yourself in the face."

He definitely noticed. He isn't showing any kind of concern or care though. *And why should he? I only met him two days ago and his whole shtick is about how much he doesn't care. How is someone who doesn't care going to save anyone?* She pulls with everything she has and a little bit extra, grabbing her hand and pivoting like Delsar instructed. His grip stands no chance.

"Good," says Delsar. "Do you see the position you're in compared to me?"

"Bent?"

"I'm pulled forward. Now you can elbow my stomach, backfist my nose, punch my throat, kick my knee, stomp on my foot. Pretty much just smash whatever is exposed and not armored."

"Like the guard's faces? You always countered for their faces because most everywhere else was armored."

"Obvious, but yes."

She's right. It's just common sense but so many people overthink things or don't even notice the obvious. It's good that she's clearly not one of those people.

"That's enough for now." Delsar extends his hand. "Let me see that map again."

"But I was just getting warmed up," says Elidria.

Delsar doesn't move or give any kind of reaction.

"It's in the carriage. I'll go get it," she says.

Delsar follows right behind her. She climbs into the front seat and grabs the map from her bag. She turns and jumps back from Delsar's unexpected proximity. "Oh? Here you go." She hands the map down to him.

Delsar grabs the map and climbs in next to her. He sits down and opens the map. "There's a town about two days southwest from us. We need to go there and acquire gear for you."

"How much of a detour is that?"

"Two days there and another day to get back on track, so about three."

"Can we afford to make such a detour?" asks Elidria.

"We can't afford *not* to. As it stands, we have no extra gear and the only weapon you have is the knife I gave you, which has done more damage to you than anything else."

Elidria peers over the map. "Which town?"

"Dukla," says Delsar.

"That's fairly close to the coast. What if we travel by boat?"

"To pull this job off, we cannot be noticed. We need precise, calculated strikes to disrupt their ranks. Stealth will be our biggest ally. We will get noticed miles away if we take a boat."

"Not if we stay near the shore," says Elidria. "This peninsula is just south of my village and it will cover our approach."

"Not if they have a lookout on the peninsula, which, if they have any intelligence, they will."

"Then we travel by boat to Fairview and walk from there," suggests Elidria.

"We have no crew," says Delsar.

"Then we charter a boat."

"I'm not traveling with random people."

"Delsar," Elidria says sternly, "if we are adding three days to our travel, we *need* to find a way to make that time back. A boat is the best way. I'll pay for a passenger boat and you won't have to talk to anyone."

"You're assuming we find a boat that has room and is scheduled for departure when we arrive. We could show up and have to wait a week before another boat departs for Fairview." Delsar doesn't stop. "On top of that, the nearest port from Dukla is in Grandell's capital. That's another three-day travel. We will lose six days if we can't find a voyage."

"This is worth the risk," Elidria encourages. "We have the money and you have me."

"What's that supposed to mean?"

"People will be more likely to say yes to me than to you. I've seen it."

Delsar grumbles but then starts to think for a moment. "Fine. You're the boss and it's your village in peril. I'll let you make this call."

Elidria hammers her fist into her palm. "Then it's south to Dukla and then south to Grandell."

"We need food for the horse as well. Make sure you have money for the trip *and* the horse," warns Delsar.

"I do," Elidria assures him. "Don't worry."

"Then speaking of horse food, make sure he gets his breakfast and then we continue your training."

"Right away!" Elidria yells, as if she is a recruit in the army.

"We depart in an hour."

During the trek to Dukla, Delsar taught Elidria a pair of forms he learned during some of his travels as Arviakyss. He stressed her stances, emphasizing the importance of proper form and smooth movements. She did struggle a bit with the sword, but he knew she just doesn't have the muscles for it yet. Any free time they had was spent working those forms over and over again.

At one point, Delsar took her hunting. He tried to teach her how to shoot but she couldn't even draw his longbow. He had to take over when they spotted a wild hog and she shot an arrow that went about ten feet. He wounded it and then tried to teach her how to kill it mercifully, but she would have none of it. She didn't mind eating it when it was smoked and cooked but she refused to kill it herself. *She was willing to shoot it but she won't kill it while it's wounded. Go figure.*

The meat was plentiful and would last a few days. Provided it doesn't go bad.

The trip was predictable. Nothing out of the ordinary. It took two days just as Delsar had estimated.

Delsar stops the carriage and turns to Elidria. "Remember, we are travelers heading for Grandell. We are here for food and supplies, specifically for our horse. You said no lying so this is the story we stick to."

"What if they question our relationship, like why we are traveling together?" asks Elidria.

"I'm training you to be a hunter. We have a hog in the back as proof," explains Delsar. "You see? We won't be lying about a thing. This is the proper way to infiltrate enemy lines anyway. The more truths you tell, the harder it is to mix up your story and the more believable it is."

"That does sorta make sense."

"I'm the best in the kingdom at this"—Delsar puts his fist on his chest—"or at least I was until I became so recognized."

For that moment, Elidria can sense real pride coming from Delsar. Pride that doesn't stem from arrogance but from real experience and truth. It warms her heart to know that there is still some human in him. No matter what he does, he can't hide that.

Delsar starts the carriage again, bringing the main gate into view.

"So where are we getting my gear?" Elidria asks, twisting in her seat with excitement.

"There is a man here who goes by the name Galius."

Elidria gasps.

"Do you know him?" Delsar asks.

"Not him," she says. "My best friend is named Galia. His name reminded me of her. I"—Elidria swallows—"left her behind. She was with me and I just left her." Elidria stares off in front of them.

Delsar looks at her out of the corner of his eyes. He's not exactly sure what to say after that.

Elidria notices his pause and can't help but smile, even after the memories she just shared. *Softy.*

"Galius is my old master," says Delsar, breaking the silence. "I apprenticed with him for two years."

"Oh? Why do you think he has what we need?"

"When an apprentice graduates, he is given a new, standard-issue set of gear. The old stuff is given to the master as trophies."

"So Galius is someone you trust?" Elidria asks.

"Nope. We're going to sneak in, find his armory, grab what we need, and get out."

"We're going to *steal* from him?" Elidria sets her hands on her hips.

"Of course," says Delsar. "He'll recognize me. Did you forget I'm wanted?"

Elidria frowns, crossing her arms.

"Your emotions are literally everywhere," Delsar states.

"At least I *have* emotions," Elidria retorts.

Delsar rolls his eyes. "Now we just have to hope he's not assigned to the gate. Speaking of…." Delsar turns in his seat to face Elidria and points his finger in her face. "We are here so swallow whatever emotions you're feeling now and get your head in the moment."

Before them is a long, wooden wall that stretches around the entire town. The wall is about eight feet tall and the gate, directly in front of them, is about ten. It has one small battlement to the left of the gate.

"Halt!" demands a voice from the battlement. There is a guard in the tower and the one at ground level who approaches the carriage. "State your name and business."

"My name is Delsar and we are in need of horse feed."

"And where are you going?" the guard questions. The other begins to inspect the carriage.

"We are on our way to Grandell. I'm a hunter and this is my apprentice, Eldra." Elidria perks up hearing Delsar call her by her preferred name, though he only used it so he wouldn't give them her real name. "We finished our training in the woods, so now I thought I'd teach her how to hunt by the water."

The second guard looks in the back of the carriage, only to see a small amount of horse feed and the dead pig. He gives the guard in the tower a nod to let him know everything checks out. He makes his way around to Delsar and eyes up his sword. "There is no hunting within the walls and your sword must remain sheathed at all times."

"Understood," Delsar replies.

"Welcome to Dukla," says the guard before shouting, "Open the gate! Let them through!" The gate, which is more like two giant half-doors, splits and begins to open inward.

"Thank you, sir." Delsar gives a slight bow from the waist before signaling to his horse to start moving. After passing through the gates, Delsar looks over at Elidria. "Nothing to it."

She glares back at Delsar with her arms crossed. "You'd better take me hunting by the coast or you'll have lied."

"What?" exclaims Delsar. "I didn't lie. We'll be hunting for boats, will we not?"

Her nose crinkles. "Taking advantage of what people perceive is still lying. Even if you speak the truth, but you know that people will perceive it differently from what you said, you're a liar."

Delsar scoffs, shaking his head and rolling his eyes. This is something he's done countless times. That's what makes a good con artist. Being able to lie by telling the truth is quite the skill to have if you want free stuff. To Delsar, though, he doesn't feel like he just lied. Even if he did, it was for the mission. They are on the clock and lives are on the line. "I'll take you fishing down by the coast if that will settle your conscience."

"It's not *my* conscience I'm worried about," she replies.

Delsar shakes his head and refocuses on the road ahead.

The town is active this morning. There are people going to and fro, pushing carts filled with different goods. There are no big businesses in Dukla, but there are many small ones and it seems like everyone in town has something to sell or trade.

As for the buildings, they are all a dark brown. The same color as the forest that surrounds the town. The rampart is also brown. Near the center of town is an elevated and flat platform with a well atop it. The platform looks like it could be a stage, but why have a well on a stage? The platform is made of dirt and has wood along the sides. It also has a small, three-step staircase that leads to the top. All along the platform are even more vendors.

Delsar is stunned by the number of people and buildings in this small town.

As if she can read his thoughts, Elidria asks, "How are we going to find Galius in all of this?"

"We ask."

"We ask? *That's* your master plan?"

"Yup. He trained four other guards before me. All I need to do is tell someone that I was an apprentice of his and that I'm surprising him with a visit. I'm sure they'll tell us where he lives."

"That's lying," says Elidria.

"I *was* his apprentice," states Delsar.

"I mean surprising him with a visit. You aren't visiting him."

"We *are* visiting and he *is* going to be *very* surprised when his stuff is missing."

Elidria closes her eyes and tries her best not to cry over such an appalling statement. "Well, leave me out of this." She sinks in her seat.

"It's to save lives, Elidria. Believe it or not, we guards would do this all the time if it meant completing the mission quickly and efficiently. That means fewer casualties."

"It's not going to work."

"Watch me." Delsar brings the carriage to a stop at the nearest cart. "Excuse me," he says to the vendor.

"Good morning! What can I do for you?" asks the trader.

"I'm looking for Galius. He's an old friend of mine. Do you know him?"

"That man has a heart of gold. Such a kind guard, though he only works about twice a week these days."

Delsar continues his interrogation with a casual air. "Do you know where I can find him?"

"And what business do you have with him?"

"I was an apprentice of his many years ago and was passing through. I thought I'd surprise him with a visit."

Elidria closes her eyes with Delsar's statement. That's the one she really has a problem with.

"His apprentice? Splendid! It's good to know there are others out there like him."

This time it's Delsar who subtly grimaces and Elidria sees it. *Regret. He feels regret. Hmm.*

The man continues, "You are actually on the right street. Just follow this one until you get to the Sheriff's Office. His is the next one after it."

"Oh? He's next to the Sheriff?"

"Yup. You can't miss it."

"Thank you very much," says Delsar as he gives a little salute.

The man gets all excited and salutes back. It's not a very good one, but he tried. "If you need any turnips, be sure to look for me," he tells them.

Elidria pulls on Delsar's sleeve and gestures her head toward the man.

Delsar shakes his head in confusion. "What are you trying to tell me?" he asks in a whisper, squinting his eyes.

Elidria rolls her eyes and smiles past Delsar. "Can we buy two baskets from you right now? Our horse, Gipsy, will love them."

Delsar is taken aback by the name she gave the horse. He is pretty sure 'Gipsy' isn't a very good name for a male horse, but whatever.

"You want two full baskets?"

"Yes, we would."

"I've never sold a whole basket to one person before, let alone two. I've always estimated my baskets to be worth one gold each, but for you—,"

"Two gold is perfect. You helped us so much already." Elidria gives him a huge grin that isn't fake by any means. She hands the man three gold pieces and Delsar hops down to load the baskets.

"Oops," says the vendor. "It looks like you gave me an extra gold piece, miss."

Elidria tilts her head. "That's for being so kind. Plus, you're going to need to buy some new baskets."

"Thank you very much, miss!"

"Mhm." Elidria closes her eyes as she smiles at him without her teeth.

Delsar finishes loading the carriage and hops back up front.

"Have a good time with Galius!" The man waves and the carriage begins to move.

"You, too!" waves Elidria, leaning over the side. "Farewell!" She sits back down, completely beaming. "What a nice man."

"You do know that he's not going to be having a good time with Galius?" Delsar questions Elidria.

"What do you mean by that?"

"You said, 'you too.'"

Elidria's face turns white. "I said, 'You too.'?" She starts to stand back up and leans out the side but Delsar grabs her and pulls her back down.

"Stop," he says. "It doesn't matter. I doubt he cares. Also, I thought you didn't like lying."

"Again, what do you mean?"

"The whole act you just put on? The flirting and the over-the-top smiling? I'd say that's lying, wouldn't you?"

Elidria rolls her eyes again and smirks. "The man was really being nice and I meant every smile. I was also only being myself. You know, nice and presentable? Kind of like you were except I *am* those things because I *believe* in those things."

"Whatever." Delsar lets out an exasperated sigh. "We should have picked food up on the way out. Not this junk."

"What are you talking about? Gipsy will love the turnips." Elidria smiles at the horse.

"Turnips are snack foods. You can't give horses more than *maybe* one per day. Now we have over four hundred! You're going to kill her."

"Him," Elidria corrects.

"I know that!" snaps Delsar. "The name you gave him doesn't help."

"Wow." Elidria looks Delsar up and down. "You're a grouchy-pants."

Delsar scoffs. "Do you take nothing seriously?"

"I take what's serious seriously." She crosses her arms. "Gipsy is just a name and the horse is just a horse. If you want to get upset over a bad name for an animal, that's your problem. Besides, if you're going to call me whatever *you* want, I'm going to call you whatever *I* want."

"Whatever," Delsar says again. "The food we have left, plus grass and a turnip each day should get *Gipsy* to Grandell. We'll buy *real* food for him then."

Delsar pulls the carriage to a stop and hands the reins to Elidria. "Drive the carriage around a bit. I'm going to see who's home." Delsar jumps off the carriage and dashes between the Sheriff's Office and the house next to it.

"Hm." Elidria watches him disappear. "Well, Gipsy, looks like it's just you and me. Walk on!" she yells.

The horse doesn't move.

"Huh?" Elidria tries again. "Giddyup!" Still nothing. She shakes the reins and then pulls on them. It has the opposite effect. Gipsy begins walking backward. "No! Go forward!" The horse stops. "You may think you've gotten the best of me." Elidria brings a hand to her chin as she begins to try and remember how Delsar makes it go. She comes up with another idea. "Yip, y—,"

"Elidria? What are you doing?" asks Delsar.

Elidria looks at Delsar who stands in the front door of the house. "Just driving the carriage. Like you asked. As best I can."

"Okay?" Delsar scratches his eyebrow. "Just come here."

"Sure." Elidria lays down the reins and jumps down. "Is no one home?" she whispers, hands clasped behind her back.

"No one. And that's not all," says Delsar, "the gear is displayed in the living room. This couldn't be easier."

"It's not hidden away?"

Delsar doesn't answer. Instead, he pulls her into the house. Sure enough, mounted on the living room wall are three sets of armor. Each one has a plate inscribed with "Arviakyss" under it. Right in the open for all who enter to see. "Look at it all." Delsar sounds excited. "Take your pick. Anything you want."

"Delsar—," starts Elidria.

"This one was my first set," he says pointing to the left. "I was thirteen when they crafted it for me." Delsar lowers his voice. "Actually, I was twelve. I think I was smaller than you are now though."

"Delsar!" Tears are streaking down Elidria's cheeks and dripping off her chin. "This isn't right!" She turns and storms out of the house.

"Elidria!" he shouts after her. He turns back to face the gear. "I'll just pick for you." He starts inspecting the gear and puzzles in his brain. *Does she need a shield? Might as well take one.* He grabs two. *Perhaps two swords as well.* He takes two swords. *I'm not sure I can carry it all. I'll just take a few trips.*

"Arviakyss?"

Delsar's face goes white and a sudden panic overtakes him. He drops the gear and spins around with his sword drawn.

"What has this world done to you?" the man asks as he steps closer to Delsar. His face betrays a worried expression beneath a well-trimmed beard.

"Stay back!" commands Delsar.

The man throws his hands up.

"Delsar!" Elidria covers her mouth, knowing she just made a mistake calling him by his name.

"Delsar? Like the Outcast?" The man seemed to put two-and-two together. "Put your sword down, son."

"Not a chance."

Elidria puts herself between Delsar's blade and the man. "Stop!" she yells at Delsar. "I brought him here. Can't you see he still loves and respects you? He has your armor on display for all to see. It even says who it belonged to."

Delsar looks directly at her. "How could you?" His eyes look betrayed, causing Elidria to feel a pain in her heart.

"Delsar, please."

"Arviakyss." The man steps past Elidria and puts his chest against Delsar's blade. "I'm worried about you. May we talk?"

Delsar begins to shake and quiver. Tears form in his eyes as he looks back and forth between the man and Elidria. He starts to stammer, "I-I-I-I ca-c-c-can't." The sword drops and the man immediately grabs and embraces him. Delsar's eyes go wide as he starts to pant. He then clenches his eyes shut and begins to grimace. He puts his head down. "I-I'm s-sorry." He begins to weep.

The man leans back and looks right at him. "I forgive you and I'm not mad at you."

"But I failed you," says Delsar. "The Queen is dead because of me."

"Tell me something." The man tilts Delsar's head up to look him in his eyes. "Did you kill the Queen?"

Delsar shakes his head. "No, but I was supposed to protect her. I failed her and this country."

Elidria can't believe what she just heard. The world didn't just turn on him, he blames himself for whatever happened almost six years ago. He's been living with that guilt and has had no one to talk to about it. She tears up, watching the two men hug each other.

"Then fix it."

Delsar looks a bit confused. "Master? She's dead."

Galius points at Elidria. "Then make a *new* right. Why does she travel with you?"

"She needs me to kill some mercenaries," he answers.

Galius looks at Elidria. "Why do you need him?"

"I need him to save my village and my people," she says.

Galius looks back at Delsar. "Go to save. That's why you travel with her. To save her and her friends and her family. Make up for what you didn't do for the Queen and save *her*."

"It's impossible," says Delsar. "I can't save her village from what she's described."

Elidria will have none of that. "Yes, you can!" she shouts. "You are the Queen's Champion! You've fought trolls, half-dragons, wyverns, entire governments! Of course you can save a small village. Plus, you'll have me. I'll make sure nothing hurts you. I'll make sure we keep fighting until we've won. The mercenaries won't stand a chance because whatever they're fighting for is nothing compared to what we fight for. We fight for hope and freedom. They will never take that from me and you can't let them keep taking it from you!" She clasps her hands over her mouth, shocking herself with her own outburst. Her words just came out after hearing Delsar has no real plans of winning. That is something she just can't stand for.

"I can help," Galius tells Delsar. "What do you need?"

"Gear," says Elidria, moving her hands from her mouth to her chest.

"Take whatever you want," he instructs her. "It does no one any good sitting on a wall."

"Thank you, sir." Elidria gives a bow.

"Take all the swords and all the shields. You never know when you may need extra."

Elidria grabs the last sword and shield off the wall and acquires the ones from the floor Delsar dropped, too. At her carrying limit, the shields crash against the wooden floor.

"You can make multiple trips," Galius says, calmly.

Elidria gives him a sheepish smile. "Thanks." She gets to the door and bows before exiting with just the swords in-hand.

"Arviakyss, why didn't you just ask for help?" Galius questions.

"Because I can't trust anyone," he answers.

"But I trust you."

Delsar perks up a bit from hearing that.

"Despite what so many have told me, I always believed you were innocent. I always knew they were wrong. And it's not just my trust you still have, it's also my love."

Delsar turns his head away from his master.

"I loved all my apprentices, but the love I had and *still* have for you is different. It's a love I reserve for my family. Ask for my help and you'll have it. I'll leave here and go with you."

"No," says Delsar. "You *do* have a family here. I have none. Hers are probably dead. We have nothing and no one to lose. If I took you away from your family, I'd feel even worse than I already do. I can't do that to them and I can't have you do that to me."

"Okay." Galius squeezes him tight. "She's about the same size you were when you graduated. Your famous 'padded' armor should fit her."

Delsar takes a deep breath and pulls away from the hug. "Thank you."

"You're welcome. Would you like help bringing the armor out?"

"I'm just grabbing the shinguards and bracers," Delsar tells him.

"Why nothing else?"

"Because she will never overpower anyone. Her only chance is her speed. We take that from her if she wears too much."

"Then how does she fight?" asks Galius.

"My way," Delsar bluntly states.

"That's good. Teach her well."

Elidria walks back in after delivering the swords. "You picked my armor for me?" she asks Delsar.

"He did," answers Galius. "And he can manage taking it to the carriage."

Delsar completely understands what his master is hinting at and walks out of the house to wait at the carriage.

"Come here, Miss—?"

"It's Eldra."

"Miss Eldra."

"Just Eldra."

Galius smiles. "Eldra it is."

"Thank you," says Elidria.

"Mhm. Come sit down." With an open hand, he points at one of his chairs.

"Um, okay, Mr. Galius."

"Please, just Galius."

"Sure." Elidria sits in the chair.

"I believe that if you didn't find him when you did, he would have become the very thing he is accused of being."

"I fear it also."

"Arviakyss is still in there and I believe he needs you as much as the world needed him. If you truly wish to save your village, you must save him from himself first."

"I know," she says. "I just don't know how."

"Remain innocent and keep sharing your love. Help him do what's right no matter what. Doing one wrong leads to another. Keep him straight and forgive him when he messes up. He needs someone he can trust and talk to. Even if what he says hurts, he needs to be heard. You must have patience and kindness, because if you lose him, who will save your village?"

"No one," she says, tearing up. "He's the only one who's said yes."

"Then fight for him, both physically and emotionally. Do not let go of him and always have his back."

"I will." Elidria nods her head. "I'll do my very best."

"Then I will take you to him." He takes her hand and helps her from the chair. "Oh, and Eldra?"

"Yes?"

"Don't stop smiling."

Elidria forces a little smile. "Okay."

"Okay!" Galius repeats, chipperly. "I will lead you to your carriage."

"Thank you, Galius."

"Anytime." He grabs the shields off the floor on his way by and leads her to the carriage where Delsar waits.

The Sheriff leans against his building and watches them approach the carriage. "So? Is everything alright?" he asks Galius.

"Everything is perfect. Thank you for letting me handle this."

"Do fill me in later. The girl seemed pretty upset when she came running into the office."

"Sorry about that," says Elidria, smiling while simultaneously tilting her head and closing her eyes.

"Yup," the Sheriff responds.

"Arv—," Galius catches himself, "are you ready to go, Delsar?" he asks, after placing the shields in the back.

"We are. Thank you again. For everything." Delsar grabs Elidria's hand and helps her up.

"Bye, Galius!" Elidria shouts as Delsar snaps the reins to get the horse moving. "Oh," she says, realizing how to make the horse go.

Galius starts to smile. He then lets out his classic, girthy laugh as they depart.

"Mhm, yes, well you folks have a good day. Oh, and don't leave your carriage in front of my office next time, please," says the Sheriff, sounding not a little miffed.

Galius can't help but laugh even more.

CHAPTER 4

THE GIRL

8 Years Ago...

Aldameer bursts into his best friend's house, pure excitement and joy shining on his face. "Guess what?" he asks.

"She didn't?" responds Raymar, standing up from his chair and slamming his hands on the table.

"You know she did! The Queen fully supports our request to start a village on the western coast."

"No way!"

"She didn't stop there," Aldameer adds.

"Oh?"

"She will be sponsoring the whole thing! The trek, the means of travel, transportation, guards, contracting, literally everything! We'll have enough to start a comfortable village and even more to cover anything else we'll need for a whole year!"

"That's," Raymar pauses for a brief moment, "fantastic. So what's the catch? This all seems a bit too good to be true."

"There is one condition," says Aldameer.

"Spill it, pal."

"Our main export is going to be snails."

Raymar stares blankly at his friend. "Let me see if I heard you right. Did you say 'snails?'"

"Turns out, the Queen's favorite color is blue and they use snails to make blue-colored dyes. This business should make us lots of money."

"That's different." Raymar begins chuckling to himself. "Raymar the snail farmer. Who would have ever thought?"

"I know it's a bit strange."

"Correction, it's *really* strange."

"Sure," says Aldameer, "it's *really* strange, but it gives us a chance to start things fresh with the people we love. We just don't have the freedoms we could have, here in the capital."

"It seems our dreams are coming true," says Raymar, staring into the distance. He snaps back. "Oh, we'll need to come up with a name."

"About that," Aldameer sounds like he is about to admit some terrible crime he once committed. "The Queen kind of needed a name so that the contract would be official."

"Then what did you say?" asks Raymar suspiciously.

"Bihnor."

Raymar can't stifle his laugh. "You mean like the name of our secret base we played in when we were kids?"

"I know it's silly," says Aldameer, "but we can change it when our contract ends."

"It's a perfect name. Bihnor was a place you and I would hide in to get away from people and have adventures. That's pretty much what we're doing." Raymar begins toward another doorway. "I'm going to find my wife and kids and tell them about the news."

"I heard everything." Raymar's significant other emerges from the very doorway he was trying to enter. "This is truly the best news I've heard in a long time." She gives Raymar a very passionate hug.

"Oh my goodness!" exclaims Raymar. "Al!"

"What? What is it?"

"Have you told your wife yet?"

"I've only told you."

Raymar looks directly at Aldameer. "You'd best take care of that right now. You should also probably pretend that you haven't told me anything. You know how wives can be if they aren't the ones who get to hear first."

Marith gives her husband a very strong pinch on his back. "You know it." Then gives him a kiss.

"I'll take your warning to heart and let her know right now." With that, Aldameer grins and dashes out of the house.

2 Months Later...

"...and check. That should be everything," says Aldameer, holding a checklist in his hand, marking off everything and everyone that is needed and ready for this departure. "Now we just need to wait for our escort."

"The Queen selected the guards herself. They won't be late," Raymar reassures him.

"I know you're right. It just seems like every little thing causes me stress right now."

"I don't know how you do it," says Raymar. "I would never be able to stay sane trying to orchestrate something like this."

"I'll tell you what, it's not easy to—," he stops himself short. "Elly! Where are you going?" he shouts to his daughter who just took off from one of the carts.

Raymar puts his hand out to stop Aldameer from taking off after her. "You're stressed. I'll handle this."

Aldameer gives him a nod and lets him run after his daughter.

"I don't want to go!" she yells as she gets further from the caravan that's about to leave. Raymar tries his best to catch up with her but she zips across a field and darts for a road that leads into the woods, leaving him in the dust.

"Eldra! Watch out!" His warning is too late as Elidria crashes into two guards coming from the same road. She falls backward and tears trickle down her face.

One guard bends down to assist her. "Are you all right?" he asks, extending his hand for hers. He can see that she isn't crying because of the fall. "What seems to be bothering you?"

Elidria looks up and sees the hand that is being offered to her. She accepts the help and proceeds to hug the guard. "It's not fair," she tells him.

"What isn't fair?"

"I live here and love it here, but I'm being forced to leave and go where I don't want to."

"Are your parents making you leave?" he asks.

"Yeah, and they don't seem to care what I think."

"Parents like making the tough decisions for us, don't they?"

"Tough? This isn't a tough decision! This is an easy decision. Our friends and our lives are here. We shouldn't have to move anywhere."

"May I ask what your name is?"

Elidria replies with the name she prefers to be called, "Eldra."

"That's a beautiful name." He places his hand on her shoulder and gives her a warm smile. "Miss Eldra, you may be leaving your friends and your home but it's a great, big world out there with tons of amazing people. Don't think of this as losing your old friends, but instead think of it as making new ones. Besides, your old friends won't be going anywhere. I'm sure you can see them again and maybe you can introduce them to your new ones."

"Galia is coming with us," responds Elidria.

"Is she your friend?"

"My *best* friend. I don't know what I'd do if she wasn't."

"Then why don't you both make new friends together? That sounds like quite the adventure." She still looks a little bit sad to the guard, staring at the ground. "Don't worry about the things you are afraid to miss out on. The world keeps moving and so must we all. Do what can be done today and be ready for what happens tomorrow, because tomorrow is something that no one has ever experienced."

Elidria looks up at the guard. "I'm sorry," she says.

"No need to apologize. That's just life."

Raymar finally catches up with Elidria. "I'm so sorry about that and thank you."

"Like I told Miss Eldra, there is no need to apologize. It's our job to protect this country. Whether from physical threats or even emotional, if someone needs help, we're on the case. Are you folks part of the caravan heading for Bihnor?"

"That's us," says Raymar.

"Lucas and I have been assigned as your escorts until Rimdale. We will be replaced by two others there. Can you take us back to your party?"

"Of course, follow me." Raymar starts to lead the guards back to the caravan.

"Thank you, um…." Elidria brings her finger to her chin. "I don't know what to call you."

The guard gives her a huge smile. "Arviakyss," he responds. "You may call me Arviakyss."

Elidria closes her eyes and tilts her head, returning his smile with her own. "Thank you, Arviakyss."

Elidria grabs Gipsy's leg and tries to force him to place it down a certain way. "No, Abi. You don't get the turnip unless you place your hoof here." She is attempting to do something with the horse that would cause most people to question the sanity of the girl.

Delsar bounds out of the trees and enters the clearing where they set up camp. "Here's the schedule for—" He stops himself short when he sees her doing who-knows-what with the horse. "What are you doing?"

Elidria stops immediately and walks over to Delsar with her hands clasped behind her back. "I'm teaching Abi how to walk silently, since, you know, our biggest weapons will be mobility and *stealth*." She covers one side of her mouth and whispers that last word.

"That's an…" Delsar breaths in, "interesting idea. Why did you change his name to 'Abi?'"

She rushes both her hands up against Delsar's mouth and hunches over. "Sh-sh-shhhh."

Delsar forcefully removes her hands from his face. "Don't do that."

She doesn't appear to care about Delsar's stern words and continues her strange antics with a glint in her eye. "We're supposed to be incognito so I gave him an alias. From now on," she gets even quieter, "call him Abi." She straightens back up and returns her voice to normal. "At least, just until we finish our mission."

Delsar begins to gesture with his hands as if he is about to say something but gives up and brings them down to his side. He is definitely one of those people questioning her sanity. He stands there for a few moments and finally pinches the bridge of his nose, shaking his head. "Listen," he starts, "in town, I was able to retrieve a schedule for one of the ferrying companies in Grandell."

"Oh?"

"We are about a day from the coast and the boat I've chosen leaves in two. It's supposedly an eight-day voyage to Fairview. From there, we will be just five days from Bihnor by land. You shaved a whole week from our trek with this detour."

"Did you hear that, Abi? We're going to be—" She suddenly has a realization. "Wait, we *can* take Abi, right?"

"The ferry I chose transports horses as well as up to two carriages. It will just be extra to shuttle them."

"Wonderful!" she exclaims. "Abi, we're going on a voyage together!"

"We will be passengers and *not* crew members. That means we will have eight days that will be perfect for training and training alone," Delsar informs her. "Speaking of, please tell me you did the sword sets I had you practicing before you started doing," he shakes his head again, "whatever it was you were doing with the horse."

"It was stealth training and, yes, I did."

"Good. Do them thirty more times."

"Each?" she exclaims.

Delsar lowers his head a bit and raises his eyebrows.

"Never mind." Elidria pulls out her sword and begins repeating the two new forms that Delsar had taught her the day before. It's the stances that Delsar keeps snapping at her about. All his corrections he keeps giving her are definitely a bit frustrating, but she can't let such things get to her. This is something she has to get good at. Her village depends on it.

Elidria wakes to the sound of rocks and dirt getting knocked around by the spinning of four wheels. It's a sound that she has completely become accustomed to. The rattling of the carriage, however, she has not. Despite that, she had no issue sleeping aboard the carriage last night. Delsar's rigorous training saw to that. He figured that traveling at night would make that time back.

Elidria rolls over from her back onto her stomach and attempts to stand. No success. In fact, she can hardly move at all. Every time she tries, her arms give out from under her. "Delsar!" she cries out. *Ouch!* Even that hurts.

The carriage comes to a stop and Delsar sticks his head in from the front. "What?" He sounds annoyed. Nothing new.

"I can't move," Elidria states, lying flat on her back.

"Why not?"

"Everything just hurts and even when I try my body won't listen to me." Elidria has never trained her body like this before.

"It's your body reacting to the training," Delsar explains. "It means you're getting stronger."

"Well, I *feel* like I'm getting weaker."

"You're just not used to what I put you through yesterday. You can have today off, but after today, you train through the pain. The enemy doesn't wait for you to feel good before they try killing you. You have to learn to fight, even when your body is telling you to give up."

Elidria gives him a blank stare. She never actually thought of that. She could lose an arm but those she fights won't care. "So, is this going to be a thing?"

"Yes, and we're in Grandell's capital," he informs her.

"Oh, uh—"

"Just let your body recover. We can get things done more efficiently if I handle setting up our transportation."

Elidria really can't argue against his plans, even if she wanted to. "In that case, I'm going to just lie here for a bit and maybe train Abi some more."

"Grandell is pretty big. We should arrive at the coast in maybe an hour."

He wasn't wrong. After about another hour of travel, the carriage comes to a stop again. Elidria can smell the familiar scent of the salty water and embraces the fresh sea breeze as the canvas on the carriage lifts from the wind. She can't help but smile as she takes a deep breath.

Delsar hops around to the back and pulls open the drape without warning. "I need your money."

Elidria fumbles and drops her canteen while also inhaling a bit of water. "Dehhl-sahr!" She coughs a couple of times. "You can't just barge in and scare people like that." She is definitely struggling a bit. "Have you ever heard of knocking or announcing your presence?"

Delsar doesn't reply to anything she just said. "I need your money for the ferry."

"How much will this trip cost us?"

"Seventy-five for you, me, and the horse. It's another fifty for the carriage."

"One hundred and twenty-five gold?" she exclaims.

"It's a pretty good deal."

"Delsar, we only have one hundred seventy gold and a pouch of silver left," she tells him. "We will barely have any left when we reach Fairview."

"What happened to you having plenty?" Delsar asks.

"I didn't realize things were this expensive."

"Making up time costs money." Delsar shakes his head. "It's whatever. We'll make up the money some other way. For now, I need you to go to town and pick up some *real* food for the horse and some fruit. The dried pig meat shouldn't be our only food."

"Will I have enough for that?"

"As long as you remember that those things are bought with silver and not gold." He reaches into the back and snatches her bag. He pulls out a pouch of silver and tosses it to her. She doesn't catch it.

She grinds her teeth and scowls at Delsar. "And now you're just rummaging through my bag."

He then pulls out the pouch of gold and places it in his own bag.

"I'm just going to take my bag with me. You didn't have to throw the silver at me. I'm going to just put it back in," she says.

Delsar barely pays her any mind. "Make sure you get this done. We get a full sleep tonight." Delsar turns to head off but has one last thing to say, "Fight through the pain."

"*Right.*" She sounds like she just gave up a little. If Delsar is starting on his job, she may as well start on hers. She grabs her bracers and straps them on. Her arms are not happy about that. "*Golly!*" she exclaims. "Why are you so heavy?" She peeks out the back of the carriage to make sure Delsar didn't just hear her say that to two inanimate objects. He's nowhere to be seen. She takes off her bracers and lays them back on the floor. "I'm not even going to bother with you either," she tells her shinguards. Just boots today. Even just bending to put her boots on hurts. "How am I supposed to fight like this, Delsar?" She listens for a moment but no one replies. She struggles to her feet but is determined to stand. "I'm just grabbing some food," she tells her body. "This will be a piece of cake." She giggles, in a bit of agony, at her own choice of words. She grabs her bag and straps on her sword. Hopping out of the carriage, she crashes to the ground. She lies there for a minute or so. If anyone is to pass by, they will likely think she's dead.

Enough is enough! She pushes to her feet and wobbles around. The docks and booth that Delsar is buying his tickets from are only a couple dozen yards from the carriage and are very much in view of each other. That means there isn't much of a theft threat. She's pretty sure he'll have his eyes on the carriage. However, that also means she has a bit of a walk to get to the market part of town.

The roads have signs that clearly mark which way everything is, so it would take someone truly "special" to get lost here. She locates the sign that reads, "Market and Lodging," and follows the road that leads away from the open beaches and seagrass and into the forest. As she continues, the trees begin to get denser and the shadows get darker. *I just need to stay on the path.* She holds both her hands together against her chest.

The smell and breeze from the ocean doesn't seem to penetrate this far into the woods. Everything seems so still and silent. The birds aren't even chirping. Delsar, or someone else with intuition, would probably have noticed that something is off. Even Elidria senses something wrong but shrugs it off as her fear of the dark. She is wrong.

"Hey there, girly." A round man in an unbuttoned vest, equipped with a club, appears from the darkness in front of her. "What is such a pretty girl like ya wandering around tha woods by ya'self fer? Don't ya know it can be dangerous?"

"He's right," says another man next to him. He's a bit taller than the first but definitely smaller in weight. His weapon is a knife. "I heard that a woman went missing in these here woods just last week."

Elidria draws her sword immediately. "Stay back!" she warns.

The bigger man with the club chuckles. "We just want to make sure ya not alone is all. We'll even make sure ya comfortable." Both men start to approach her.

Elidria makes a slight attempt to run but her ankle rolls. *I have no strength left.* She points her sword directly at the man with the club but he swats it away. She is unable to keep hold of her sword and it crashes down a few feet from her. She turns but the man grabs her wrist and pulls her closer to him.

"Why would a looker like ya resort tah something so violent?"

"I guess we'll have to be violent with her ourselves," says the taller one.

Elidria pulls against the man but is unable to break his grip. She begins screaming for help as loud as she can.

"Ain't no one gonna hear ya out here."

Elidria's heart begins to pound and her chest starts to burn. "The thumb!" she exclaims out loud. With that, she pivots on her right foot, away from the attacker, and pulls up and away with her arm. The man is unable to keep his hold and loses his balance trying to get it back. He leans in towards Elidria and she uses his own momentum, driving her left fist into his mouth.

The man shrieks as his front teeth pierce through his lip and he stumbles backward, dropping his club.

The taller man gets upset over her fighting back. "You moo!" he yells, fully enraged.

"Moo?!"

The man charges at Elidria, holding his knife above his head.

What am I supposed to do now? She steps to the side and the man overshoots her by a few feet. He is slow to turn around and is now unbalanced. He looks like he could be drunk. *Delsar said I can't win with my own strength.*

The taller man begins running at her again. Elidria steps into what Delsar called a 'forward bow,' dropping her weight and her shoulder towards the man. It was one of the many stances Delsar had her do over and over. The man's hip crashes into Elidria's shoulder, sending him toppling over her as she crashes backward from the impact. She feels something dig into her back when she hits the ground. It's the hilt of her sword. She spins over and snatches it before standing back up.

The bigger man, mouth dripping blood, has his club in both hands and he does not look happy. He charges at Elidria and swings his club straight for her head. It's clear that he doesn't care whether she's dead or not anymore. She drops into another stance she practiced and slashes his thigh as the club passes harmlessly over her head. He topples over from the pain but quickly tries to get back up.

"Stay down!" Elidria commands, placing her blade against his neck.

He has no choice but to do as she says. The taller thug, back on his feet, takes off into the woods.

The sound of heavy footsteps and clanging metal approaches them and two guards appear, running from the market district. Both have their hands on their swords, ready to draw them if needed. Seeing Elidria with her weapon out, the guards draw their own. "Drop your sword, miss. We can handle it from here."

Elidria throws her sword to the side, away from the thug.

The guards are pretty sure they know what just transpired but they decide to secure the scene before they jump to any conclusions. One of them grabs the sword while the other keeps watch on Elidria and the man. "We heard a girl yelling for help, though it seems you didn't need any."

The thug immediately tries to formulate his own story in an attempt to throw the guards off. "I was walkin' to da port when dis girl assaulted me. I think she was after mah money."

The guards both look at Elidria and begin laughing. "Do you see the club and dagger?" one asks the other.

"I do," the other guard answers as he walks over and picks them both up.

"It just so happens," the first guard begins to explain, "that women have been getting assaulted in these woods recently. 'Club and Dagger' is what people have been calling them. Funny how there's a club, a dagger, and a woman here. Where's your friend? He can't be far off."

Elidria points into the woods where he ran. The guard nods to his partner and takes off in a sprint, disappearing into the forest.

The other guard secures the club and the knife in his pack. He then wipes the blood from Elidria's blade with a rag and hands it back to her. "That's a nice sword. It looks like an older model we used to use."

Elidria grabs it from him and sheaths it. "Thank you. A friend of mine gave it to me."

"Oh?"

"Yeah. He also taught me how to defend myself."

"That's a good skill to have." He grabs the thug by his vest and forces him to his feet. "Are you going to the coast?" he asks Elidria.

"I'm going to the market."

"That's a shame," he replies. "If I didn't have to take this guy the other way, I'd escort you there."

"It's no problem. I started my walk alone, so I might as well finish that way." It really isn't fine. The feeling of being alone in the woods after an encounter like that doesn't sit well with her. The whole experience is starting to pull on her heart.

"Thank you for what you've done. You've made Grandell a safer place. May I get a name for my report?"

"It's Eldra."

"Okay, Miss Eldra, you have a safe walk."

Elidria just nods in response. She holds her right hand tight to her chest.

"Let's go, punk. Your scumbag days are over."

Elidria stands there and watches the guard disappear down the road with her assailant. She finally turns and continues her way to the market. She takes a deep breath but can't hold back the tears from racing down her cheeks. She even starts weeping audibly as she shivers uncontrollably. The pain in her muscles begins to return as her adrenaline completely dissipates. She feels new pain in her shoulder and her left hand, although that's not why she's crying. The walk to the market from where she is isn't far. In earshot, in fact. Despite that, the walk feels long as she continues saddened and completely alone.

"Next!" The dockmaster ushers Delsar to the counter. "And what can I do for you?"

"I need tickets for the 'Hasty Wake's' departure tomorrow for Fairview," says Delsar, getting straight to the point. No attempted flattery whatsoever.

"Fairview you say? That's a popular one." She begins looking through her notes. "There's a bit of room left. Will it just be you?"

"Me, a girl, our horse, and our carriage."

"You're in luck," says the dockmaster. "They have room even for your carriage."

Delsar gives no form of response.

"How do you wish to pay?" she asks.

"Gold."

"Okay, then. Your total is one hundred thirty-five gold."

"Now wait a minute!" Delsar snaps at the woman. "The tickets should only add up to one twenty-five. Where did this extra ten come from?"

"Running a dock isn't free. It's an extra five for you and the girl which goes straight to the docking company. It allows the ferries to dock here for free."

"I didn't see anything that mentioned this addition," Delsar says, crossing his arms and huffing.

"It's just business, hon. I don't make the rules, I just work here."

Delsar doesn't say anything more. He breathes out a very exasperated breath and begrudgingly hands her the full payment. Perhaps he could have attempted a negotiation, but at this point, he just wants to be done here and get the tickets.

"Make sure you don't lose these." She slides him two tickets and two different permits. "You will of course need them to board the ferry, but they're your insurance, too. Should something happen that cuts your voyage short, the company will refund you entirely. That is assuming you still have your tickets. You will also be fully refunded if you cancel at least one night before departure. You will not be refunded if you cancel tomorrow unless the ferry can fill your spots. Do you understand?"

Delsar just gives her a nod.

"Make sure your permit for your horse is visible and place the one for the carriage on its seat."

Delsar responds with a, "Yup," and walks off. *She talks as much as Elidria.* He tries to imagine the two of them getting in a conversation together but then realizes that they are pretty different. The dockmaster probably has to say those same lines to everyone who buys from her. Meanwhile, Elidria is very much spontaneous and not even an Elven-fortune teller would be able to guess her next words. *Ga!* He's just happy he doesn't have to deal with the dockmaster anymore. But then again, he doesn't like dealing with anyone.

Delsar pulls his pocket watch from his satchel. The line took longer than he had originally hoped but he should still have time to grab those extra things he wants for Elidria. He just wants to make sure he's back at the carriage first. He begins wandering the docks, looking for any kind of tavern or diner. *Where there are people, there is usually food.* That's true pretty much anywhere. He begins following a small group who just finished loading one of the boats. *They probably just finished a job and are now looking to grab a bite to eat.* Delsar is treating this like some sort of stealth mission when all he needs to do is just ask. It's just more proof that he is very uncomfortable interacting with other people.

He follows them for only a minute. That is all it takes to confirm his deductions. The group of men enter a building built right on the docks, over the water. The big sign above reads, 'Salty Crustacean.' He enters right after them. He then weaves his way through the group as they all decide to conglomerate right at the entrance. *What a pain.* After his successful maneuvering, he walks up to the main bar. "Barkeep?"

"Yes?" replies a burly-looking man.

"Do you have potato products?" Delsar asks.

"Uh, yeah. Baked potatoes, sweet potatoes, sliced potatoes. We do potatoes," he replies. "They go great with our lobster. Mashed potatoes specifically."

"That's nice." Actually, Delsar doesn't care. "Do you throw your bags away when you're done with them?"

"What are you? Some kind of census man?"

"No. I just want the bags."

"Tell you what, if you try the lobster meal, with mashed potatoes, I'll grab you a couple of bags."

"I need four, but your offer is fine."

"Roki! One lobster meal with mashed potatoes!" shouts the keeper to the kitchen. "And what to drink."

"Water."

"Water is free so your meal is just three silver." It's a bit more expensive than the meal he never ate back in Eskor, but that's seafood for you.

Delsar hands him three of his own silver pieces. Elidria has the pouch they usually use for these kinds of purchases.

"Your food will be out in fifteen minutes," the barkeeper tells him.

"Thanks." The word "thanks" just slipped out.

Elidria is back at the carriage, sitting in the front seat by the time Delsar returns from his meal. "Here," he says, tossing her the four burlap sacks he acquired from the bar.

"What are these for?" She holds them up for inspection.

"The horse's hooves. They will muffle his walking."

"Delsar."

"Hm?"

"Thank you." She holds them against her chest as if they are a precious family heirloom that has just been returned to her.

"Right." Delsar doesn't appear to understand her reaction to such an immaterial gesture of throwaways. He has no intention of using the horse once they get close to Bihnor so they will likely never use them.

However, to her, they are even more proof that he does have a heart in there somewhere.

Delsar gets back to making sure everything is on track, "Did you grab the feed for the horse and fruits for us?"

"I did, though I couldn't carry it all, so I had to hire someone which did cost a bit extra."

"The price for the ferry was ten more gold that it was supposed to be as well," Delsar informs her.

"So how much gold do we have?" Elidria asks.

"Thirty-five."

"Oh?"

"Never mind that. You should get yourself a *real* meal." He points toward the bar he just came from. "There's a bar on that dock. Go and eat something."

"Would you like to come eat with me?" she asks.

"I just ate so I'll stay here and make sure nothing is missing."

She tries again. "Can you walk me there?"

"Both of us going would be a waste of time." He points again at the dock. "It's right there on—"

DELSAR

"Delsar, please! Please just come with me." She looks terrified and on the verge of crying.

"Okay," he responds. "You're the boss." He gestures for her to lead the way.

The walk there only took about a minute but it felt long and awkward. Neither of them said a word until entering.

The barkeeper greets them with a huge amount of energy. "Hey! Potato Sack! Welcome Back! I see you've brought someone with you."

"Just get her anything she asks for and deliver it to our booth," instructs Delsar.

"I just want whatever you had, please."

Delsar looks at the barkeeper to see if he heard her.

"Right." He did. "Roki! Another lobster meal with mashed potatoes! And just water to drink?"

Elidria perks up. "Actually, do you have, like, um, apple juice?"

The burly man gives her a warm smile, likely realizing something is bothering her emotionally. "Sure, and for you, the juice will be on the house. Three silver, Potato Guy."

Delsar rolls his eyes, realizing that Elidria is again getting a better deal than he did just for being her. He hands him the silver and escorts Elidria to a booth, far from everyone else. He lets her sit first before sitting across from her. "All right, what's going on?" he asks.

Elidria begins her story about what happened in the woods and fights back her tears as she does. "On my way to the market, two men attacked me."

"What?" exclaims Delsar. "How did you get away?"

"Well, I sort of, um, beat them up."

Delsar gives her a surprised, yet almost proud look. "Oh?"

"Yeah, and I think I broke my hand." She holds up her left hand for Delsar to examine.

He leans over the table to take a good look at it. "The back of your hand is definitely swollen. Did you punch one of their faces?"

"Yes, but I won't do it again," she quickly says.

Delsar pulls a bandage from his bag and slides out from the bench. He drops to a knee next to hers and reaches for her hand which she lets

61

him take. He is about to start wrapping it but looks up at her watering tears first. "Tell me, what is *really* bothering you?"

Elidria grimaces, not from the pain in her hand, but by the thoughts that keep playing in her head. "Those men—." She stops, barely keeping it together. "The guards said they attacked other women before. I don't think they were there to just randomly attack me." She can't hold her streams of tears back any longer. They begin flowing violently off her face. "What if they were going to do something to me that was worse than death? What if they already did it to those other women?"

Delsar sits on his knee completely shocked. His mouth drops a little as he tries to think of something to say, though her experience was something he knows he can't ever identify with. He slides onto the bench next to her. She wastes no time and grabs him, burying her head into his side.

"Elidria, you feel now the burden of f-fighting evil," he stutters, periodically. "The toll it has on your s-soul. There are people going through unspeakable things right now and no one is around to save them. A woman will walk through those woods and not even know that she was in danger because you already saved her. Think of those people, the ones you saved, not the ones you couldn't."

"No," says Elidria, still with her head tucked away. "The ones we failed are the ones we should think about and strive to rescue. I escaped and this is how *I* feel." She looks up at Delsar. "Imagine those who couldn't escape. The pain they are in even now. If we fight for only good feelings then we are no different than those men."

The words from Elidria are like nothing he's heard before. He used to save people because it made himself happy. To him, there isn't a real difference between someone doing what most consider is right versus someone who many label as a villain. They both are only doing it to feel happy. At least, that's what he's always thought. "For every wrong in the world, there are a dozen more opportunities to make a right," he finally says.

"I won't forget those who suffered just because it hurts a little," she tells him. "I'm going to save my village and I will do it regardless of my hand or my feelings." She makes a fist with her left hand and stares at Delsar.

Whether she said those things just to hear them for herself or because she truly wishes to live by them, Delsar is certain her convictions are very much set in stone and no one can change her mind about them. He gently takes her left hand. "That doesn't mean you can't heal. You will fight better if your hand isn't broken."

"And I will fight just as hard either way." She opens her fist and lets him tightly wrap it with the bandage.

"I know you will." Delsar ties a knot in the bandage and lowers her hand.

Elidria wipes away her tears and looks at the table. "The food is here."

The barkeeper somehow managed to place the meal and drink on the table without either of them noticing. It was kind of him to not interrupt them. "Hey!" exclaims Delsar.

Elidria startles.

"It took them over fifteen minutes to prepare my meal! It's been like five for this one!"

"They just like me more." Elidria gives her eyes-closed, head-tilted smile.

"I'm going to have to write a complaint about this. Picking favorites," grumbles Delsar. Delsar takes in a deep breath. "Just enjoy your meal now."

Elidria already has her lobster flipped over, digging for the juicy parts.

Delsar ponders everything that was just said in his mind. Despite how terrible her experience was, it was probably one of the best things that could have happened to her. Now she feels the burden of combat and the emotions that go with it. Considering what she said, she experienced even more than just that. This was something she needed before getting to Bihnor.

Elidria gobbles down her meal and leaves no lobster meat.

"That was definitely not your first lobster," Delsar states.

"I live in Bihnor, remember?"

"I thought snails were your—"

He is interrupted by a man crashing through the door and entering the bar. "Help me!" he cries. "My town! My family!" He starts to hyperventilate and is unable to give any clear message.

One patron rushes over to the man. "Sir, what is happening to your town?"

The man is able to compose himself enough to deliver his plea. "There are trolls in my town! At least six of them. They killed our guards and anyone else they saw. My family is still there. I couldn't get them out!"

Elidria turns to Delsar. "We have to—"

"No."

"But—"

"We don't have time. Our boat leaves at noon tomorrow. We can't miss that."

"We can't just turn our backs on his town! They need our help."

"We turn our backs on *your* village if we do help," says Delsar.

"We'll make the time back some other way. We have to help them!"

"It might feel that way but there are others who—"

"Do what can be done today and be ready for what happens tomorrow, for tomorrow is something that no one has ever experienced."

Delsar is taken aback as he recognizes his own words.

"We can't help my village today but we can help his," she continues. "I will not let them experience tomorrow like this."

"Eldra," is the only word Delsar is able to respond with.

"Yes, Delsar. That's me." She smiles and tears up at the same time. "We *can* save them."

"And we can make it back," he tells her. *We can make it all back.* He turns to the man. "How far is your town?"

"I-I think I've been running for the last two hours," he claims.

"We'll take my carriage. You tell us where to go."

"Let's go then!" he exclaims.

Before he follows him from the bar, Delsar turns to the rest of the patrons. "Will anyone else join us?" No one answers. "I'll ask again. Will any of you help us?" Still no one. The thought of fighting six trolls that just killed the well-trained guards doesn't sit well with any of them. "Very well. Elidria?"

"Of course," she replies.

"Wait!" A man, darker than the barkeeper, steps out of the kitchen.

"Roki?" questions the barkeeper.

"This is something I need to do," says the cook who looks about Delsar's size.

"Then let's go. We leave now." No one else says anything or offers any kind of aid. Delsar leads the team of four from the bar as fast as they can run. He looks over at the dockmaster's booth. *If I cancel now, I'll get all our money back.* He thinks about it for a moment before letting the thought pass. That will waste precious time. Plus, there is still a line.

The group all pile into the front of the carriage. "Which way?" demands Delsar.

The man points at the eastern road. "That road will take us straight there."

"Come on Gipsy! Show us your worth."

CHAPTER 5

THE TROLLS

15 Years Ago…

"Just hang on a bit longer!" Roki has his friend's arm over his shoulder as he practically drags him back to his village.

Roki and Hirro had been crossing a narrow river about waist deep, but when Roki tripped over something while crossing, it was still deep enough to sweep him off his feet. In hopes of rescuing his friend, Hirro allowed himself to be swept by the current as well. He grabbed onto Roki's collar but could not regain control. Simply standing up was all that was needed but every time they tried, the water would just push them back over. In a desperate attempt, Hirro pushed off the riverbed and launched the two men a few feet over and into a fallen tree.

Roki was dazed by the impact but quickly grabbed his rescuer as the water started to drag him back under. He pulled him across the tree and back to dry land before coughing up a bit of water. "Thanks for the save, chum," he said while also letting out a bit of a stress-relieving laugh.

"Roki," responded Hirro weakly.

That's when Roki looked over and saw the branch protruding from his chest. "Hirro!" He grabbed his friend and helped him to his feet. "I'm going to get you back. I promise!"

That was two hours ago. The two of them had gone on a one-night hunting trip a few miles from their village. Roki could never have imagined such a routine endeavor could have gone so wrong. "I can see the light from our village! We are almost there!" he informs Hirro.

Hirro just lets out a bit of a groan as acknowledgment.

"I just need to get you down this hill." Like wearing a cape, Roki wraps both of Hirro's arms over his shoulders. "I'm taking you down like this, okay?"

"Uh-huh."

If I didn't slip in that river, we wouldn't be in this mess. It's not just the guilt of slipping. He was the one that convinced Hirro to cross the river at that spot instead of looking for a safer location in the first place.

He leads Hirro down the hill with his feet dragging behind. "Help! We need help!" Roki shouts.

People scramble from their houses and huts to respond to his cry for help. "Roki?" says one man, surprised by his return. "What happened?" He helps turn Hirro over and picks him up by his legs.

"He's impaled." Anyone can see it, but Roki is stressed and doesn't have time to explain the story. They need to get him to the local infirmary, right now. Another villager leads the way and opens the door for them.

"Lay him over here," the Doctor instructs. He is still in his nightgowns and probably just woke up because of the commotion. Roki and the other villager lay him on the table.

"He has a branch in his chest, Doc," Roki tells him.

"How long ago did this happen?" the Doctor asks.

"Maybe one or two hours ago. I'm not sure."

The Doctor starts to cut open Hirro's shirt but stops to check his pulse before lowering his own head. "I'm sorry, Roki," he says without looking up.

It's obvious what he means but Roki will have none of it. "Don't stop now! He was just okay a minute ago!"

"Then he was lucky to have even survived for that long."

"No, look!" Roki pushes the Doctor aside and rips open Hirro's shirt. "I left the branch in so he wouldn't bleed out. Keep working!"

"And he didn't bleed out," says the Doctor. He points to the bit of blood around Hirro's mouth and nose. "He likely drowned in his own blood. I'm so sorry, but there was nothing either of us could do."

"Then get the blood out so he can breathe again."

"We don't have any way of doing that here and even if we could, it wouldn't do any good now. He's gone." The Doctor looks at Roki. Even when it's just impossible, he still feels guilt for anyone that dies on his table.

"But he can't be. Not like this." Roki starts to completely break down. "It's all my fault. It's all my fault. It's all my fault. It's all my fault."

"It's not your fault, Roki. I'm sure it was an accident," the Doctor tries to reassure him.

"I messed up!" snaps Roki. "He saved me but I couldn't save him! I should have listened." He begins to repeat, "What have I done? What have I done?"

"Roki! Get a hold of yourself!" The Doctor grabs him by his shoulders. "As sad and tragic as this is, you can't keep blaming yourself. You can mourn for him but please don't do anything stupid. You can still live for him." The Doctor has seen plenty of people in the field go crazy because of events just like this one. They would blame themselves and enter into an inescapable depression. Sometimes, they would even take their own lives.

"But it *is* my fault. *I* did this to him."

The Doctor slaps him across the face. This completely shocks him. "If you truly blame yourself, then make it up to him somehow. Do for someone what you couldn't do for him."

Roki's desperate breathing starts to slow a bit. He looks at Hirro's lifeless body. "I can do that," he says. "I can." He closes his eyes. "I will make this up to you, I promise."

Delsar pulls the strap that secures Elidria's bracer to her left arm. She can't help but wince as he tightens it. "Are you good?" he asks her.

"Once I start moving, I won't feel a thing," she tells him.

"Don't get yourself killed trying to be like me," he warns. "You could hardly stand earlier. If you can't go on, say so. I'll sit you out immediately."

Elidria shakes her head. "I'm not here to be you. I'm here to save these people."

"Don't get overconfident because you beat two random thugs who had no training."

"It's not confidence, Delsar. It's determination and I have no intention of dying today."

Delsar doesn't respond to her after that. He only glances at her as he checks her other armor plates.

"What? Do you disagree?" she asks.

"Determination may push you past what you thought possible but it won't save you from being dead. If you really have no intention of dying, pack up and leave."

Elidria scrunches her nose and scowls. "You're incredibly encouraging before a battle of life or death."

"And you haven't seemed to grasp the actual horrors that await you. The trolls are going to try to kill you. You *will* have to kill if you—"

"I get it," Elidria says, stopping him from continuing. "These aren't defenseless hogs and they're killing people, so I do get it."

Roki interrupts their "gear-check," sticking his head through the back of the carriage. "The horse is all set. We're ready to go."

"Fine," says Delsar, without looking back at him. He glares at Elidria with an unreadable stare before giving her a nod. "Let's go."

They both jump out of the carriage and Glade, the man who summoned them, hands Delsar Gipsy's reins. "The burlap sacks are on nice and tight," he says. "Good luck, you two."

Delsar flips the reins over the horse's head and turns to face Elidria. "You're in the front," he tells her.

"What?" she exclaims. "I've never ridden a horse before. You should be in the front and I'll just hang on."

"No, you're riding front. I'll kick and move the horse, you only need to steer."

Elidria swallows hard and approaches the side of Gipsy. She starts to examine him and stands on her tiptoes to look over his withers.

Delsar rolls his eyes. "I can give you a boost."

"Please," she replies.

Delsar bends down and interweaves his fingers for her to step on. She places her right leg on his hands. "Unless you wish to ride backward, I suggest you use your left leg."

"Oh, right." She does just that and Delsar gives her a bit of a lift, allowing her to swing her right leg over the horse. Some of her hair flips into her face, forcing her to move it out of her eyes.

"The women in the army wear their hair up so that doesn't happen," says Delsar.

"Or you could be like me and just cut it all off," Roki chimes in.

"Well, I'm not *in* the army and I've never mounted a horse before, so forgive me if I'm not perfect."

Delsar removes his shield and straps it to his arm before gracefully mounting behind her. He pulls his sword out and gives everyone one last reminder. "You two follow Elidria and me into Orange Peak on foot. We'll clear the market and move for the houses. Glade, you said the houses are in a 'target' formation?"

"Yeah," confirms Glade. "It's four rings of houses that circle inside of each other."

"Then we have three alleys to clear. After Elidria and I clear the first ring, you two will go from house to house and evacuate any survivors you find back here. Do not engage with any trolls. Elidria and I will handle any that need to be killed. Once the houses are cleared, we bang out. Everyone understand?"

"I do," says Roki, "but what happens if we have no choice but to fight?"

"You both need to engage at the same time. Get to opposite sides of the troll and only get close when it's looking the other way. Tag-team it and go for its heel and then throat."

Glade begins to repeat, "Heels and throat," to psych himself up. The extra sword and shield Delsar gave him from Galius' set shake in his hands.

"Stick to the plan and you won't have to fight any," says Delsar. He puts his head next to Elidria's ear. "Are you ready?"

She grips the reins in her left hand and pulls out her sword with her other. "I won't be if we take any longer."

"Then we ride. Let's go!" Delsar kicks the horse and they take off in a gallop for the town. Ahead of them is a flat bridge that crosses a low river, connecting the outside world with the market part of town.

Amongst the tents and market stalls, they spy a lone troll that appears completely oblivious to the fact that a horse is careening toward it. Gipsy's hooves plod across the wooden bridge but the sound isn't as sharp as it would have been without the burlap sacks. The troll still hears it and turns around only to be immediately met by Delsar's blade slicing into its throat. It tries to cry out but only a bit of gurgling is produced by its severed throat before it falls to the ground.

"Pull on the reins," Delsar tells Elidria.

She does and Gipsy comes to a stop. Delsar hops off first and gives Elidria a hand. She slides down but looks a bit concerned. "What if they kill Gypsy?" she asks.

"He can outrun them. He'll be fine." Delsar flips his shield over his back and points at a road that cuts through the rings of houses. "We're taking the first left. Come on." Delsar takes off in a sprint and fully expects Elidria to lag behind but she effortlessly keeps his pace. This allows them to zip through the first set of houses in barely a minute.

They exit the alley on the opposite side of the road they started from. Roki and Glade are just now passing the dead troll and Delsar silently points at the first ring, letting them know it's clear. The two men start the tedious task of clearing each house.

The second alley is as barren as the first. House after house they sprint past before emerging, yet again, on the center road. However, Delsar catches a glimpse of a troll entering the third and final alley. Delsar picks his speed up and disappears into the alley with the troll.

Elidria races after him only to see the troll already on its knees. She charges it but before she can do anything, a blade slides out of its head before disappearing again. The troll falls forward and Delsar whips his sword through the air, splattering some of the grey blood from his blade on the surrounding houses. It was a quick takedown. One Elidria wishes she could have seen despite the surge of bile burning the back of her throat. She swallows, forcing it down. The killing churns her stomach, but she does her best to shake her emotions off, reminding herself that this is to save innocent lives.

Delsar says nothing and turns back around, continuing his rotations.

Elidria staggers and feels nausea surge through her body. She catches herself on one of the houses and shakes her head. *It was just a troll,* she thinks to herself. She looks up at Delsar, whose lead keeps expanding, and takes off after him. This time, she is unable to keep his pace.

Delsar exits the last alley, clearing the housing district. He turns back toward the market to start clearing the rest of the town. However, a troll stands blocking their way back. It lets out a huge squeal, alerting anyone or anything to their presence. "And so it begins," says Delsar as Elidria finally catches up.

The troll rips a lamppost from the ground and raises it above its head. It starts making quick little grunts, pumping the post up and down.

Elidria sets herself, ready to fight the beast head-on, but Delsar has other plans. "Lead it into an alley. Go!" he shouts.

She gives Delsar a quick glance but then follows his instructions. She runs at the troll, stealing its attention, and then darts into one of the alleyways.

The troll chases after her. In a straight line, she would stand no chance, but weaving through the narrow alley proves difficult for the troll and its improvised weapon keeps snagging on the houses as well. Finally, the post gets caught on two houses and the troll drops it. It turns around to pick it back up but has its thigh immediately slashed by Delsar as he slides past. The blade was so ineffective, the wound doesn't even bleed, but it does take its mind off Elidria and onto Delsar.

"Eldra!" Delsar shouts as he jumps back and avoids a crushing strike from the troll.

Elidria jumps out from between two houses and approaches the troll from behind. She swings her sword like an axe and chops into the troll's Achilles. The troll screams and twists around to swing at Elidria. She finds herself completely flatfooted because of her attack and is unable to react. The troll strikes but gets its arm caught on one of the houses. Elidria readjusts herself and bounds away.

Though the chop was not the brightest idea, leaving Elidria completely defenseless, it still proves effective as the troll starts to fall over and crashes through the side of a house. Much of the house begins to fall, sending debris and rubble all over the alley where Elidria was. The troll lands on its back with its upper-half through the house.

Delsar tries to get in close for the killing blow but the troll keeps swinging its arms around wildly. It's like fighting a cat on its back. Delsar removes his shield and straps it to his arm. "We've got this," he says. He charges the troll and tries to reach its throat but the troll smashes its arm into Delsar's shield, sending him back. He tries again but gets the same result. That arm has to go. He charges with his sword at the lead, hoping to remove the arm that keeps thwarting him. He swings down with all his strength but his blade never meets the troll. The troll sticks its hand out and catches Delsar's arm. The momentum of his swing jars Delsar's sword from his hand. He drops his shield and frantically reaches for his knife that resides in his satchel. The satchel that rests against his right hip. The troll raises Delsar's right arm even higher, making it impossible to reach across and grab his knife. He gives up and smacks the troll's thumb with his fist.

The furious troll lifts Delsar up even higher. It is clearly about to slam him to the ground, ending Delsar's life. He squirms and tries to break free.

"Hey, there."

The troll freezes and tilts its head back. That's what Elidria was hoping for. She plunges her sword straight down into its eye. She adds another push, sliding the sword even deeper into the troll's head.

The grip on Delsar weakens and he frees himself, crashing to the ground. He scampers to his feet and grabs his sword, preparing for the troll to be angrier than ever. But the troll's body is now a lifeless corpse.

"Don't worry, Delsar. I got it." Elidria stands in the house, next to the troll's head with her sword deep in its eye.

"Wait." Delsar swallows and catches his breath a bit. "How did *you* get there?"

"They left their door unlocked."

"Oh?"

"And I can't get my sword out." Elidria pulls at her sword as a demonstration.

"All right." Delsar grabs his shield and slides it on his back. He climbs across the troll and grabs hold of Elidria's handle.

"You called me Eldra," she says as he pulls the blade out.

"It was quicker to say," he tells her as he wipes the blood from her sword.

"It's a start." She retrieves her sword from Delsar.

"Time to run again. They know we're here now."

"Right."

"Let's go!"

"Is anyone in here?" shouts Roki. He and Glade have already cleared countless houses and haven't found a single survivor. "If anyone is, we are here to rescue you."

"I'm going to head over to the next house," says Glade. "There are still a lot of houses and it will go faster this way."

"No way, man. Delsar said to stay together at all times. I know you're concerned about your family, but to save them, you have to be alive first."

"But this is taking too long!" It's clear just how frustrated Glade is with all the negative results. "The survivors are probably at the stronghold. That's where we should be looking. Not here."

"Delsar hasn't cleared by the stronghold yet." Roki places his hand on Glade's shoulder. "We stick to the houses and we stay together. That's how we'll find your family."

"If Delsar really has cleared the houses, then there should be no reason we can't split up."

Both men whip around and direct their attention to rumbling by a table. They ready their shields and point their swords.

"Glade, is that you?" Part of the floor flips open to reveal an older woman atop a ladder.

"Miss Wanda!" exclaims Glade.

"Are you really here to rescue us?" she asks.

"Y-yes, we are. Where's my family? Are they down there?"

"I'm afraid not." Wanda climbs out with the help of Roki and is followed by seven others. "The town split up and hid here, at the Mayor's house, and in the windmill."

"Then we have two more places to check. Come on, Roki!"

Roki grabs Glade by the shirt and halts him. "Hold on. Let's get these guys out while the market is still clear." He turns to Wanda. "What about the stronghold? Is anyone there?"

"It got overrun by the trolls. We dared not hide there."

"Here's the plan. Glade and I are going to escort you guys out. Glade, do you know where the Mayor's house is?"

"I do."

"Then after we get these guys out, we go there. Got it?"

Glade nods his head. "Then let's do this quickly."

"That's fine," says Roki. He opens the door and leads the survivors out. "Come on! Hurry up!"

Glade's order didn't do anything. Everyone is already running from the house as quickly as they can.

They run past the first troll that Delsar killed in the market. Some of the survivors look away or cover their mouths as they go around it.

Roki stops at the bridge and points across it. "Come on guys. Just keep running and follow this road until you get to the carriage. We'll be back with more survivors."

The eight survivors continue on their run. Some say "Thank you," while others don't even look back.

"Take us to the Mayor's house," says Roki.

"If the houses are safe, we should go to the windmill first."

"Are you crazy? Just stick with the plan."

"That's easy for you to say," snaps Glade. "It's not *your* family that you're trying to save."

Roki grabs Glade by both his shoulders. "Believe me, I *have* been in situations like this. There is a right way and a wrong way to go about things, even if you're being noble. I made the biggest mistake of my life trying to do what's right. Let's follow Delsar's instructions and save your family *his* way."

Glade looks like he's about to reply to Roki's speech but instead points past him and screams, "Troll!"

Glade jumps out of the way but Roki stands there, frozen in fear.

"Get out of the way!" Glade warns.

Roki raises his shield. He looks like he's going to try to stop the one thousand pound charging monster with just his circular shield.

Glade pushes Roki out of the way and takes the full force of the charging troll, sending Glade and the troll through the guardrails and into the river below.

Roki snaps back to his senses. He runs to the ledge and peers into the water a few feet beneath him. "Glade!" Bubbles pop up to the surface, but no Glade or troll. "Oh, please, not again." He starts frantically looking for anything he can use but keeps drawing a blank. "Help!" he starts to shout. "Delsar!"

Another cry from a troll emanates from the upper-market. Roki sets himself back up, this time ready for the troll. The cry is cut short and it sounds like it may have crashed to the ground.

Delsar and Elidria both bound down the market stairs. Delsar runs up to Roki and Elidria watches their back. "What happened?" Delsar asks.

"Glade fell in the river with a troll," says Roki. "I haven't seen either of them come back up."

"Trolls sink." Delsar quickly removes his many accessories and lays them on the ground. "Elidria, stay with Roki." He dives in with only a knife.

"Delsar!" screams Roki.

"He can handle this," says Elidria. "Since the one troll I killed, he's been killing them faster than I can move." Elidria just witnessed him kill two trolls in the upper-market as if they were nothing. She had no time to do anything. He just ran in and killed them. He's becoming exponentially more efficient with each troll he fights. Watching him amazes her.

Roki doesn't respond to Elidria. He has his eyes fixated on the still water. "Come on," he repeats a couple times. Roki catches movement a few feet from where Delsar dived in. Glade's head, followed by Delsar's, burst from the water. "There they are!" Roki points.

Elidria can't help but look.

"Help us find a way out of here." The river doesn't flow but it is still about six feet below the market. The walls of the river are lined with smooth bricks making climbing up nearly impossible.

"You could just wait for high-tide," jokes Elidria, trying to lighten the mood.

"Watch your back," Delsar reminds her with a flat tone.

She turns back around to watch for any more threats. "I'm pretty sure I saw some stairs in the upper-market that lead down to the river," she says without looking back.

"Got it. Watch my stuff."

"I can't do both."

"I was talking to Roki."

"How is Glade?" Roki asks.

Delsar rolls his eyes. "I'm swimming now. Talk later." He begins his short swim with Glade resting atop his chest.

It only takes a couple minutes to reach the stairs. Glade starts to wake up as Delsar drags him from the water and up the stairs. "Wh-wh-what? Delsar?"

"Are you all right"? asks Delsar.

"Stop!"

Delsar stops immediately. "What's wrong?"

"I think my whole right side is broken."

"What about your legs? Can you walk?"

"I think I can."

Delsar backs off and lets him stand back up.

He grimaces as he does. "My whole arm hurts hanging like this."

"Then you're done."

"What do you mean?"

"We don't need you anymore," says Delsar. "Go back to the carriage."

"But I'm on my feet."

"You lost both your sword and your shield in the river, your arm is destroyed, and the pain you don't realize you're in will immobilize you at any moment." Delsar gives him a hand down the market stairs. "You're a liability now."

Glade stops halfway down the stairs. "But I haven't saved my family. I have to find them."

"Shut up, Glade!" snaps Delsar. "We are doing things my way and you are no longer a part of my plan. If your family is still here, Elidria and I will find them. Just back off!"

Glade's face turns white and he says nothing to counter Delsar. Instead, he submits, following him back to the others.

"Roki, take Glade back to the carriage and then come back," Delsar instructs while reequipping.

"Leave him to me. Oh, yeah." Roki remembers something. "There are two more sets of survivors. One is in the Mayor's house and the other is in the windmill."

"Where are those, Glade?" asks Delsar.

"The Mayor's house is on the center road. It's the one closest to the center on the right. It has the King's flag so you can't miss it."

77

"And the windmill?"

"That's on the east side of town. In the farming district, beyond the wheat field."

"Elidria and I will grab the survivors from the mayor's house and meet back here. Then, the three of us will take on the windmill and bang out of here. Got it?"

Elidria nods.

"Come back here when you're done," Delsar says to Roki. "Keep up." Delsar takes off and Elidria chases after.

"All right, Glade." Roki walks over to assist him. "Let's get you out of here." He tries to help, but Glade grimaces again.

"Can you try and find something that I can use as a sling? I'm not sure I can make it back like this."

"Sure thing, bud." Roki peeks in the nearest market stall and begins rummaging around for any kind of clothing to support Glade's arm. "This looks like it will do." He holds up a shirt for Glade's approval, except he's not there. "Glade?" Roki looks around and sees him running east, away from the bridge. "Wait!"

It's no use. Glade has only one thing on his mind.

Roki hops out of the stall and chases after him. They run past the houses and then past a couple various buildings. Glade pushes into the wheat field and gets further ahead of Roki. He fills his lungs to call out, but the sound catches in his throat as the top-half of a troll appears above the wheat heads. Panicked, he ducks into a thick part of the wheat field.

The creature lets out an all-too-familiar battle cry. The same cry one made before slamming Glade into the river. Roki gets back up and readies his sword, except the troll isn't after him. It's chasing Glade. "Watch out, Glade!" Roki shouts but isn't heard.

Glade tries to open the windmill door but it's locked, so he starts pounding on it instead. "It's Glade! Are my wife and son in here?"

"Dad?" a voice from inside responds.

"Yes! It's me!"

The door opens to reveal about ten individuals, excluding the boy, all hiding in the corner.

"Look out!" shouts the boy, maybe thirteen, grabbing Glade and pulling him in.

The troll slams into the entrance, sending brick and mortar into the survivors. Glade and his son are thrown to the floor. The troll steps through a new hole, bricks falling off its shoulders and stone crushing underfoot. Everyone starts crying and screaming for their lives as it enters and blocks any way for them to escape. The troll lets out another deafening cry, knowing it found its prey.

"Hey!" shouts Roki, hurling a rock into the back of its head. The troll turns around and Roki slides past it, placing himself between the troll and the survivors. "Everything is going to be okay!" he exclaims. "I'm going to make things right."

CHAPTER 6

THE SHIFTER

3 Years Ago…

"Just let me leave and the girl gets to live," demands the shifter.

"Not going to happen," responds the guard. "You're wanted for illegal experimentation and conspiracy against Ithendar. Give me the girl and come peacefully." He extends his hand for the retrieval of the hostage.

The shifter forcefully pulls her away. "Not on your life!" he snaps. "What I'm doing goes beyond what you could *ever* understand."

"Then tell me about it." The guard does his best to keep the shifter's mind off the girl. "Maybe you can help me understand."

"Do you take me for a fool? I am not dumb enough to fight a guard on my own. I will be taking this girl out of town. When I feel no one has followed, I'll let her go and be on my way. No one else needs to get hurt," the shifter says, pointing at the other guard.

The partner had been unfortunate enough to not realize that this man was a magic-user until it was too late. Some townspeople are doing their best to treat an ugly wound in his chest.

"You will pay for what you've done to him, along with your other crime!" says the guard, losing his patience.

"You're the ones that cornered me," the shifter reminds him. "What, you thought I would simply let you take me? I'm on the verge of a breakthrough! Your lives are meaningless compared to the work I'm doing."

It is clear to the guard that this shifter has no care for human life and that he probably has no intention of letting the girl go alive. If the guard is going to do something, it has to be now. The guard lunges his sword for the hand that holds the knife against the girl's neck.

The shifter casts his own image over the girl in hopes of confusing the guard. He pulls the girl and steps out of the way.

"I won't fall for the same trick twice!" the guard exclaims, sending a bolt from the crossbow at his hip, straight into the hand of the shifter's opaque body.

The shifter shrieks and the image he threw over the girl vanishes.

The girl breaks free and runs behind the guard, who now points his sword directly at the shifter. "You've lost. Give up or die."

The shifter's black image laughs. "That was a good trick. Unfortunately for you, I am *much* better at such deception."

An arrow screams through the air and strikes the guard between his breastplate and abdominal plate, shocking him. He stands there for a moment before dropping his sword and collapsing to the ground.

Roki bounds up to the girl and crouches down to her height. "You're safe now. He won't be hurting anyone again."

"What did you do?" screams the girl.

Roki steps back, confused by her anger. "What do you mean?"

"You saved me," says a voice directly behind Roki. Suddenly a sharp pain befalls his leg as a knife slashes through it.

Roki drops to his knees. He whips around to see a shadow of a man running toward the woods. Roki grabs for another arrow but there are none there. The shadow snatched them before running off. "What was that?" he asks out loud. He twists back around to face the man he just shot, except it's not who he thought it was. The image of the shifter disappears and reveals the guard instead. He shot and killed the guard that already saved the girl. "What have I done?"

The troll throws its head back and gives one massive cry. It charges Roki and swings straight for his head.

Roki throws his arm up and the strike splinters his older, wooden shield. The force of the blow sends him back. His feet slide and stumble through the rubble. He catches himself, plants his feet, and sends a wide swing at the beast's midsection.

The troll catches the blade in its hand and Roki slides it right out, leaving a huge gash in its palm. It shrieks and tries to push Roki further away with a kick.

Roki points the tip of his blade at the oncoming foot, but the troll's underfoot proves too tough. The foot knocks the blade aside and slams into Roki's chest, sending him ten feet on his back.

A couple survivors run to Roki and help him back up. "When I say run, you guys run! Go straight to the market entrance. Got it?"

The survivors give him a mix of blank and scared looks, showing that they've lost all hope.

"Just run when I say!" Roki goes on the offensive but stays further from the troll than last time.

The troll starts getting more aggravated with every swing it makes because Roki simply steps back, putting more and more slashes into its arms. Tired of the pokes and pricks, the troll enters deeper into the windmill, hitting its head on the chandelier. It rips it down and hurls it at Roki.

Roki spins out of the way but gets met by the troll's massive arm, and violently crashes into the wall. He staggers back to his feet, dazed and bruised. He shakes his head to clear his vision. "You're going to have to hit harder than that," he says, not for the troll to understand, but for the survivors to know he isn't done yet. "This is it. Get ready!" he yells to them.

Roki and the troll charge each other at the same time. The troll with both arms raised above its head and Roki with both hands grasping his sword, shield still strapped to his left arm. Roki's dash is quicker than what the troll expected. He stabs his sword into its stomach. It stumbles back, allowing Roki to slide it back out.

For a moment, the troll looks sad. The sad face is quickly replaced with pure hatred. It drops one huge hand down to crush Roki.

Roki drops his sword and braces his shield above his head with both arms. The massive fist shatters the shield into pieces and Roki drops to his knees from the force. His left arm screams from the impact.

With its other hand, the troll picks Roki up, wrapping around his neck and chest.

"Run!" shouts Roki with what will likely be one of his last breaths. "Now!"

The survivors are stunned watching the fight. Glade is the first to say anything. "He's giving us a chance! Let's go!" He starts for the big hole in the side of the windmill and the survivors follow.

The troll sees them moving and runs after them.

"No one else dies today!" Roki sticks his hand in one of the troll's many gashes on the hand that grasps him.

That does the trick. The troll completely forgets about the survivors and stops to yank Roki's arm from its wound. With an effortless squeeze, the creature crushes his wrist and forearm, popping tendons and reducing his bones to splinters.

Roki screams and digs his teeth into the troll's arm.

The troll slams him onto his back and pulls his arm, dislocating it. It releases its grip and places its massive foot against his chest.

Roki feels his breath being forced from his lungs as he gasps, trying to inhale with no success. He can feel his chest buckling and his ribs being pushed out of place. In one last desperate attempt, he reaches out with his left arm and tries to grab his sword. The handle sits only a few inches from his fingertips. This is it. There is nothing else he can do. *Did I buy enough time for the survivors? I wish I knew.*

THWACK! Something hard smacks into the back of the troll's head and lands next to Roki. He tries to focus on what it was but his eyes refuse to work.

The troll releases a bit of pressure to face the annoyance. It immediately takes another rock straight to the face.

Glade's son stands at Roki's defense, hefting another rock. He is not alone. Every survivor from the windmill begins rushing the troll. It steps off of Roki and swings its arms wildly. A few of the survivors get knocked around but others grab onto its arms and legs. One even manages to get behind it and jumps on its back, putting it in a chokehold.

Roki gasps for breath and his eyes rattle around in his head before they refocus. He quickly gets his bearings back as oxygen surges through his body. He rolls over and grabs his sword with his barely functioning left arm.

The troll shakes the people from his arms and grabs the man on his back, throwing him into a pile of hay in the corner. They get right back up and begin pulling on its arms again. The troll kicks a woman right at Roki, who for a moment, almost tried to catch her. In his current condition, he decides against it and steps out of the way. The troll watches Roki get closer and desperately tries to free its arms but more begin grabbing them and don't let go.

Roki easily avoids the slow-moving arms and slashes its heel, bringing it to its knees. It brings its arms in front of its face, but the people pull back. Even the woman who got kicked is back up, and that is all the troll can handle. Its arms drop and with one well-aimed strike, Roki's blade passes cleanly through the troll's throat. Its eyes go wide and it begins to waver before finally falling hard on its face.

Roki stands there, dismayed, catching as much breath as he can.

"You saved us," says one townsperson. "What is your name?"

"His name is Roki!" exclaims Glade. "Let's hear it for Roki!"

Before anyone can start cheering, Roki stops them. "No! Don't! There may be more. Let's get out of here before they show up. Is everyone okay?"

"We can all still move if that's what you mean," says one woman.

"But can you run?"

No one responds with any form of negative.

"Then we run." Roki dashes out of the windmill with eleven others at his heels.

"Run!"

Two trolls chase after Delsar, Elidria, and the sixteen survivors from the mayor's house. The survivors are all scrambling in a full panic and the trolls are bearing down on them, closing any space they have between them.

"Elidria, we stop the trolls here!" He spins around at the end of the houses and lets the survivors run past him. He has no intention of letting those trolls into the market.

Elidria starts pushing through the panicked townspeople and races for Delsar's side. Her eyes start rattling and she stumbles on her feet. Delsar says something but she can't make it out. "I can't hear you!" she shouts. His lips move again but now his voice isn't even muffled. The nauseous feeling she felt a few minutes ago surges through her. She drops her sword and everything around her feels like it's closing in. *I have to keep going!* Everything turns grey and her eyes feel heavy. Her knees tremble and everything turns black as she collapses to the ground before making it to Delsar. Her time is up. She is well past her limit. The training from yesterday and the assault from earlier were already too taxing on her. She pushed herself further than she thought possible, but now her body is taking over. And it has had enough.

"Elidria!"

There is no time to help her. The trolls are only strides away. One troll runs at Delsar while the other has its sights on the unconscious girl. Delsar hurls his dagger at Elidria's troll in hopes of stealing its attention. It bounces off the troll but it does the trick. Both trolls are now fixated on him. "Bring it!" he shouts, psyching himself up.

'Hit and run' tactics will leave Elidria vulnerable, so that is out of the question. Can he stand his ground against monsters nearly twice his own height? He drops into the very stance Elidria used against her taller attacker in the woods, except Delsar puts all his weight forward and braces his blade against his arm plate in hopes of tripping the troll and sending it tumbling.

The first troll's shin connects with his blade and Delsar adds a bit of a push and lift to help the troll off its feet. The move works and the troll trips over Delsar. Even with his near-perfect stance, he is unable to stay upright because of the troll's force on impact. He falls back on his right knee and then rolls sideways to avoid the second troll. He slashes at the troll's heel but only hits the calf, doing no damage.

He jumps to his feet and charges the troll. He needs to kill it before the first troll gets back up. *Fighting two at once is difficult,* he thinks to himself, *but fighting just one, that's easy.* He slides past the troll and slashes again at its heel, this time cutting clean through.

The troll drops to a knee and swings wildly, but Delsar, knowing the troll was going to use the same strike all the other ones have been using, had already moved. The creature panics, losing sight of Delsar and whips its head around to find him. It finally catches sight of him, but only after the blade passes through its throat. It grabs at its neck but it's no use. Air seeps from the slit, bubbling the blood rushing out before the troll's life leaves it.

Delsar backs away and lets it fall to the ground. He turns back for the first troll but it is still on the ground, holding its shin. He never would have been able to do that much damage swinging at the troll's leg on his own. The force of the troll's weight and speed were just what he needed.

The troll is too fixated on the pain in its leg to notice Delsar walk next to it. Delsar raises his sword and plunges it into the troll's eye, killing it in an instant. He quickly pulls it out and scans the ground. "Elidria?" *Where did she go?*

"Delsar," says a male voice from behind.

Delsar whips around, sword pointed at the possible new threat.

"That's what the girl called you, right?" A man in red robes holds Elidria's limp body, with his arm tucked under her right shoulder and a knife to her throat. "You're upsetting my plans."

"So these are your trolls?" It's a question he doesn't need answered. It's obvious to Delsar that this man is responsible for the monsters.

"They aren't just *trolls*," says the mystery man. A sadistic grin creasing angular features. "They are *Rock* Trolls. My own creation. Named after the thickness of their skin."

"That seems like a bit of an overstatement. I can still slice them like any other troll." Delsar starts to circle the man. The man keeps pace with Delsar's flanking maneuver, keeping Elidria directly between them. Keen eyes regard Delsar in a casual manner. Delsar can feel them studying him, watching him. Calculating.

"You are very right. I have some more work to do before they are perfect, but watching you has helped me a lot. The trolls are too uniform. Too predictable. They killed the six guards with no problem, but not you."

"I'm a quick learner," Delsar says, picking up his dagger from the ground. "What exactly is your play? Why attack this town?"

"I know what you're doing, boy," snaps the man. A sudden scowl darkens his face. "You're stalling until you find a way to kill me."

"Can you blame me? You've had plenty of time studying me. It only seems fair that I return the favor."

"I would be offended if you didn't. The four of you managed to kill my twelve trolls, so I'd rather not let you analyze much longer. Because of that, I'll keep this brief. My work here is done and I will be on my way. However, my trolls are *far* from perfect and you will make the perfect testing subject. Come with me and fight my trolls until I make one that can kill you. Should you not, I'll have to take this girl instead. It will hardly be fair."

"That's your proposal? Who would ever agree to that?"

"Do you not care about the girl? Does she mean nothing to you?"

"You've miscalculated the situation. She's just my employer. I can always get a new one."

"Then I guess I made a mistake," says the man. "Such a pity it has to be like this. You've seen my face so now you must die. So will she, but a lot slower, I'm afraid."

Delsar wastes no time after hearing the man's comment. He hurls his dagger at the hand holding the knife to Elidria's neck, but the blade passes clean through his hand as if he's not even there.

Delsar's knife stabs into Elidria's collar. She wakes up and screams.

Delsar is completely mortified. "Elidria!" he cries.

Elidria smashes her head into the man's nose and sends him stumbling back.

Delsar rushes the man and runs past Elidria. He strikes for the hand that still holds the knife but the blade passes through and does no damage. Frustrated, Delsar charges shoulder lowered to tackle him at the waist. He crashes to the ground, surprised as his entire body passes through.

Elidria pulls the knife from her collar with her right hand and spins around, punching the man in the face with her left. She then grabs him and flips him over her shoulder, slamming him to the ground exactly where she first went unconscious. With one final jab, she knocks him out.

Delsar gets back up and tries to assist her. "Are you all right?" He reaches for her left hand but she pulls away.

"Don't touch me," she says, stepping back.

"But your collar."

"You mean the one that had the knife that you threw in it?" She points at her collar to reveal a wound that already stopped bleeding.

"I don't get it. What about your hand?"

Elidria holds up her right hand for Delsar to examine.

"Your broken one," he corrects.

"Oh, yeah." Elidria holds up her left hand, revealing no new injuries. It doesn't look any worse at all. "I forgot about the pain after I felt the knife stabbed in me." She gives Delsar a forced smile.

Her light jokes did always lighten the mood, even if Delsar never shows it. However, she didn't sound happy and her comment only made him feel worse. "Look, I'm really sorry. I don't know what happened."

"Stop, Delsar. I heard you say I'm replaceable, so give it a rest."

Delsar's heart drops hearing her repeat it, and it's true, he did say that. He straightens up. *This is why I stopped caring.* "Help me find his knife," he instructs.

"I have it right here." Elidria pulls the man's knife from her belt.

"How?"

"You don't know all my tricks."

Delsar's mind puzzles and a dark feeling surrounds him. This whole situation just feels wrong but if he says anything, he may offend and hurt Elidria more than he already has. "I guess not."

Elidria grabs the man and hoists him over her shoulder.

"Wow. Do you have him?"

"You think I can't handle this guy?"

"It's not that," says Delsar. "I just couldn't touch him earlier. Some kind of magic field or something."

"Clearly I can, so just leave him to me."

Delsar grabs Elidria's sword off the ground.

"Delsar!" Roki runs past the housing district with a multitude of people with him. "This is everyone. Let's get going."

"Why aren't you at the bridge?" Delsar eyes Glade and gives him a stern look.

"I'll tell you later. Let's get clear first." Roki walks over to Elidria and eyes up the man over her shoulders. "Who's this guy?"

"The trolls are his doing," Delsar says. "He's some sort of magic-user."

Roki gets closer to get a better look, but Elidria steps back, a pool of blood at her feet. "Are you okay?" Roki asks.

"Ask Delsar," she snaps.

"I've seen this guy before!" Roki exclaims, pointing at the man.

"This exact guy?" asks Delsar.

"I did and he *is* a magic-user. He's specifically called a shifter."

"*What* is a shifter?"

Glade interrupts. "Hey, if it's all right, we're going to the carriage."

"That's fine." Delsar waves them away but still focuses on Roki's answers.

"I'm going with them," says Elidria. "I'll have one of them take a look at me."

"Have someone take that guy for you."

"I can handle him," she says, again.

"All right, Elidria. So, what *is* a shifter, Roki?"

"Shifters can throw their image around and even place it on other people. It's a good thing you got this guy when you did."

"Are their images physical?"

"They're just images. You'll pass through it unless there is something underneath."

"If they can throw their image around..." Delsar whips out his bow and nocks an arrow. He spins around and points it at Elidria who now holds the man upright with a knife to his throat.

"I suppose I bit off more than I can chew," she says. Both her image and the man's begin to fade, revealing the man holding an unconscious Elidria. "Funny. This situation feels familiar, but now I know you *do* care for the girl."

"Let her go," demands Delsar. "You have nowhere to run." He aims his bow directly at the shifter's head.

"I could kill her right now."

"Then I *will* kill you. There is no circumstance where you get out alive unless you let her go."

"You're wrong." The shifter sports a smug smile on his face. "You need me for information, so you see, I'm going to take her—" He gets cut short as the arrow from Delsar's bow strikes him in the face, causing him to drop the knife and Elidria. He and Elidria fall to the ground.

Roki runs over to Elidria.

Delsar nocks another arrow and stands above the shifter. "Actually, you're wrong." He draws it back and points it at the shifter's head. "I need her more than I need you."

"You killed him," says Roki. He points at some of the townspeople who had turned back around, hearing the commotion. "Leave it at that. There's no need to shoot a dead man. Help me get Eldra back."

Delsar stares at the arrow lodged in the shifter's cheek and closes his eyes. He takes a deep breath and places his bow and arrow away. "Fine." Delsar points at one of the town's men. "You! Help Roki get her to the carriage."

"Where are you going?" Roki asks.

"I'm going to make sure there are no other trolls. Once you get Elidria to the carriage, bring everyone back."

"You think the town is clear, then?"

"I do. I don't think he planned on ever revealing himself." Delsar hands Roki Elidria's sword. "I think his attack failed so he planned to kill us all in our sleep posing as Elidria. It might have worked if you didn't recognize him."

"Then good luck, Delsar. Watch your back out there." Roki turns to lead the man carrying Elidria. "Let's get her out of here. What's your name?"

"I'm Thoms."

The two men cross the bridge and begin their walk back to the carriage.

Delsar bends down to examine the shifter and pulls down his collar, revealing a bloody knife wound. Even though there was no blood while he looked like Elidria, the shifter could not change what was underneath. Delsar then checks to see if the shifter is breathing. Satisfied, he leaves the body and climbs to the market's second level.

The town isn't the biggest, so it doesn't take Delsar long to find the harbor. It's not a large harbor but there is room for one dock, two small boats, and one large one. All still present but damaged enough to not escape on. That was likely done to keep the townspeople from leaving. One of the smaller craft looks like it could still sail, but probably not far. He clears the docks, a crane, the boats, and anything else that may be hiding someone or something. He only finds the carnage left over by the trolls' attack.

The stronghold is near the water. Delsar locates the small, castle-looking structure and makes his way inside. There are bodies thrown all over the inside and even a couple guards. Anyone who thought the stronghold would be their salvation paid for that assumption with their lives.

Delsar sighs and sheaths his sword. The town really is clear. He takes a different route even though he's certain there is not another living thing in this town other than himself. He waits at the bridge for a few minutes until the carriage finally comes into view. Four men from the town are pulling it and Gipsy is being led next to it. Delsar runs across the bridge. "What happened to my horse?" he exclaims.

Roki greets him. "Your horse has a mighty limp, Delsar. I'm afraid we ran him lame today."

Delsar brings his hands to his head in frustration. Not only are they likely going to miss their voyage tomorrow, but now their ground transportation is down.

"Eldra is in the back of the carriage," says Roki, "though it's not going to fit across the bridge."

Delsar is running all sorts of different ideas through his head to make up the time they lost and doesn't give Roki a very insightful solution. "It's whatever. Just leave it there. The boat!" he suddenly exclaims.

"The boat?" questions Roki.

"We can use the one at the harbor to make up time." Delsar is clearly excited but Roki doesn't understand why.

"What do we need to make up time for?"

"Not you. Elidria and I can use the boat instead of the horse."

"I don't know where you're trying to go but the town may need their boat."

"They can live without it. Besides, I'm sure they will be more than happy to help me since I helped them."

"Listen, Delsar, the sun will be going down soon. Whatever is on your mind about tomorrow, let it be. Get some sleep, and on a fresh mind, I'm sure you can figure out your horse problem."

Delsar responds with a "Hm" and turns to the four men who finished pulling the carriage. "Two of you take Elidria to the Mayor's house and lay her in a bed."

Roki and Delsar cross back over the bridge, into town.

"I assume the town is clear?" asks Roki.

"It is."

Delsar and Roki step to the side to let the others pass.

"Thank you, Delsar."

"I didn't save *your* town."

"But you did save me."

Delsar thinks back. "At what point did I ever save you? You seemed well-in-hand the whole time."

"You saved me from myself," Roki explains. "I've made some mistakes and have been a problem for others in the past. You gave me the chance to make those mistakes right again."

"Like whatever happened between you and the shifter?"

"I never said anything about having a problem with the shifter."

"The fact that you studied up on him tells me otherwise."

Roki can't help but smile. "You're quite perceptive."

"I just pay attention to the obvious." Two people carrying Elidria walk by. They aren't fumbling her or anything like that, but Delsar can't help himself from snapping at them anyway. "Be careful with her! Take her straight to bed and make sure she's comfortable." Delsar catches Roki looking at him funny. "She can't pay me if she's dead," he says.

"That makes perfect sense. What did you do with the shifter's body?"

"I didn't do—" Delsar's brief and calm serenity with Roki is replaced with dread. *So much for me being perceptive.* "Come on!" He takes off for the harbor and Roki follows after, albeit a bit slower as he tries to keep his shoulder still.

"What's going on?" Roki shouts to Delsar who bounds up the market stairs in just a couple of strides.

"The boat!" he yells back, disappearing from Roki's view.

Roki runs as quickly as his body will allow. His arms scream in agony, but relief is going to have to wait. He rounds a corner and Delsar already has his bow drawn and pointed at a boat sailing away. He watches the arrow release and fly through the air before passing through the red robes of the shifter and striking the small boat's mast. The image fades and returns to the shifter himself.

"You had me earlier, Delsar!" the shifter shouts across the harbor. "It's too bad *he* stopped you from finishing the job," he says, referring to Roki.

Delsar fires another arrow but the shifter has ample time to move.

"You blew your chance," the shifter says as the boat moves further away. "Next time I will not be so easy. Next time you and the girl will die. I promise you that."

Delsar shoots one last arrow that has little chance of connecting at such a range. "And I won't miss next time!" Delsar yells in retaliation.

"You didn't miss! My face will never look the same and I hold you personally responsible! Mark my words, Delsar, I will make even those you trust most turn on you!"

Delsar can't do anything but watch the boat drift farther away. He lets out a frustrated cry and drops to his knees.

Roki runs to his side. "Delsar, don't worry about him right now. You won. You stopped him."

Delsar looks at Roki, fists curled tightly. "I didn't win. He's getting away and Elidria is down. According to him, this is merely the beginning and now I've made an enemy with someone I don't even understand."

In the eyes of Roki, this is a victory. They set out to save the town and they succeeded. However, he has never been marked for death before. He will never understand the feeling of dread, regret, and failure that Delsar feels now. "There's a book," Roki says.

"What book?"

"In the Grandell library. It's how I learned about the shifter. I'll take you there."

Delsar closes his eyes and nods his head. "That would be a big help, Roki. Take me to this book."

CHAPTER 7

THE COOK

2 Months Ago...

"Things are now in motion."

A man walks into Renon's laboratory, interrupting him from reading his book filled with notes.

"Is the first batch ready?"

"Of course it is." Renon places his book on a table covered with paper, viles, and other apparatuses used for both science and magic. "Twenty-four of my beautiful creations are ready to deploy."

"Two dozen trolls isn't enough."

"These aren't your ordinary cave trolls," Renon explains, a self-satisfied smile on his face. "I call them Rock Trolls. Their skin is thick and near impenetrable by sword, spear, or bow. They will be more than a match for your typical guard."

"They had better be. If they fail—"

"They won't fail. Besides, I have even more in the works that are better than these. Everything I make is always better than the last."

"And when will those ones be ready?" the man asks.

"Two months. Even with all the magic and science I'm using, they still take a bit to grow. Of course, it's much shorter than it would take naturally, but they still take six months from birth."

"They had better be as tough as you say they are. I need them to wipe out Orange Peak and I want maximum casualties." The man sweeps his arms across his body as if to illustrate his words.

"You say you need them, but really you mean your master needs them. I would certainly like to meet the man paying my bills," says Renon.

"He's a very secretive person. I don't even know the man at the top."

"Interesting. Very well. I will be accompanying my trolls on their rampage. I'd very much like to learn as much as I can about them, so I can improve them later."

"The origin of these trolls must remain a secret. You may observe but no one must ever see you."

"Please," Renon scoffs, "I'm a shifter. No one will ever know I'm there."

"Then wrap up what you are doing," the man instructs. "I'm deploying the trolls tomorrow. You will go to Orange Peak by boat and you will be accompanied by twelve of your trolls."

"Why only half?"

"The other twelve will be dropped in random locations in the south. This is to further push the theory that these are random troll attacks. Will my men be able to control them?"

"Of course. They will follow you and anyone else that is loyal to you."

"How does that work?"

"It's simple magic, really. They are loyal to the same cause you are, even if *you* don't know what you are loyal to."

The man gives Renon a confused look. It appears he doesn't understand or believe what Renon has said.

"I value my life and my work," says Renon. "I would not risk either of them. I know you will have me killed if they don't perform adequately. I would not give them to you if I didn't think they were ready. The spell I used is sound. They will do whatever your will is."

Renon's explanation seems to do the trick. "Good. I value your life, too. It will be nearly impossible to find someone else with your talents to take your place." The man turns and leaves the laboratory.

Renon lets out an exasperated sigh.

Moments later, another man, in red robes like Renon, enters the laboratory.

Renon greets him. "Nikarat, what brings you to my lab?"

Nikarat looks at a couple notes scattered across the tables before answering. "Your trolls are impressive. Your work always astounds me."

"I know you're not just here to compliment me. What news do you have?"

Nikarat closes the door and walks up to Renon. "I understand they wish to attack Orange Peak."

"Yes, and I will be accompanying them."

"You must not leave any survivors. Grandell must not find out about this attack until it is too late."

"So then we *want* to attack Orange Peak?" Renon asks.

"I'm the one who suggested it to these mercenaries and told them I want *you* there," says Nikarat. "I'll join you with my own boat in case you wish to grab *test subjects*."

"The younger the better. Tell me, Nikarat, what is our play?"

"Did you use the spell on the trolls?" Nikarat asks.

"I did."

"Then we do what the mercenaries ask for now. When the time comes and our plans change, so will the trolls' loyalties. The pendulum will swing in our favor very soon."

"It's about time," says Renon. "These simpleminded mercenaries are a pain to deal with."

"Just be patient a bit longer. Our era will once again return to Ithendar."

The sun shines through the window and hits Elidria's face. She stirs a bit before opening her eyes only to blind herself. "Gah!" She puts her hands in front of the sun. Two annoying white dots now sit in the middle of wherever she looks. Her eyes begin to adjust and that's when she realizes she is not alone in this room. A boy, about thirteen, sits in a chair a few feet from the bed Elidria slept in. He's eating some sort of porridge. "Uh, hello?"

The boy looks away from the wall he was staring at to meet his eyes with hers. "You're awake!" he exclaims which makes Elidria jump. He must have been lost in thought to not notice her waking up until she said something.

"I am," she says as a matter of fact and sits herself up.

"I'll go tell the others!" The boy starts to run for the door but suddenly remembers something, or in this case, forgot something. "Um, they told me your name but I forgot it already."

Elidria is still trying to figure out exactly what is going on. She gives him a confused look and answers, "I'm Eldra. Who are—"

"Great!" The boy runs from the room. A few moments later, she can hear him shouting, "Eldra is up! Guys, she's awake!"

"I'm so confused," Elidria says out loud. The boy returns with two others. She recognizes one of them. "Glade?"

"Eldra!" He exclaims. "I'm so glad you're all right. Thank you for everything you did for my town and my son."

"Did we win?" she earnestly asks.

Glade nods and smiles. "You went down right at the end. The last two trolls stood no chance against Delsar."

Elidria eyes Glade's sling. "What happened to your arm?" she asks.

"Remember when I got knocked into the river?"

"Oh yeah." More memories of that day versus the trolls begin returning to her. "What about Delsar? Where is he now?"

"He and Roki left for the capital not one hour ago. Something about needing to find a book with information he needs. Roki apparently knows where it is."

"Did he say when he is going to get back?"

"He thinks tomorrow. He said if he's not back by then you should practice your stances."

"Rats." Elidria changes her attention to the others in the room. "And who are these people?"

"My apologies," says Glade. "I should have introduced them. This is my son, Cade."

Elidria can't help but grin hearing his name. "You're Glade and your son is Cade? What, is your wife named 'Jade' or something?"

"That's my sister," Cade answers.

Elidria lets out a quick snort and bites her bottom lip at Cade's quick-witted response. She brings her hand to her mouth. "I'm sorry. You can continue with your introductions," she says, trying not to laugh.

Glade gives his son a wink and then continues. "Yes, and this is Miss Wanda. We've all been taking turns keeping an eye on you but it was Miss Wanda who's been taking care of you."

The elderly woman walks up to the bed and extends her hand. "I'm very grateful to have finally met you." She shakes Elidria's hand. "Thank you for saving our town. I'm afraid we'd all be dead today without your help."

"I don't think I really did much." Elidria feels a bit of disappointment for collapsing in the middle of combat. She must have been a huge burden on Delsar and not a help.

"Nonsense!" Glade chimes in. "You were the glue that held us all together, or at least, Delsar. The way he stood up for you when the shifter tried to take you, tells me that you're the reason he fought so hard." He throws a couple punches in the air.

"The shifter?"

"I forgot you were already asleep for that. You see, the trolls were not here by accident. They were actually—"

Wanda interrupts. "I'm sure Delsar will fill you in later. For now, just enjoy your day off. Here are your clothes, all nice and clean." She lays a set of folded clothes on the bed. "We already cleaned up the trolls and much of the town, so don't feel like you need to help. Come down when you're ready."

"You cleaned them that fast?"

"We burned them yesterday, my dear," Wanda informs her as if she can tell Elidria isn't sure what day it is. "The attack was two days ago. You slept through yesterday in its entirety."

"Crud!" A realization dawns on her. "We missed the boat because of me!"

"Delsar told us about your boat troubles. We're fixing one up for the two of you that should be ready by tomorrow evening. Whatever may worry you right now, let it go and enjoy today."

Elidria sighs in relief and gives Wanda a courteous bow from her waist. "Thank you."

Wanda smiles at her. "Your gear is all at the foot of your bed, should you feel the need to have it with you." She then grabs Glade and Cade by their shoulders. "We'll leave you be now. Take your time."

Elidria gives a little grunt as acknowledgment and the trio leave the room.

"I don't know if I want to change," Elidria says to herself with a smile. "These clothes are pretty comfortable." Elidria examines the clothes Wanda swapped hers for. Nevertheless, she finds herself changing back into the same clothes she wore when she first set out from Bihnor. This is the first time they have been cleaned since that fateful day. She also straps on her belt with sheath and blade, and applies her armor plates. They are a part of her now. She is going to make sure they become as natural to her as her own two feet.

"Thanks for taking me with you, Delsar," says Roki, walking next to Delsar who is pulling a cart.

"I can literally see the 'Grandell sign.' Why do you decide to talk now?" Delsar asks with an annoyed tone.

"We are just walking. We may as well talk about something."

"I hate unnecessary conversations, and I'm only taking you with me because you know where the book is."

"I've never had anyone swear they would kill me before. That must feel weird."

Delsar rolls his eyes. "Are you still talking?"

"So what if I am? Talking won't hurt you."

"That doesn't mean you should."

"Wow. You really need to lighten up."

That is the second time in just over a week that Delsar had someone say that to him and this time it doesn't sit well with him. "And you need to shut up!" If he wasn't pulling the cart, he would definitely have his finger pressed against Roki's chest right now.

Roki is taken aback by Delsar's outburst. "What business does a nice girl have with someone like you?"

"It's always about the girl, isn't it?" Delsar shakes his head. "Our business isn't your business. Got it?"

"Interesting, but just so you know, I care for both Eldra *and* you."

"You want something to talk about?" Delsar asks, raising his voice. "What is *your* play? Why did a random cook abandon his job to help a bunch of people he doesn't know? I don't get you, Roki."

"My business is my own," Roki responds with his chin up.

"Don't you pull that!" snaps Delsar.

"Oh, I'm sorry. Do you enjoy being a hypocrite?"

"This is why I hate useless conversations. They always turn into this. Unless you have something useful to say, don't say anything at all!"

"That must be a 'you' problem," Roki says. "My conversations are usually quite pleasant. You should try being nice sometime. You might actually enjoy it."

Delsar grinds his teeth but says nothing in response, further adding to the awkwardness of this walk.

It's Delsar who finally breaks the silence after a few minutes. "Everyone has an agenda," he says. "Good or bad, it doesn't matter, they just want to feel good. Perhaps the world isn't about feeling good."

"So you've decided to live your life in misery so you aren't like everyone else?"

"Don't talk." Delsar is very stern but doesn't look at Roki. "The world will disappoint you if you pursue happiness. One moment, everyone agrees with you and wants to see you succeed. The next, someone else says something that everyone thinks will make them even happier so they abandon you and everything you worked so hard on, even if this new opinion is just a lie."

"What does this have to do with Eldra?" Roki asks.

"Who said it has anything to do with her? Maybe I'm just trying to fill this time so I don't have to hear *you* talking."

Roki grumbles and grinds his teeth. "Everyone has an agenda. Here's my story." Roki clears his throat, but before he can begin, Delsar stops him.

"I don't want to know your story," he says, plainly.

Roki jerks his head back. "You wanted to know why I chose to help. My story explains why."

"Despite what I *may* have said, I actually don't care. I don't want to hear someone else's *sad story*."

"So yours was sad, too?" Roki figures.

"Forget it," Delsar says, rolling his eyes.

"You're not very pleasant company, Delsar."

"That's because you badgered me into talking. Silence is *very* pleasant."

"I helped because I need to make up for my past mistakes," Roki explains.

"Oh, you told me anyway," Delsar says, rolling his eyes again and sighing. "Thanks for the information that was *super* obvious."

"I'm trying to bond with you, Delsar."

"I didn't *ask* to be bonded with."

Roki squints his eyes. "You're a mysterious person, Delsar."

"Good."

Roki tilts his head observing Delsar's aggravated expressions continuously evolving. "Do you even have the muscles required to smile?" he asks.

"Shut up."

"Smiling is free and contagious. Sharing a smile with others will always make your day a little bit better."

Delsar scoffs. "Are you *trying* to be Arviakyss?"

"And what's so wrong about that?"

"He murdered the Queen and betrayed the kingdom. Not very heroic if you ask me."

"You're right, Delsar. He's a bad guy, but I can still remember the good he did and model what I do after that."

"Is that who you're pretending to be, Roki? Are you trying to hide your shame by pretending to be someone better?" Delsar asks, looking directly at Roki.

Roki's face completely changes and this time it's his voice that sounds aggravated, even offended. "There's nothing wrong with trying to be better. You can't get any further once you've settled. I've chosen someone who *is* better than me so now I have something to work towards."

Delsar has no words to respond to what he just heard. Always striving to become greater than he was is what made Arviakyss, the Champion, who he was. He never settled, even when he was at the top. Roki might just be copying Arviakyss, but copying something that works isn't a bad idea.

"He was an inspiration," says Roki. "I think a lot of people still believe in who he was and strive to be like him. Perhaps Eldra is inspired by him, too."

Delsar scoffs. "Oh, I doubt it."

"And why is that?"

"Because she's a better person than he ever was."

"That doesn't mean she can't look up to him. It's like a master and an apprentice. The master trains the apprentice to be better, but the apprentice will still look up to his master."

"Or maybe she just had good parents." Delsar brings the cart to a stop at the entrance to Grandell's capital and his tone completely flips. "Roki, do you think he could be innocent?" he asks full of sincerity.

Roki looks past the sign welcoming them to Grandell. "So I'm not the only fan?"

"I used to be," says Delsar. "Now I'm not so sure."

Roki gives Delsar a very thoughtful look. "That is something I've probably asked myself every day since I heard. I assume you think he is?"

"I guess I wouldn't have asked if I didn't." Delsar's young age escapes through his voice.

Roki puts his hand on Delsar's shoulder. "Maybe, one day, we'll meet him. Then we can ask him."

Delsar nods his head and gives a subtle smirk. "Wouldn't that be something?"

"Please, we insist." The man keeps trying to get Elidria to take the bag of money he's holding.

"I said 'no' so please stop asking. We didn't help because we thought we'd get paid."

"But this is the price Delsar agreed on."

"Wait, this is Delsar's idea?" Elidria asks, a bit shocked.

"Twelve hundred gold and ten percent of this year's crop for each of you."

"What?!"

"The crop won't be ready until harvest, though. Oh, and the boat is yours."

"That one I knew. Listen, Nomar, keep my cut and put it towards rebuilding, please." She pushes the large bag away.

"Are you sure, Mistress Elidria?"

"Mistress Elidria?" she exclaims. "It's just Eldra and I'm very sure."

"Miss Eldra," Nomar corrects himself, "should you reconsider, come find me. Our offer of thanks will still be on the table."

"The name I won't be reconsidering." Elidria didn't mean for her comment to come off as a joke, but Nomar bursts out laughing anyway. Elidria can tell that it is his way of hiding the fact that he is still scared. Not just scared, but also overwhelmed with grief and loss. Losing the money will only add to that stress. They need it now more than ever.

Elidria bows and bids the man farewell, then she heads to the harbor. She wants to take a look at the boat she just acquired. Before she can make it, Glade and his son Cade run into her.

"Eldra!" shouts Glade, clearly excited about something.

"Hello, Glade and Cade." Elidria brings her hand to her mouth and giggles. She bites down on her lip.

"You know," starts Glade, "some would consider that rude."

"I do know and I can't help it. Every time I think of your names, I think of Cade's stellar comeback."

"That'a boy, kid!"

"Speaking of your *sister*, where is she today?" Elidria asks, knowing full well she doesn't exist.

"Jade is out hanging with Uncle Wade," Cade replies.

A grin shoots across Elidria's face as she jerks her head back. She bites her lip again and closes her eyes. "Okay," she says, taking a breath, "a name like yours would be awesome."

"We have our fun," Glade confirms.

"What has you both so excited today?"

"We just helped with identifying the dead, but my wife and many of the children aren't among them."

Elidria's very happy expression quickly leaves her face. "Oh, I'm so sorry."

"No, no, no." Glade throws his hands up. "This is good. According to Miss Wanda, there was another boat with men blocking our boats from escaping when the trolls attacked."

"Oh, my. Do you think they were working for the shifter?"

"Probably, but that's beside the point. They were taking prisoners aboard their boat. Since she's not here, she must be there!"

"What do you think they're doing with them?" Elidria covers her mouth the moment the words spill out of her. That's probably something they don't want to think about right now. She doesn't think much about her village for the same reason.

Glade doesn't appear to mind. "All that matters is that they might still be alive. Cade and I are going to do what we can to find them. Miss Wanda got a good look at the boat so we thought we'd walk the coast and ask around a bit."

"The whole coast?" Elidria remarks.

"As far as we need to go until we find some answers."

"Wouldn't it be faster to sail from port to port?"

"For sure, but we don't have another boat," he replies. "One got stolen, another got completely wrecked, and then we're giving that last one to you."

If Elidria wasn't feeling bad about taking the boat before, she is now. "Can you buy one in Grandell?"

"Technically, but a used one that fits our needs will probably run us three hundred or four hundred gold. We don't have the funds for something like that."

Elidria gets hit by an idea. "Guys, come with me." She runs back the same way she just came from and quickly locates Nomar who still holds the bag filled to the brim with gold pouches. "Hey, Nomar!"

"Miss Eldra?"

"I'm here to talk about that offer."

"Oh, you are? That's good."

"But I do have new conditions, which I think are more than fair."

"And what might those be?" Nomar inquires.

"I want six hundred, I don't need the crop, and when Glade goes out to find his wife, you are to send someone with him. Preferably someone who isn't thirteen and doesn't have a broken arm."

"Where are you going with this?" Glade asks.

Elidria holds her hand up to Glade but continues to engage with Nomar.

"That seems less than we offered," says Nomar. "Are you sure about this?"

"Completely."

"All right." Nomar reaches into the bag and pulls out six pouches, each one holding one hundred gold pieces, and hands them to Elidria who wraps her arms around them. "When you are ready to depart, Glade, I will go with you."

Elidria turns to face Glade and smiles with her eyes closed and drops the pouches at his feet. "This is for you. Go find your wife."

"Wait, all of it?"

"Now you can buy the boat you said you need."

"But, if we're smart, a boat will only cost us three hundred."

"There will be other expenses along the way. Believe me. The other three hundred will pay for supplies and anything unexpected." Elidria is speaking from experience. She thought she had plenty to get Delsar back to Bihnor with her, but she's already nearly out, and she brought a lot.

"This means so much." Glade sheds a tear. "I don't know what to say."

"Then don't say anything. Just accept this gift and use it for good."

Glade hugs her tightly, trapping her arms awkwardly at her side.

"Oh?" She was not expecting this. "Nomar," she struggles to say while being squeezed, "make sure the other six hundred goes toward rebuilding. Maybe even buying a new boat for the town."

"Of course, Miss Eldra." The burden of needing to pay Elidria is finally off his back. He gives her a true, genuine smile.

"Roki!" The burly bartender is more than happy to see his fellow coworker.

"Hey, Jaysahn."

"I see you brought Mr. Potato Sack back with you."

Delsar opens his mouth to say something but quickly decides against it.

"I was wondering when you were going to return to work." Jaysahn eyeballs Roki's bandaged right wrist. The same arm is also in a sling.

"You're a bit worse for wear from when you left, I'd say. What exactly happened?"

Roki sits at the counter while Delsar stands in his usual "overwatch mode."

"Trolls!" exclaims Roki. "Twelve to be exact."

"Twelve trolls?" Jaysahn repeats, already drawn into the story.

"They were tearing up Orange Peak."

"What did you do?"

"We had to kill them to rescue the survivors from their shelters. Actually, I only killed one. Delsar pretty much killed the rest."

"Did he?" Jaysahn looks up at Delsar. Delsar's face doesn't change. "Wow."

"That's not all. They were being controlled by a shifter."

"A shifter? You've mentioned those things before."

"That's why we're here in town today. There have been trolls popping up in all sorts of random locations. We think the shifter and his trolls are going to become an even greater problem."

"Anything I can do to help?" Jaysahn asks.

"There is," Delsar cuts in. "Tell our story to as many people as possible. I don't think the shifter intended there to be any witnesses. If people find out about him and what he did, it may deter him from another attack."

"I don't think I could keep my mouth shut if I tried." Jaysahn looks back at Roki. "You're not coming back to work, are you?"

Roki holds up his left arm to reveal even that one being bandaged. "I don't think I would even if I could. Something evil is afoot. Something I can help stop. I hope you understand."

"You're a fine cook, Roki. What kind of person would I be if I didn't support you on something so noble? Go. You have my blessing."

"Thank you, Jaysahn. I'll see you again."

"Likewise."

Roki gets up from his stool and turns to Delsar. "Whatever you and Eldra have gotten yourselves into, count me in."

Delsar scoffs and starts to leave the bar. "Not happening."

Roki runs after him. "Oh, come now. The shifter wants to kill both you *and* Eldra. You'll need someone with you he *doesn't* want to kill."

"What we're doing has nothing to do with the trolls *or* the shifter. Besides, you can't even fight." Fighting isn't the issue here. Delsar doesn't want to deal with any randoms or unknowns.

"So the end of your journey does lead to a fight. If I'm not going to get a yes from you, I'll just have to ask her. She is the boss, isn't she?"

"What, are you, twelve?" snaps Delsar, pushing through the exit. "One parent says 'no' so now you're off to ask the other one?"

"I was twelve at one point in my life, so I have practiced."

"Here's the deal," Delsar spins around and jams his finger into Roki's chest, "in the off chance she does let you join, I'll be placing you in charge of logistics. No fighting, because guess what? I am in charge and I will not be having you slow us down. Got that?"

"Crystal."

"I didn't ask if it was clear." Delsar whips back around and grabs his cart. "Weaponsmith. Where is it?"

"Follow me." Roki leads Delsar away from the docks and up the road where Elidria was attacked.

Near the center of the market district lies a building with a kite shield as its emblem. "Shouldn't we be picking up the heavy stuff on our way out?" Roki asks.

"It doesn't matter," says Delsar. "We'll just put it all in the cart. Where's the library from here."

Roki points to the next building over. Overhanging the door is a sign that reads, "Grandell Library."

"I'm still buying a sword first," Delsar states. He and Roki walk in and are greeted by walls covered with various types of weapons. Swords, spears, glaves, bows, knives, shields, clubs. Enough gear to arm a small army. Delsar wastes no time picking out a sword and he takes it out of its sheath to examine it. It's slightly longer than the issued sword Elidria uses, yet it's much lighter and the blade is very fine. The handle is also slender with room for two hands if desired. The hilt has a golden color to it and so does the small counterweight.

After deciding, he moves over to the shields. Again, he finds what he wants right away. A kite shield, a bit smaller than the one he wears. Not just made from old wood like the circular ones they grabbed from Galius. This shield is layered; the inside, where the straps lie, is made from a tough wood, while the outside, and its edges, are plated with iron to help with structural integrity.

One last thing is needed before purchase. Delsar approaches a crate with arrows bunched in groups of twenty. He places the sword and shield on top and grabs the whole crate.

Roki can't help but comment. "Are you planning on fighting the whole army?"

Delsar doesn't respond to the comment because he deems it unimportant. He checks out and the cost totals three hundred ten gold. Fifty for the arrows, sixty for the shield, and another two hundred for the sword. He pulls the total out of the pouch Orange Peak had given him as payment for saving the town.

Delsar loads it all in the cart before moving on to the library. "What's the name of the book?" he asks.

"It's Chapel's Journal," Roki replies. "He was a guard back during the Great Magic Divide."

"Let's grab it and go. I want to get back to Orange Peak before it gets too late."

Roki leads Delsar to the shelf where he found it three years ago. They peer at a bare spot on one of the bookshelves. "Huh," Roki says. "This is where it was." They search the surrounding shelves and Roki even rifles through the 'children's section.'

Delsar leaves Roki to his own devices in hope of finding it himself.

"Excuse me, miss," Roki says, grabbing the attention of the librarian at the front desk.

"Are you checking something out?" the librarian asks.

"I'm actually looking for a book that I've read here before. Chapel's Journal. Do you know where I can find it?"

"Someone else checked it out just yesterday. If you'd like, I can let you know when it gets returned."

"I would appreciate—"

"It doesn't matter," Delsar says, creeping up behind Roki.

"Huh?"

"It's not coming back."

"Why is that?" questions Roki.

"When was the last time it's been checked out before yesterday?" Delsar asks the librarian.

She doesn't even need to look at any records to answer. "Three years ago by you, Roki."

"That's what I thought. It was the shifter who grabbed it. His intelligence is going to be a problem."

Roki isn't completely convinced. "How did he even know about it?"

"The same way you did. He looked for it." This is a huge blow. They need that book to learn as much about this new enemy as they can. Now the only knowledge they have on him is what they've seen and whatever Roki can remember from when he first read the book.

"Are you sure you don't want to take me with you?" Roki asks. "I'm the closest thing to that journal."

Delsar knows he's right. Taking him with them will allow Delsar to siphon as much info from Roki as possible. "Elidria," he says. "She'll decide your fate."

CHAPTER 8

THE CONTRACT

15 Years Ago…

"That's a beautiful pyramid of logs," Bekka says, uncovering her eyes after being instructed to open them.

"Not the logs. Look at me." Glade is sporting very cheaply-made platemail, covering his entire body. He looks stiff and uncomfortable as he tries to move around.

"Why are you wearing that ridiculous outfit?"

Glade begins climbing the pile of firewood, knocking some down and stumbling quite a bit on his way up. He resembles a foal trying to stand for the first time.

"What are you doing? You're going to get hurt," Bekka warns.

He begins climbing on all four while simultaneously delivering his speech. "For years, I've been— Gah! Wait." One of his legs gets stuck between some of the logs. He struggles to yank his leg from its entrapment and nearly tumbles backward when he does pull it free. He flails but catches himself.

"Glade!"

"It's okay," he assures. "Let me try that again." He resumes his ascent to the top. "For years, I've been—Wha!" His arm plunges through one of the gaps, causing him to smack his face against one of the logs. "Hehe. Good thing I'm wearing this ridiculous outfit."

"If you weren't, you'd be at the top by now. Save your speech for when you get there."

Glade begins again. This time, concentrating on climbing and not delivering his speech. After much effort, he stands triumphantly at the top. He draws his very dull sword and extends it onward, as if he just conquered a mountain or defeated a powerful foe. "For years— Oh nuts." The pyramid starts to rumble and shake. Glade wobbles and loses his footing as it all collapses beneath him. He crashes down on his back as more logs fall around and on top of him.

"Glade!" Bekka runs over and starts pulling logs off of him.

He just lays there, still with his sword in his hand and something else clutched tightly in his left. "Ouch."

"Oh, Glade. Why don't you ever think things through?"

He begins groaning before giving his response. "Actually, I think I did this time." He opens his hand and reveals a ring.

Bekka's face lights up, admiring the shine of the stone atop the ring. "Is that my grandmother's?"

"Your father gave it to me yesterday when I went to see him." He puts the sword down and feels around his waist. "I had another one, but I think I dropped it somewhere in these logs." He rolls over and pretends to frantically rummage through the logs.

Bekka picks up a log and taps his back with it. Glade turns around and sees her with her eyebrows up, giving a slight nod. "Well?" she asks.

"Huh?"

"Are you going to get on with it? Just ask the question."

Glade holds the ring between his thumb and index finger, extending it towards Bekka. "Bekka?"

"Yes, yes?" She hugs the log against her chest as her heart pounds.

"Do you," he pauses for a moment to catch his breath, "think your grandmother has any more of these, because this one is a bit small on me?"

"Glade!" She slams the log into Glade's chestplate. Not enough to hurt him, but definitely enough to get him focused.

"Okay." He takes another deep breath and closes his eyes. He only opens one to ask the question. "Will you marry me?"

"Of course!" She drops the log and extends her left hand. "If you can deal with my bad breath, I'm sure I can deal with your crazy shenanigans."

Glade pulls the ring back. "Bad breath might be a dealbreaker."

"It was a joke, you mook. Just put the ring on."

Glade releases a huge grin and places the ring on her finger. He hugs her and says in her ear, "That was a pretty good proposal, wasn't it?"

"You're a dunce."

"At least I executed my plan pretty well."

"I'm pretty sure your plan executed you."

"Then it's a good thing you were there to rescue me." Glade kisses her on the cheek.

"Now you can return the favor."

Arm in arm, the two walk back toward town. "So, how many kids do you want?" Glade asks. "I've already picked out names."

"Excuse me?!"

Even though the main gate was cleared the day before, Roki and Delsar still use the smaller, market bridge to enter Orange Peak. The market is the main hangout in town since the troll attack. Elidria and a few others are already there, discussing various things. Elidria notices them crossing the bridge and halts her conversation, making a beeline toward them.

Delsar gives no clear expression but Roki is very happy to see her. He steps ahead of Delsar and waves his less-broken left arm. "Hey, Eldra!"

Elidria pays him no mind and storms past him. She walks up to Delsar, who still lugs the cart behind him, and slaps him across his face.

Delsar drops the handlebars and brings his hand to his face. "What is with you and hitting me?"

"You made these people pay you twelve hundred gold *and* ten percent of their crops?"

"Of course I did. I said we'd make our money back. That's the only reason I agreed to help."

"No you didn't. You said we'd make it *all* back, and that was under the context of time."

"I meant our money. Did you think we were going to do something like this for free?" Delsar asks. "We were low on money so we took the job. People tend to be very generous after you've saved them."

"You're an idiot and a liar! You purposely made it sound like you were talking about time," Elidria says as a crowd begins to gather.

"No I didn't. I meant money and that is *all* I had on my mind."

"We did it because it was the right thing to do. No one offered us any payment. They've already lost so much, and you're willing to take even more?"

"Their population has dropped seventy percent. I'm sure they can do without ten percent of their crops."

Elidria gasps and slaps Delsar again. He grabs her wrist and attempts to wrench it, but she immediately pulls away from him and delivers her own push to his chest. "You're not just an idiot and a liar, you're also a huge jerk! What's wrong with being the good guy? Why is it so hard for you to do what's right?"

"Because being the good guy is irrelevant. All it takes is one mistake before no one cares how *good* you were."

"You told me people used to call you humble. I see now that they were wrong."

Delsar gives his usual scoff but doesn't reply.

"You fell, and you fell hard," Elidria continues. "Not because of what others did to you, but because of what you did to yourself. You cared too much about what others thought of you, even if you never admitted it. When they stopped giving you the love you *thought* you deserved, you fell into a void of your own regret and discontentment. That's called pride, Delsar. People will always hate you, no matter how good you are. On the other hand, there will always be those who love you, regardless of what others say is true. Just like Galius. Maybe it's time you stop caring about what others think and start caring about how *you* think. You don't need to be loved by others to love others yourself. But people *do* love you. Why can't you share that love instead of pouting in your own world of darkness that *you* created?"

Everyone watches and waits for Delsar's response. He gives none and watches her turn around and storm away, through the crowd. He doesn't know what to say. Typically, he's the blunt one. To have it turned around on him caught him off-guard. Elidria disappears from Delsar's view before he scoffs again and shakes his head. "Get this stuff ready for departure," he says to no one in general. He throws up his hood and walks away, toward his assigned house. "You can keep your crops!" he yells without looking back.

Everyone stares and tries to process what just happened. It's finally Glade who breaks the silence. "So, Cade, what do you think he has in the cart?"

Roki changes his shocked expression to an awkward smile. "Come on over and I'll show you," he says. "You're going to love this new sword he got." Roki pulls off the cover and shows the spectators the new gear.

Elidria paces back and forth in her room. Sleeping isn't an option. *How can Delsar be so smart and yet so dumb at the same time? Did he only pretend he cared about what happened to me on the road?* "Of course he did!" she exclaims. She brings her hand to her chest. "At least, I hope he did." All sorts of thoughts and scenarios keep racing through her head. She feels some sort of comfort answering them out loud. *Is he really our best chance?* "Why did you say I could trust him and no one else?" She tries to imagine how her father would respond, but every time she starts to talk for him, her own thoughts of resentment fill her consciousness.

Someone knocks on her door and she whips around to face it. "If that's you, Delsar, leave me be!"

"It's Wanda, my dear."

"Oh, I'm sorry." Elidria pulls open the door. "Please, come in."

Wanda obliges. She saw and heard most of the confrontation Delsar and Elidria had in the market. She figures Elidria might need someone to talk to and she is spot on. "It's no worry. I think a break from Delsar will do you some good."

"I had all day without him."

"Then he can wait another night." Wanda sits on Elidria's bed and gestures to her to join.

Elidria takes the offer and sits next to her.

"Tell me anything you'd like. I'm here to listen," Wanda tells her.

"Where do you want me to start?"

"Just tell me whatever's bothering you."

Elidria rolls her eyes, much like how Delsar does. "Well, it's obviously Delsar. He used to be such a kind man. He always did his best to make those around him safe and feel happy. Since I started working with him, I see he clearly wants to do what's right, but at the end of the day, he's either stealing from you, lying to you, or taking advantage of you. He is so, *gah*, just annoying! Why can't he be more like how he was and just get over what happened to him?"

Wanda closes her eyes and nods, thinking about what Elidria had to say. "I don't know who he is or what his past was like. It sounds to me you want him to be more like you. No one else is you and no one else is him. Everyone must deal with their own faults and tribulations in their own way. The best we can do is be there for them when they need help. To set an example and maybe even inspire. He has a respect for you so he will follow you if you continue to lead."

"I'm no leader and I don't want to be. He also only cares about me because I'm paying him."

"He put himself between you and both trolls when you went down, and he stood his ground. He also fully expected us to pay him after clearing the town. He didn't need you to get paid."

"Well, you don't know him."

"Maybe I don't, but maybe you just need to give him time."

"My village doesn't have time!" Elidria's frustration with Delsar and her hidden anxiety about her home comes out. Those are words she had no intention of sharing with anyone.

"What's happening in your village?"

"Please, Miss Wanda," Elidria begs, "don't mention this to anyone. I don't want your town to feel they need to help. You've all suffered so much as it is."

"If that's what you want; however, you should be letting us make that decision for ourselves."

"Delsar says our team needs to remain small and stealthy, so even if you wanted to help, it likely won't be for the best. As far as combat and tactics go, he's proven to know what he's talking about."

"He did do what our guards couldn't with just the four of you. I'm fairly certain Glade never used a sword in combat before that day," says Wanda.

"He's good at what he does, that's for sure. I just wish he was good in other places, too."

"I'm not going to pry about your village then. Whatever is going on, it sounds like Delsar already has a plan, and telling us isn't part of it." Wanda places her hand on Elidria's shoulder. "Is there anything else you need help with?"

Elidria thinks for a moment. "Actually, there is one thing. How's your paperwork?"

Wanda gives a confused look. "Paperwork?"

The people of Orange Peak scuttle about, carrying crates and mixed emotions. It's been three days since the troll attack but none of them have been given any time to mourn their losses. They've been put straight to work cleaning, rebuilding, and making sure Delsar and Elidria are ready for their voyage. They are, after all, the saviors of Orange Peak. Mourning can wait.

"No, put anything non-perishable in the hull. The cabin needs to fit four hammocks, fresh food and water, and our essential gear." Delsar is a man with a plan. Right now, he's trying his best to stuff more than this small four-person boat can hold.

Elidria left early in the morning to practice her forms, without Delsar. Neither of them have spoken or even seen each other since the night before.

Departure is now scheduled for noon since the boat finished its repairs earlier than expected. Elidria is cutting it close and probably doesn't even know about the time change.

Roki is the perfect middleman and his mission is a definite success as Elidria follows him back to the docks. She flounces her way up to Delsar and shoves a piece of paper in front of his face.

"What's this?" Delsar asks.

"A contract. You never signed one, remember?"

"An agreement is all I need."

"Well, not me." She pulls it back down and begins examining it. "It states what you get with your employment and what you're agreeing to do and not to do, during this time."

"You're going to have to be more specific. A contract will make this official. What about all the days prior to this? I believe this is my eleventh day working for you."

"I covered it all," she says. *"You are to escort Elidria,* that's me, *to Bihnor, in hopes of freeing its people from mercenary oppression. All expenses during the journey will be reimbursed by Bihnor. Under no circumstances is the employee to take on any other jobs in which the employee receives other payments of any kind, unless approved by his employer.* That's also me. *Should this rule be broken, the employer may deduct pay as she sees fit or terminate the contract, forfeiting all unreceived payments. The employee will be paid 500 gold on arrival to Bihnor and another 1,000 for clearing the village of all insurgents. He will also be paid another 100 gold for each day on and each day prior, since verbal agreement in Eskor."* Elidria finishes her reading and looks sternly at Delsar. "All you need to do is sign. Roki is our witness."

"One thousand what?" Delsar asks.

"I don't understand what you mean."

"It states that after I clear the village, I receive another one thousand. That one thousand could be anything."

"Look, I'm not a lawyer and this isn't perfect." Elidria points her finger right at Delsar. "You and I both know what it means and that, of course, would be gold. You know I'm not going to lie to you so when I say 'it's gold,' it's *gold.*"

Delsar extends his hand and takes the contract from her. The face he's giving her she can't figure out. "I'll hold you to your word," he says.

"And I'll hold you to your signature." Elidria pulls a charcoal pen from her bag and hands it to him. She looks up at him with the top of her eyes and doesn't tilt her head back.

Delsar signs the paper. "Here you go, *boss.*"

Elidria snatches the paper and scrunches her nose, stuffing the contract in her bag. "What's all this stuff everyone is carrying onto our boat? Let me guess, more payment for saving them?"

"You really don't trust me, do you?"

Elidria shakes her head. "No, and I don't know why I ever did." She doesn't give him time to respond before turning away from him, heading back toward the market.

"I'll just add you to my very long list of people who don't!" he retorts. "And don't go far. We leave at noon."

Elidria's face quivers as she brings her hand to her chest, clenching it in a fist. Her tears only fall for a moment. She quickly wipes them away as Roki chases after her.

"Eldra, wait," Roki says, jogging up next to her.

She whips around to face him. "What?" she asks, very exasperated.

Roki comes to a stop next to her and ignores her tone. "The town didn't give him those supplies."

"Then just *where* did he get it all?"

"He bought it all. With the reward money," he explains. "He even bought the boat that they already gave you."

"What?" Elidria can't believe it. She shakes her head. "He wouldn't give up his precious gold for something he can just take."

"He did, though. I don't know him like you do, but I do know that he hears you. On the way to Grandell, he would hardly let me get a word in. For you though, when you talk, he listens."

"Because I'm paying him, Roki!" She jams her finger into Roki's chest but quickly retracts it, realizing she got that from Delsar. "I'm sorry. I didn't mean to snap at you." She sighs. "He just doesn't care."

"Then why did he pay the town back?"

Elidria closes her eyes and thinks about it. "I don't know."

"I think you do," Roki states.

"What do you want, Roki?"

"What do you mean by that?"

"My best friend's little brother would always butter me up and try to get on my good-side before asking for something. So, what is it you want?"

Roki releases a subtle smirk. "You are as sharp as Delsar. It's astounding."

"You're still doing it."

"I am. You're right. I'll just get to it." Roki takes a breath. "I got to hear you read the contract so I know what's happening to your village. I want to help, for free."

"No."

Roki's envisioned plan pops and his face is completely blank after hearing her bluntness. He was sure that she would consider it. "B-b-but..."

118

"Delsar doesn't want any other members in our group. I trust his judgment."

Roki is taken aback. "What happened to you *not* trusting him?"

Elidria's eyes go wide and her heart drops. She covers her mouth with her hands. "I just lied to him!" she exclaims, about to burst into tears.

Roki immediately realizes his poor choice of words. "No, you didn't. You trust his judgment, not him."

"You believe in a person for what they do. To trust his judgment is to trust him." She turns and starts to power-walk back to the dock.

"Wait!" Roki grabs her by the shoulder. "You can't just apologize to him. He wants your trust. You should make him earn it back."

Elidria pulls her shoulder away. "I'm not going to lie to him. I can tell you care about both of us, but I'm going to go about this the right way. He can have my trust now and *we* can fix anything else later." She resumes her walk.

"We, like you and I?"

"No, like me and Delsar."

"Eldra!"

"Leave it, Roki!"

Roki doesn't try to stop her but he does follow her back down.

"Delsar!" she shouts.

Delsar starts to turn around. "You're just in t—" He gets cut short by Elidria's embrace.

She wraps around his torso and places her head against his chest. "I'm sorry," she says, breaking into tears. "I lied to you and for that, I am *so* sorry."

"The one thousand g-gold?"

Elidria looks up at him. "No. I told you I don't trust you anymore, but that wasn't true. I do trust you." She buries her head back in his chest. "Forgive me." She starts to audibly weep.

Delsar's jaw drops open as he tries to process what's going on. "E-e-elidria, I'm not usually offended by people not t-t-trusting me," he awkwardly stutters. "You d-d-don't need to hug me. Th-th-thank you for c-c-clarifying. Can you just let go?"

Elidria looks up and lets him go.

Delsar straightens his cloak. "You're officially my boss now and typically, bosses don't hug their employees. Let's try to be professional."

"That's how I apologize." She sniffles and wipes her nose. "I guess you should hope I don't lie to you again."

"Or you could just *not* hug me."

"You let me in Grandell."

"That was different," Delsar says, placing his hand on the back of his head. "Look, I'm sorry for losing your trust, even if it was for only a moment."

"Forgiven." Elidria tilts her head and closes her eyes, giving him a smile.

"Okay. Let's not do that again." Delsar looks at Roki. "So, did she say yes?"

"What?"

"About letting you come along?"

"She said 'no.' How did you know that's why I went to get her?"

"Because you said you would ask her yesterday." Delsar sounds annoyed again. "It's not magic," he says, rolling his eyes.

"You were going to let me decide?" Elidria asks.

"You're the bill-payer. It's too bad you said 'no.' I'm not babysitting Glade and Cade, so that just leaves you."

"What?"

"Sorry we're late!" shouts Glade, running with a few bags in hand and Cade at his heels. "Cade got his head stuck in the banister," he says, stopping next to the trio.

"That was you, Dad," Cade corrects.

"Oh yeah. It was me. Hey guys."

Delsar brings his hands to his face. "Elidria, please just let Roki come. I need him so I never need to interact with these two."

"Then, yes!" She gives Roki a huge grin and grabs his hands. "You can come!"

"Thank you!" Roki hugs Elidria.

"This man likes hugs," she says, being squeezed and lifted by Roki.

"I'm so happy for the both of you," Delsar says without a tone change. "If we're done lollygagging, why don't we get aboard?"

"Wait, just like that?" Elidria asks.

"Don't ask that. I've been working on getting things ready all morning. Just get on board."

"Sure, Delsar."

The five of them walk across the dock and board the boat. Nomar is there checking the sail.

"Are we good to go?" Delsar asks.

"Everything is where it needs to be, Captain."

"Thank you, Nomar." Delsar turns to face the other four with his chest puffed out. His voice almost sounds like it could be an octave deeper. "You heard him. I am Captain now. You will all do as I say and call me as such. We are sailing for Fairview where Roki, Elidria, and I will depart and travel by land. Nomar, Glade, and Cade will continue by boat in search of the shifter. To get there, we will be split into teams of two. Roki and Nomar, Glade and Cade, me and Elidria. One team will be working the sail and wheel, one will be sleeping, and the other will be having free time. We will rotate every eight hours unless otherwise told. Roki and Glade are not to work the sail because of their broken arms." Delsar looks down at Cade. "That means you will be working the sail eight hours a day for eight days. Got it?"

Cade salutes. "I got it, Cap!"

Delsar closes his eyes and grinds his teeth. "Everyone, please watch Nomar as he adjusts the sail, so we can depart."

"Right this way, guys." The group follows him to the sail but Elidria stays behind.

Delsar walks over to the rope that connects the boat to the dock and begins untying it. "What do you want?" he asks her.

"I didn't need a contract, did I?"

"The contract was a good idea."

"But you were planning all this before I gave you the contract."

"So what?" He pulls the rope in and walks toward her. "Boats don't work on land so we may as well give it to Glade. It just makes sense."

Elidria smiles. "It does."

Delsar stops in front of her and looks down at her. "How heavy are you?"

Elidria's smile disappears. "Excuse me?"

"How well can you swim?"

"What is the meaning of these unrelated questions?"

"These are completely fair questions." He steps back and looks her up and down. "I'd say you're one hundred pounds."

Elidria gasps. "As if! I'll have you know, I'm one hundred and *twenty* pounds."

Delsar looks her up and down again. He shakes his head. "No, you're definitely one-oh-five."

Elidria sticks her hand out and turns her head away. Blood rushing to her cheeks. "Stop! Why do you want to know something so personal?"

"I'm trying to decide if you should wear your armor or not. I can't have you sinking to the bottom of the ocean if you fall in."

"I can swim just fine."

"Fifteen pounds of iron says otherwise." Delsar snaps his fingers. "Ah-ha! That's where you got one-twenty. You weighed yourself with your armor on."

"No," she says, "and stop. I'll take them off if you say I must."

"Take them off whenever you're not training."

"How often will I be training."

Delsar gives what she interprets as an evil glare. "Your training will be your free time."

Elidria's heart sinks, but only for a moment. "Very well," she says, sticking her chin up. "I'll take these off."

"Good. Go learn how you use the sail." The boat starts to move so Delsar bounds up the stairs to the helm, leaving Elidria to her thoughts, and grabs the wheel.

"Wait, Delsar!" Elidria yells. "We can't go yet. I didn't say 'goodbye' to anyone."

"Come up here then."

Elidria climbs the stairs and Delsar points behind him, without looking back. Elidria looks beyond the aft to see the shore lined with the townsfolk, all waving and cheering. Elidria runs to the guardrail and returns their waves with her own. "Goodbye, everyone!" she shouts.

The town returns a mix of "goodbyes" and "thank-yous."

Elidria finds Wanda in the crowd and gives her a special wave.

Wanda nods, with a huge smile on her face, and doesn't stop waving.

Satisfied, Elidria turns away. She scans the boat, looking from person to person. They are laughing and joking, with Nomar trying his best to teach them how to use the sail. *Can we do this for my village?* she thinks to herself. She finishes her scan and looks at Delsar. *It all rests on you.* "I'll stand with you," she says out loud.

Delsar turns his head slightly, indicating he heard.

"Please..., stand with me."

CHAPTER 9

THE VOYAGE

40 Days Ago…

The sound from Bihnor's steeple bell rings throughout the village, letting the people know that trouble has come. The bell isn't the only warning anymore, the cries and screams of the villagers are enough to alert anyone of the terror outside

Aldameer bursts into the room that hides Elidria and Galia. "Girls, you need to go now!"

"Where are the guards?" asks the panicked Galia, who is barely holding herself together.

"They're gone." Aldameer reaches out his hand and tries to help up his trembling daughter. "I need you to run."

"I can't," says Elidria.

"Yes you can. Come on."

"Where did they go?" Galia continues to question the whereabouts of the guards, only adding to Aldameer's stress.

"I don't know. They left us." He grabs Elidria's arm with both hands, pulling her out from under the table. "Let's go!"

"Where? How am I going to get out? They'll just shoot me like they did Treye and Raielyn!" exclaims Elidria, eyes wide with terror.

"Not if you go now. The sun is rising above the ridge. It will blind them."

"Who are *they*?" screams the equally frightened Galia.

"Mercenaries. We don't have time for this." Aldameer pulls Elidria to the front door. He takes his satchel off and puts it on Elidria. "This

124

is full of gold and supplies. Run east as fast as you can and don't look back. Find Arviakyss, he can save us."

"He's a murderer," says Elidria.

"No," Aldameer snaps, "he didn't. Trust him and no one else."

"Well, how am I supposed to find him?"

"He goes by the name 'Delsar' now. They call him the Outcast. Track his work and you will find him." Aldameer grabs the door's handle but remembers one more thing. "Tell him we're being attacked by the Darkened Wanderers and offer him any payment."

Elidria nods as she tries to process everything her father just said.

"I got it," Galia says. "Come on, Elidria. We can save our village."

Aldameer opens the door as an arrow whizzes past the entrance, hitting someone trying to fight back with a hoe.

Elidria screams and brings both hands to her mouth.

Aldameer grabs her arm again and forcefully pulls her outside. "Find the Outcast!" he shouts, pushing her in front of him.

"But what about—"

"Go!" he yells. "I'll keep them away from you."

Elidria backs away from her father, stunned and unsure what to do.

Galia grabs Elidria's hand and starts to run. "Let's go, Eldra! The village needs us to do this."

Elidria gets spun around and stumbles, trying to keep up. She looks over her shoulder but gets yanked back forward by Galia. "Dad!" she cries. She pulls against Galia and breaks free of her grip. "I'm not leaving him!"

Galia turns to stop her but gets struck in the chest by an arrow, dropping her to the ground.

Elidria drops to her knees by Galia's side. "You're okay," she tells her, trying to help her back up. "Just get up and run."

Galia grabs Elidria's hand and squeezes it tight. She grimaces from pain she never could have imagined. "No," she says, shaking her head, "you must run." Tears stream down her face. "Run and promise me you'll come back and save us."

Elidria starts to phase out as her face turns ghostly white. "Galia," she says, already thinking she's dead. Her lips begin to tremble.

Galia squeezes Elidria's hand with what little strength she has left. "RUUUUUN!!!"

Elidria falls back on her arms, startled by her friend's desperate attempt to get her going. "I promise," she says, still in shock.

Two men with bows see them and quickly nock their arrows, pointing them at her. She scrambles to her feet and starts running up the ridge. She gets bombarded by the light of the sun as it crests over the ridge. She hears an arrow zip by her ear and feels dirt splash into her leg from another hitting the ground. She continues to run, despite being blinded by the sun, but no more arrows even come close to her. She never looks back but the scream from her friend causes her to hesitate for a moment. She closes her eyes and takes a breath, her tears are like uncontrollable rapids. She opens them again and sprints away. She runs and doesn't stop. Away from the village. Away from the mercenaries. Away from Galia.

"Galia!" Elidria shouts, waking up from her memories. Her heart pounds and sweat coats her palms. The rocking of the boat doesn't help with anything.

"Eldra, are you all right?" asks Roki, looking up from rummaging for a quick bite in the cabin.

Elidria takes a few breaths and composes herself before answering. "It was just a dream," she says.

Roki drags a barrel next to her hammock and sits on it. "Delsar couldn't sleep either. It seems we all carry our demons."

Elidria's mind drifts for a moment because of Roki's comment. Demons are exactly what they are, but these feelings are something she's going to have to live with. It's the price of doing what's right and it's not about her, it's about her village and those she left behind. "Demons or not, we *all* made our choices."

"You're talking about Galia?"

Elidria closes her eyes and nods her head. She didn't realize she shouted her name so loud. "I will save her, and I will save my village, and I will save Delsar, and I will save anyone else that needs help, even if they don't ask for it."

"That's a tall order."

"Well, I'll try."

Roki leans back. "I understand that feeling all too well. I want to make it up to the people I've failed by saving someone that no one else can. I want to step into an impossible situation and tell them they will be fine."

Elidria sits up in her hammock. She squints her eyes and tilts her head looking at Roki. "There's something more to you. Your usual over-the-top enthusiasm sometimes feels forced."

Roki's eyes are all Elidria can see of his face in this dark room, but they say it all. He stares back at her without uttering another word.

"We smile to hide how we truly feel from others," Elidria says as if reading his mind. "There's pain deep down inside us and yet we still tell others we're fine. Sometimes it feels like death is the only thing that will free us of this weight. Perhaps taking on an impossible mission and dying a hero's death is the best way to go about it."

"What do you mean?" Roki asks, trying to sound chipper.

"You said you understand how I felt," she answers. "That means you feel what I feel, do you not?"

Roki's chest gets heavy as he feels a guilt overcome him. "I'm such a coward," he says, burying his head in his hands.

Elidria places her hand on Roki's shoulder and slides it under his chin. She lifts his face up, gently forcing him to look at her, and she smiles at him. "We *all* have our demons."

Roki shakes his head. "If we're both feeling the same thing, why does your smile feel real to me?"

Elidria tilts her head and lets a tear roll off her face. "It wasn't always. After I met Delsar, and even you, the hole I felt was replaced with hope. I realized how much I have to live for and how much *more* I have to give."

Elidria's words again leave Roki without a response. He audibly swallows, killing his silence.

"If you want to talk about it, I'm open to listen," she tells him.

Roki opens his mouth but takes a moment to say anything. "I don't want to be judged," he finally replies.

"And that's why you don't talk to anyone about this?" Elidria places her hands on Roki's. "If you should ever change your mind, you come find me. I'll listen to you as a friend."

Roki closes his eyes and starts to weep. He has never come close to talking to anyone about how he feels. About his end desire. He always thought the judgment of those who heard would make him feel even worse. That they would push him past what he could handle and expedite his end plans.

"Everyone on this boat is human, just like you," Elidria says, lifting Roki's head with her words. "Remember that."

Roki takes a deep breath and nods. "I'll take you up on your offer, one day."

"That will be nice."

"Can I hug you, again?"

Elidria smiles. "Of course you can."

He leans in for the hug and drips a couple tears on her shoulder. "I'll try not to disappoint you," he says.

Elidria squeezes him but remains wary of his dislocated shoulder and snapped wrist. "I won't be disappointed."

He breaks from the embrace. "One day, why don't you talk to me about Galia?"

"I'll talk about her now if you're—"

"Roki!" Delsar storms into the cabin. "What happened to grabbing a quick snack? You're supposed to be at the wheel and yet you're here dilly-dallying with Elidria."

"Sorry, Captain." Roki scrabbles to his feet. "I'll get back to it."

"Delsar!" Elidria scowls at him. "Can't you see we were having a heart-to-heart? Why don't *you* go back to the wheel and let us finish."

"No, it's all right," says Roki.

"Nonsense. You didn't even get to eat anything. Delsar, he must eat."

"Fine! But if I'm on the wheel, you're on the sail."

"Delsar—,"

"It's Captain!"

"Then I'm Eldra, *Captain!*"

Delsar stares sternly at Elidria and she returns the glare. "Fine, *Elidria*, have it your way." Delsar moves from the door and ushers her to exit up the couple of stairs.

"Thank you, *Delsar*."

Delsar rolls his eyes and locates Glade and Cade, both leaning over the guardrail, having some sort of conversation. "Glade! It's your turn at the wheel. Cade, take the sail from Nomar and let him know he can grab some sleep."

"Aye-aye, Cap!" Glade salutes.

"It's *Captain*! You are the last person I'd let shorten it." Delsar sighs and looks at Elidria. Her arms are crossed. "What is it now?"

"Nothing, really. I just thought you and I were going to do that."

"It's not our turn. We have a cycle that we should stick to."

"So, free time for us?" Elidria asks.

"We are not skipping your training again. You aren't going to be seasick again like you were yesterday, are you?"

Elidria's eyes go wide and her face turns red as she quickly looks down at Delsar's feet. "N-no, I think I'm over it."

"Good. Come with me." Delsar leads her back into the cabin. He walks over to a crate and pries it open, revealing hundreds of arrows.

Nomar walks into the cabin and greets them. "Good morning, Captain, Eldra."

Elidria bows but Delsar doesn't even look over. "Nomar, what happened to the crate with all the gear I got in Grandell?"

"A crate that looks just like that one got placed in the hull. Someone must have mixed them up."

Delsar pinches the bridge of his nose but only remains annoyed for a moment. "Elidria, I'm going to need you to crawl around the bowels and find it."

"Why me?"

Delsar's head jerks back. "Why? Because you can fit and because I said so."

"Cade is smaller than me. Maybe you can have him do it?"

"He's working the sails and you need to start training."

"I'll do the sails while he crawls under."

It dawns on Delsar why she is so reluctant. *She's claustrophobic.* "Are you going to be okay on this boat for six more days?"

Elidria grimaces, realizing her secret is out. "We aren't far from shore. If I really needed to, I think I could swim for it." They are traveling parallel with the coast, just a mile out. A swim is definitely possible.

"This is something you need to overcome. I'll ask Cade to go, but please go with him."

Elidria squeezes her eyes shut, thinking back to the traumatic event that caused such fear. "Could you?"

"Go down? It's too small for—" Delsar stops himself but it's too late. He made things worse. Elidria's face says it all. "Let's go talk to Cade. We'll figure something out later." He lets Elidria exit before him.

Because of the boat's size, it only takes a couple strides to reach the mast that holds the sail. "Hey, Cade," Elidria says, giving him a chipper wave and smile. "Delsar has something he'd like to ask you."

"Yes, Captain Sardel?" Cade asks.

Glade bursts out laughing from behind the wheel. Whatever it meant, he likely put his son up to it.

"That's not even funny!" Delsar shouts back to Glade.

"It is now!" Glade starts to wheeze.

Delsar looks at Elidria in hopes of an answer. She shakes her head and shrugs her shoulders.

"This is stupid," Delsar says, pinching the bridge of his nose. "Elidria, I believe it is *you* who has something to ask Cade."

"Could you, please?" She uses a more hushed tone.

"Um, why?"

"I don't like asking for things unless I'm paying for it."

"Then what do you call what you've been doing with me?"

"I'm paying you," she replies. "Did you not just hear me? I'm your boss so I can ask you for anything *I* want."

"For someone who doesn't approve of pride, you seem to have a lot if you can't even ask for help." Delsar is sure he's right, but this is a quick bout he is not going to win.

Elidria slams her fists on her hips. "I'm not being prideful. I'm being afraid," she says loud enough for even Glade to hear.

Delsar rolls his eyes and scoffs. "Fine," he says with his fingers on his nose again. *No one with even an ounce of pride would ever admit to that,* he thinks, looking over at Cade. "Cade, if I take that rope for you, will you grab the contents of a certain crate for me?"

"You want me to crawl into the hull and squeeze my way through all the barrels and stuff, in the dark?"

"That sums it up."

"Sweet." Cade hands the rope to Delsar. "What does it look like?"

"It's a bigger one, so it's probably in the back and under some *stuff.*"

"So it's square."

"It's a crate, so, yes."

"I'm just making sure."

"Oh," Delsar whispers something in his ear. "Just bring it up. Take as many trips as you need."

"Sure." Cade stares at Delsar.

"What?"

"You're standing on the trapdoor."

Delsar looks at his own feet. "This is a design flaw." It really isn't. Delsar only needs to step to the side and work the sail from there. Once he moves, Cade lets himself under the deck.

"It's pretty dark and spooky down here."

Elidria bites her lip but says nothing. Neither does Delsar. If Cade wanted a verbal response, he's not getting one.

"Good thing you chose me," says Cade, continuing his adventure below. "It looks like I can just slide over these barrels." The sound of scuffling emanates from the trapdoor. "Hey, I think I found it!" He is clearly heard shimmying and grunting. "Yup, this has to be it. There's a super-heavy barrel on top, so I can't open it." He struggles to hoist the barrel. "I'm going to just push it off."

Delsar finally breaks. "We don't need a play-by-play!"

Cade goes silent. A loud crash under Delsar's and Elidria's feet interrupts the silence, followed by the sound of rushing water. Cade doesn't say anything.

"Are you going to tell me what you just did?" Delsar asks, both annoyed and curious.

"You said no more play-by-play."

"This is an exception! Tell me!"

"Okay, so there is a barrel down here, or at least, there was, and it looks like we were using it to store water. Emphasis on *was*. It no longer holds or has the ability to hold water. Also, my socks need drying."

Delsar shakes his head and repeats, "He's thirteen," over and over again to himself. He looks over at Elidria. "You do know I was an apprentice when I was thirteen, right?" he asks her, more so to confirm it with himself that Cade is a dunce.

"I do," she replies.

"I'm just making sure."

"Actually," shouts Cade, "I'm going to need to dry my everything!"

"You are your father's son."

"That'a boy!" yells Glade from behind the wheel.

"That's not a compliment, Glade!"

"Maybe not to you."

"Can you get inside the crate now, Glade? Gosh! I mean, Cade." Delsar runs his hands through his hair as Elidria giggles. "This is only day two," he says. "I don't know if I can do this."

She brings her hand to her mouth and tries to cover her ear-to-ear grin.

"You won't think it's funny when he's done," Delsar snaps.

Elidria breaks out in laughter. Any amount of torment from training is well worth it to see Delsar suffer like this.

"Um, Captain Del—"

"Don't you dare!" shouts Delsar, cutting Cade off.

"Delsar, sir?"

"That's better. I appreciate the 'sir' because you're thirteen and *I am older than you!*"

"Captain, Delsir?"

Delsar throws up his hands, completely giving up. "What does Glade's child want?"

"The crate's lid has been nailed down. I can't open it."

"Why is this so hard?" Delsar asks Elidria, not expecting an answer, but he'll happily take one. "Come back to the door," he yells down to Cade. "Elidria will hand you a crowbar." He looks over at Elidria. "It's by the crate with the arrows."

"On it." She runs into the cabin and returns moments later. "The crowbar was really easy to find and a cinch to acquire," she says, throwing a bit of salt on the wound.

"That's a first."

Cade's head pops out next to Delsar's feet. He's completely soaked.

"Did you go swimming down there?" Delsar can't comprehend how he managed to get drenched from head-to-toe in water that's not even ankle-deep.

"What? You thought I *wouldn't* enjoy my time down here?"

"I. Don't. Know. What. That. Means. Take the crowbar and go back to your antics that I don't want to know about in the bowels of my boat."

Elidria hands him the crowbar and he disappears back under.

"I think Glade cloned himself," Delsar says, looking beyond Elidria with terror in his eyes.

"That means there is another wonderful person in this world."

"Your definition of wonderful must differ from mine."

"He left his home to find help before returning, saving his son and his town." Elidria's face drops. "I understand now. I had to leave." She hugs Delsar under his arms. "Thank you, Delsar."

"Woah! W-what happened to *not* hugging me?"

She backs away and gives him her usual head-tilted smile. "You're just really huggable."

"You know that crate I said was nailed?" Cade asks from below.

"Oh no. Elidria, hug me really tightly around my neck."

Elidria raises an eyebrow and squints her other eye at him.

"It wasn't actually nailed," Cade continues. "It was only latched on the other side. That's why I didn't notice it."

"So what does that mean, exactly?"

"It's broken. It won't work anymore. It's dead. I killed it. But it is open now!" Cade sounds excited with that last sentence.

"That is the result we were looking for."

"Hey! These are really nice."

"Don't get them wet!" Delsar commands.

"Oh. I wish you told me earlier."

Delsar looks at Elidria. "I'm very sad I decided to switch posts early. But that is the *only* thing I am sad about."

Cade finally emerges with a kite shield in his hands. It's smaller than the one Delsar wears now. "Here you go. I'll grab the other thing now."

Elidria grabs it from him and examines it. "This is beautiful! It looks so much better than the one you use now."

"Ouch. I really like my shield."

"But this one will make you look like a good guy. It's so shiny and silver." Elidria straps it around her arm. "It's lighter, too."

"Just so you know, I would *never* give up my shield. She stays with me and is certainly not getting replaced."

"She?" Elidria giggles with her hand by her mouth.

Cade emerges again. This time, with a sheathed sword. "Here you go."

Elidria leans the shield against the mast and grabs the sword. "This handle is really nice. Gold and silver are a great touch."

"Cade." Delsar gives Cade his spot back and takes the sword from Elidria. "Grab the shield." He says as he leads her to the bow of the boat.

"Thanks, Cade," Elidria says, knowing that Delsar won't. She grabs the shield and follows Delsar about ten feet before they run out of room.

Delsar slides his shield off. "Put that on my back, will you? I already screwed in some straps."

"Sure." Elidria tries to slide the metal straps over his shoulders. "It won't fit. Maybe if you take off your cloak?"

"This won't do. Give it to me." He snatches the shield from her. "Of course," he says. He almost sounds exasperated, but not quite. "I used the wrong measurements. Turn around."

"Okay?" Elidria obliges.

Delsar slides it on Elidria's back and it fits perfectly. "At least it won't go to waste."

"What do you mean?"

"The shield fits you so I guess you should keep it."

"You could just get new straps."

"Elidria, it's yours. I already have one."

Elidria's face lights up and she covers her smile with her hand. "This is for me?"

"I figured, if you're going to fight like me, you should be geared like me. Oh," Delsar extends the sword to her, "this is yours, too."

Elidria is at a loss for words. She slowly and carefully grabs the sword from Delsar. She stares at it and then pulls it out of the sheath. The biggest grin Delsar has ever seen creeps across her face. "Woah. It's longer and yet lighter than the guard sword I use."

"Stabbing and slashing. That's what this one is better for. No hacking or chopping and try not to parry too much with it. We're going to work on your movement today. You'll do your forms and, randomly, I'll swing at you with my sword. Just duck and dodge and whatnot. I'll get faster as you get better at it."

"Wait, Delsar, I don't know any dodges."

"That's okay. I will help you. How did you defeat those men in Grandell?"

"Well, one of them I slashed in the leg. The other just gave up and ran."

"When you slashed him, were you attacking?"

"No, it was reactionary."

"So you dodged?"

Her movements during that fight dawn on her. "Yes! I guess I did. How did I do that?"

"Dodging and countering really is just reactionary. If you think too long, you'll die. You just have to *do*. That's what the forms are for. Your body gets used to doing them over and over. That way it instinctively drops into a stance or a move when needed."

"Wow. Thanks for making me do my forms so much, then."

"Yup. We'll work on dodging and countering. I assume you dodged toward your opponent?"

Elidria gasps. "I did! How did you know that?"

"That's how you were able to counter. Toward danger is away from danger."

"That's weird."

"Don't worry about it." Delsar pulls his pocket watch from his bag. "We still have seven hours and fifty minutes before our shift change, so I'm going to drill your movements into you."

"Oh, boy. Delsar, eight hours is insane."

"I'm not a monster. We'll have a break here and there."

Elidria takes a huge breath. "All right. Let's do this."

"Bracers and shinguards."

Elidria sheaths her new sword. "I forgot about those. I'll be right back."

"Cade's log: Day 6 of his intrepid journey - I sit here bored out of my mind. I am in charge of making sure the wind is always hitting our sail. However, for the last six hours, the wind has not changed so I sit here, waiting for a need to adjust it.

"My entertainment isn't very interesting either. Our strange Captain and Eldra have been doing the same thing for hours. Even in my sleep, I dream of working the sail and watching them do their dances over and over.

"I'm afraid my sanity is starting to slip from my consciousness and that very soon, I will become a maddened brute who resorts to mockery and insults for pleasure."

"Cade!" yells Delsar. "Can't you see we're working? Write in your head!"

"During my sail shift, this morning, my uncanny Captain made threats toward his favorite thirteen-year-old crew member. His voice was stern and his intent unclear. Cade now fears that should the boat run out of supplies, our anomalous Captain will choose Cade's delicious flesh to satisfy the appetite of the rest of the crew. The only question is, who will he choose next?"

Delsar storms over and snatches the journal from Cade. "I said do it in your head! If you don't, I *will* make your fantasy into your reality."

"I already dream the same thing over and over, so I guess I am living my *fantasy.*"

"Delsar," says Elidria, "he's right. Everyone's been doing the same thing over and over again. We aren't trained sailors so we're not used to this. Even my training is the same every day and my partner is the same for all my shifts. Perhaps we could mix some things up?"

"The female made some good points. Her words are like a sharp knife that cuts into our peculiar Captain's chest. He stands there dumbfounded, wondering how he didn't think of these things and how he's going to make it right."

Delsar swipes another journal from Cade. "Why do you have two?"

"I have three," scoffs Cade.

"Fine!" Delsar turns to Elidria. "And what do you have in mind?"

"Just a simple switch. I'll have Glade as a partner, you can have Nomar, and put Cade and Roki together."

"I still need to train with you."

"Then work the sail while I'm on free time. Then you can do both."

"I'll think about it. We *are* only two nights from Fairview."

"Can we at least change up the training a bit? Your movements are too predictable now. I know when I need to dodge before I think you realize you're attacking."

"You're getting cocky, huh?"

"It's not just the dodging. The forms are boring now, too."

Delsar thinks for a couple moments. He draws his sword. "Then let's fight."

"What?" exclaims Elidria. "Are you crazy?"

"My previous assumptions are confirmed by the female. Our queer Captain is truly no longer fit to lead. His mind is like a bag of potatoes, mashed into soft oozing paste, ready to drip from the ears. At least the 'Sail Shift' is about to get a little more interesting."

"I know that's your last one, Cade. Don't make me take it from you."

"I'm done."

"You'd better be." He reengages with Elidria. "It's a friendly spar. You'll get to fight a live opponent instead of just going through the motions. It will be good for you."

"If you say so. I just don't know if I trust myself."

"You'll be fine. Oh, and try not to parry. You don't want to scuff your new sword and not everyone will attack you with a blade. Work on dodging and countering. Your low height *is* your advantage."

Elidria holds her sword in front with both hands. "Then let's do this."

Delsar smirks and readies himself. "I won't make this easy."

"Why do you have to say things that scare me?"

"Just count us in, Cade."

"I got you." Cade stands up from sitting against the mast and holds up his hands. "Over here, on the starboard side, we have the implacable and delightful Eldra! And on the port side, we have the dour and loathsome Captain!"

"Just say 'go.'"

"Three-two-one-go."

Elidria moves first but tumbles over and almost falls overboard. She crashes into the guardrail and so does Delsar on the other side.

Cade falls on his hands and knees. "It wasn't me," he quickly states.

"No kidding." Delsar stands himself back up. "Glade, what did we hit?"

"I'm not sure, Captain!"

Nomar and Roki exit the cabin. Both of them look like they just woke up.

"Nomar, do you have a clue?" Delsar asks the fisherman.

"If I had to make a guess, I'd say we hit a sandbar. I don't usually sail far from town, but I've never had *this* happen before."

"How could I be so stupid?" Delsar runs his hands through his hair. "I was so concerned we should sail close to shore, in case of a storm, that shallower water completely slipped my mind. Do we have solutions?"

Nomar shakes his head. "I'm only self-taught. This is something I also never thought of."

"Could we wait until high tide?" Roki asks.

"This is high tide," Nomar states.

"Then this is only going to get worse. No idea is a bad idea! Everyone, brainstorm!" Delsar orders.

"I can swim to shore and get help," Elidria volunteers.

"By the time you get back, this sandbar is going to be an island."

"What's another day at sea?" Glade asks.

"Delsar and Eldra are fighting against the clock as it is," says Roki. "Plus, I wouldn't trust these waters. I've heard too many stories during my time in the *Salty Crustacean*."

"Can we dig it out?" questions Glade.

The whole party looks at him.

"I thought you said no idea is a bad idea?"

"We'll save yours for later. Anyone else?" Delsar asks.

"Why don't we make the boat lighter?" Cade finally gives his two-copper and hits the nail on the head.

"That could work," says Nomar.

"Dump all our perishables. We'll hit the next town we pass and buy more." Delsar starts to formulate a plan. "Nomar, you and I will pull stuff from the hull. Water, food, and anything else we can just buy. Roki and Glade will do the same but in the cabin. Elidria and Cade, you two toss whatever we drag up. Everyone understand? We have to get going before the water drops any lower."

"Sounds easy enough," says Roki. "Let's do it."

Nomar opens the trapdoor and hops down. "I'll just hand you the stuff. There's no room for both of us."

"Understood."

Nomar hands Delsar both crates and barrels full of bread, fruit, water, wheat, horse feed, and other various items. Delsar hands them off to Elidria and Cade who double-carry them to the starboard side and toss it all over.

"If the boat starts moving, Elidria, I want you to grab the wheel, and Cade, make sure the sail is getting wind."

Because of her heavy load, Elidria gives a grunt in acknowledgment.

"This is the last one!" Nomar yells up.

Delsar grabs it from him and helps the others with dumping everything. The boat shifts a tiny bit before settling again. "Just a bit more!" They toss the last crate and the boat begins to move. It scrapes against the sand and then stops again.

Cade leans over the side. "What else do we have that isn't essential?"

Delsar looks over the side with Cade. "The sandbar doesn't look like it extends that far. We only need to go another hundred feet or so." He grabs a rope and hands it to Cade.

"What's this for?" he asks.

"Don't let go." Delsar proceeds to push Cade overboard.

"What was that for?" cries Elidria.

"Grab the wheel. Glade! Your son fell overboard! Go get him!"

Glade bursts out of the cabin. "What?" He runs next to Delsar and spots his son. Cade doesn't look panicked, but that doesn't mean Glade isn't. Without a second thought, he jumps in after his son.

"Glade!" shouts Elidria. "He's got a broken arm, you idiot!" She jabs Delsar in the shoulder but he doesn't seem to care.

"He'll be fine." He leans over the rail to talk to Glade. "Grab a barrel if you're having trouble and hold onto that rope, too."

The boat begins to move again but still scrapes the sand.

Nomar climbs from the bowels, completely oblivious to the shenanigans.

"Nomar, do we need anyone on the sail?" Delsar asks.

"The wind is with us so we should be fine."

"Good. I need you to jump overboard."

"Come again?"

"Get in the water and grab the rope." Delsar begins removing his own accessories.

"All right. If that's an order." Nomar jumps in and grabs the rope with the other two.

Delsar ties his end of the rope to the guardrail and gives Elidria a little salute before joining the rest in the water. The boat completely breaks free, so Delsar must quickly grab the rope before it gets ahead of him. Now four men, one being Cade, are being towed through the water, across a sandbar.

Roki exits the cabin and beholds the unforgettable sight. "Why am I not part of this?" he shouts to the towed.

They don't answer. Perhaps it's humiliating, or maybe they're enjoying it too much. Glade breaks the strange silence. "You know, this is how I met my wife."

Despite Bellrock's small size, Delsar still insisted on splitting up to replace the lost food and water. He and Nomar are finalizing a few things before heading off to find food. He just sent Glade and Elidria to fetch fresh water.

"One hour really isn't enough time for my usual antics," Glade tells Elidria.

"We're getting water. What possible antics could you be referring to?"

"The messing with people kind."

Elidria brings a finger to her chin and tilts her head. "Messing with people?"

"Yeah. Every day is different from the last. Cade and I always make sure we do something that we'll remember for the rest of our lives, every day. The more fun or random it is, the easier it is to remember."

"Is that why Cade was so excited about crawling under the boat?"

"It was also why he didn't complain about getting tossed overboard. It was a new experience. A new memory."

"So, what do you mean by 'messing with people?' I assume it's another way you remember the day."

"It is, indeed," confirms Glade. "Buying things can be so boring. Been there, done that. I like to take on a character. One time, I pretended I was from the future when I was buying bed covers. I remember exactly what it was I was buying *and* I remember exactly what the girl looked like who was selling them. I'm pretty sure she'd remember me, too."

"That's kind of lying."

"Nonsense, Eldra! It's a performance. You wouldn't claim a stage actor to be lying, would you?"

"I wouldn't, but people know they're acting."

"If I'm going to be honest, Eldra, I'm pretty sure she knew I was acting." Glade stops Elidria before entering *Bellrock Voyage and Supplies*. "The point wasn't the story. It was the memories. It's a day I will never forget and I'm sure the girl will never forget either. I even remember the lunch I had that day. It was tuna."

"Well, I'm not an actor, nor do I wish to do *anything* like that." A bit of Delsar seems to be rubbing off on Elidria. She turns to enter the store. "Let's just get the water and get back."

"It doesn't have to be a character. Let me think." Glade snaps his fingers. "I've got it! Every time someone says 'water,' we say 'glub glub' or jump in the air."

"That's stupid," Elidria says, without looking back.

"Come on, Eldra. It will be fun."

"It *literally* won't be."

"*Memories*," Glade whispers, loudly.

"People will think we're crazy."

"Who says we aren't?"

"I'm not!" Elidria spins around and almost jams her fingers into his chest, but she stops herself. "Glade, let's just be normal people."

"Then something simple? Something that will only raise an eyebrow?"

"You're going to tell me anyway, so you may as well just spill it."

"Great! How about, you have to be standing on the right to talk?"

Elidria turns back around and starts toward customer service. "I don't know what that means."

"Like, we stand next to each other when we talk to the clerk, but only whoever is on the right may speak."

"We have to switch places if we wish to talk?"

"Exactly!" Glade definitely lives for embarrassment.

Elidria tilts her head down and shakes it. "We should be acting like professionals, not children."

"No one remembers a professional."

"And I don't want to be remembered as a fool."

Glade runs in front of her. "Come on. You won't see these people ever again. It will be fun. I promise."

"You're not going to stop, are you?"

Glade's grin is his only response.

"Whatever, but we're only doing the switchy thing. I'm not saying 'glub glub.'"

"Splendid!" Glade leads her to the counter and stands himself on her right.

The clerk greets them. "Welcome. Are you looking for anything specific?"

Glade begins his escapade with a terribly fake accent. "Hello, my fine sir. We are looking for your *goodest* water."

Elidria's face goes beet-red immediately and she brings her hand to her face. *Why is this happening?* She gives Glade a look, which in her mind means "Don't do that," but he interprets it as "I'd like to talk now."

Glade steps around her and gives her a reassuring smile.

"We just want freshwater," she says. "Please make it fast."

"Of course. We sell it in barrels if that's what you're looking for," the clerk informs.

Glide slides past Elidria and puts on a different accent. "And how much will that be costin' us?"

Elidria notices the clerk's head jerk back as a reaction. She feels her face become warm and prickly before looking away from the clerk. *My heart is beating faster than when I fought the trolls. This is so dumb!*

"They cost three silver per barrel of water with a two silver refund on the return of the barrel." He looks at Elidria who is too embarrassed to return the look. He looks back at Glade who now sports the biggest smile known to man. "We deliver to the docks for free. I just need the name of your boat and I can have the water there in ten minutes."

Glade slides back to Elidria's left, smiling at her with the same giant grin.

Elidria reaches into her bag and pulls out six silver pieces. "We just need two. Thank you," she says quickly.

"And the name of your boat?"

Glade jumps back to the right. "I'm afraid our boat has never been blessed with a name." He uses another accent.

"Is that true?" asks the clerk. "I can't tell if you're being serious."

Elidria breaks. "It is true and unfortunately he is being serious. Will you be able to recognize us if we stand outside our boat?"

"I don't think I'd be able to forget the two of you," he says.

Elidria pinches Glade in his side. "I will forever be a fool to him," she grumbles quietly to Glade.

"No, it was different," says the clerk. "It was entertaining and brightened my day a little."

"See?" Glade exclaims. "Success!"

"Then we are done here. Thank you, and I'm sorry." Elidria grabs Glade and starts dragging him out.

"You're welcome, and it wasn't a bother." The clerk waves to them.

"Wasn't that great?" Glade asks, still being pulled by Elidria.

"No. It was stupid, and foolish, and childish, and dumb," Elidria huffs. "It was everything I said it would be. I've never been more embarrassed in my life."

"If that was the most embarrassing thing you've ever done, then you really need to get out more."

"Not with you. Delsar was right."

Glade laughs. "But did you see his face? This is a day none of us will ever forget."

"But I *really* want to forget this one."

Glade puffs his chest out. "You'll be thanking me when you have stories to tell your grandchildren."

"Oh, I have stories to tell and I can assure you that this one is the *last* one I'll ever be telling."

"You're saving it for last? That's so sweet."

Elidria lets out an annoyed grunt. "Next time, I'll stay on the boat and Cade can go with you."

"Now you're excited about getting back on the boat? I guess my work here is done."

Elidria stops them in their tracks. "You did that because I was feeling stir crazy?"

"Yup."

"That had to be the *worst* way of going about it."

"But it worked," Glade says assuredly.

"Only because now I want to pout to Delsar." Elidria takes a deep breath and shakes her head. She even scoffs before continuing. "You're right. I am excited about getting back to the boat. Even if your tactics were *unusual*, so thank you." She starts walking back toward the boat. "But just so you know, Cade is much funnier than you."

Glade laughs again. "The apprentice has become the master."

"Captain, look at this." Nomar points to the giant wooden map at the end of the dock. "According to this, we're just one day from Fairview."

"That can't be right." Delsar takes a look for himself.

"Think about it, we've hardly needed to adjust the sail because the wind was blowing with us the whole time. Instead of needing to zigzag with the wind, we've been able to sail completely straight."

"Six nights to Fairview from Orange Peak. That's pretty good. Let's grab what we're here for." Delsar doesn't waste any extra time thinking about their quick journey. He leads Nomar to what looks like a market.

Delsar grabs various baskets of food, paying all the merchants the requested money. No hassling or unnecessary conversations.

"Captain, I've never been able to personally thank you for what you did for us," says Nomar.

"That's five copper," the baker demands.

Delsar hands the man his money before responding to Nomar. "Your population went from one hundred and ten to just over thirty. I don't think you should be thanking anyone. If anything, you should be in mourning, yet I haven't seen any of you shed a single tear."

"I'm sure they're mourning now. With our saviors in town, we wanted to celebrate. I'll find my own time to mourn, later."

"Then who did you lose?"

"Glade's wife is actually my cousin, though she is more like an older sister to me." Nomar's voice drops. "My father hid in the stronghold."

"I'm sorry to hear that," is Delsar's response, yet his tone doesn't sound any different from before.

"What about you?" asks Nomar. "Have you ever lost anyone?"

Delsar continues his determined walk from merchant to merchant. He doesn't even look at Nomar. "Everyone," he says.

That wasn't the response Nomar was expecting. He's not sure how to continue. "I didn't know."

"How could you?" Delsar hands money to another merchant.

"What about Miss Eldra?"

"What about her?"

"You still have her."

"She's just my employer. I make it a point not to form attachments anymore."

"So you don't lose them?"

"What happened in my past is my business," scolds Delsar.

"I wasn't going to ask about it. I make it a point not to pry."

"This is why I chose to go with you today," says Delsar.

"I was wondering about that, Captain. I'm with you and you sent Miss Eldra with Glade. Why was that?"

"This was Elidria's idea and I'm not going with Glade. That just leaves you."

"What about Roki and Cade."

"Someone has to stay with the boat, plus Roki has two busted arms and Cade is a child. I don't want to spend more than an hour here and children are easily distracted."

"I think Glade is more easily distracted," Nomar says, chuckling a bit after. "I wonder what kind of stupid things he's having Miss Eldra do with him."

Delsar interrupts their own conversation. "This is enough. If we are only a day out, we won't need any more."

"What about food for a horse?"

145

"I'm not getting food for something we don't have. That was a mistake I made in Orange Peak. I'll get food when I get a horse."

"That's fair." Nomar uses Delsar's segue to ask a question he's been wondering since the start of their voyage. "Tell me, Captain, where *are* you and Miss Eldra going?"

"What happened to not prying?"

"Unlike you, I have formed an attachment to you both. I'd hate to see you two get hurt. You train her every day which means you *are* expecting to fight. Whatever it is, Orange Peak can help. Just like you both helped us."

"No," Delsar says as blunt as ever. "I can't pay you like you've paid me and I never owe anyone anything."

"If you say so."

"I respect you, Nomar."

"Huh?"

"You seem to be the only person on the boat who actually listens. You even call me 'Captain.'"

"What do you mean by that?"

"You take everything I say and you leave it at that. Everyone else would be begging for more information."

"It's not my place to know everything, nor is it possible. That's what my dad used to say, even though I'm pretty sure he would say it because I would ask him things he had no clue about. If people want to tell you something, they will. Asking more than once is rude."

"That last part sounds like something a mother would say," Delsar speculates.

"It kind of was. It was Bekka's mom, my aunt, who was the motherly figure in my life."

"Bekka?"

"Glade never told you?"

Delsar's questioned look answers that.

"Bekka is Glade's wife. I'm surprised he never mentioned her name."

"I may have forgotten." Delsar isn't usually curious about the affairs of others, but Nomar has piqued his interest. "What about *your* mother?"

"Now *that* is something I don't want to talk about."

"Very well." Delsar starts walking on the dock.

"Captain, please don't let anything happen to Miss Eldra."

"Why is everyone concerned about her and not me?"

"Because she's cute and pretty. She also has an innocence about her. You're a bit of a ruffian. Not very likable."

"Wow." Delsar is slightly shocked by Nomar's own bluntness. "That's an honest answer. I might actually miss you, Nomar."

"I'm flattered."

"Hey," Roki says, leaning over the boat's guardrail.

"What's up, Roki?" Nomar replies.

"Glade and Eldra are back already. They ordered two barrels of water which will be delivered in a few minutes."

"Make sure everyone is ready," instructs Delsar. "When the water gets here, we depart."

"To Fairview," Nomar says to himself, sighing.

Delsar looks at him and nods. "To Fairview."

CHAPTER 10
THE DECEIT

11 Years Ago…

"You catch anything, Nomar?" Soren approaches his son, looking anxious about something.

"Actually, quite a few." Nomar points to a basket he has on the dock, next to where he stands. It looks like it holds about five or six fish, slimy and dripping over the sides.

"May I join you?"

"Of course."

Soren sits on the dock next to Nomar. "You should sit for this."

"What is it?" asks Nomar.

"Please." Soren gestures and Nomar obliges. "I was talking t-to Aunt Freya and she thinks it's time you learn about your mother."

Nomar can hear his father fumbling with his words. His mother's past has always been kept a secret. He never pried or sought the answers for himself. There is likely a good reason they didn't want Nomar to know. "It's okay," he says to his father, placing his hand on Soren's shoulder. "I've gone fourteen years without knowing and I'm doing just fine."

"N-no. You d-deserve to know." Soren takes a couple deep breaths. His lips quiver. "Just bear with me."

"Would you like a line?"

"Yes, please."

Nomar runs off, fetching another fishing rod and handing it to Soren.

"Thanks," says Soren, trying his best to smile.

Nomar sits down and they both cast their lines out. It remains this way for a few minutes until Soren finally works up the courage to start his story. "I loved your mother very much. So much, in fact, that we got engaged. The night after I proposed, I took her to a nice restaurant in Grandell. I even paid for a top-class carriage to take us."

Soren pauses for a moment, expecting his son to comment, but he says nothing and intently listens.

"After our meal, and some aimless wandering of the town, we returned to the carriage. That's when your mother realized she left her earrings back at the restaurant. To this day, I don't know why she took them off. Regardless, I was a fool and should have gone back with her. Instead, I waited for her at the carriage. Five minutes turned into twenty. I told our driver he could go and I set out to find her. It was getting late, so I figured Taiana and I should just rent a room for the night."

Soren tears up and sniffles a little. His heart starts to race thinking about what came next. "I never found her that night. It wasn't until the late next day a guard found her in the woods, beaten, bruised, and left for dead." Soren breaks and begins to weep.

Nomar is stunned. He knows the story isn't done but it doesn't take a genius to figure out the rest. He squeezes his father's shoulder. "You don't need to continue."

Soren looks at his son's eyes with his own watery, red eyes. "Perhaps sharing this with you will help me more than it will help you." This is a secret he's been hiding for years and the anxiety of such a secret has been building up since the day it happened.

Nomar nods.

"The night I left her was also the night she became pregnant with you." Soren drops his head as he says it. He feels so much shame and like he just failed Nomar.

Nomar squeezes his eyes shut and tries to process everything Soren just shared with him, but one question keeps popping into his mind. "Are you not my father?" he asks.

Soren shakes his head. "Not by blood. I'm so sorry."

Nomar pulls his arm off Soren and makes a fist. Now it's his voice that betrays a tremble. "What about mom? What happened to her?"

"We never got married. After she had you, she left, leaving only a note. She wanted to start over and every time she looked at you, she was reminded of the man who defiled her. She left you with me and I never saw her again."

For a moment, Nomar feels like throwing a fit and screaming at Soren or anyone for what he just learned, but he doesn't. He composes himself and hugs him instead. "Thanks, Dad."

"W-what?" Soren is thrown off by Nomar.

"For not abandoning me."

"You seem okay with all this."

"I'm not exactly okay with it, but no one chooses where they came from. 'It's always now and it's never yesterday or tomorrow.' That's what the Queen says, and right now, I've got a pretty neat dad."

"But I'm not—."

"It doesn't matter," says Nomar, stopping his father. "What you've told me doesn't change what you've done for me for fourteen years. Most kids can't say they were chosen, but I can. You chose me, so thank you."

Soren buries his head into Nomar's shoulder and begins to sob. "Then you're welcome," he says as best he can. The two of them embrace each other for a while until Soren finally straightens back up. "Um, may I still call you 'son?'"

"I'd be sad if you didn't. Hey, Dad?"

Soren sniffles once more. "Yeah?"

"I think a fish stole your bait."

Soren lets out a forced chuckle and finally smiles. "So one did," he says, confirming Nomar's observation. "Hand me another worm."

"You got it, Dad."

A thick haze obscured the boat's vision all last night and most of this morning. It wasn't until the sun heated the air that the fog dispersed.

"Wow!" exclaims Nomar, amazed by Fairview's breathtaking sight.

Glade gives no witty remarks or bad jokes and neither does Cade. Both are also astonished by the walls of this great city.

"Go wake up Delsar," Nomar instructs to no one in particular. He can't take his eyes off Fairview.

"Delsar!" Glade shouts. His feet stuck in place.

Some annoyed grumbling, followed by a thud, is heard coming from the cabin. Delsar pushes open the door and is followed out by Elidria. Delsar's sleep lines and Elidria's frizzy hair indicate they both just woke up.

"What is it now?" Delsar asks, but he needs no answer. His jaw drops beholding the city. "Woah," he says silently enough so only Elidria hears.

"What is it?" she asks, rubbing her eyes and squinting one open. Her eyes are taking their time adjusting to the sun's light. "How can you already see?" she whispers to Delsar.

"Lady and gentlemen, I give you Fairview." Nomar opens his arms wide and starts to laugh.

Elidria blinks a few times and really tries to focus. She is hit by awe and drops her belt and sword. Before her and everyone else are massive, white cliffs with a giant wall built on top, making the cliffs' already monumental presence even more astounding. Spires of rock jut from the ocean. Most are shorter but some reach as high as the cliffs. Atop many of them are battlements and watchtowers with long suspension bridges connecting them and the wall together. Running down the wall are dozens of pulley systems and cranes. Just as many staircases go up and down from multiple docks and harbors. One more massive tower stands above everything else. Extending from the wall, it sits in the very south-west corner of the continent, overwatching the entire city and its surrounding waters. "Fairview Tower," Elidria says under her breath.

Delsar pulls himself from the trance and calls up to Roki at the wheel. "Take us in."

"Aye...aye," he responds, a bit flabbergasted. The smaller towers in the water have men with flags. The man in the nearest tower signals Roki directions. He follows a few more towers and guides the boat into a cove full of smaller vessels like the one they're on.

"I hope nothing falls on us," Glade says, half-joking and half-serious.

Upon docking, men from a nearby building immediately start tying off the boat. Another man with a notebook greets them. "Welcome to Fairview!"

Elidria leans over the guardrail and waves to him. "Hi!" she shouts, also smiling.

The man returns her smile with a nod.

Delsar exits the boat and approaches the man.

"You must be the Captain," he assumes because of Delsar's lead.

"I am," Delsar confirms.

"What is your name and the name of your boat?" he asks.

"My name is Delsar, but I won't be leaving Fairview on this boat," Delsar informs the dockmaster. "Put Glade as Captain. I'm transferring ownership to him."

"Oh? That's new." He looks at Delsar's company. "Which one of you is Glade?"

Glade raises his hand. "That would be the handsome one."

The dockmaster looks Glade up and down. "Not you, then."

Glade laughs at the dockmaster's quick-wittedness. "Okay, so maybe the ugly one."

The dockmaster gets right back to business. "Are you taking ownership of this vessel?"

"Yes, I am."

"And do you have a name for her, Captain Glade?" he asks while writing a few things down.

"*Bekka's Fury*," Glade replies. "She's named after my wife."

"Lovely," says the dockmaster. It sounds like he truly cares about the name, but it might just be his job. "Where are you traveling from, Captain?"

"Orange Peak."

The dockmaster pauses and looks up from his notebook. "Orange Peak?" He examines the ragtag group and spies the mix of bandages and slings on Elidria, Glade, and Roki. "I've heard rumors from others that have docked here. Are they true?"

"Unfortunately," says Glade.

"Oh my. If you are in need of medical assistance, we have the best physicians in the country."

152

Delsar interrupts the socializing. "We appreciate your concern for our wellbeing, but some of us are on a tight schedule."

"Of course. I must ask you, Captain, what is your business in Fairview?"

"We're looking for any clues on the whereabouts of the man that attacked my home," Glade answers.

"If it's a boat you're looking for, Fairview Tower keeps meticulous records of every boat that docks here and even records descriptions of those that pass. Fairview will be more than happy to help those from Grandell's borders."

"Thanks, dockmaster."

The dockmaster changes his attention over to Delsar. "If your business is different, I must know."

"Supplies," Delsar responds, "then Roki, Elidria, and I are traveling to Bihnor by foot."

"Bihnor? Ah, yes. In Lar."

"That's the place," Elidria cuts in.

"Then I have almost everything I need from you folks." He rips a slip from his notebook and hands it to Glade. "Docking here is one silver per night, plus one on arrival. Just return with this slip and the payment, and you'll be all set."

"Thanks." Glade grabs the slip.

"As for you, Master...?"

"Delsar."

"Master Delsar, I've never had anyone transfer ownership like that before, but I'm fairly certain that you must pay the arrival fee since you owned the boat when you docked."

Delsar hands him the silver without opposition.

"One last thing, weapons *are* allowed but may not be drawn unless on the very rare occasion of self-defense."

"Understood."

"Then you are all set. Enjoy your time in Fairview." The dockmaster shakes Glade's hand and immediately greets another tenant waiting for service. "Captain Jahvess! I'm glad you got that fixed. Are you ready to depart?"

Delsar grabs his group's attention. "Glade, Cade, you two head to Fairview Tower and look for any info on the boat that attacked Orange Peak. Elidria and I will head into the city and scout for supplies we will need for our trek to Bihnor. Nomar and Roki, you both stay with the boat."

"You had me stay with the boat in Bellrock, too," interjects Roki.

"Logistics," says Delsar. "You want to be a part of *my* team, so this is what you do."

Roki shakes his head, a bit frustrated and Elidria mouths him the word, "Sorry."

"Elidria, we're looking for a cheap carriage and horse. When we find those, we come back for Roki and the rest of our gear."

Elidria embraces the unsuspecting Glade.

"What's this for?" he asks.

"If we return before you, we may not see each other again. I'll miss you."

"In that case, I accept." Glade hugs her in return. "Thank you for everything, Eldra."

"Cade." Elidria gestures to Cade who joins the hug. "I'd like to thank both of you, as well."

"You wish to thank us?" asks Glade.

"For being so wonderful and an inspiration."

"I don't think anyone has ever called my dad 'wonderful,'" Cade states.

"Hush now. Let me bask in this moment." Glade gives a forced sniffle. "Good luck, you three. I wish you a successful adventure. Whatever it may be."

Elidria escapes the hug and grabs Nomar. "I'll miss you, too."

Nomar laughs. "If you're coming back to the boat, I'll see you again."

"Then I'll have to hug you again."

"And I'll accept it."

"Elidria, go put your gear on." Delsar's ability to interrupt such beautiful moments knows no bounds. "You're allowed to wear it so you will."

"Yes, Delsar." She runs aboard the ship before turning to wave at Glade and Cade one last time. "Goodbye!"

"See ya," is Glade's response while Cade just waves.

By the time she returns with her gear, Glade and Cade are long gone. Off on their own mission.

"You ready?" Delsar asks.

"Yup."

"Nomar, Roki, we'll be back in an hour."

"You got it," is Nomar's reply.

"I'll still be here," is Roki's.

Delsar shakes his head and starts his way toward the nearest stairs.

"Bye, guys." Elidria gives a quick wave and jogs after Delsar.

He starts the long ascent, up into the city. "He's like a kid," he says to Elidria, without looking back.

"I think he's a doer, Delsar. He doesn't like being sidelined."

"He can't fight *and* he's hurt. If he can't come to terms with that, then I'm not sure I even want him here anymore."

"Roki's been through a lot. We need to be—"

Delsar spins on the stairs and cuts her off. "Don't talk to me about a rough life." He tries to jam his finger into Elidria's collar, but she skillfully deflects it with her own hand.

"Everyone handles things differently," she says without paying any more mind to Delsar's forceful behavior. "Stop comparing everyone to yourself."

"Why? Because I'll be disappointed?"

Elidria rolls her eyes and walks past Delsar, leading the way up the stairs. "The world is disappointing if *you* decide it's disappointing. Try finding something you like about him instead of complaining all the time."

"The same can be said about him," Delsar says, following Elidria up.

"But it can start with you. You don't need to wait for him to figure things out before you figure things out."

Delsar scoffs. "You're like that little voice in my head. It can be really annoying."

"At least your voice has reason. You should listen to it more."

The rest of the climb is done in silence. They emerge on the inside of the wall. Everything is made from the same stone that was used for the towers and the wall. The wooden doors, flags, and various flowers would be the only things breaking up the grey color if there weren't so many people around. A couple different street performances have gathered quite a large crowd in this area. There is a pair of guards in almost every direction Delsar and Elidria look.

"Where do you think they keep the horses in all of this?" Elidria shouts through all the commotion.

"The edge of town," Delsar responds. "We can buy one now and pick it up on the way out."

"Why do you think there are so many people?" Elidria asks, weaving through the path Delsar is rudely creating.

"Probably some sort of event, and don't ask me what event it might be, because I don't know."

"Fair enough."

"Hold onto your bag," Delsar warns. "This is a prime pickpocketing situation."

Elidria reaches down and grabs her bag tightly. "That would be mean."

"Pickpockets don't care about your feelings."

"I'm used to that."

"Ask someone where the stables are," Delsar instructs.

"You've finally decided to use my womanly charm to help get what we need?"

"No, you won't get recognized as enemy number one."

"*Okay*, Delsar."

Delsar can't tell if she didn't quite believe his reason or if she was just being respectful confirming his request. He grabs her by the shield as she walks by. "Don't waste our time flirting with anyone."

"I don't flirt. I'm just a happy, easy-to-approach kind of person."

"Yeah, whatever."

"There's a nice looking lady over there. I'll talk to her if that will make you feel better."

"I'm not your father. I don't care *who* you talk to."

"You're a bit inconsistent, Delsar." Elidria approaches the taller woman and taps her on the shoulder. "Excuse me, Miss?"

The woman turns around and, with a very masculine voice and face, responds, "What you want?"

Elidria is shocked for a moment and Delsar looks away, likely trying to hide his laugh at Elidria's shock and the woman's clearly aggravated annoyance.

"Um, I was just wondering if you know where the stables are," Elidria says, sheepishly.

"What do I look like to you? A map? I'm trying to watch the play. Leave me be."

"Oh, okay. Sorry." Elidria turns to Delsar. Her face completely aghast.

Delsar smirks and gives his own go. "Good morning, ma'am."

The woman again turns to face Delsar and Elidria. "What is it n— Oh." She looks Delsar up and down. "And what can I do for you?"

"I'd like to apologize for my rude friend."

Elidria's jaw drops and she slams her hands on her hips but says nothing.

"Rude, indeed. You'd think she was never let out into public before."

"She *is* a snail farmer," says Delsar.

"That explains it. You know how those people can be."

"Do I ever?" Delsar shakes his head and pinches the bridge of his nose in agreement. "I saved her from some troll and now I'm stuck with her."

The woman looks at Delsar's sword and shield. "You fought a troll?"

"I had to. The snail farmer decided to drop a knife on her foot, alerting the troll where we were."

Elidria's face is now red and her nose is crinkled. She looks like she's about to explode.

"Really? I've never seen a troll before."

"Let's hope you never do. They're tough, but I'm tougher."

The woman gives a bit of a smirk. "You look it."

"Yup. I'm actually here in Fairview looking for a horse to continue my adventure. You don't know where the stables are, do you?"

"You're asking the right person. Just follow the western wall to the edge of town. You can't miss the stables."

"Thank you, Miss…? I'm sorry, what was your name?"

"Millicent."

"Oh?" Delsar almost coughs but controls himself. "Sorry again about my companion. I hope you enjoy the rest of your show and thank you."

"Any time, hon."

"Yeah." Delsar quickly turns and grabs Elidria by the sleeve, pulling her with him.

"How am I the rude one?" Elidria asks, not resisting the pull.

"You interrupted the nice lady trying to enjoy the show."

"You're a jerk."

"I've been told."

"You were also very flirty back there. You were nicer to her than anyone I've ever seen. You like her," Elidria teases.

"Like anyone would ever fall for that enchantress."

"Someone will."

"Whatever."

"Also, you could have just had me ask someone else. You didn't need to try to get info from her."

"It was training. I just showed you how to interrogate an unwilling informant."

"Yeah, *that's* what you did." Elidria doesn't try to comprehend. She understands what just happened and doesn't need Delsar to confirm it, not that he would. "I feel like acting nice when you're not is kind of fibbing. I also feel like she only helped you because she thought you looked handsome. That makes me feel like I was *never* going to get anything out of her. And *that* makes me feel like—"

"Elidria," Delsar whispers, cutting her off and ignoring her rant.

"Hm?"

"Two guards have been following us since our interrogation."

"Maybe because you're still dragging me by my sleeve."

Delsar lets her go.

She straightens her sleeves and her top. "That's better." She then turns to confront the guards. "Good morning," she says.

"Halt!" one of them responds.

"I'm already not moving."

"You too, pal."

Delsar turns. "What can we do for you?" he asks.

"You both need to come with us."

"Why?"

"You are being investigated for the conspiracy against Orange Peak."

"You can't be serious." Delsar almost laughs.

"Yeah, we were the ones that stopped the troll attack," Elidria states, stomping her foot.

"As I said, it's an investigation. Please hand over your weapons and come with us."

Delsar's hand curls into a fist.

Elidria can see the tension in his jaw and the glint in his eye. *He's debating,* she realizes. *Go with them or fight.* Instinctively, she wraps her hand around her sword hilt. Fighting the city guards would be morally wrong, not to mention illegal. She opens her mouth to say so and reaches for Delsar's sleeve, but his hand moves first. Delsar's sword sways on his hip and drops from her view.

"Fine. I hope you can resolve this quickly," he says, handing his belt over to the guard. "We have very important places to be."

Elidria lets out a huge sigh before doing the same.

"Now, come with us." One guard leads the way while the other follows behind. They head back where they just came from.

A man is leaning against part of the western wall and Elidria recognizes him immediately. "Nomar!" she shouts. "Tell them who we are."

"Is this them?" asks a guard.

Nomar examines them both thoroughly. "That's them!" he exclaims. "They're the ones that attacked my town!"

"What?" both Elidria and Delsar exclaim in disbelief.

The guards grab hold of them and cuff their hands behind their backs. "You two are under arrest for the massacre of Orange Peak."

Delsar is almost frozen. He makes no attempt of defending himself or stopping the guard from taking his shield.

Elidria begins crying as her guard also takes her shield. "But Nomar, I don't understand." Emotions begin flooding her consciousness. "Why are you doing this?"

Elidria can't help from pacing around the cell while Delsar sits on a cot with his hands on his knees. He seems more annoyed than panicked.

"How can you be okay with this situation?" Elidria asks, completely aggravated.

Delsar looks up at her. "I'm not *okay* as you put it. I got too lax with my crew and now I'm paying for it."

"*And...?*" Elidria's stress levels are much higher than usual. Who can blame her? "We're supposed to be getting to Bihnor, but now we're stuck in here! For something completely stupid, too."

"Elidria, just take a seat."

"I'd rather not."

"They won't hold us long," Delsar starts to explain. "They know who we are now so I'm sure they'll get to the bottom of this."

"But how long is that going to take?"

"Calm down. Please, just sit."

Elidria slams down on top of her cot, crossing her arms and legs, and huffing. "This is stupid."

"So you've said."

Elidria rolls her eyes.

One of the guards who arrested them enters the office. "Elidria of Bihnor, daughter of Aldameer, and Delsar, mercenary and the Outcast, reports from Grandell have confirmed your story. You both are free to go." The guard opens the cell and points at the gear laid on the desk. "You can take all your stuff with you."

Elidria bursts through the door and grabs her stuff as quickly as she can.

Delsar leisurely stands up and walks out, giving the guard a subtle nod.

"Sorry for the inconvenience," says the guard.

"Don't fret. You were doing your job."

"Maybe do your job better next time," says Elidria, sliding her shield on.

Delsar gives her a stern look but says nothing. He turns back to the guard. "Could you lead us out?"

"I can." The guard waits for Delsar to acquire his gear before leading them from the guard office and through a hall built into part of the main wall. "I'm sorry again," he says. "Please enjoy the rest of your time in Fairview."

Despite her annoyance, Elidria's natural habit kicks in and she gives the guard a bow, thanking him. Delsar is already off in his chosen direction, so she must run to catch up. "Delsar!" she yells, panting. "Delsar, wait!"

Delsar whips around. "What was that all about?" he demands.

Elidria stops in her tracks, somewhat confused by Delsar's sudden outburst. "What do you mean?"

"'Just do your job better?' That was their job and they did fine."

"Since when do you care?"

"I *was* a guard so I *do* appreciate their work. What if the accusation against us was true? If they didn't hold us until they figured everything out, we could have escaped and caused mayhem elsewhere."

"I didn't mean to," she says. "I'm stressed knowing that every moment we aren't traveling is another moment we aren't helping my village. My apologies for being freaked out."

"I don't need your apology." Delsar begins his walk again. "It's whatever. I have something else on my mind."

"Roki?"

"Not Roki. Those charges were never going to stick. I want to know what Nomar's deal was."

"Well, Roki wasn't with him. We should probably check on them."

"That's *obviously* where we're going."

"I'm speaking out loud, Delsar. You don't need to be rude."

"Thinking out loud."

"Huh?"

"Forget it."

"I'm a snail farmer, remember? I guess I'm not perfectly attuned on how to speak like you are." Elidria grabs Delsar's sleeve. "Wait a sec. Try to be understanding with Nomar. I'm sure there is a logical explanation."

"Of course there is," Delsar agrees. "I trusted and I got burned. Roki is off the team. I'm not having another potential enemy following us." Delsar pulls his arm from Elidria and continues his determined walk.

"They're our friends, Delsar. Don't treat them as less."

"They're *not* my friends and even friends can hate you. Believe me. I know."

"Why should I believe you? If trusting people is so wrong, then maybe I shouldn't even trust you."

"That's probably the smartest thing you've ever said," Delsar replies.

That's not the response Elidria was hoping for. She wanted to trap him with his own words, but him agreeing with her won't do it. "What about Galius? Even with everyone's reality changing around him, he stayed true to what he believed."

"That makes him wrong."

"But he was right." Elidria follows Delsar down the stairs. "What others believe and say doesn't matter if it's not true, sure. I understand that, but he *is* right and he *does* still love you. He's your friend if you let him."

"Is that my conscience speaking? Sorry conscience, I stopped listening to you long ago."

Elidria scrunches her nose. "You're impossible!"

"Then leave. I know you *think* you can change me to how *you* want me to be, but I'm the way I am because that's how the world made me."

"Delsar, you can be molded and influenced by your past, but you can't let that define you. You choose who you are."

"Then I've chosen."

"Well—"

Delsar holds his hand up and stops her. He expected the dockmaster to greet them upon reaching the bottom of the stairs, but he's nowhere to be seen. In fact, no one is. "Something's not right," he tells Elidria while drawing his sword.

Elidria senses it, too. "Roki and Nomar!" she exclaims. She pulls out her sword and takes off for the boat.

"Elidria, wait!" Delsar tries to catch up but her speed is too much for him.

Elidria dashes up the ramp to their boat, out of sight.

Delsar hears her scream, "Nomar!" before he's able to catch up with her.

There is a pool of blood on the deck with Nomar lying in the middle of it. Elidria runs to him and drops her sword in the pool. She slides to her knees and tries to tend to him. It doesn't matter. The multiple stab wounds in his chest were too much for his body to handle.

Delsar switches into soldier mode. "I'll check the rest of the boat." Delsar hears Elidria begin to weep uncontrollably as he spies blood on the cabin door. Entering, he sees Roki staggering to his feet with a gash on his forehead. "Roki!" Delsar is about to give him a hand when a commotion from outside steals his attention.

"That's her! She's the one!" comes the voice.

"Delsar!" Elidria shouts.

Delsar runs from the cabin and is immediately taken down by two guards. "What is the meaning of this?"

"Just stay down!" orders one of the guards.

"He was with her," says the dockmaster. "They're the ones who assaulted me."

"What?" Elidria exclaims. Two more guards grab her off her knees. "Let go of me!" she demands. She struggles and kicks, her feet dangling in the air.

Roki emerges from the cabin, hand on his head.

"Roki, tell them what happened!" demands Delsar.

Roki looks down at Nomar and then at Delsar and Elidria. "She came running in, yelling at Nomar about betraying them or something. I tried to intervene, but that's when Delsar grabbed me and bashed my head against the door. Then he threw me in the cabin. I can only imagine what the girl did to Nomar."

"Roki?" Elidria can't understand why he would say something like that.

"You are both under arrest for two assaults and one murder." The guards stand Delsar up and begin stripping them both of their gear.

Delsar struggles against them but they completely overpower him.

"We did none of those things!" cries Elidria. "Roki, why won't you tell them?"

Two more guards run onto the boat to assist Roki with his gash.

"Don't touch me," he says, backing away from them. "I'll let a real physician handle it."

Don't touch me? Delsar knows he's heard that before.

"Take these filth away," orders a guard. "Find out if this guy had any family."

"He did," says Roki. "They were."

Elidria's head drops from the comment and her feelings of dread and loss take her over. Tears stream down her cheek as she audibly cries.

The guards bring them back to the very office they were just released from and search them much more thoroughly this time. They remove Elidria's shinguards and bracers, restrain her hands behind her back, and forcefully shove her into the cell.

Another guard enters the office with Elidria's sword, covered in Nomar's blood. He whispers something to the guard who just searched Elidria and places it on the desk with her other stuff.

"You people make me sick," says the first guard before searching Delsar. He removes Delsar's armor plates and even finds another knife in his boot. He also takes off his cloak and finds a bandage around his ribs. "What's this?" he asks.

"I broke my ribs a couple weeks ago," Delsar responds.

The guard peeks under, revealing purple and blue splotches on Delsar's side, confirming the story. "Wrapping your ribs like this doesn't help. It only constricts your breathing," says the guard, trying to be helpful even to those accused of murder.

"You heal your way and I'll heal mine."

"Very well." The guard restrains Delsar's arms and pushes him in with Elidria. He slams the cell shut and shakes his head before sitting at his desk. He starts writing a few things down, taking inventory of what was pulled off of Delsar and Elidria.

Elidria drops to her knees and begins vomiting uncontrollably. She starts gasping for air and doesn't stop crying as her body drains her of anything physical and emotional.

Delsar looks away and closes his eyes. For a moment, he thinks about helping Elidria but he decides to let Elidria do what she needs to do.

After a minute, Elidria is able to compose herself. She stands back up and looks at Delsar with her watering eyes. "I made him come and help Glade," she says. "He's dead and it's my fault."

Delsar grimaces from her words. The feeling of regret is something he knows all too well.

"You have a visitor," says a guard, entering the room with Roki.

Roki walks up to the cell, bandage around his head. "Can you leave us alone for a moment?" he asks the guards.

"You have three minutes." The guards leave the office.

Delsar initiates the conversation. "Tell me, *Roki*, what is the girl's name?"

Roki frowns. "You are very perceptive. I'll give you that. How you tracked me here, I can't figure."

"I'm going to be an even bigger problem for you than you could ever imagine," says Delsar.

Elidria's eyebrow raises as she tries to make sense of the men's confrontation. The more she listens, the more she puzzles.

"I said I'd kill you *and* the girl. I assure you that I will keep my promise."

"We'll be getting hung and not by you."

"Yes, well, you getting hung as a result of *my* genius counts."

"I thought you wanted to create a troll to kill me."

"I still can. I only want one that *can* kill you."

"This cell won't hold me. I *will* be the one killing *you*."

"I don't doubt you escaping. Just know this, if you continue to follow me," he points at Elidria, "*she* will be the one who pays for it and I will take something dear from her."

Delsar tries to spit on Roki through the bars but the spit passes through Roki's head and lands on the floor. Delsar then gives him a smirk.

Roki storms out of the office.

"I don't understand what's going on," says Elidria.

"That wasn't Roki," Delsar says, still watching the door where Roki exited. "*That* was the shifter. He's about your size which is why my spit passed through his head."

"Now I'm really confused. Who was who?"

"He posed as Nomar to get us arrested. That was to buy himself time to assault the dockmaster as you and then kill Nomar. He played everyone perfectly. He even gave the guards a reason to believe why we'd kill Nomar. They thought we killed him because he had us arrested earlier."

"That's a stupid reason to want to kill someone."

"But it worked."

"What about Roki? Where is he?"

"The shifter likely took care of him while posing as you." Delsar removes his hands from his back, revealing that he escaped the cuffs. "We'll worry about him later. Right now, we *need* to get out of here. Are you going to be sick again?"

"I have nothing left," she says, sticking her tongue out with a bad taste in her mouth. "What if he killed Roki?"

"I don't think so. I need you to pretend to be sick."

"Pretending is lying."

"Elidria!" Delsar yells. "Get on the ground!"

Elidria crinkles her nose but obliges, lowering herself to her knees and dropping her head so her hair covers her face.

"Guard, help!"

A guard rushes in.

"I think she's really sick."

The guard spies the vomit on the ground and Elidria looking dazed. "Get in the corner!" he commands Delsar.

Delsar steps back.

The guard unlocks and enters the cell. "Are you all right, Miss?" He bends over to help Elidria and Delsar jumps on his back, putting him in a chokehold. The guard quickly flips Delsar over his shoulder and reaches for his sword.

Laying on his back, Delsar kicks the guard's foot, sliding it back. He grabs his arm and pulls the guard down with him. The guard lands on his hands and knees, over Delsar, and Delsar smashes his elbows against the guard's wrists, bringing him down on top of Delsar. He then grabs the back of the guard's belt, flipping him over his head and switching positions. Delsar presses his knee against the guard's neck.

The guard grabs a fistful of Delsar's inner-thigh. He squeezes and twists, causing Delsar to pull his leg away. As he does, the guard kicks him off.

Both men race to their feet and begin circling each other.

The guard charges at Delsar in hopes of grappling him, but Delsar suspected as much. Delsar drops his weight and lunges forward with his shoulder in front. The guard's top-half bends over Delsar as his legs come to an abrupt stop, slamming into his shoulder. He lands on his back and quickly blocks Delsar's kick, aimed for his face. He grabs a hold of Delsar's leg and starts to roll over it.

Delsar has no choice but to comply or let the guard snap his leg in two with his weight. Delsar falls on his back and the guard positions himself atop his chest. Delsar throws his arms up to protect his face from the impending punches, though they don't come.

Elidria jumps at the guard, slamming her chest into his back, knocking him forward.

That's all Delsar needs. He thrusts his hips up making the guard catch himself by placing his arms by Delsar's head. Delsar slides his arms around the guard's braced arms and tucks them in, rolling over and switching positions again. He keeps the guard's arms tucked in his own and drives his forehead down into the guard's nose. The guard shrieks but Delsar doesn't let up. He does it again and then releases him before driving his elbow straight into the guard's eye, knocking him out.

Delsar wastes no time standing back up. He dashes from the cell and grabs his shield from the desk. He takes it and stands against the wall next to the office door.

A few moments later, another guard runs in to investigate the commotion but is immediately met with a shield to the face. His legs swing out from under him and he crashes to his back, smacking his head against the ground. He doesn't move after that.

Delsar runs back to the cell and unlocks Elidria from her restraints. "How did you get out?" she asks.

"I'll tell you later. Grab your stuff." Delsar equips his gear much faster than Elidria does. He grabs her sword and wipes the blood off with his cloak before handing it to her. "We have to leave town *now*."

"What about Roki, or even Glade and Cade?" Elidria asks, genuinely concerned. "They're going to get back to the boat and be really confused."

"Glade is a grown man. He can figure it out." Delsar equips his shield on his left arm and grabs Elidria's hand with his other, pulling her from the office and down the hall.

Two more guards are already there, blocking the way to get outside. "Halt!" one shouts.

Delsar releases Elidria's hand and braces his shield with both arms. He plows into the guards before they have the chance to draw their weapons and knocks them down. Delsar stumbles as he steps over them, and Elidria runs around them.

Delsar dashes out the door but before Elidria can escape the wall and into the city, something cracks into her shield. She screams from the startle, and looking over her shoulder, she sees one of the guards just fired a bolt from his crossbow that lodged itself into her shield. Her shield was enough to stop the lethal projectile. She dashes out of the hall and meets up with Delsar. "Which way now?"

"North, along the wall. Watch our backs," he says, taking off with Elidria chasing his heels. He leads her into the crowd of people watching the various performances. "The guards won't shoot with all these people," he tells her.

"Right!"

Delsar isn't the tallest, but he is still taller than most. He catches a glimpse of a guard pushing through the crowd from the right. "Take the lead!" he yells to Elidria. Delsar lags to the right and lets her pass. The guard breaks through the crowd and is met by Delsar, using his shield and his bodyweight to again bowl over another guard. He slows for a moment and so does Elidria. "Don't stop," he says, picking his pace back up.

Elidria tries to push through a group of chatting individuals but one of them notices and tries to block her. "Delsar!" she shouts as two of them try to grab her.

Two others also try to stop Delsar but he pushes one back with his shield and kicks the other in his gut.

The kicked man falls back into Elidria, knocking her into the clutches of her two "good citizens."

The other man Delsar pushed grabs onto his shield and pulls.

Delsar gives no resistance and allows his shield to be pulled from his arm.

The man tumbles back, having expected Delsar to put up some kind of fight, and crashes into one of the men holding Elidria. He lands on his back with Delsar's shield on his chest.

Delsar jumps on his shield, knocking the wind from the man. He quickly grabs the shield off the man.

With now only one man grabbing her, Elidria easily pulls her arm from him and drives her heel into his foot. She jumps around the downed men and follows after Delsar.

Delsar slides his shield over his back and pulls Elidria into an alley to avoid three guards from the front. "They're going to shoot now!" he prophetically shouts.

Another bolt cracks into Elidria's shield, but even with Delsar's warning, she can't keep herself from screaming. She turns left to follow Delsar through another alley, and right as she does, another bolt whizzes past her head. "They're trying to kill us!" she exclaims.

"So much for people being wrong not mattering!"

"That's not what I meant!"

"Yeah, I know! Don't stop running!" A guard jumps out in front of Delsar with a shield and crossbow equipped. Delsar strikes the bow with his sword and slams his own body into the shield, knocking the guard down. Delsar trips trying to get past as the guard grabs his leg. He falls forward but rolls back to his feet in one fluid motion. "Draw your sword!" he commands Elidria.

"I'm not hurting these people," she says, running past Delsar.

"Then stay behind m—" Another guard grabs Delsar's shield and yanks him back. Delsar smoothly puts his sword away and drops his shoulders, allowing the shield to detach from his back. This confuses the guard long enough to allow Delsar to get a few strides ahead of him. He pulls out his bow and puts an arrow into the guard's unprotected thigh.

Delsar sends another arrow at a guard behind the first but he strikes him in the pauldron. The arrow bounces off but does throw the guard's aim askew and his return bolt hits a building instead of Delsar. Delsar shoots for his thigh this time and takes him down. He spins back around to catch up to Elidria. "I lost my shield!" he yells. "Take the rear!"

Elidria is much further than Delsar but slows to let him catch up and eventually pass.

The alley ends and opens into a park of lush grass and a few trees, very spread apart. Civilians jump out of Delsar's and Elidria's way. More people should mean less shooting.

Guards pile out of the alley from behind and two more block them in the park.

Delsar nocks another arrow but Elidria stops him. "Don't!" she shouts.

"I'm not going to kill them."

"Don't risk it." She dashes past Delsar and breaks to the right.

One of the guards runs after her, leaving just one in front of Delsar. The guard readies his sword and shield, but at the last moment, Delsar slides under the shield, taking out his ankles with his feet.

Without losing any momentum, Delsar gets right back up and runs after Elidria and her guard. Without his shield, he quickly catches up. He grabs the guard from behind and yanks him back.

The guard is quick on his toes and spins around with a retaliatory strike.

Delsar throws his arms up and blocks the blade with his bracers. He slides his arms down the sword and jabs the guard in the nose, stumbling him back. Delsar breaks away and does his best to keep up with the incredibly fast Elidria.

She runs out of the park and past some stables. The stables are supposed to be at the edge of town. They must be close to escape.

Fairview City's only threats come from the sea. Because of that, the giant wall only runs along the cliffs to the south and west. There is no wall or gate threatening to keep them in.

Running through the stables, Delsar spies three figures with bows and uniforms on a smaller wall to their left. "Archers!" he shouts to Elidria.

An arrow, aimed for Elidria's exposed legs, glances off the side of her shinguard. She stumbles and another arrow zips past her. There's no doubt the second arrow would have hit her if she didn't stumble.

Delsar sends his own arrow at the third archer, making him duck for cover and stopping the sniper fire for a crucial moment. He and Elidria cut into a grove of trees, which intercept another arrow intended for Delsar. "Go right," he tells Elidria.

The archers ready their shots, aimed at the north end of the grove, but Delsar and Elidria emerge from the east, using the trees to obscure the archers' sight. They all fire anyway but none of them hit.

Delsar and Elidria enter into a giant field slanting downward. At the end of the field is a tree with a huge canopy and a tall watchtower next to it.

A bell rings from the city, notifying the tower of their presence. A single archer is seen atop the battlement and four guards exit from below.

"Watch the tower!" Delsar warns Elidria.

She sidesteps an arrow that digs into the ground behind her. "Thanks," she says.

"Run for the tree!"

The guards notice their direction change and run for the tree to engage them.

The archer continues his volley but the range makes avoiding the arrows very easy.

Delsar and Elidria make it to the safety of the tree. Ignoring Elidria's earlier plea, Delsar fires an arrow at one of the guards waiting for them. It strikes his thigh and he drops. Delsar tries again on another but the guard wises up and catches the arrow with his shield. Delsar slides his bow away and draws his sword. "We need to be quick," he tells Elidria who finally draws her own blade. The guards from the city may have fallen far behind, but they will catch up eventually.

One guard breaks from the other three and goes after Elidria. He strikes diagonally at her, which she had avoided a thousand times back on the boat with Delsar. She does so again, stepping in and ducking under while also delivering her own strike across the guard's leg. She spins around him and kicks him in the back, knocking him down. She checks on Delsar who is having his own problem fighting two at once.

He parries their strikes but they then decide to lead with their shields. Trying to disengage, Delsar trips over a root and falls backward. The guards circle him, preventing any kind of escape.

Elidria runs behind one of the guards and slashes his leg. She tries to kick him down like the first one but this guard is much bigger than the last and only seems aggravated by the slash and kick. He turns around and whacks Elidria's sword from her hands with his own.

Delsar blocks a strike from the guard above him. The guard swings down at Delsar who catches the sword with his own. Delsar grabs the guard's arm to pull him down but the guard pulls back. Delsar uses the guard's pull to stand himself back up and tucks the guard's sword under his arm. He grabs the guard's shield and kicks the inside of his knee. The guard howls and drops his sword. Delsar releases the shield and lets him topple to the ground.

The bigger guard swings again for Elidria. She ducks in and drops to her knees, jabbing the guard's thigh a couple times. The guard kicks her away and slams his shield to the ground, infuriated by her speed. Despite the guard's extra mobility and using two hands on his sword, Elidria is still able to dodge and counter. She punches him where she slashed him earlier and this time he does feel it. He drops to a knee and Elidria sends the palm of her hand up into the guard's chin.

Delsar adds his own punch into the man's neck, knocking the behemoth down. Delsar puts his sword away and pulls his bow back out. He nocks an arrow and aims it at the base of the tower.

The door opens and the archer runs out, only to be met with an arrow to his lapel.

"Let's go!" Delsar takes off again.

Elidria grabs her sword and runs by his side. The other guards from the city begin drifting further and further away. Running across a bridge, through the farming district, and up hills and ridges, they don't stop. Even as their bodies scream, the only thing on their mind is escaping. Every stride they take is more distance between them and Fairview. They won't stop until their own bodies give up on them.

CHAPTER 11

THE SHERIFF

1 Day Ago...

"It was a doozy getting that out. I'm afraid you may never see with your right eye again." The physician hands Renon a mirror to inspect his face.

"That's quite the shame." The mirror shows a bandage covering much of his right cheek and eye.

"I'm sorry I couldn't do more."

"You're not the one I blame for this."

The physician grabs some fresh bandages. "Take these and make sure you replace them every morning and anytime they get wet."

"Very well. Your services will do for now." He hands back the mirror and snatches the bandages.

"I recommend you avoid anything that requires depth perception until you get used to using only one eye."

"Thank you, Nurse."

"It's Doctor."

"They give that title to anyone these days, don't they?"

"I'm not sure I follow."

Renon smirks. "No, you wouldn't."

"I guess not." The Doctor opens the door. "You're all set. Please leave your payment at the front."

Renon hops from his chair and exits the room without any form of 'thanks' or 'bye.'

"Have a good day," the Doctor wishes.

What a pain. Renon leaves two gold with the receptionist. *How can a man like that be called a 'doctor?' I could have fixed this by myself back in my lab.* He pushes through the crowd outside the office and then down the stairs to the docks. *At least that's where I'm heading.*

"I named it after my wife."

"Lovely. Where are you coming from, Captain?"

"Orange Peak."

What? Renon looks over at the dockmaster and examines the group that just docked. "Delsar," he says too quietly for anyone to hear. *Did he track me?*

"We're looking for any clues on the whereabouts of the man that attacked my home."

He did. So be it. I'll just have to kill him and the girl here. Renon watches and formulates a plan in his head.

"Captain Jahvess?" asks the dockmaster.

"Huh?" Renon responds.

"I was just asking if you are ready to depart."

"I was, but I think I forgot something. I may have to stay another night."

"That's not a problem. Just keep track of that slip I gave you."

"What happens if I lose it?" asks Renon.

"I'll have to put effort into my job." The dockmaster chuckles at his own comment.

"Funny." Renon isn't nearly as amused. "I need to grab something from my boat."

"Of course. I'll leave you to it. Until later." The dockmaster gives a salute and bumbles away.

Renon returns to listening to Delsar's crew.

"I see you're pairing up with Miss Eldra again," says Nomar.

"Do you have a problem with that, Nomar?"

Nomar? He'll do just fine. Renon bumps into Nomar as he walks by.

"Hey!" exclaims Nomar.

"Sorry, sir. One eye," Renon says, altering his voice and pointing at his bandage.

"Don't worry about it."

Too easy. Renon walks on and examines the identification card he snatched from Nomar. *Nomar of Orange Peak, son of Soren. Perfect.*

"Sorry, what'd you ask me, Delsar?"

"Forget it."

"Sure."

"You ready?" Delsar asks Elidria running down the ramp.

"Yup."

"Nomar, Roki, we'll be back in an hour."

"You got it."

"I'll still be here."

Delsar walks off and Elidria says, "Bye, guys," before joining him.

Nomar turns to Roki. "Logistics?"

"That's what Delsar's calling it. It's because both my arms are messed up."

"I can teach you how to read a star map if you'd like. I'm sure Delsar will appreciate that."

"Knock yourself out. Anything is better than nothing at this point." Roki follows Nomar aboard a ship, disappearing from Renon.

Renon casts Nomar's image over himself and follows Delsar and Elidria.

Up the stairs, he keeps his eye on them and locates two guards. "Guards, help," he says, doing his best to sound distressed.

"What is it?" one of the guards asks.

"My name is Nomar and I'm from Orange Peak." He holds up Nomar's identification. "I came here to grab medical supplies for my town, but I think I just saw the very two people who led the trolls. The very two people who orchestrated it and killed so many of my friends."

"Are you sure? Where are they now?"

"I am. They went that way." Renon points through the crowd. "A man and a woman. They both wear shields."

"We'll grab them." The guards leave Renon to pursue the accused.

"And I'll be here," says Renon, but not to be heard. He leans against the wall and waits.

It doesn't take long before they return with both Elidria and Delsar restrained.

"Nomar!" Elidria shouts. "Tell them who we are."

"Is this them?" the guard asks.

"That's them! They're the ones who attacked my town!"

"What?" they both exclaim.

"You two are under arrest for the massacre of Orange Peak." The guards strip them of their shields and start leading them away.

"But Nomar, I don't understand," says Elidria. "Why are you doing this?"

One of the guards stops for a moment to talk to Renon. "We'd like to ask you a few questions later, if that's all right."

"That's fine. My boat is at Dock G," he tells the guard who nods and continues. *This is too easy.*

He walks back down the stairs and changes into Elidria as he does. A separate image of Delsar appears behind him. He walks straight up to the dockmaster's office and pounds on the door.

The dockmaster opens the door and greets them. "Master Delsar and Miss…, I'm sorry. I seem to have forgotten your name. What a terrible host I am."

The image of Elidria pushes the dockmaster into the office. "How could you possibly forget my name?" it asks, angrily. It then punches him in the face and knocks him down. Elidria jumps on top of him and begins beating his face repeatedly. "You really are a terrible person and we both hate you! Right, Delsar?"

The image of Delsar just nods.

Elidria jumps off the dockmaster who stirs as he goes in and out of consciousness. "Just stay there for a bit," says Elidria before turning into the dockmaster himself.

The image of Delsar also fades.

"Listen up!" Renon shouts as the dockmaster, exiting the office and grabbing the attention of all the workers. "Some important politician is coming to this dock. The guards are taking over so everyone out!"

The workers quickly finish whatever they were doing and leave the dock as ordered.

Renon walks over to Delsar's ship and calls out, "Hello? Anyone aboard?"

Roki and Nomar exit the cabin and greet him. "Hey! What's up, Dockmaster?" asks Nomar.

"We have someone important coming in so I need to make sure any kind of weapons are secured."

"Sure thing. Come aboard," Nomar invites him.

Renon walks up the ramp and eyes up the cabin. "Anything dangerous in there?"

"We have a crate of arrows in there, but I'll throw it under the deck if that's needed."

"Just make sure it's nailed shut."

"You got it." Nomar starts for the cabin.

"Wait a second," says Renon, stopping him. He looks at Roki. "Could you handle it for him? I have a question for Nomar."

"Sure." Roki leaves them and enters the cabin.

"What is it?" asks Nomar.

"Is this yours?" Renon holds out Nomar's card.

"Oh my! Where did you find that?" Nomar grabs it and starts to examine it. Suddenly, he feels a sharp pain in his chest. He tries to scream but Renon presses his hand against his mouth. The knife gets pulled out before sliding back in again and again. Nomar crashes to his back and the world fades from his eyes.

Renon separates from the dockmaster's image, leaving it above Nomar, and runs next to the cabin door. His voided image stands and waits.

Roki exits the cabin and sees the dockmaster hovering over Nomar, knife in his hand. "Get away from him!" Roki exclaims but his head gets slammed against the door before he can do anything. He drops to the ground, completely dazed.

Renon's black image looms above him. He bends down next to Roki.

"Are you going to kill me, too?" Roki asks.

Renon laughs. "You're a nobody. You're not worth the time. I'd much rather watch you self-destruct because once again, someone else dies and you get to live." He slams Roki's head against the ground, knocking him out and leaving him with even more regret.

The King's Private Quarters...

"Who's there?" demands the King.

"Malgo, my Lord."

"Come in then."

The two giant doors open and the King's advisor enters. "Have you heard about the reports from Grandell? The attack against Orange Peak?" Malgo asks.

"They are most troubling."

"Then did you hear about the magic-user who led the trolls?"

"Yes."

"I suggest you have him killed silently. Use your best operatives to find and eliminate him."

"No."

"My Lord?" questions Malgo.

"I can use this." The King stands from his chair. "I'll have my guards find him and bring him here. Then I'll make an example of him and execute him publicly."

"What if he talks?"

"The people will have no reason to believe him."

"Then it is a wise decision, my Lord." Malgo bows.

"What about Bihnor?" the King asks.

"There are no reports from there."

"That's unfortunate. Notify me immediately when they do."

"Of course. Is there anything else you need of me, my Lord?"

"You're the one who knocked on *my* doors. If you have nothing else to report, leave me."

"There is one more thing."

"What?"

"Another troll attack. There were no survivors."

"Where?" asks the King.

"A small hunting village." Malgo swallows. "Boforest."

The King turns away. "My Queen's village."

"Yes."

"Set up a meeting with the council immediately. I must inform them of the news."

"Right away, my Lord." Malgo bows and departs from the chambers.

The King looks out his window. "How truly unfortunate."

"Delsar, are you awake?"

Delsar moans before answering. "I wish I wasn't," he says, flat on his back.

"I know what you mean," Elidria relates. "My everything hurts and I can't move my legs."

Delsar stirs a bit and gives up. "Same."

"How far do you think we ran?"

"Too far. I think if we were horses, we would have died."

"What time do you think it is? Everything is so dark in this forest."

"I don't know. Wait, I'm still wearing my bag." Delsar slowly turns his head toward Elidria. "And you're still wearing your shield."

"I think I slept on it."

"That probably didn't feel good."

"I don't think it made a difference."

Delsar slowly pulls his pocket watch from his bag. "It's noon. We need to eat."

Elidria closes her eyes and begins to tear up. "Nomar," she says under her breath. The events from yesterday begin playing in her head. "Delsar?"

"Yeah?"

"You thought I was one hundred five pounds but I told you I was one-twenty."

"I remember."

"I think you were right." Elidria struggles onto her side and faces Delsar. "After I escaped Bihnor, I couldn't stop throwing up. For days, nothing I ate stayed down. I almost gave up on everything." She shakes her head. "Why are we doing this? Everyone in Bihnor is dead."

"It does matter what people believe," Delsar says, "*even* if they're wrong. The only reason you travel for Bihnor is because you believe there is still hope. Even if you're wrong, this is right."

"Delsar, that was kind of nice for you to say." She rolls to her back and looks up. "I didn't expect anything like that from you."

"Don't get used to it. I'm mellow when I'm weak."

"I'll keep that in mind." Elidria shakes her head and squints one eye as she puzzles. "How *did* you escape your restraints?" she asks.

"That was easy. All issued restraints use the same lock. All you need is a key. I keep one under the bandage around my ribs. The fact that I really *did* break them helped with hiding it."

"That's clever, but thinking about the escape reminds me of something."

"And what's that."

"Come close to me, Delsar."

"*Okay?*" Delsar struggles to his hands and knees and crawls over to her.

"Closer," she says.

Delsar leans in. "W-why am I so c-close?" he asks with a stutter.

Elidria slaps him across the face.

Delsar flips onto his back. "Why do you do these things to me?" he exclaims.

"Don't *ever* ask me to lie for you again!" she says, pointing her finger at his face.

"It was necessary," he defends.

"If you ever do, I'm going to be *very* put off."

"What does *that* mean?" Delsar rubs his cheek. "Look—" He stops there and rolls his eyes. "Forget it."

"Don't you roll your eyes at me! We're supposed to be the good guys."

"And yet we're treated as the bad."

"Then stop being the bad guy."

"We didn't *do* anything wrong," says Delsar. "They arrested us *before* I had you lie."

"Just because they treated you badly, doesn't mean you have to treat them badly. Stop giving people a reason to hate you. A reason to call you the *bad guy.*"

"I told you I made my choice, Elidria. I'm not Arviakyss anymore. If that's who you wanted to help save your village, then that's too bad. He's dead."

"Why are we always bickering?"

"Why are *we* bickering? It's because you disagree with *everything* I do. Stop trying to fix me and we'll get along just fine."

Elidria crosses her arms. "I'm not going to have a thug work for me. Remember who's working for whom."

Delsar rolls his eyes again. "Whatever."

"I think you need to get those checked."

"Get *what* checked?"

"Your eyes. I think they're loose. They keep wobbling around."

"You're a child."

"Hey," Elidria starts, "a child who beat two guards in combat."

"That *is* impressive," Delsar says. His tone sounding proud all of a sudden. "It's your speed. You're faster than even me. You won't lose many fights if you use it. Just remember, if you ever do come across someone as fast or faster than yourself, you need to be clever. Just put the slightest bit of thought into your combat and you'll come out on top."

"I like you as a teacher, Delsar. You have the ability to turn everything into a learning experience."

"Is that the only reason you like me?"

"At the moment." She turns back on her side and leans on her elbow. "So now you. What do you like about me?"

Delsar thinks for a moment. "You're like a dog," he says.

Elidria's head jerks back and her nose crinkles. "Excuse me?"

"Let me finish." Delsar sits up and rests against a tree. "You're a grouch, but you still do what you're told and you do it well. You're also very loyal. So, you're like a dog."

"I've never met a grouchy dog," Elidria states.

"Mine was. There was something mentally wrong with her. That's another thing you both have in common."

Elidria tilts her head against her hand and scowls. "If you weren't so far away from me, I'd slap you again."

"You could throw something at me."

"Why are you telling me how to hurt you, because I likely will."

"I don't want you to be single-minded is all. If something won't work in combat, you have to adapt or you'll die. When the guard blocked my arrow, I switched to my sword."

"I get it."

"I'm also thinking about spitting on you."

Elidria stops blinking and raises her eyebrow. "That's weird, random, and I don't want you to do that to me."

"Just hear me out. When I tried to spit on the shifter posing as Roki, the spit passed through his image and left no wet spot on him. When I threw a knife into his collarbone when I thought he was you, his image of you also had no blood, even though he did leave a trail. I believe he struggles altering the images he casts. Water might be the perfect way to tell who is who."

"You threw a knife at the shifter thinking he was me?" she exclaims.

"I threw a knife at him that was actually just an image of him, so the knife passed through him and hit you who was actually him."

Elidria squints her eyes. "Interesting. Also, if you spit on me, I spit on you."

"No way. I'm definitely Delsar."

"I think the shifter would say that."

Delsar rolls his eyes.

"Stop doing that! They're going to get stuck," Elidria warns.

"No they won't."

"My mother told me they would."

"She lied then."

Elidria sits up and hurls her bag at Delsar, striking him in the chest. "Don't you say such things! She would never lie."

"Whatever! And, I'm not going to spit on you. That, as you like to say, would be stupid. I don't think it's feasibly possible to act like you."

"Well, I don't know about you, Delsar. You've been almost nice to me today. I think the shifter may have replaced you in my sleep."

"He also killed you in your sleep then."

Elidria brings a finger to her chin. "That's a good point. Can I have my bag back?"

"Stop hurting me and then *maybe* we can negotiate terms."

Elidria extends her hand. "No promises."

Delsar tosses her the bag. "A purse doesn't fit my physique, anyway."

"It's a military-grade satchel. It's almost identical to yours which means yours must be a girly one, too."

Delsar rolls his eyes and tries to stand up. He stumbles around like a newborn fawn.

"See? Your equilibrium is all off because you keep rolling your eyes."

"Oh, shut up," Delsar says, very much annoyed.

"But, seriously, what are you doing?" she asks.

"At the moment, trying to remember how to stand."

Elidria scowls.

"I'm going hunting."

Elidria perks up. "Can I come with you? I'd rather not be left alone right now. Our talking has taken my mind off of what happened yesterday."

Delsar shakes his head. "No. Stay here. You need to ponder what you've seen and what's happened. I'd rather you do that now instead of later. Mourn for Nomar. He was a fine man." Delsar turns to leave but doesn't get very far. He tries to lift his foot to step over a root but his foot only drags against the ground and stubs against the root. His legs give out and he tumbles back to the ground. "On second thought, perhaps we can talk about him together?"

Elidria can't help but smile. She crawls over to Delsar and leans against the tree he tripped over. "I'd like that very much."

"I don't actually look evil, do I?" Elidria asks, pointing at two wanted posters on the news board of Midori Trails. One with a very evil-looking version of her and one with Delsar.

Delsar grabs the posters and rips them down. "This won't do."

"How are they moving north faster than us?"

"They needed to print them, too. We can't enter this village looking like this."

Elidria looks down at her blood-stained skirt and torn sleeve. "How are we going to get new clothes if we can't be seen in these ones."

"I'll sneak in and grab some."

"You mean steal?" Elidria crosses her arms. "I'll deduct your pay if you do and that will cost you more than just buying some."

"Fine." Delsar removes his bow, cloak, and quiver, revealing his very dark-brown tunic and satchel. "I'll go in like this and buy some. Then I'll come back and you can change. Sound good?"

"Hmm. Are you *sure* no one will recognize you without your cloak?"

"Not at all." He tries to hand his stuff to Elidria. "Hold on to these while I'm gone."

"I'm not holding all that. I can barely stand as is. Just place it behind those trees. I'll wait for you there."

"Whatever." Delsar lays his stuff down and turns to enter the forest village.

"Be careful, Delsar."

Delsar looks over his shoulder but says nothing in response.

"You have nothing to watch your back anymore," she says, but Delsar doesn't respond.

"Excuse me, sir?" A villager approaches Delsar. "I can't help but notice you've walked by me twice. Are you looking for something?"

"Uh, yeah." Delsar was certain he'd be able to find a tailor on his own, but nothing in this village is marked. "Do you have a tailor?"

"Phillious usually makes our clothes. Outsiders mostly just pass through and don't usually look for clothes. I'm not sure he'll have anything for you."

"Can you at least point me to where I can find him? I pay well."

"He's probably at home. His house is the third one on the right, down that road." The man points.

"Thank you." Delsar almost bows but stops himself.

"Anytime." The man lifts his hand up but doesn't wave it.

Okay? Delsar walks from the man, but peers over his shoulder from time-to-time, keeping an eye on him. He reaches a house at the end of his directions and knocks on the front door. Someone begins scuttling around inside before the door opens.

"Hello?" the stranger asks.

"Are you Phillious?"

"I am he. Who might you be?" the man inquires.

"I'm, uh, Galius. I'm in need of some clothes. I was told you're a tailor."

"I don't have anything ready," he responds, already starting to close the door.

"Please." Delsar places his hand against the door. "I can pay well."

Phillious brings his hand to the bridge of his nose, just like Delsar does, and sighs. "What do you do, Galius?"

"I'm a hunter but I'm from Grandell. My brown doesn't work well around here."

"Green is what you need."

"I can see that."

"All right. Just come in."

Delsar enters past Phillious to see his living room filled with shelves, books, a comfortable-looking chair, and a wooden desk. "Nice place," Delsar says, looking around with his hands clasped behind his back.

"It's finally how *I* want it so please don't touch anything." Phillious walks next to Delsar and looks him up and down. "You look about my size, Galius. I think I have something you can use."

"A hand-me-down?"

"Not necessarily," Phillious replies with his finger extended upward. "My ex got me some hunting gear before we broke up. It came with clothes that I doubt I will ever wear. I'll give them to you for five copper."

"I don't have any copper," says Delsar. "I do carry silver."

"That hardly seems fair. These clothes are not worth silver."

"It's fine. I'm willing to pay silver."

"No, we should figure something fair out."

"You said your wife got you a hunting set?" asks Delsar. "Does that include arrows?"

"She's my ex, but yes. I have ten arrows that will never touch a bow."

"Throw those in. Will that be worth my silver to you?"

"My arrows are worth nothing to me, but I think that's fair. One silver for the clothes and the arrows."

"Deal!" Delsar flips him the coin. "One more thing."

"Yes?"

"You mentioned your ex twice. Did she leave any clothes behind?"

"Delsar, you're green," Elidria remarks, tilting her head as she examines Delsar's new attire. His pants are still a dark brown but now his tunic is a dark green. So dark that it could be mistaken for black in this shadowy forest.

"Like everything else in this village." Delsar tosses more clothes to her. "Put these on."

"These are heavy," she says, catching them.

"They come with a leather kama."

"A what-now?"

"Just go change."

"Sure." Elidria disappears behind the tree. "These are nice," she says, coming back into view with her new outfit. Her top is now a dark blue with adjustable stitching by her left lapel that extends down about three inches. Around her waist are two pieces. The first is a loose, brown skirt that extends down to her knees. On top of that is the kama Delsar mentioned. It's made of a thick leather that's a darker brown than the skirt. It covers the front of her thighs and extends around her like the skirt but is open at the front. It's also slightly longer than the skirt, so only the gap in the front reveals the skirt underneath. Her boots and shinguards are now clearly visible. "This must have cost you a fortune."

"Why is that?"

"The blue top. I farm this stuff and it's not easy to come by. Also, what is the point of this extra piece?" she asks, lifting up the kama.

"It will protect your thighs from being slashed."

"Why don't guards use something like this?"

"They used to, but since guards mostly police now, they lost their thighplates for added mobility. Officers use kamas though."

Elidria twirls. "Cool. You did pay for this, didn't you?"

"Of course I did. One silver for all of this and ten arrows."

"One silver!" exclaims Elidria. "That's pretty much stealing."

"Don't give me that. The man wanted less."

Elidria tilts her head and smiles. "It's a bargain, for sure. Good job."

"Your approval means the absolute world to me."

Elidria frowns. "Your sarcasm needs work."

"I don't care. Grab your gear."

Elidria and Delsar fetch their things from behind the tree and begin their walk into the village.

"Do you want to know something?" Elidria asks.

"Not really."

"I'm twenty today," she says.

"So, you decided to tell me anyway."

"The big 'two-zero.'"

"That's completely random."

"Birthdays usually are. I don't think I know anyone who chose when they were born."

"Obviously."

"Wait a sec!" Elidria stops Delsar in his tracks.

"What?" he asks, annoyed.

"How long were we at sea?"

"Six nights."

Elidria sighs in relief. "Oh, that's good. Today *is* my birthday then."

"I'm so glad you cleared that up. I would hate for today to proceed as normal."

"What about you?" Elidria asks.

"What about what?"

"When's *your* birthday?"

Delsar shakes his head. "Who cares?"

"I do. So, when is it?"

"I'd rather not, right now."

"Come on," Elidria pleads. "Telling me won't hurt anyone."

Delsar rolls his eyes but then shrugs. "Whatever," he says with a sigh. "I turn twenty-three at sunset."

"Wait, like sunset tonight?"

"Yup."

"Woah. What are the odds?"

"Probably about as likely as us surviving Bihnor."

Elidria pumps her fist. "So definitely possible."

"So not *probable*."

"Tomato, tomato."

"You just said the same word twice."

"Because we're going to *do* the same thing twice. We crushed a town full of trolls. What are some lame mercenaries going to do against us?"

"They're not going to get killed by the same trick over and over like the trolls. That's what."

"Oh yeah." Elidria's enthusiasm disappears. She changes the subject. "What are our plans here in Midori?"

"Sleep. I found lodging so I thought we'd have an early night."

"Wait, what time is it?"

"Four in the afternoon."

"What? I'm only twenty. You can't be treating me like I'm old already!"

Delsar spins around to face Elidria and scowls are her.

She grins back at him. "It was from a play," she says.

"I've seen it."

"Then you get it."

"Just stop."

"Stop what?"

"Being happy! It's really annoying."

Elidria brings her hand to her chin. "Hmm, nah. Being happy is fun."

"Then keep it to yourself."

"*Grumpy-pants.*"

"What?" Delsar asks.

"You heard me."

Delsar shakes his head and grumbles.

"So, what kind of lodge are we staying in?" Elidria asks, getting Delsar's mind off her.

"We are actually here," Delsar says, staring at Elidria for a few more moments before turning and extending both his arms toward the front of the building.

Elidria looks up at the overhanging sign. "Sheriff! We aren't seriously sleeping in the jail, are we?"

"Oh no. You suddenly sound like you aren't happy."

Elidria scrunches her nose and points her finger in Delsar's face. "My tone means nothing. I'm a million of the brightest torches on the inside."

Delsar rolls his eyes and scoffs. "Listen, there are no inmates and the sheriff said it's fine for the one night."

"It's just, this is going to be my third time in a cell with just a one-night separation," Elidria says, holding up three fingers on one hand and one on the other.

"You're not going to have PTSD are you?"

Elidria crosses her arms. "I don't know. You tell me."

"The village only ever holds one drunk every once in a while. Because of that, Margret, the caretaker, put a nice bed in one of the cells for him. It's actually a luxury."

Elidria leans forward and pokes her finger into Delsar's arm. "You realized you said *a* bed in *one* cell." She crosses her arms again and lifts her nose. "I'm not sleeping on the floor."

"I'm sure they have a cot. I'll sleep on that. Come on." Delsar opens the door for her and follows her in. "Hey, Sheriff."

"Oh hey, Galius. This must be Elly." He walks over to Elidria and extends his hand.

"Actually," says Elidria, "only my dad calls me Elly. Everyone else calls me Eldra." There is a touch of annoyance in her voice and she looks at Delsar with the corner of her eye.

"Nice to meet you, El—,"

"One other thing," she says, interrupting the Sheriff. She points at Delsar. "Everyone calls him *Delsar*. I'm not sure why this jerk suddenly likes being called *Galius*, because that is *not* his name."

"Two separate cells then?" the Sheriff asks.

"If you could, that would be great." Elidria gives him a smile.

"No one else is using them."

"We're actually exhausted," Delsar informs. "You wouldn't mind us turning in early, would you?"

"I can't be treating you like you're old already!" the Sheriff exclaims.

"I like this man," says Elidria, her face beaming.

Delsar pinches the bridge of his nose and shakes his head.

The Sheriff smiles back at Elidria. "I'll finish my day on patrol. The cells are open so take your pick."

"Thank you." Elidria bows.

"I hope you two can sort things out. Have a nice sleep." He tips his hat and leaves the office.

"Elly and Galius!" Elidria shoves Delsar.

"We need to keep our identities a secret, or did you forget we're wanted for murder?"

"Stop worrying about what others think and just tell the truth!"

"They mean to hang us."

"I know that. That doesn't make it okay to lie."

"Yes it does."

"Bad guys lie and I don't want to be a bad guy." Elidria enters one of the cells. "This one with the bed is mine. You can sleep in that one."

"Fine." Delsar grabs a key before entering his cell.

"What's the key for."

"To get out if the doors accidentally close."

"Smart. In that case...." Elidria slams her cell door.

"I'm the one with the key."

"It's the principle." Elidria lays in her bed and pulls up the nice covers. "I'm going to sleep now."

"*Okay?*"

"I hope your dreams make you regret what you did." Elidria rolls over. "Oh, and happy birthday."

Delsar scoffs and stifles his laugh. "Yeah. Good night, Elidria."

Both Delsar and Elidria wake up, startled as Delsar's cell door gets slammed shut.

"You thought I wouldn't recognize you." It's the Sheriff with his arms crossed. "Well, I didn't, or at least not until this morning."

"What are you talking about?" Delsar asks, getting up from his cot.

"Some hooligan ripped down some wanted posters from our news board yesterday. I just finished replacing them. I was given a few spares, you see, and this time I actually took a good look at them. Boy, was I surprised when I realized the two people on those posters are the very two people sleeping in *my* jail."

"Oh?" Delsar inquires, a smirk creeping across his face.

"Oh indeed. You chose Galius as a cover name, which was smart, but you, missy...."

"Me?" Elidria presses her fingers against her chest.

"Yes. You chose the name Eldra *and* you gave away your partner's name. Not very good moves, *Elidria*."

"Not you, too. Don't you agree that lying is never the answer?"

"Of course, but neither is murder."

"And so do I," Elidria states.

"I'm sure you do. You two will be stuck in here until the guards arrive. You won't be escaping on *my* watch."

"You're much too keen for us," Delsar says. "Hold up. We still have our swords. Would you like us to hand them over to you?" Delsar starts unbuckling his belt.

"I do." The Sheriff stops himself from approaching Delsar. "Wait.... Actually, I don't. I heard how you escaped Fairview. I won't let you trick me."

"You caught me."

"I'm going to summon some guards. Don't even *think* about trying to escape. These locks are from the new series. They're uncrackable and unbreakable."

"I'm stumped then." Delsar sits back on his cot.

"Who'd have thought that I'd capture two fugitives in *my* jail? Ha!" The Sheriff exits the office to fetch guards from the nearest outpost.

Delsar stretches and stands back up. "How are your legs today, Elidria?"

"They still hurt but they seem to be functioning well," she says while squatting.

"That's good. Shall we be on our way?"

"I'll miss this bed, but I think I'm good."

Delsar pulls the key from his bag and unlocks his cell. He does the same with Elidria's and places the key on the desk. "Make sure you have everything."

"I do."

"Then north we go."

"I'll even let you lead." Elidria opens the door for Delsar.

"When don't you?"

"Fairview."

"Ouch." Delsar walks from the office. "Come along then."

They head back to the tree they hid their extra gear and old clothes behind. Delsar throws his cloak on and Elidria slides her shield into place. "Unfortunately," says Delsar, "with the Sheriff's report, they will know we're heading north."

"What does that mean for us?"

"No more villages or towns or even people. We have clothes now so we hunt for food and camp at night."

"More like *you* hunt for food. I can't even draw your bow." Elidria watches Delsar start his way back toward Midori Trails. "Shouldn't we go around?"

"The Sheriff won't be back anytime soon. This will be faster."

"That's quite the risk you're willing to take." Elidria follows despite her concern.

"Not really. I don't think this sheriff has ever dealt with a real criminal, or at least, not for a long time. We are *way* out of his league."

"That's not very humble."

"But it is the truth. I'm just telling you why I'm willing to take such a risk."

"Hmm. I'm not so sure."

"Let me put it this way, everyone has different strengths and weaknesses. To beat your opponent, you must find their weakness and use your own strength. That means admitting what your strengths are. That is perfectly fine, Elidria. The Sheriff is our opponent. I know he isn't prepared for us in the slightest. I'm going to use that to slip past him faster. Make sense?"

"I guess it does tactically."

"Good."

They slip through the village without any problems. The occasional villager would stare but that was probably because, to them, Delsar and Elidria are strangers in their village. No one talked to them or even approached them.

"This road goes north." Delsar stops and faces Elidria directly. "We are three days from Bihnor. Are you ready for this?"

"We've come so far and have been through so much." She passes Delsar and starts down the road. "Nothing is going to stop me."

Delsar follows. "Is that why you finally drew your sword in Fairview?"

"If they stopped us, Nomar would have died for nothing. All the sacrifices made for me would be in vain. I'm *going* to save my village. No odds are going to stop me."

CHAPTER 12

THE ROAD

6 Years Ago...

"Arise, Aldameer, winner of the Deadliest Draw."

Aldameer stands up from his kneeling bow, raising his head up. "It was an honor to have the chance to shoot in your presence, my King."

"Your skills are astounding. The archers of Fairview pale in comparison to what I just saw from you. Absolutely breathtaking."

"Thank you, my King. Your words are too kind."

"Enough with such formality. You don't have to call me King every time you speak. You are our guest and winner of the tournament."

"As you wish," Aldameer replies.

"My Queen has something for you and I'm sure she wishes to say her own words. Taharial, if you would." The King steps aside to let his wife speak with Aldameer.

"Thank you, dear." She stands up from her opulent chair that was used for overseeing the tournament and approaches Aldameer. "Young Aldameer," she says, "your archery skills today have not only impressed me, the King, and everyone who witnessed it, but they've also inspired me. I have for you a prize and an offer. First," she takes the Elven recurve bow from the table that sits between her and the King and hands it to Aldameer, "please accept this for winning against the finest marksmen in the kingdom."

Both Aldameer and the Queen bow to each other with the exchange. "Thank you, my Queen. Such a beautiful bow will be cherished in my household and its magnificence will every day remind me of you."

The Queen blushes. "I know you're just being kind with your flattery, but do be careful. My husband might hear you."

Aldameer has a moment of fear in his face and bows to the King. "I apologize, my King. Forgive me. I meant no disrespect to you."

The King laughs. "Taharial, stop toying with our champion."

The Queen smiles at Aldameer. "As a woman, I do appreciate your kind words. The hate from the people who disapprove of how I do things weighs heavily on my heart. Even just your adulation is a huge blessing to hear."

"I'm glad to help then."

"I'm happy to hear that because that is exactly what I'm looking for. I have an offer for you, Aldameer, son of Conah."

"My ears are open."

"Hey, Aldameer," says the King. "Talk to us like normal people. You don't have to try and sound fancy."

"As you wish." Aldameer looks back at the Queen. "I'd like to hear your offer, please."

"I'm putting together a team of extraordinary individuals. Your talents and perhaps your morals are exactly what I'm looking for." The Queen smiles close-mouthed. An eyebrow twitches up, making her look as though she plans to do something clever.

Aldameer raises his own eyebrow. "To do what, exactly?"

"It's a small task force. One that will answer directly to me. You will be known as the Queen's Shield, but you will not be ordinary guards. You will have special privileges and not have all the same restrictions the King's Guard has. I'm hoping a small team of men with a high moral value will be willing to do things differently and execute operations with love."

"Love?"

"Currently, the guard and army are supposed to strike fear into the hearts of our enemies and potential criminals. I want to do things differently. I wish to strike courage and inspiration into the hearts of our allies and our people. That is my proposal to you."

"How many others are on this team?" Aldameer asks.

"Currently, Arviakyss is the only one on my team. You'd be number two."

"Arviakyss." Aldameer's mind wanders upon hearing such an honor. "That's an amazing offer. To hear I'm your second choice after the Queen's Champion means so much to me. I have to talk to my wife about it though."

"Take your time," the Queen tells him. "Oh, and I would love it if you yourself would hand-deliver your dyes to me whenever you have a shipment ready. That way we can talk about this more."

"You remember who I am," says Aldameer, surprised that she could remember a simple snail farmer.

"I paid for your village so of course I remember who you are."

It's not just because of that. The Queen tries her best to remember every citizen in her country that she meets.

"Your blues are exquisite," she adds.

"I personally thank you for everything you've done for me and yet you still offer more. I don't know what to say."

"You don't have to say anything right now. Go to your wife and give me your answer when you return with my blue."

"I will." Aldameer bows one last time. "Thank you, again. From the bottom of my heart, I thank you."

Elidria stretches and takes a deep, relieving breath. It's the first morning since Fairview that she woke without muscle pain. It's also much earlier than usual that she's up. Not even Delsar is awake. She stands and walks over to him. She spies an open book on his thigh and she carefully removes it. Looking in the pages, the first words she notices are "Elidria is." She quickly closes it and places it back on his lap. *Perhaps another time*, she thinks to herself.

She suddenly realizes where she is. If everything goes well, they could arrive in Bihnor by late tomorrow. She shudders for a moment. *A bit of time to myself will do me good*, she decides. She grabs her sheath and wipes the mildew off with her underarm. She straps her belt on and grabs her bag. In the bag, she pulls out her charcoal pen and rips a piece of paper from her own journal. A journal seldom touched since leaving her home. "*Couldn't sleep*," she begins to write, "*Went east about two hundred feet. Just clearing my mind a bit.*" She places the note on her shield where she was sleeping and lays it down with a rock.

The forest roof is still very thick, much like it was back near Midori Trails. This does make it very difficult to tell what time of day it is. The darkness and croaking of frogs suggest it's still very early in the morning.

As she walks, she notices some light cutting through the trees. *It must be a clearing*, she decides, and walks toward it. A fresh breeze blows through her hair and she takes another deep breath, appreciating such a beautiful feeling in this stressful time. She pauses and closes her eyes. *Is that water?* She perks up and realizes the sound of running water is coming from the clearing she is walking toward. "Don't mind if I do," she says out loud and smiling.

Reaching the clearing, she can't help but take her boots and socks off before entering the small creek. She instinctively lifts her skirt though this one is much shorter than her last so there is no real reason to. The water only goes slightly past her ankles. The cold water feels wonderful on her aching feet and the bright light from the moon and orange glow from the rising sun just add to the little piece of paradise. She finds a rock large enough to sit on and does just that, extending her legs to let the water flow between her toes. She leans back and enjoys the feeling for a few minutes. "Delsar," she says, aloud. *He's walked just as far as me. Perhaps he will enjoy this, too.*

Elidria stands back up, ready to go fetch him, but something on the other side of the creek catches her eye. "A flower?" A flower isn't usually strange to see but there isn't another flower in sight, and the orange color seems different. She tilts her head and walks toward it. She bends down next to it and begins examining it. She notices black spots on the petals and decides that maybe Delsar can tell her what kind of flower it is. She reaches down to pick it but it pulls itself underground and disappears.

"What?" Elidria is more than surprised. Flowers don't usually do things like that.

The flower pops up again but is ten feet further past the creek.

"You're an interesting fellow," she says, approaching it again and trying to pluck it.

It pulls under again and then reappears even further past the creek and in the forest.

"This is so weird." She follows it into the woods but it disappears again. "Where'd you go this time?" She looks around and notices it popping out right beneath her. "What are you?" She reaches out again but pulls her own hand back this time. "Something's not right." She starts to back away from the flower but it's too late.

The flower bursts out of the ground with a huge vine attached and it wraps itself around Elidria's ankle.

She screams as it pulls her off her feet and begins dragging her across the ground, deeper into the forest. "Delsar!" she cries, while desperately reaching for her sword. She kicks at the vine with her other foot and manages to pull her sword from its sheath. She whacks the vine, chipping it, and it lets her go before disappearing into the darkness of the forest.

Elidria scrambles back to her feet. Another vine shoots out of the darkness but she steps to the side and severs it with her sword. Two more careen toward her. She chops one but the other grabs the hilt of her sword, trying to pull it from her. She holds on as another wraps around her leg. It pulls and she falls backward. Hanging desperately to her sword, the vine around her ankle pulls her through the air.

She grabs the sword with both hands and pries it from the first vine. Her back crashes to the ground as a result, and the vine around her leg continues to drag her deeper.

"Delsar!" she cries again while grabbing hold of a small tree. She wraps both arms around it and screams as the vine starts pulling harder. The bark rubbing against her arms and chin starts to pinch her skin. Elidria releases with one arm and swings at the vine. She can't quite reach it but its pull suddenly lessens. Her relief is only for a moment as it quickly pulls even harder, jarring her from the tree.

The dirt, mud, roots, and rocks all scrape at her as she helplessly slides along the ground. With all her strength, she bends her knee and swings her sword, clipping the vine. It releases and Elidria tumbles to a stop. She gets to her knee and takes a moment to catch her breath. Her hair feels matted and twisted, filled with leaves. She staggers to her feet but two vines burst through the ground and wrap both her wrists. They pull her back to her knees and squeeze. Elidria screams and drops her sword.

Another vine grabs around her waist and lifts her up while the other vines let her go. It carries her toward a fat tree, much shorter than the other trees but still very thick. It also looks much different than all the other ones. It starts to sway and a deafening sound of wood creaking and snapping rings out as the trunk begins to split. Hundreds of wooden spikes line the new opening, which makes the hole resemble a mouth.

Elidria's face goes white, realizing that is where she is getting pulled. She grabs at the vine around her waist but another wraps around her neck and starts to squeeze. She grimaces and slides her fingers under its grip. Two more vines grab her arms and pull them away. Her neck gets squeezed tighter. Her eyes start to roll back and they feel like they're going to pop out. Everything begins to fade and her body goes limp. She has nothing left and even if she did, there's likely nothing she could do. To travel so far only to be killed by a tree. *Please..., be a bad dream.*

Her stomach churns from a jolt. The vines shake her wildly and startle her back to consciousness, though everything is still a hazy gray. One of her hands comes free and she grabs at the one around her neck. It slams her against a tree and then into the ground. She gasps and coughs uncontrollably, realizing the implication. It had released her. Her vision slowly begins to return, along with a huge headache. She winces in agony trying to move. One of her eyes closes and the other only squints open before also closing. They start to jostle around as she tries to open them back up.

"On your feet and fight!" comes a voice but it sounds muffled and distant.

Elidria groans.

"Elidria, get up!" the voice commands again.

It clicks in her mind who it is and her adrenaline suddenly surges through her body. She rolls to her hands and knees and looks up. Delsar stands between her and the tree. He has his sword and her shield in his hands.

"Get up and grab your sword!" A vine shoots at Delsar and splinters against the shield. He quickly slashes down on another, severing it from the tree.

Elidria climbs to her feet and is suddenly hit with nausea. She staggers around as her eyes refocus. Locating her sword, she snatches it from off the ground and asks, "What do we do?"

"Run!" he says. "Back to camp!" Another vine strikes the shield and knocks him back.

Elidria starts to run and shouts, "I'm going!" over her shoulder.

Delsar turns and runs after her, swatting the occasional vine.

The tree lets out the most unearthly cry as the ground begins to rumble. Vines everywhere erupt from the dirt, tripping up Elidria and Delsar. The tree itself begins traversing the ground, using its giant roots to drag it across the ground, making it resemble an octopus. It thrusts one of its roots at Delsar who blocks it but gets knocked down by the impact.

Elidria turns. "Delsar!"

"Just run!" Delsar jumps back on his feet and starts pushing Elidria along.

They duck and dodge trying to get back to the camp. The tree continues its chase and swings its vines wildly. Another root juts out of the ground and trips Delsar. A vine wraps around his ankle but Elidria quickly severs it. She helps him back up but he stumbles a bit more, allowing Elidria to reach the clearing first.

She trips through the ankle-deep water but catches herself with her arms and makes it to the other side.

Delsar reaches the clearing but gets tripped by another vine. This time, he goes down hard.

The tree closes its distance and looms above Delsar.

Delsar places the shield in front of him as two more vines shoot toward him. He braces for the impacts but they never come. The vines shrivel up and turn to dust before they reach him.

The tree shrieks again and shakes violently.

Delsar climbs back to his feet and dashes across the creek. He turns, ready for another attack but the tree doesn't move. It stands at the edge of the clearing as if it had never come alive.

"Delsar!" Elidria runs to his side. "Why doesn't it move?"

"I think the sun hurts it," says Delsar. "Grab your boots. Let's go."

"Right!" Elidria scans the ground for her boots, but then she notices an orange flower at Delsar's feet. "Look out!" she warns as she shoves him out of the way. A vine shoots out of the ground and impales Elidria through her left upper-arm before exploding into dust. Elidria screams and so does the tree as it disappears back into the darkness of the forest.

"Elidria!" Delsar grabs her before she can fall over from the shock.

She begins whimpering. Her lips quiver and tears stream down as she clenches her eyes shut.

Delsar sheaths his sword. "I'm getting you back to camp." He wraps his shielded arm around her and grabs her boots on the way by. He periodically checks over his shoulder along the way, but the tree doesn't ever show itself again.

In the camp, he sits her against a tree and grabs a knife from his bag. He cuts her sleeve off and pulls out a bandage to wrap her wound.

Elidria's eyes go wide and she flails her legs. "Stop!" she screams as he starts wrapping her arm. "That hurts!" She starts to whimper again.

"You have to let me stop the bleeding. Bite your thumb if you have to."

"Don't be stupid," Elidria says while pushing his hands away.

"Elidria," Delsar says sternly, "bite your thumb."

She sticks her thumb between her teeth and clenches down. Her eyes go wide again as Delsar wraps and she begins biting even harder, but she makes it through. "I can't believe that worked," she says in a pant. Her face tightens up again and her eyes shut. "It burns!"

"Is it sharp at all?" Delsar asks.

"No, it just burns!" she yells through her teeth.

"That means it didn't sever your bone and only got flesh. This is good."

"But it still hurts!"

"Getting stabbed will do that." He grabs around her other arm. "We need to get out of here. Who knows if it's trying to find a way around that clearing."

Elidria groans trying to stand up. "Everything hurts. Not just my arm, and I can barely see. Delsar, I feel really nauseous."

"You have to stay awake." Delsar grabs her bag and sheaths her sword. "Talk to me about something," he says as he lugs her back toward the main road.

Elidria starts shaking her head. "I don't know," she says weakly. "Why doesn't it like the sun?"

"I think it's a cursed creature."

"I don't understand," she says, quieter than before.

"It's what we called them in the guard," Delsar explains. "They're creatures that get killed when in sunlight. Orcs and Vampires are examples."

"Where did they come—" Elidria snaps out for a moment. "Where did they—"

"Elidria, stay with me. Elidria!" It's no use. She goes completely limp in his arm. He lowers her down and starts to shake her. "Elidria, wake up. We have to keep moving."

She can hear nothing. It's not exhaustion that knocked her out this time. Instead, it's from the amount of trauma her body has taken. Her body being tossed around like a ragdoll and being slammed multiple times almost did it. The stab was the last straw. Her body shut itself down and simply shaking her will not wake her back up.

Delsar turns his head away and squeezes his eyes shut, stopping the tears from falling. "Eldra," he says, mostly to himself. "You rest now." He hoists her body over both his shoulders. "I'll stand for you."

The path of destruction left behind by the boar Delsar is tracking indicates that it is likely a big one.

Delsar still has Elidria draped over his shoulders and carries everything they both had when they fled from Fairview. He did, however, put Elidria's socks and boots back on. This was to make carrying everything a bit easier.

Every once in a while, she would stir and mumble, but she was never responsive and would go still moments after. The vine piercing her bicep was probably the worst of her pains but Delsar is much more concerned with the heavy blow to her head when she was slammed against the tree. Having her brain deprived of oxygen from being choked likely made things worse. She's probably not going to be very comfortable when she does eventually wake up.

Delsar silently places Elidria and her shield down to draw his bow. Pulling an arrow back, he sets his sights on his prize. A two hundred pound boar a mere thirty yards away.

The boar makes nary a sound, plopping to the ground with an arrow through its skull. It likely didn't even feel it.

Delsar picks Elidria and the shield back up and carries them over to the carcass before placing them back down. He's carried wounded soldiers before, but only ever to safety. Having to repeatedly pick Elidria up and place her back down to do anything is definitely slowing his usual progress.

He pulls the arrow from the boar's head, and for a moment, thinks about wiping it off and placing it back in his quiver. He shakes his head and tosses it in some bushes.

A low rumbling sound emits from the bushes. Delsar spins, recognizing the rumbling instantly.

From out of the bushes, a large, grey wolf steps cautiously. His lips are curled in a threatening snarl. Deep gold eyes look into Delsar's, single-minded certainty reflecting in its depths.

Delsar can't shake the feeling this predator had been stalking him and chosen now to move in for the kill.

Another growl joins the first. More wolves emerge, padding softly over the forest floor and spreading out to form a semi-circle around Delsar, Elidria, and the boar.

Delsar draws his sword and grabs Elidria's shield. He stands himself directly above Elidria and shouts, "Back off!" He clenches his teeth, knowing full well that these wolves will be more than happy to kill him for the meal. Would they leave him be if he leaves the boar to them? Picking up Elidria will leave him vulnerable to any form of attack. Standing and fighting is his best choice.

He scans the dogs in an attempt to count them, but before he can, two jump at him. Delsar bashes the first dog with the shield and lets the other impale itself on his blade. The wolf clearly didn't understand what the sword was designed to do.

The sword catches something in the dog's chest as Delsar is unable to pull it out when the dog falls to the ground. The deadweight at the end of his blade jars the handle from his hand.

Another dog jumps and bites at the shield. Delsar pushes back and delivers a nasty right hook, clocking the dog across its face. The wolf retreats, whimpering because of its more-than-likely broken snout.

Delsar grabs Elidria's sword from his belt and draws it. Scanning the wolves again, they appear to be second-guessing their decision to steal this boar from this bipedal. Delsar raises his sword and shield, screaming as loud as he can.

A few of the dogs step back and the one with the broken snout completely disengages, running from the pack. Two others watch their pack member leave and follow after.

The momentary lull in combat allows Delsar to get a proper count. Three still circle, three run off, one is dead at his feet, and one stands with its tail between its legs. It's the one that got bashed by the shield at the start.

One of the three dogs that still circles is bigger than the others. Likely because it always gets to eat first, meaning it's the alpha. It growls at Delsar, so Delsar returns the favor. "Bring it!" he shouts, bending his knees and bringing the shield to the bridge of his nose.

A wolf from behind lets out a gurgled bark as it lunges at Delsar.

Delsar spins around and brings the edge of his shield to its neck, knocking it into the boar.

The alpha launches with Delsar's back turned.

Delsar whips back around, bringing his left foot up and striking with an inverted roundhouse kick. His shinguard meets the wolf's teeth as it clenches down on his leg and shakes its head wildly.

Delsar drops off balance and the third dog finally joins, grabbing hold of Delsar's sleeve under his right bracer. Both dogs pull, putting him in the unfortunate position of not being able to reach either of them with the shield. He shimmies the shield from his arm and hurls it at the dog on his leg. The shield hits and the wolf releases. He readjusts and grabs the wolf on his sleeve by the hair of its face, yanking it over his shoulder and into the alpha.

Both dogs crash into each other and that's when they finally give up. The alpha gives a quick yip and the four dogs, still able to move, dash away into the woods.

Delsar lets out a battle cry, settling much of the adrenaline surging through his body and claiming victory over the pack of wolves.

He catches the sound of more whimpering and looks down at the dog by his feet. It's still breathing, despite the stab wound. "I know you were just hungry," Delsar says, raising Elidria's sword, "but so am I." He drops the tip of the sword through its neck, ending its suffering.

He slides his swords out and wipes both blades off with a rag before resheathing them. He then sets up a fire and finally begins carving and cooking his prize.

"It's time to eat," he tells Elidria, shaking her.

She stirs and produces noises, indicating the pain she's in. Her hand starts to move as she brings it to her head. "It hurts," she says before going back into shutdown mode.

"Later, then?" Delsar sighs. "I'll save you some." He eats what he needs and wraps the extras in another bandage, storing it in his bag. He checks for all his items and Elidria's before hoisting her back up and over his shoulders. Shield on his arm, he begins his walk back to the main road. How far he traveled tracking the boar, he's not sure. He does know the direction he came from, so he's bound to come across the road again.

Something catches Delsar's ears. *A carriage!* The thought of help about to pass him by on the road races through his head as he takes off running through the woods. Another thought comes to him during his sprint, *What if they're guards?* He slows down and crouches at the edge of the road right as the carriage passes him by.

It sounds like an elderly man is singing up front and every so often, an older woman harmonizes with him. They aren't guards but they could still turn in Delsar and Elidria.

Delsar wrestles with the number of ways this goes bad, but a drop of blood from Elidria's arm landing on his hand settles it. "Help!" he shouts, entering the road behind them.

The singing and the carriage stops. The older man peeks his head around the carriage and then disappears. The couple starts talking to each other but Delsar can't make it out.

"Please," he tries again, "she's hurt."

The man jumps off the carriage and begins running at Delsar with the woman following behind him.

Delsar steps back and covers Elidria with the shield. Their aggressive movements send a fear through Delsar, making him momentarily think that they mean to attack him.

"Are you all right?" the man asks, still in a run.

"I have a blanket," the woman shouts.

Delsar didn't even realize he was holding his breath. If it was a fight they wanted, he wouldn't have lasted long.

"What happened?" the man asks, trying to get a look at Elidria.

Delsar lowers the shield and lets him examine her face and arm.

"She shouldn't be held hanging like that," the man says upon further inspection.

Delsar wants to say something about needing to carry her this way, but he's too out of breath from the run.

"Lay her on the blanket," says the woman, catching up. Delsar complies and the woman wraps her up. "Honey, you carry her back to the carriage for this man."

"It's fine," Delsar interjects between breaths.

"Sorry, boy. Once my Lindsia decides upon something, there's no changing her mind." The man picks Elidria up under her arms and legs.

Delsar lets him without interjecting this time. "Thank you," he says.

"It's no problem." The man heads back toward the carriage.

"You look awful," says Lindsia. "How long have you been carrying her?"

"Sunrise."

"Goodness gracious! It's after six now!" She sticks her arm through Delsar's and stands beside him. "Come. You should get in the carriage, too." She leads Delsar to the back of this smaller carriage.

The man lays Elidria on the part of the floor that doesn't have luggage and Delsar sits on the bench that extends from back to front. The man examines Elidria more closely this time. "Dear, can you grab a fresh bandage for her arm?"

"Of course." Lindsia climbs in and rummages through the luggage. "Now, boy, tell me exactly what happened."

"It was some kind of monster in the woods," Delsar says as his heart starts to slow down.

"What kind of monster?"

"It was a—" Delsar stops, realizing just how unbelievable it's going to sound.

"A what?"

"A tree."

The man is taken aback and even his wife looks confused after pulling out the medical supplies.

"I know how strange that sounds, but it was. It grabbed her and tossed her around like a toy, slamming her into other trees and the ground. Its vines choked her and the whole thing even tried to eat her. That wound is from one of the vines impaling her."

The man continues to stare, but his wife snaps him out of it. "We're in a very unexplored region. There could be lots of mysterious creatures in these woods."

"Right." The man replaces Elidria's bandage. "How did you escape?"

"Its vines turned to dust in the sun and it wouldn't follow us into the clearing." Delsar brings his fingers across his eyes and to the bridge of his nose.

"We're very glad you escaped," says Lindsia. "If you need some rest, my husband and I will take care of her. Where are you both heading?"

"Bihnor, up past Lar."

"We're on our way to Stalton. It's the next town on this road."

"That's fine. Thank you, again."

"We'll be there in about two hours." Lindsia puts a pillow under Elidria's head and hands another to Delsar. "A comfortable rest is what you both need. Would you like a blanket?"

"If it's no bother."

"Not at all."

"You both should stay at our house tonight," says the man. "Heck, maybe even two nights. She's gonna need it."

"We'll likely take you up on that offer." Delsar grabs the blanket from Lindsia. "Thanks."

"I'll get us moving again." The man hops out the back.

"Wait," says Delsar. "What are your names?" He doesn't care so much about them, but he's sure Elidria will want to know when she wakes up. Delsar might have them move on before she does, so getting them now makes sense.

"I'm Ellis and this is my bride, Lindsia."

Delsar gives a nod. "It's a pleasure and I really mean that."

"It's nice to meet both of you...?" The man tilts his head.

"I'm...Delsar and she's Elidria."

"Well, Delsar and Elidria, I'll get you both to town in no time." Ellis waves and disappears around the carriage.

"What have you had to eat?" Lindsia asks out of the blue.

"I cooked up a boar a few minutes ago."

"You need more than meat. You need fruit, sugar." The carriage starts to move and Lindsia climbs along the bench toward the front of the carriage. "Honey, can you hand me a couple apples?"

"Sure thing!" Two apples stick through the carriage lining and Lindsia grabs them.

"Thanks, babe." She hands them to Delsar. "Save one for her if she wakes up."

"I will."

"I'm going up front with Ellis so you can catch some sleep."

"You've been very kind to us. It's something I'm not used to."

The woman smiles. "Kindness is contagious. We're just spreading it from someone else." She reaches past Delsar and pulls the back lining down, giving them privacy from the outside. "Rest easy." She crawls back toward the front. "I'm coming out."

"You do remember what happened the last time you attempted this maneuver, don't you?" asks Ellis.

"So help me this time."

"I've got you."

She disappears through the front and their singing from earlier resumes.

Delsar takes a bite from his apple and slowly drifts into darkness, listening to their songs.

Delsar wakes up, sensing the carriage coming to a stop.

Armored boots approach and Ellis' voice is heard. "What can we help you with?" he asks.

It's definitely two pairs of boots and they walk past the carriage from both sides. "We're tracking two fugitives that have likely been traveling this road."

Delsar silently tightens Elidria's shield. "Wake up," he whispers to her.

Her condition doesn't seem to have improved much over the last hour. She doesn't so much as stir from Delsar's request or shake.

"A man and a woman?" Ellis asks the guards.

Delsar peeks out the back. Another carriage sits about ten yards from this one. Two more guards are with it. One holding the reins and the other just hopped down and is on his way. Delsar can't sneak out the back with them there, but staying is just as bad.

"That's right," the guard replies to Ellis' question. "They escaped from Fairview three days ago and Midori Trails two."

"Really? We just picked up—"

Delsar bumps the shield on the floor picking Elidria up and the guards notice. "Did you hear that?" The guard signals to his partner to check the back and he gets joined by another guard.

"There are two folks back there that we picked up on the road," Ellis informs them. "The girl is very injured."

"Stay here," the guard instructs. He draws his sword and raises his shield, ready to defend the civilians if necessary. "Clear it," he commands the two ready at the back.

"Come out peacefully!" orders a guard.

Delsar pulls on the stack of luggage, causing much of it to tumble down and crash out the back.

The guards step back to avoid the boxes and cases. "That's it! We're coming in!" In perfect unison, both guards push into the carriage with their shields held out in front. Delsar's not there. Only toppled luggage and a slashed hole on the wall of the carriage.

"He ran out the side!" the guard holding the reins shouts.

Delsar dashes into the tall grass field that grows amidst the forest, creating a bit of a clearing.

One of the guards runs after him but quickly loses sight of him because of the grass and darkness as the sun sets lower in the sky.

"Wait!" the guard with Ellis and Lindsia warns. "We can't go in there not knowing where he is. Go fetch the dogs."

Hiding Elidria in the grass to fight the guards isn't going to work now, and running will be impossible. He's going to have to fight, even with her over his back.

Two dogs howl and dart into the grass, disappearing from view, but the two paths of grass getting knocked down are heading straight for them.

Delsar repositions Elidria over just his left shoulder so he can grasp her with the same arm and have her covered by the shield. The first dog bursts through the grass and Delsar punches it straight in the face, causing it to let out a squeak. Delsar pulls out his sword and stands ready for the second, but it doesn't engage. It instead stands a few feet from him and just barks, over and over. Delsar starts running but the dog follows, keeping his position revealed to the guards.

There's no point running. Delsar stops suddenly and spins around, surprising the dog. He kicks the dog, knocking it to the ground but two of the guards are on him in an instant. He tries to keep one between him and the other but he can't while carrying Elidria. He parries one strike from one side and lets another clatter with the shield. He's not going to last long like this.

Delsar pushes headlong into one of the guards, crashing shield-against-shield. The extra weight with Elidria only adds to his momentum, allowing him to overpower the guard and push him back. The guard trips over something and they both tumble to the ground. Delsar drops Elidria and quickly scrambles to his feet before stepping on the guard's shield, pinning his arm down. Delsar delivers a kick with his shinguard into the guard's head. Even with a helmet, a blunt blow like that isn't going to feel good.

The other guard swings for Delsar, but no longer holding Elidria, mobility isn't an issue. He ducks under the strike and attempts to lunge in. However, the guard at his feet is still conscious and grabs Delsar's leg, pulling him off balance. He stumbles and is forced to block the next strike instead of countering. The sword glances off his shield and

Delsar shakes his leg free, stomping on the guard's arm and kicking him in the head again.

The other guard swings for Delsar again. Delsar slides away and right back in, retaliating with his own strike for the exposed thigh.

The guard reacts by lifting his leg and catching the strike with his own shinguard. He swings back at Delsar who spins out of the way. The two reset and recompose themselves.

"We didn't kill anyone," Delsar states. His mouth dry from exertion.

"Save it for the trial," says the guard, breathing heavily.

"We can't go with you. Bihnor is under siege and we plan to help."

"I would have heard something about it if that was true."

"You can't know everything."

"Are you finished?" the guard asks.

"Always." Delsar sets, waiting for the strike.

The guard charges, but not with his sword. He leads with his shield this time.

Delsar jumps to the side to avoid and counter, but the guard opens up with his shield and clips Delsar's wrist. The initial shock and force knocks his sword from his hand. It flies into the guard's breastplate before dropping harmlessly to the ground. Delsar quickly grabs the guard's shield and starts twisting it like a wheel.

The guard tries to knock Delsar off with his sword but Delsar's shield is in the way. The guard whacks Delsar's shield but realizes his arm is going to pop if he doesn't go with the twist. He tries to fight against the twist but does so in vain. He flips over and lands on his back.

Delsar pins the guard's shield with his knee and his sword hand with Elidria's shield. He then starts driving the heel of his hand into the guard's face repeatedly. The guard struggles but Delsar doesn't stop.

Elidria screams and Delsar pauses for a moment.

"Enough!" booms a voice from behind.

Delsar looks over his shoulder and sees the guard who was giving the orders, with Elidria clutched by her hair. She's not asleep anymore. Delsar raises a fist this time to finish his guard off, but the other guard pulls harder on Elidria's hair and she screams again.

"Get off him now!" the guard commands.

Delsar opens his fist and slowly puts his hands up. The guard on the ground pushes Delsar off and proceeds to punch him in the face, knocking him to the ground. The guard rolls him over, removes the shield, and restrains him.

"Let her go!" Delsar yells from the ground. "Can't you see she's hurt?"

"I hardly care." He lets go of Elidria's hair and she immediately whips around with a punch. The guard blocks her strike, catching the bandaged part of her arm.

Elidria cries out again and drops to her knees.

"Elidria, stop!" Delsar shouts as his guard stands him up. "They have us."

Elidria looks at Delsar with the corner of her eyes and begins to weep.

The guard grabs her by the chin and stands her back up. "You're a feisty one."

Elidria slides her head down and digs her teeth into the guard's leather glove.

The guard howls and releases her.

Elidria steps back and puts one hand up, ready to fight. Her other arm sits limp at her side.

The guard has enough and clenches both fists.

Delsar knows what's about to happen. If Elidria takes another big blow to the head in her fragile condition, she may never wake up again. The guard raises his fist while Delsar slides his toe through the shield at his feet. He kicks out, sending the shield into the guard's leg, stealing his attention away from Elidria.

"Keep control of him!" he shouts at Delsar's guard. He turns back to face Elidria and grabs her arm, completely overpowering her. "You both are under arrest for Nomar of Orange Peak's murder, multiple assaults, including royal guards and Fairview Archers, and evading arrest." He pulls Elidria's arm down behind her back and forcefully cuffs her.

She clenches her eyes and grimaces from the pain.

The first guard, that got knocked out by Delsar, stands back up. He staggers about as he looks around at his surroundings.

"Gareth," shouts Elidria's guard, "grab the dogs and everything else! Bring it all back to the carriage."

The guard snaps from his bewilderment instantly. "Roger!"

"No more tax money will be spent on either of you," the guard informs Delsar and Elidria. "The governor of Fairview has deemed both of you guilty. We're taking you to Stalton where you'll be hung in the morning."

"What?" exclaims Delsar. "What about our trial?"

The guard starts laughing as he leads them back to the carriage.

Elidria lowers her head and begins crying again, from both her pain and the feeling of dread. She lifts her head again and her glistening white eyes look at Delsar's. "What do we do?"

Delsar shakes his head in complete despair. "I don't—, I don't know."

CHAPTER 13

THE GIBBET

6 Years Ago...

"That was some of the most fun I've ever had. I should go with you on your missions more often," the Queen says as Arviakyss starts unstrapping her armor from her body.

"I don't think the King will approve when we brief him about what happened," says Arviakyss.

"I'll deal with him, and, Captain, my right bracer is really irritating. Could you get that one off first?"

"Yes, ma'am." Arviakyss begins twiddling with the leather straps that keep her bracer on.

"You even recommended I get padded bracers like your own. I'm not sure why I didn't have that order expedited."

"I'm sure they have them finished by now." Arviakyss removes the bracer and pulls something sharp from the leather. He holds it up for the Queen to see. "Though, I don't think it was the bracer that was irritating your arm."

"Is that from the wyvern?" she asks, extending her hand and retrieving the tooth from him.

"Unless something else bit your arm that we don't know about."

"Astounding." She tries to hand it back to Arviakyss but he puts his hands up.

"It was your arm it wanted. That will make a fine memory."

"A trophy," she says admiring it more closely. She holds out her other arm but doesn't take her eye off the tooth. "My other bracer, if you please."

"Right." Arviakyss removes her other bracer and gets to work on her breastplate. "Thank you," he says.

"Thanks goes both ways for us, Arviakyss."

"But you've made the promise I made for my mother a reality. Nothing would be the same without your help and support."

The Queen smiles. "It was the choices *you* made and your hard work that got you here. Being humble is good, Captain, but don't ever forget where you came from."

"You mother me too much," Arviakyss comments.

"You're seventeen and I'm in need of practice. I also believe one should never turn down a word of wisdom."

"Perhaps. Stand up for a moment, please, your Highness?" The Queen stands for Arviakyss and he removes her breastplate. "You can sit back down." Arviakyss kneels down and begins working on her armored boots. "It's a great talent to teach. It's an even greater talent to listen," he says.

"More words from your mother?"

"Always."

"I so badly wish I could have met her. I feel she could have made a wonderful advisor."

"It's a shame you don't have any of those," Arviakyss says.

"The different opinions of many outweigh the governed opinion of one. They never seemed to understand that."

"No, no," Arviakyss defends. "I'm not saying you were wrong firing them. I was just pointing it out."

"I know that, Captain." The Queen brings her hand to her chin and crosses her legs, making Arviakyss need to adjust himself to get back to work on her boots. "You're a Captain without a team, Arviakyss."

"There's you," he replies.

"Yes, but I am your overlord." She gives Arviakyss a smirk. "No, you need a real team. One with the same principles as you. Each one having an exceptional skill to offer."

"And what would this team do?"

"What you do but better. People you can depend on. Who will do what you need them to do. You're great at almost everything you do, Captain, but you aren't the best at any of it."

"No one ever is."

"Someone *always* is," she retorts. "If saving the world is our goal, the best should be doing it. An archer, a swordsman, a negotiator, a medic, a navigator, a hunter, a spy. People whose specialties are more singular. You have 'A-class' abilities in all those skills, so you can relate to them all. That is why for this team, you will be leader. A real captain."

"A team would be nice. Do you have people in mind?"

"I have a few candidates," she tells him. "The Champions. That is what I'd like you *all* to be called. There shouldn't be just one champion for the kingdom."

"I have no problems with that, though I doubt I have a say."

"You're right. My mind is already made up. This isn't a fantasy of mine. It's already on paper and being put together."

"How long until this project is ready?" Arviakyss asks, pulling off one of her boots.

The Queen gasps as he does and falls back in her chair.

"My Queen?" Arviakyss gets up. "Are you—" he doesn't finish his question. An arrow, his arrow, rests high through her chest. "Taharial!" he exclaims this time, dropping next to her and turning her on her side.

She lays there gasping for air with the tip of the arrow sticking out her back. It only stopped because of the backrest on the chair.

Arviakyss pulls bandages from his pack and tries to apply pressure to both the wounds around the arrow. "Help!" he yells while also scanning the Queen's quarters. There's no sign of anything. Looking where he thought the arrow came from, he sees nothing. No window or tapestry or hidden door. There are no holes big enough in the walls to make such an accurate shot.

Arviakyss looks back at the shocked Queen. Her eyes are wide and her breathing slows. "Just hang on," he says. "Please, don't you leave me."

#

The Council of the Six Powers of Ithendar...

"All are present, my Lord. The meeting will begin at your request."

With the council having only six members, plus the King, it is clear that everyone is present. Despite that, it is still Malgo's job to inform the King of the attendance.

In this square room are nine chairs. Three on each wall, minus the entrance wall. One seat for each of the Six Powers, one for the King, an empty one on his right for the Queen, and another empty one on his left for the Seventh Power of Ithendar, although they do not attend such meetings anymore.

"Then we shall begin." The King looks over at the representative from Grandell. "Grandell, please let the other council members know what happened in our borders."

Grandell stands up. "I'm sure most of you have heard about the troll attack in Orange Peak and of the random trolls popping up all over the south. Unfortunately, I regret to inform you all that these attacks are not random. There are stories going around stating that a magic-user led the attack at Orange Peak, though he was thwarted by a small group of mercenaries led by the Outcast. The governor of Grandell deployed a company from his army to help rebuild Orange Peak."

"This is old news," says Nallendar's representative. "Why call us here for something we are all aware of? The attack, as sad as it was, did fail. We sent a company of soldiers there to reinforce the border, you don't need us."

"Let him finish," the King scolds him. "There is more."

"Yes, there is." Grandell swallows hard and continues. "Another two companies were deployed to Boforest to hunt and exterminate another group of trolls that wiped the village out. They found no survivors."

"What?" exclaims Fairview's representative. "Then the royal bloodline is lost! The King must find a new queen."

"I agree," says Lar. "As it stands, Sire, you have no family," he tells the King. "You and your wife never bore a child and now her bloodline is no more. Should something happen to you, we have no one to take your place that the people will approve of. The governors and lords will all want the throne and I fear this united alliance between the Six Powers will fall if you die with no successor."

"He must pick a wife who has a family," says Malnera.

"It's decided then." Agla stands up. "My King, you must pick a new queen. Someone young who can bear you a child. If you do not choose a queen in three months, the council will pick one for you."

"Very well. In three months' time, I will have a new queen. Now, we have the trolls to figure out."

"It's a perfect job for the Queen's Guard," says Grandell.

"The Queen's Guard failed," interjects Fairview.

"That's because the project was never completed," Grandell defends. "My King, I suggest you put together a small task force as your previous wife tried. A team of your best men. Allow them to get to the bottom of this. Magic must not be allowed to return."

"We beat magic when it was strong and rooted in these lands," the King says. "A small incursion of trolls is nothing to fear. Fortify your defenses for now." The King stands up. "That is all. You are all dismissed. Notify your governments at once."

Sleeping was out of the question last night. Even if he wanted to. An accelerated heart rate and palpitations plagued Delsar's chest all throughout the evening and into the morning, for this is the day he and Elidria are scheduled for execution. No defense, no forewarning, no trial. Just swift, fraudulent justice.

Delsar looks over at Elidria whose broken body wouldn't let her stay awake last night, even in the uncomfortable position of sitting against the cell bars with her right arm chained above her. It's no way to spend your last hours, but Delsar has no way of getting to her and any amount of noise he made was likely ignored by her brain's subconscious. At this rate, she's going to wake up only to be immediately hung.

The thought makes Delsar shudder. It was he who decided to ask the couple from the carriage for help and it was he who dropped her in the woods. If he hadn't let that guard grab her, he's sure he could have taken them all on. But now they're here, with four guards watching their every move. Everything was stripped from them except the bare minimum of clothing. Delsar's tunic and pants, and Elidria blue top and light-brown underskirt. No socks, or boots, or belts. Nothing that could risk allowing them to escape, not that a pair of socks would help.

"Elidria," Delsar says, his nose stuffy and his voice shaking. Once again, his voice falls upon deaf ears. He turns away and sniffles as he starts to choke up. He wipes his tears with his shoulders and closes his eyes.

The sun's light passed through the small window about an hour ago. Eight o'clock is definitely close. The wait of such an impending fate is worse than anything he's ever experienced.

Loved ones passing away was bad, but that is often sudden and you have no say in the matter. This is completely different. He also has no say but it hasn't even happened yet, and there is no moving on or getting over it. It feels like being trapped in a small, white room with no windows or doors. He must sit and wait for an impending doom while also being lost in his own thoughts of regret. The feeling in his heart tells him that even if a miracle takes place, he will never truly heal from such emotional trauma.

The Mayor of Stalton walks in and is accompanied by eight armed guards, though they are not for him. "Your time has come," he says to Delsar and the unconscious Elidria.

Delsar takes a deep breath and goosebumps formulate all over his body. His teeth chatter and his heart hastens even more. "I f-forced her," he says. "Elidria. I saw her beauty and I stole her from her family. I told her she had to do whatever I asked of her or that I'd kill her family."

The Mayor shakes his head. "A noble lie, but it's too late. Take them," he orders the guards.

"Please," Delsar pleads as the guards open his cell and one grabs him, restraining his hands behind his back, "there must be something I can do so that you'll spare her."

"Bring the man you killed back to life and fix all the guards you maimed." Another guard picks Elidria up and the Mayor leads them out into the town square.

There is a crowd of people gathered. "Move!" yells one of the guards. The crowd parts and reveals a gibbet with two nooses and a lone, masked executioner atop it.

Delsar shakes his shoulders but the guards grab even tighter. A battle of strength against even just one of these guards will not go in Delsar's favor.

They push Delsar to the stairs of the gibbet and he trips and stumbles his way up. He turns around at the top. "You can't kill her while she sleeps. That's not allowed," says Delsar.

"I am very aware." The Mayor snaps his fingers and a guard hands him smelling salts. "String them up."

They force Delsar back and on top of a trapdoor. Despite his squirming, they manage to get his head through the noose. "She's innocent!" he cries. "I swear it! Nomar did not fall by her hands!"

The crowd boos and some even start throwing things.

The Mayor steps in. "There's no need for that," he tells the crowd. "These scum will get what they deserve. There's no reason to make a mess of things." He walks over to Elidria who also has a noose around her neck and is being held up by a guard. "It's time to wake up," he says, waving the salts under her nose.

Elidria wakes up with a start and flails her legs apart, trying to keep her balance. Her eyes roll around and refocus. Her mouth drops and her heart is immediately filled with dread. "No, no, no," she says quickly and her eyes fill with tears. "Wait, please! Don't!"

"We gather here to witness the execution and justice of two murderers from Fairview," the Mayor starts. "On Friday, these two individuals murdered their own crew member and assaulted two others before crippling multiple guards. Their crimes are beyond just. May their deaths serve as an example to those who wish to follow in their footsteps and wipe away the shame they brought upon their families." The bell from the town clock starts to sound and the Mayor gives the executioner a nod.

"Last words!" Elidria cries. "Please, just allow us those." She closes her eyes and starts shaking her head, fully expecting the floor to drop out from beneath her. "Please, please, please, please."

The Mayor holds his hand up. "It is customary that we allow such requests. You have one minute each."

Elidria looks over at Delsar, her teeth chattering, but it is Delsar who speaks first.

"Eld-dra," he says with a nervous stutter, "I'm s-sorry. I'm sorry f-f-for not getting you where you asked— Where you asked me to get you. I'm sorry for n-not b-b-being the man you needed or wanted. I'm sorry for not even c-calling you what you've been asking me to call you since we m-m-met. You aren't just a name to me anymore. You're s-something m-much more. A champion fights and wins, but that is where they stop. You've g-gone above and beyond, not just to get back to help your village, b-b-but also to help everyone you could along the way. You gave Roki a reason to fight. You gave G-glade hope. You inspired Nomar to act and m-m-make a d-difference. It was you who put t-together the team that saved Orange Peak. You did all of that without expecting anything in return. Not even a simple thank you. You are something I never could be. Something I wish I was. You are a hero. *My* hero. It sounds selfish, I know, but I needed saving and I didn't even know it. *You* did, though. Not from the physical, but from something darker. From somewhere only I could have put myself. You were the light that shined even when I tried to snuff it out. Even though I couldn't save you and *can't* save you, I thank you. Thank you, Eldra, for saving me."

Elidria tries to formulate words to say but she gets overwhelmed with emotion. Her head drops and she starts to sob. "I forgive you," she finally says. "I always have." She doesn't say anything after that.

"Since you're done, we shall proceed," says the Mayor.

"Let her finish her minute!" Delsar yells. "It hurts no one."

The Mayor nods and everyone goes silent, watching Elidria stand there with her eyes closed. She takes a deep breath and finally looks up at everyone. "I'm ready."

The Mayor looks over at the executioner. "Pull it," he says.

Both Delsar and Elidria tense up and clench their teeth. Their eyes close again as they wait for the floor to open and their necks to snap. That's if they're lucky. If their necks survive the drop, five minutes to five hours of choking torment awaits them.

The executioner places his hands on the lever and squeezes the safety. "Forgive me," he says.

"Don't you pull that lever!" yells a guard, pushing through the crowd on horseback.

The executioner quickly takes his hands off.

"Don't listen to him," says the Mayor. "Just pull it."

The rider pulls out his crossbow causing every guard to do the same. "Don't touch the lever. I have new information from Fairview. You are *not* to kill them."

"Lower your weapon," a guard tells him.

"Not until the Mayor acknowledges."

"Lieutenant!" the guard raises his voice.

"Mayor," says the Lieutenant, "I have papers with me. If they die up there, you will be charged with two accounts of murder. I promise that won't help with getting you a seat on the council."

The other guard grabs the paper from him and reads it.

"We have our own orders from Fairview," says the Mayor. "They are to be hung at once. They *are* guilty. Pull the lever, now!"

The Lieutenant fires his crossbow into the executioner's shoulder, sending him falling back and off the gibbet.

The other guards start running at the Lieutenant and one even fires his own bow, the bolt striking him in the armguard before harmlessly bouncing off.

"Wait!" yells the guard who had snatched the paper. "Everyone, stand down! What he said is true. Stand down. Someone assist the executioner."

The guards all stop and the Lieutenant gently kicks one away from his horse. He then dismounts and readjusts his breastplate as he approaches the gibbet.

"Don't stop!" shouts the Mayor. "Stop this fool!"

"That's enough," says the Lieutenant. "I am Lieutenant Telrus and I come from Fairview. New evidence has proven their innocence. I'm here to secure their safety and help them back on their way."

The Mayor blocks the stairs but Telrus sweeps his legs away with his arms, making him tumble to the ground. "They're hardly innocent!" he yells from the ground. "What about the guards they hurt?"

"Pardoned," Telrus says without looking back. He removes the noose around Delsar and does the same for Elidria.

Both of them run to each other and drop to their knees, embracing each other with just their chins to their shoulders.

Telrus removes the cuffs from their arms and they immediately wrap their arms around each other. "I'm sorry you got put through that," Telrus says. "Take your time up here. I have some words to say to the Mayor."

Delsar just nods his head.

"Alright, folks!" shouts Telrus. "Nothing to see here. Go back to work!"

Delsar and Elidria sit embraced for what feels like minutes before Delsar finally says something. "How can I be like you?" he asks. "You find joy where there hate. You find courage where there is no hope. You find peace when there is only distress. You live in a world that only wants to tear you down, yet you always get back up. You put people like me to shame."

Elidria leans back and places her hands on his cheeks. "No, I'm just like you," she says, wiping his tears with her thumbs. "As a kid, I've lied, cheated, stolen, disobeyed, and recently I've even given up and not given my best. The world deserves our best. Deeming someone's mistakes worse than your own is just a way to exalt yourself and put others down. It's what leads to a world you described. One where everyone is afraid of being wrong and scorns those who disagree. Forgiveness, Delsar. Not just for those who wronged you, but also for yourself. I forgave you for your blemishes, but you don't feel any different, do you?"

Delsar shakes his head, tears streaming down.

"Then start here." She places her fingers on his heart. "Forgive yourself. Everyone makes their own mistakes, big and small. You need to accept it, both theirs and yours. Once you realize your own mistakes, it's much easier to help others with theirs instead of judging them and casting them aside."

"But I know of my mistakes."

"Then you already feel what so many others don't. Humility. Now accept that humility." Elidria stands up. "Wait!" she yells to the people still dispersing.

Some ignore her and keep walking while others stop and look like they're interested in what she has to say.

"I forgive you," is all she says.

Most just turn away and continue on their ways but some smile.

"I do, too!" shouts Delsar, standing to his feet beside Elidria. He then looks down at her. "If this is what it takes."

She tilts her head and smiles, covering her mouth with her hand. "It is," she says as she breaks into tears and embraces him. "We'll do it together. As heroes."

Delsar places his hand on the top of her head. "The two heroes."

"I like that. No thugs here," she says before giving a little giggle.

Delsar starts to laugh, too, though it sounds more nervous than anything. Before long, they both sound like they just heard the funniest joke ever, helping relieve them from the anxiety that they just went through.

"He can't be a guard and it's because of them!" yells the furious Mayor. "His dream was ruined!"

"You mean to say that you almost had two people killed over some dream?" Telrus isn't backing down. He's not going to let the Mayor get the final word in this argument. "Perhaps you aren't fit to be mayor if you let your personal feelings get in the way."

"There's nothing wrong with personal feelings."

"There is when you kill people who don't deserve it. Since when is an execution order made so early?"

"I got orders from Fairview and I followed them. How was I supposed to know it was from some shifter? Do you expect me to question an order?"

"If the pieces don't fit, yes. The execution didn't belong here. You should have sent them back to Fairview to have them handled. Instead, you wanted the satisfaction of killing them yourself. Just because your son broke his knee."

"My son didn't break his knee," says the Mayor. He flings a stubby finger in Delsar's direction. "That man broke his knee."

"How conceited can you be?"

The Mayor's face turns red. "Your mission was a success," he says, spit flying from his mouth. "What you set out from Fairview for is done. Your services here are no longer required. Hop back on your horse and ride back to Fairview."

"My job is *far* from done," Telrus interjects.

"Get out of my sight and out of my town! That's an order!"

"I don't recognize your authority right now."

"How dare you! I'll have you court-martialed for this!"

"And then there will be a full investigation of what almost transpired here. Remember that seat on the council you want? The kingdom doesn't like stuck-up mayors having a say how it runs."

"Are you threatening me?" the Mayor asks.

"Maybe I am." Telrus gets in his face.

"Are we interrupting something?" Elidria asks, Delsar with her.

Telrus doesn't move. "No. The Mayor was just about to grab all your items to give back to you. He also said there's a nice diner around the corner where you can eat, on him."

The Mayor tries his best not to back down but eventually gives in. He lets out a heavy breath, seeming to deflate as he does. "Bart!"

"Yes, sir?" A guard runs up and salutes.

"Go grab the items from the hold. Make sure these *fine, innocent* people get their stuff back."

"Right away, sir." The guard grabs a partner and runs off.

"They could also use an apology, *Mr. Mayor.*"

"Oh, that's all right," Elidria cuts in. "We already forgave him."

The Mayor turns his head toward Delsar and Elidria. Elidria stands with her hands behind her back, smiling, while Delsar stands completely straight-faced. The Mayor lets off the subtlest of growls. "Just do whatever it is you came here to do. While in *my* town, they are *your* responsibility." The Mayor begins storming off. "If I ever see you again…," he grumbles.

"You'd best hope not!" Telrus yells after him. "If you ever do see me again, I'll likely be leading the investigation myself!"

The Mayor doesn't respond but instead keeps walking with his back turned.

"It sickens me that people like that are the ones in charge," says Telrus.

Elidria looks up at Delsar. "His hate makes him no different from what he accused us of. To the heart, hate and murder are the same."

"I apologize on his behalf." Telrus removes his leather gloves and shakes Delsar's hand. "I'm Telrus and I'm here to get you whatever you need so you can get back on track."

"And I'm Eldra," Elidria says, bowing deeply.

Telrus returns the bow.

Elidria gasps. "I didn't think anyone else bowed anymore."

"It's something people don't do much since the Queen died, but I still think we should. It's a sign of great respect."

"And I agree. It's great to hear that from someone else."

"If you both aren't busy," says Delsar, "what did you mean by getting us back on track? Just what do you know?"

"Probably more than you're comfortable with," Telrus says, placing his hand on the back of his neck. "Let's go somewhere we can talk privately." Telrus summons another guard. "Keep an eye on my horse. Another guard will return with their gear. Make sure he leaves it here with you."

"And who are you?" asks the guard.

"I'm the one giving you the easiest job in the kingdom. Just get it done." Telrus gestures for Delsar and Elidria to follow. "This way please."

Telrus leads Delsar and Elidria to a table in a diner specifically designed for confidential conversations. He lets them sit down and pulls a med kit from his pack, kneeling next to Elidria. "May I have your arm, Miss Elidria?"

"Um, sure. Thanks." Elidria allows Telrus to gently take her arm and replace the decrepit, tainted bandage with a new one. "Why did you go so far out of your way for us?" she asks, wiping the last bit of her tears away with her other hand.

Telrus smiles while wrapping the arm. "Why did you go out of *your* way to help Orange Peak?"

Delsar and Elidria both look at each other, shocked. "Just how long have you been tracking us?" asks Delsar.

Telrus finishes and sits on the other side of the table. "Long enough to know you're heading to Bihnor."

"She's Elidria of Bihnor, daughter of Aldameer. You're going to have to come up with something more than just reading her identification."

"Long enough to know that you're heading to Bihnor *and* expecting a fight."

"What *do* you know?"

"Something is going on in Bihnor. Something we guards aren't supposed to know," Telrus explains.

"Mercenaries attacked and likely killed most of my people," Elidria's states.

"We aren't allowed past Lar's capital city. Something is amiss in the kingdom, Mr. Delsar and Miss Elidria. Something I fear to be very sinister."

"And you want us to know?" Elidria asks.

"You're the only people who seem to be doing anything about it." Telrus waves in the waitress and lets her serve Delsar and Elidria their breakfasts before he continues. "I'm not allowed past Lar. I want to help you in Bihnor but I can't make any promises. However, I can get you anything you may need. And I do mean anything. I can also share my intelligence with you."

"Just how smart are you?" Elidria asks.

"He means military intelligence," says Delsar.

"Oh. That does still make him smart, right?"

"I should hope I got my job because I'm smart," says Telrus.

"What's in it for you?" Delsar asks.

"My country gets to live another day."

Elidria looks at Telrus wide-eyed.

Delsar's face doesn't change. "Continue," he says. "I won't be interrupting again."

Telrus nods. "I believe everything started about eight years ago, with the creation of Bihnor. I call it phase one. Two years later was phase two. The Queen's murder. Phase three is happening now which are the troll attacks and Bihnor. I fear what phase four may be."

"You think the troll attacks and Bihnor are related?" Delsar questions.

Elidria elbows him and brings her finger to her lips. "Shhh," she says. "You said you wouldn't be interrupting again."

"It's all right," says Telrus. "It's a good question to ask. Orange Peak wasn't the only attack. Boforest was wiped out last week. The same day you arrived in Fairview."

Delsar's shocked. "But that's—"

"The Queen's home village. They weren't lucky enough to have people like you around. We found no survivors."

"But there weren't any trolls in Bihnor," says Elidria.

"True, but every one of these events has one person in common, the Queen. She is from Boforest, she created Bihnor, and now she's dead."

"Someone is trying to cover something up!" Elidria shouts.

Telrus holds his hand up to quiet her. "Specifically the Queen's murder. But I asked myself, 'Why cover it up when everyone already knows who did it?'"

"Because he didn't."

"Spot on, Miss Elidria. Arviakyss was set up and I believe someone in Bihnor knows more than they're supposed to. The trolls are just a diversion. They're supposed to be thought of as random attacks so the attack on Bihnor can be blamed as a troll attack, too."

"But why hire mercenaries?" Delsar asks. "If they wanted Bihnor wiped out, they could have just used trolls like they did for Boforest."

"Because there's another piece that's missing. The one person who knows *without a doubt* that Arviakyss is innocent. It's Arviakyss himself, of course."

"But he doesn't live in Bihnor," Elidria states.

"No, they're trying to lure him in and kill him. No one has been able to find him for almost six years. The only way they'll find him is on *his* terms."

"Like that's going to work," scoffs Delsar. "Bihnor is a random village. Why would he help them?"

"That is something I've been trying to wrap my brain around," says Telrus. "I was hoping you could shine some light on it, Mr. Delsar."

"What makes you think I have the answer?"

"They are trying to lure in one person and one person alone. Out of everyone in this entire country, only one person answered the plea for help. You did, Mr. Delsar. They set the trap and you are falling right into it."

Delsar reaches for his sword, forgetting he doesn't have it.

"Relax. I know you're innocent. Whoever is behind the Bihnor attack is the one responsible for the Queen's murder."

Delsar motions Elidria to leave but she ignores him. "Do you think there are any survivors left in Bihnor?" she asks.

"I do," Telrus answers. "I believe they are keeping many as hostages. Again, that's why they are using mercenaries over trolls."

Delsar settles back down. "Why wait six years to cover this up?"

"You ask the important questions. This is something I've thought a lot about. I believe that this coverup is not the end of the plot. I think they want, or *need*, Bihnor for something more. Two birds with one stone." He looks directly at Delsar. "You can't save the village without the King's help. You need to get in, find any survivors, and get out without ever being detected."

"Hmm." Delsar leans back. "It's been a while since I had good intel. Tell me, Telrus, how old are you?"

"So much for Delsar asking the important questions," says Elidria. "I thought you didn't like useless information?"

"I'm only curious."

"I'm nineteen," says Telrus.

"And where's your partner?"

"He sent me ahead. I travel faster. If I was even two seconds slower, you'd both likely be dead."

Elidria shutters. "That's a terrifying thought. Let's not talk about that anymore, please."

"My apologies, Miss Elidria."

Delsar's mind drifts away.

Telrus interrupts his train of thought. "I became a guard because of you. I chose intelligence because I believed I could clear your name."

"You don't know me."

"I know *about* you. You weren't just a guard. You were an inspiration. The greatest champion this country had ever seen. Not just in battle but also in the community. If I can save you, you can save the country."

"Saving the country is a bit extreme."

"Delsar," Elidria nudges him, "can we talk?"

"I can go if you both need to talk."

Delsar nods.

Telrus stands up. "I'll go pay for your meals. Wave me back when you're ready."

Elidria waits for him to get out of earshot before speaking. "Delsar, you do realize that he is a random guard who figured out you're innocent all on his own? Your face tells me you don't trust him."

"Like you said, he's a random guard."

"Tell me, Delsar, those things you said on the gibbet, did you only say them because you thought you were going to die?"

Delsar doesn't respond right away. He instead leans against his elbows on the table. "Words *are* just words." He looks over at Elidria. "I guess we're just going to have to wait and see."

Elidria crosses her arms. "You forgave the people, now trust *him*. He saved you from death when he didn't need to. His story is well thought out and makes plenty of sense. If trusting him is so hard, then trust my judgment."

Delsar laughs. "You do realize you have a concussion, right?"

Elidria scowls. "It's not just about you! He has offered help. My people need every chance we can give them. I say we trust him and I hope with all my heart that you do the same."

"I'm not against him. I just don't completely understand his convictions."

"That's because you don't know what it's like *not* being you. You didn't know Arviakyss as an inspiration but as yourself. Wanting to clear your name isn't that hard to believe."

"For you, I'll give him a chance, but remember, there is such a thing as being too trusting."

"Ask him then," says Elidria.

"What?"

"Ask him why he does what he does. Ask him what his convictions are instead of trying to figure them out by yourself. I want you to trust him because *you* deem him trustworthy."

"What happened to it not being about me?"

"Oh, he's helping regardless of how you feel. It's the slicing of the cake to have you trust him, too."

"*Icing* on the cake." Delsar sits back in his booth. "Very, well. Telrus!" Delsar gave him a wave and a nod.

"Yes?" he asks, returning to the table.

"Have a seat."

Telrus sits back down in the same spot as before, across from Delsar and Elidria. "I imagine you have more questions?"

"You say Arviakyss inspired you. For what? What didn't you have the courage for until he showed up?"

"Mr. Delsar, I love my country," he begins, "and I'm proud to call myself Ithendarian. I want nothing more than to serve and protect. Unfortunately, I'm not very big. I barely passed the physical to graduate as an apprentice. As far as defeating threats to the kingdom, I'm not the one for the job. I'm not even quick on my feet like you were. As a boy, I discovered that I'm really good at noticing the littlest of things. Like the narrow threads that connected Orange Peak, to Bihnor, then to the Queen, and then to you. *That's* how I serve and protect. Arviakyss was incredible. Trying to be like him would be impossible. However, I *can* support him and make sure he has everything he needs, including intel. That is how I will save my country. He inspired me to do my best. Intelligence *is* my best. That's what you wanted, right? My convictions? My county is my conviction."

"But it's your country that wants Arviakyss dead."

"And it's wrong," says Telrus. "I plan to save it from its belief."

"If what you told us is true, you're into some dangerous work," Delsar warns. "These people want this covered up. They *will* try to silence you."

"Truth is dangerous. I'm willing to die for it."

Elidria notices Delsar close his eyes and his face shutter for a moment. Even his nose starts to turn red from Telrus' comment.

"That's enough. I've heard what I need," Delsar states as if whatever thought he just had never happened.

"Then what about you, Mr. Delsar?" Telrus asks. "What made Arviakyss tick?"

"I've never even told Elidria."

"So we're back using 'Elidria'?" she questions.

"Force of habit. I've been calling you that for over three weeks."

"That's fine."

"Well, Mr. Delsar? What about Arviakyss?" Telrus asks again.

"Why should I tell you?"

"Because *I* told you."

"Not gonna happen," Delsar says, shaking his head.

"That's hardly fair."

"*Life* is hardly fair."

"If at all," Elidria adds.

"Arviakyss is truly dead then." Telrus looks down at the table. "Such a shame. You have some pretty big boots to fill, Mr. Delsar. I hope they fit."

"I only need to squeeze into one." Delsar looks at Elidria.

"Oh? I guess I'm boot number two." She grabs Delsar's collar and pulls him in. Whispering, she asks, "Are you sure it wasn't *you* who hit your head? Every encounter we've had so far, I would have died without you and I haven't saved you once. Sure, you can fit in my boots but I fail in comparison."

"Pale."

Elidria scrunches her nose. "I'm not here to fit in anyone's boots. I'm a girl so they likely will be too loose. However, my boots fit just fine."

"Are you trying to make a point?" Delsar asks.

"Kind of, but my point even got lost on myself."

"Elidria, I wasn't born like this. I practiced and worked hard. I gained experience and was saved countless times by Galius. You've only been practicing for three weeks, yet if I didn't know you, I'd assume you were in the army. An army recruit trains three *months* before they graduate. I'm not the one saving your town. It will be *both* of us. The two heroes, remember?"

"You're just trying to flatter me," Elidria says, unable to keep herself from blushing. She wipes her nose and her slightly tearing eyes. "Golly."

"You cry too much," says Delsar.

She lowers her head and smiles at Delsar. "It's because I'm so sweet."

"Or a child."

"Hey! I'm not the youngest one here anymore. Not with Telrus around."

"I didn't say you were the youngest."

"Hush now," she says holding up her hand. "I'm going back a few sentences before we get too far off-track." She leans in for a hug. "Thank you, Delsar." She quickly disengages after wrapping around him. "My arm!" she exclaims.

"Can you make a fist?"

Elidria closes her eyes. "No."

"This isn't good." Delsar looks over at Telrus. "We accept your help. The first things we need are two rooms. The best rooms in town. She needs a *real* night's sleep. Her head needs a break before we go anywhere."

"Consider it done."

"Oh-oh," says Elidria, back to her chipper self. "And a bath. And of course, we need our clothes cleaned and repaired. My left sleeve seems to be missing. Wait! Scratch that. We need *two* baths. Delsar is pretty stinky, too. And as it sits, I need my feet rubbed."

"It's *as it stands*," Delsar corrects.

"I can't have my feet rubbed while I'm standing, now, can I?"

Delsar looks back at Telrus. "Infirmary?"

"Yeah. That's a good call and it's paid for."

"Thanks, Telrus. It's like being in the guard again. You are a blessing."

Elidria looks up at Delsar with the corner of her eye. It was Delsar who just initiated that 'thanks' and it wasn't an act.

"Is this everything?" Telrus asks.

Delsar throws on his cloak after equipping his belt. "It is."

"Good. There should be two hundred extra gold in each of your bags. Apology money, though I'm sure going through that was not worth the two hundred gold."

"Not really," says Elidria. "If anything it makes things worse. Now every time I go to buy something, I'm going to be like, 'Oh, look. I'm using my hanging money to buy an apple. Here, mister farmer. Take this money that only reminds me of my deep, lingering trauma.' Then he's going to be like, 'Gee, thanks, but I don't even know what you're talking about.' And then I'm going to sound like a fool."

Delsar looks at her strangely. "Concussions and you don't mix well."

"Who do they mix well with?" Elidria drops her right bracer. "I can't tie this, Delsar. It's really aggravating."

"Don't worry about that today. You just heal. It's Lar tomorrow and Bihnor in the evening. Here. Just put them in my bag."

"Works for me." Elidria places her bracers in Delsar's bag. "What happens if I can't fight tomorrow?"

"Tomorrow is just reconnaissance. I don't plan on fighting at all."

"How so?"

"Get in, find the survivors, get out. Two versus an unknown number of enemies doesn't sound fun."

"What about the treasury?" Elidria asks.

"Do you really think the mercenaries haven't found it by now? There won't be any money there."

Elidria tilts her head. "Are you still willing to help?"

"You can pay me back later. You said you'd pay me and I know you're not one to lie."

"Perhaps," is Elidria's response, though something else is clearly on her mind.

"Mr. Delsar! I just remembered I have something that you lost."

"Huh?"

Telrus pulls a blanket from off his horse and grabs a shield from under it. "I'm not sure how I almost forgot."

"There she is." Delsar's face goes white. "I can't believe she came back." He grabs the shield from Telrus.

Elidria looks sad at Delsar being reunited with his shield.

Delsar walks over to her and hands her his shield. "*It* came back."

"Huh?"

"That's all it is. A shield. You stand with me so now I don't need it."

Elidria shakes her head, but quickly brings her hand to her temple and grits her teeth. "You're an idiot," she says in pain. "You do realize how dumb that is tactically, don't you?"

"I'm not getting rid of it. It was a metaphor." Delsar turns away. "Just put it on my back."

"*You're* the blunt one. You expect me to suddenly realize you're not being serious?" Elidria slides it on his back. "I stand by my first statement."

"You asked for *my* help. What does that make you?"

"Compassionate. I feel bad for dummies like you."

"So you must be a dog person," quips Delsar.

"Funny," Elidria says, crossing her arms.

"I'm just being serious."

"Oh, so *now* you are. I'm the inconsistent one, Delsar. Not you."

"Do you guys need a room where you can settle this?" jokes Telrus.

"We've been over this. We need two rooms."

"And a bath," says Elidria.

"And you're standing post," Delsar tells Telrus.

"I...I was just kidding."

"And when I say post," says Delsar, "I don't mean tree."

Elidria jabs Delsar in his side.

"Gah! I accept that one."

"Do you think this is funny?" Elidria asks, pointing at her bandaged head.

"No."

"Don't you lie!" she exclaims, startling Delsar. "I got attacked by a tree, in the woods, surrounded by trees!" She drops her voice. "It's a little bit funny." She smiles at Delsar before looking past him and going serious again. "And scary."

"Um, I'm confused." Delsar is confused.

Elidria smiles again. "Inconsistency, Delsar. That's my specialty."

"What?"

"I like you two," says Telrus. "Don't die in Bihnor on me."

"Then we'll just die in Lar," Delsar says, completely straight-faced.

Telrus bursts out laughing. "You got me." He shakes his head and lets out a sigh. "Although, Miss Elidria, I don't see how fighting a tree surrounded by trees is funny. It makes you sound, you know, a bit off."

Elidria pouts and looks away. "I guess you just had to *be* there."

"Maybe so." Telrus snaps back into escort mode. "If you're all set, I'll show you to your rooms."

"No, I'm taking a bath." Elidria forces her belt and bag on Delsar. "You can show Delsar to our rooms."

"Your rooms have baths, Miss Elidria. Stalton has some of the best plumbing in the west."

"Wait, really?"

"Yup."

"Is the water warm?"

"There's a tray of coal under the tubs. Just try not to cook yourself."

Elidria brings her hand to her chin. "That wouldn't be a good way to go."

"You could just get out of the tub if it feels too hot," says Delsar. "It's not that hard."

"Unless I fall asleep."

"A lunch and dinner will be delivered," says Telrus, changing the subject back to what's important. "You're free to wander around town and get your own meals if you don't want the catering. There are robes on your beds so you can leave your clothes by the doors. Someone will pick them up and clean them."

Delsar pulls a blue, bloodstained sleeve from his bag and tosses it to Elidria. "Here."

Elidria catches it and looks at her bandaged arm. "These sleeves are skin-tight. I don't think a sleeve will be very comfortable over the bandage."

"Then just keep it in your bag for later."

"You can handle all of this in your rooms. This way, please. I have much to do to get you prepped for tomorrow," Telrus gestures to get them going again.

"Thank you, Telrus," says Elidria.

"You're welcome, Miss Elidria."

"You make me sound so old. Please, just call me *Eldra*."

"Okay, Eldra. I can do that."

CHAPTER 14

THE PREP

3 Days Ago...

"It was the same guy who attacked Orange Peak," Roki says, sitting up in his bed at this Fairview hospital. "A shifter. It had to be him."

"You think he came here after the attack?" Telrus asks, looking up from his notepad with just his eyes.

"I'm sure it was him. What do I need to do to help pardon them?"

"Your testimony will be enough to have this case looked at again, but the big issue is the guilty verdict the governor gave. If they get caught before we can completely clear them, they *will* be hung."

Roki's eyes widen and his breathing shallows. He starts shaking his head. "You can't let this guy get away with this!" he exclaims to Telrus. "Not again."

"I don't plan to."

"Lieutenant!" shouts a voice, bursting into the recovery room with a paper in-hand. "Sir, we found him."

Telrus turns around and notices the paper in his hand. "Did he sign it?" he asks, reaching out his hand for retrieval.

"Yes, sir. He completely pardoned them."

Telrus snatches the orders and reads them to double-check. "That was incredibly easy."

"He was found tied in his closet. He said someone who looked just like him attacked him and that it wasn't him who ordered the fugitives' executions."

"They're not fugitives anymore." Telrus folds the paper and slides it into his bag. "Junnsun, let my partner know that I'm leaving without him. I'll travel faster this way."

"Uh, yes, sir!" Junnsun salutes and lets Telrus by. "Ah, sir?" he says, stopping Telrus in the door. "Do you know where you're going?"

"North. That's where they're heading. I'll just hope to run into them."

"Bihnor," says Roki. "That's where they're going. To stop the mercenaries."

"Mercenaries?" Telrus grinds his teeth for a moment and straightens his breastplate. "I guess that's not a surprise. Junnsun, what's the fastest way there?"

"The northern road that cuts through Stalton and Lar's capital is fastest, sir, but going past Lar is forbidden."

"I'll catch them before they make it that far." Telrus takes his helmet off and starts to give Roki a bow, but as he does, he gets shoved aside by another individual.

"Roki!" Glade exclaims, running into the room and hugging Roki.

Telrus straightens up and readjusts his breastplate again. "That was a bit rude," he states.

"Sorry, sir and excuse me," says Cade, waiting for Telrus to give him space through the door before entering, unlike his father.

"That's better." Telrus moves, letting the child pass.

"Who's this geezer?" Glade asks, gesturing his head toward Telrus.

"This is Lieutenant Telrus," Roki tells him. "He just cleared Delsar's and Eldra's names."

"Which won't mean anything if they're dead already." Telrus bows again. "Thank you for your time," he says before straightening.

"Hold on." Glade holds out his hand to shake Telrus'. "Thanks for your help, sir, and sorry."

Telrus grabs it and gives it a quick squeeze before backing out the door. "Don't think of me as rude trying to leave so suddenly."

"I get it." Glade grabs the frame of the door and watches Telrus start running down the hall. "Tell them 'good luck!'" Glade shouts after him.

"And that we'll be continuing the mission," Roki adds.

"And that we'll be continuing the mission!" Glade repeats.

Telrus raises his hand and waves it without looking back. He disappears around a corner and the sound of his clanging metal fades as he gets further away.

"Did you say there are mercenaries attacking Bihnor?" Junnsun tries to confirm with Roki.

Roki looks straight at the guard and nods. "That's what I said."

Junnsun gives a bewildered look. "If that's true, restricting the guards from going past Lar doesn't make any sense. This is something I have to report to the Governor. Do you have any kind of evidence with you?"

"Does a contract from Elidria work?"

"Is she the girl from Bihnor?"

"Yeah, and she mentions the mercenaries in the contract."

"It's something." Junnsun extends his hand. "May I? I'll get it back to you as soon as the Governor has seen it."

Roki pulls the contract from his pocket and hands it to the guard. "You can keep it. I'm not sure I'll be able to fulfill it anymore."

Junnsun grabs it from Roki and reads it. "Perfect." He gives Roki a nod with his mouth half-open. "This is…," he stops and just turns for the door. He looks over his shoulder and says, "I wish you a swift recovery."

"Thanks. Good luck with your report."

Junnsun leaves the room and closes the door behind him.

"What kind of conspiracy have we gotten ourselves into?" Glade asks, staring at the door.

"I don't know, Glade. I really don't know."

Elidria rummages through what is more a cart than a carriage while Delsar holds a checklist he whipped up before leaving Stalton. "The arrows are here," Elidria reports.

"All five bunches?" Delsar asks.

"Hold on." Elidria fumbles as the cart hits a bump. "Yeah, five."

"That's everything. Come back up front."

"Remember," starts Telrus, "in Lar, I can get you anything you don't have or forgot you needed."

"Speaking of," says Elidria, climbing up front and sitting between Delsar and Telrus, "how long until we get there?"

"Less than a mile," says Telrus.

Elidria looks at Delsar and tilts her head. "You never told me our plan in Lar."

"Find a map, lay out a strategy, leave for Bihnor. We won't be there long."

"If we didn't get caught, was our plan to be in Bihnor already?"

"With no complications, yes," Delsar confirms. "However, even if we didn't get caught, you needed another night to recover. Getting arrested kind of worked out."

Elidria crosses her arms a slouches back. "Speak for yourself. Just thinking about yesterday makes me cry. I was never so scared in my life."

"What about your long-awaited bath? That must have brought some form of enjoyment to yesterday."

"It was miserable," she bluntly states. "The water touching my arm felt like someone sticking a hot prong through it."

"Such is the life of Miss Eldra," says Telrus.

"It's a good thing this guard came so far just to save us," Elidria says, hugging Telrus.

"Oh, hey! You're confusing my horse." Telrus gently pushes her off.

"You've never called *me* brave," states Delsar.

"As far as rescues go, Telrus has you beat."

"But I've saved you at *least* four times."

Elidria starts counting on her fingers. "I'm only getting three."

"The troll outside of Eskor," he reminds her.

"Oh yeah. That feels so long ago. Back when I was—"

"Useless?" Delsar interrupts. "Clumsy? Accident-prone? A noodge?"

Elidria scowls at Delsar. "Choose your words, Delsar. Those ones aren't very nice."

"I'm not the one who dropped a knife on my foot."

"You dropped a knife on your foot?" exclaims Telrus.

"It was a stressful morning," says Elidria. "Have you ever awoken to a troll trying to kill you?"

"As I recall, you dropped the knife *before* it was trying to kill you."

"Tomato, tomato," she says without changing either word. "I thought you didn't see it happen?"

"I heard the squeak you made when you did."

"There's nothing wrong with a squeak from time-to-time."

"There is when you're trying to hide," says Delsar.

Elidria narrows her eyes even more, giving Delsar what now looks more like a death stare.

"I've changed my mind, Elidria. You're more like a horse than a dog."

Elidria tilts her head again. "I'm afraid to ask why, but I realize that I love horses, so really, I do want to know why."

"Loyal, like a horse, but they'll randomly want to kill you for some unknown reasons. *That* is what you are."

Elidria raises an eyebrow. "Hmm. Okay, Delsar. I'll allow that one." She starts to giggle. "I'm fast like one, too."

"Ah, you know what?" Delsar asks.

"What?"

"You can't be a horse."

"Why not?" Elidria sounds concerned over the metaphorical comparison.

"Horses don't throw up."

Elidria scrunches her nose and crosses her arms again. "The cat's out of the bag now."

"Wow. You got one right, though I don't know any who would put a cat in a bag. It would throw up though."

Telrus smiles. "You two have had quite the adventure."

"Elidria wouldn't know. She's been asleep for half of it."

"Three days, Delsar!" she exclaims, holding up three fingers. "Only three days and *maybe* a half."

"What was going through your head when we fought the wolves?" Delsar asks.

"What wolves?"

"And the couple who picked us up. Ellis and...," Delsar thinks for a moment. "I can't remember the woman's name but at least I remember them."

"See, now I think you're making stuff up," says Elidria.

"No, really, I had to fight off a pack of wolves trying to steal the boar I killed," he explains. "There were eight or nine of them."

"Um-hm." Elidria doesn't sound like she's buying it.

"I'm being serious."

"I'm with Miss Eldra on this one," says Telrus. "You need to come up with more believable stories. Like Miss Eldra getting stabbed by a living tree. Oh, and make sure you have names ready before you make anyone up."

"You expect me to remember the names of every person I ever meet? Good luck with that."

"I can," states Telrus.

"Not all of us are walking libraries."

Elidria grins from ear-to-ear listening to them talk.

"What's so funny?" Delsar asks.

"I do remember the wolves," she says. "Well, kind of. I was in-and-out all day. I thought they were a dream."

"Whatever," Delsar replies, rolling his eyes. "Getting back to relevant things, how's your head?"

"It's doing much better. It still hurts if I shake it though," she says as she shakes it.

"Then don't shake it! What are you, nine?"

Elidria's grin gets even wider. "I think my head will be perfect by tomorrow."

"That's the unpopular opinion. What about your hand?"

"It's my *arm*, but I know what you mean. I can close it now," she says, "but it still hurts a lot."

"Could you fight today if you had to?"

"Are we planning to?"

"No, but things happen."

"Absolutely," she answers. "Knock me down and I'll bounce back up."

"You're a bit too bony to bounce."

Elidria frowns and looks down. "Some women would kill to look like me," she pouts, barely audible.

Delsar changes his attention back over to Telrus. "Tell me, Mr. Encyclopedia, do you know anything about shifters?"

"I do. Of course, many years ago, magic-users were banned from Ithendar."

"Spare us the history lesson."

"Sure. A shifter's image has no mass. It's not actually there."

"We know the basics."

"Do you want my intel or not?"

"Yeah, but skip the obvious."

Telrus shakes his head and starts again. "The amount of images that can be cast at once or their sizes is unclear. It's believed that the more they practice, the more they can cast at once. Well-trained shifters can do voices and sounds, too."

"The one we fought can definitely do voices," says Delsar. "Other sounds and modifying his projections on the go was definitely something he wasn't good at."

"Don't let his past restrictions fool you," warns Telrus. "A bit more practice and could probably run a whole play by himself if he wanted. Special effects and all."

"What were they good at?"

"Infiltration and government manipulation were their specialties."

"The one from Orange Peak seemed different than that," says Delsar. "Some kind of mad scientist or something."

"Yes, I don't think he is the mastermind behind this."

"Agreed. I got the impression he was there to observe. I think Elidria and I threw a wrench in his plans."

"A wrench, Delsar?" says Elidria. "My cat makes more sense."

"*Since*," emphasizes Telrus, stopping Delsar from responding to Elidria, "it's just us and I'm sure you won't be going to the King with anything I say, I do have a few treasonous theories."

"I'm not a fan of treason," says Delsar.

"The penalty for treason is hanging!" exclaims Elidria, burying her head under her arms.

"Just theories then. My apologies. Let me just get to them." Telrus takes a breath and sighs. "To afford these trolls and mercenaries, it has to be someone with plenty of money," he explains. "It also needs to be someone with a heavy influence to convince the King to restrict travel to

Bihnor. Likely a mayor from one of the bigger towns, a lord, a governor, a council member, one of his advisors, or even the King himself."

"The gibbet!" says the freaked Elidria.

"Then don't repeat what you hear," says Delsar. "What about a family member?" he asks Telrus. "Does he have any?"

"He does not. His firstborn would be next but he never had any kids. The Queen was considered an equal upon marriage, so the bloodline switches to her until he remarries."

"Boforest was wiped out. Did her family still reside there?"

"They did," Telrus confirms.

"Then who's in line?"

"Right now, no one. Should the King die, the council will choose a new one. Likely a governor."

"This isn't a plot against the Queen," says Delsar. "It's a plot against the entire royal family."

"Only one remains. Either he did it, or he's next."

"Lar!" exclaims Delsar. "The governor of Lar would have plenty of influence to restrict travel to Bihnor since Bihnor is part of its district. Plus he would have the funds *and* he is likely going to be one of the council's top candidates."

"Lar is growing faster than any other district. Its strength is only rivaled by Fairview," Telrus adds. "The new king would likely come from Lar or Fairview."

"You have to warn someone," says Delsar. "If this is true, they will kill the King before he can remarry."

"Unless it's his future wife orchestrating all this. That's my next theory."

"She kills him after marriage and gets the throne to herself." Delsar shakes his head. "So far, both of your theories kill the King. Who else have you told?"

"Just you."

Delsar squints. "That's not true, is it?"

"I'm not going to tell you who else I've told, plus I can't really tell anyone about this. All my theories only work if you're innocent. Your innocence connects the thread between Orange Peak and Bihnor. I have to clear *your* name first. Don't die in Bihnor, Mr. Delsar. Your country needs you alive."

Elidria cuts in. "Delsar, if you truly are this important, maybe you shouldn't come to Bihnor."

Delsar's heart skips hearing those words from Elidria. She would put the nation ahead of those she loves, although Delsar is pretty sure she would try to save Bihnor on her own if he left.

"Nonsense!" says Telrus. "The attack on Boforest was tactical and so must be the one in Bihnor. Any one of those hostages may have the key to unlocking the truth behind this plot. It is equally important that the people of Bihnor are saved. Mr. Delsar is the one who can get it done. Plus, if he is to become Arviakyss again, he must always do what is right, regardless of the situation. That's the hero we need."

"Arviakyss was a champion, not a hero," corrects Delsar.

"Champions don't lose and you've lost. Heroes rise."

Elidria smiles at Telrus' comment. *That's exactly what he's doing.*

"This conversation doesn't matter," says Delsar. "I have every intention of going to Bihnor and no intentions of dying. Back to your theories. Boforest and Bihnor make sense as targets. What about Orange Peak."

"The only thing I can come up with is that they used it as a testing ground for their trolls, but that's just me saying I don't know. Hold up." Telrus brings the cart to a stop at a Lar checkpoint.

Two guards approach the cart. "What is your business in Lar today?" one asks.

"We're on official business. An investigation," explains Telrus. "Unfortunately, that's all I'm at liberty to disclose."

"Who are these with you?"

"This is Elidria of Bihnor and this is Delsar, the Outcast," he answers. "They are my consultants."

"No one is permitted in Bihnor if that is where you are heading," the guard informs.

"Correction, *we* aren't allowed. The consultants have free reign."

"That's the first I've heard of this," says the guard.

"Here." Telrus hands him his identification. "I'm intelligence. There is a possible illegal military presence in Bihnor that brings me here.

That's already more than I'm allowed to say. Whatever is there, I must report it to Fairview *and* the King."

The guard examines the card. "This is enough," he says, handing it back to Telrus. "You have access to our barracks and any gear you need. Welcome to Lar. Good luck, Lieutenant." The guards both salute.

"Thank you, Corporal." Telrus returns the salutes and then has his horse walk on.

The guard who never finished his search of the cart walks over to his partner. "I don't like it," he says.

"Letting them through?"

"No, not that. They brought enough arrows and food to both feed *and* fight off a small army. Whatever they think is going on in Bihnor, I don't think the three of them can handle it."

"Two," the other guard corrects. "The Lieutenant can't go with them."

"Then they will need more than just luck."

Telrus rolls out a giant map of Lar with its surrounding villages and towns on the table. He inspects it and becomes immediately displeased. "Is this really the most updated map you have?"

"It was printed earlier this year," informs the secretary.

"Then where's Bihnor?"

"I know where it is," says Elidria. "It's right here. Right on the coast."

"Just north of Willow's Peninsula. How could you forget to add a village a mere ten miles from here?" asks Telrus.

"I'm not the cartographer," says the secretary.

"It doesn't matter." Delsar procures a charcoal pen from his bag and hands it to Elidria. "Can you mark any buildings and structures?"

"Sure," says Elidria, about to scribble on the map.

"Uh, *no!*" exclaims the secretary. "She can't do that!"

"She's updating it," says Telrus. "You're not even supposed to be in here anymore."

"The Governor has asked me to observe."

"Unfortunately for you, you can't." Telrus gently places his hand on her shoulder to escort her out.

"You can't kick me out!" she complains. "I'm the Governor's representative!"

"Then you can represent him on the other side of this door." Telrus pushes her through the doorway. "Thanks for the map," he says while bowing. He then closes and locks the door.

"You can't do this! In Lar, you answer to the Governor!" she yells through the door.

"Considering he doesn't know what we're doing here, the King likely never told him," Telrus explains. "Since he hasn't told him, he must not be on the need-to-know list."

The secretary says nothing. Instead, she huffs and can be audibly heard storming away.

Telrus turns to Delsar and Elidria. "Actually, the King isn't even on that need-to-know list."

"Then is this even official?" Elidria asks, crossing her arms.

"It's my job to identify and investigate anything that is a potential threat to country or village," says Telrus. "If I discover anything, I am to report my findings to my superior, or even the King. I'm allowed to use my own discretion and initiative. If I deem it official, it's official."

"I wonder if that's a white lie," says Elidria.

"Huh?"

"It's a thing she does," Delsar explains. "This is his job, Elidria."

"Actually, Miss Eldra, I've been trained to deal with people like that secretary. Don't give them an inch, we're told. There are people like that everywhere. They think they know better than you or are allowed where they aren't just because they know someone or have done it before. Don't worry about it. I didn't lie."

"It's true," Delsar confirms. "Intelligence Investigators in the guard kind of have a free pass. It helps them get information quickly. Waiting for authorization could allow a culprit to get away or a terrorist attack to slip through."

Elidria squints one eye. "Very well. Shall we get back to this?"

"Yeah. How tall are the cliffs?" Delsar asks.

"Thirty feet," she answers. "There's a carved staircase that leads down to the beach. It's a treacherous and slow climb and descent."

"You could probably get down plenty fast if you fall," Telrus jokes, but is only welcomed with a glare from Elidria.

"Are there any other ways up and down?" asks Delsar, cutting the tension.

Elidria points further north. "Up here. About one mile from the stairs. The cliffs get low enough to simply climb up or down. High tide can become an issue though. The water extends all the way to the cliffs then. During low tide, the beach is flat and extends two hundred feet from the cliffs."

"What about ports?"

"Just one dock. It extends across the beach so that it sits a couple feet above the water during high tide. It goes out another hundred feet across the water during low tide."

"So it's three hundred feet long?" Telrus questions.

"Wow. Little Intelligence Boy can do math," Elidria jeers.

"I apologize for my joke before," says Telrus. "I didn't mean to be offensive."

"It's fine," she replies. "You didn't know and it was my choice to be offended, so I'm sorry, too."

"If you both are done," Delsar says, annoyed and not quite understanding what just transpired, "there is more to fill in. Are there any buildings on the outside of this ridge?"

"No, Bihnor is built completely within this crest." After a few more minutes, Elidria finishes constructing a top-down model of her village. At least, one as accurate as she can remember.

"This hill will be our staging point," Delsar explains. "The mercenaries will likely only patrol to this ridge. We won't be seen here. Then we wait until nightfall before you sneak in through this seagrass. Then, it's building-to-building. Stay in the shadows and take your time. Take all night if you have to. Find any survivors and make contact with them. Don't try to escape with any. You will be tempted to, but if we can't get them all out at once, it will make things much more difficult. They will likely be locked up so perhaps the keep or the treasury. Keep track of how many mercenaries you see and where. Then, get out. Tomorrow night we will both go in by whichever way you deem fit. That will also be the route we escape from. If we have to fight, we do like we did in Fairview. Evade and eliminate one at a time. I will try to take out a few of them silently before we even enter. Got it?"

Elidria crosses her arms. "I'm not killing anyone."

"What?"

"You heard me."

Delsar scoffs. "These are the bad guys. They murdered the people you love and are enemies to the kingdom. Their extermination is justified."

"And *we* are the good guys," says Elidria. "I'm not sacrificing *my* humanity because of what *they* did."

"You said murder is the hate in your heart. We aren't killing them because we hate them. We're killing them because it's needed."

"I know the difference between murder and justified killing. I still won't do it," she says again.

"Then what do you suppose we do?" Delsar asks.

"Citizens' arrests."

"You can't be serious."

"Very. Then we take them back here to be fairly tried by unbiased individuals."

"Everyone is biased," says Delsar.

"Well, this is how we're doing it."

"Capturing them all isn't even going to be possible. There's likely going to be at least a dozen of them. It's just going to be you and me."

"You're going to have to figure something out, Delsar."

"Okay, spook, do you have any ideas?" Delsar asks Telrus.

"I respectfully call you Delsar so I'd appreciate it if you would call me Telrus." He starts to pace around. "I've got nothing," he finally says.

"You can get us anything standard-issue, right?" Delsar inquires.

"If I deem whatever it is needed for the investigation."

Delsar gives a subtle smirk. "Then I *do* have an idea."

"Oh?"

"Mr. Delsar," Telrus says, grunting and heaving a small, but heavy crate.

"Telrus?"

"A little help."

"You astound me," Delsar tells him while also helping with the crate.

"You should have seen the guy's face," Telrus says, starting to chuckle.

Delsar and Telrus hoist the crate into the cart. "Hey, Elidria. Come over here."

Elidria snaps from her pacing and the burden that awaits her. "What's this?" she asks.

"Take a look." Delsar opens the latched crate to reveal a couple dozen restraints and just as many keys. "For all the citizens' arrests we may have to perform."

A giant smile explodes across Elidria's face. She rushes her hand over her mouth and starts to tear up. "This is incredible. Thank you, Delsar."

"No one remembers the guard," says Telrus.

"And no one remembers to call me Eldra."

"Fair enough. Hey, Mr. Delsar, can I talk to you for a moment?" Telrus grabs Delsar by his sleeve and starts to pull him away from Elidria.

"Uh, sure," Delsar says, though it doesn't feel like Telrus was going to take no for an answer with his forceful pulling. "I'll be right back, Elidria."

"See what I mean?" Elidria exclaims.

Telrus leads Delsar a few strides from the cart before using a hushed tone. "You aren't seriously going to be arresting them, are you? These, in your own words, are the bad guys. You can't risk everything because the girl is afraid of a little blood."

Delsar rolls his eyes. "I'm not an idiot. If we have to fight, arresting them will be the least of my concerns. As soon as she realizes the situation, her fight instincts will kick in. I'm just humoring her to keep her focused."

"You'd better. Don't forget just how important the survivors of Bihnor are and just how important *you* are. You *need* to stay alive. No matter what it takes."

"I'll do what's needed. I can assure you of that."

"I'm also not an idiot, *Delsar*. Don't let your loyalty to her innocence get you killed."

"I'll do my job," says Delsar, "and she's the boss. The cuffs are there *if* I deem them usable. My priority will be keeping her and myself alive."

"Don't change what works, Delsar. Arviakyss was ruthless versus his enemies. That's what made him so effective in combat."

"Arviakyss only killed when there were no other options. He also did things no one else did and didn't practice traditional combat. *That* is what made him effective."

"Then *do* that," Telrus says, pressing two of his fingers against Delsar's pec. "I've said what was needed. I'm sure you'll find a balance, Mr. Delsar."

"I appreciate your concern though I can't tell if it's because you care, or because I'm important to your theories."

"That's *my* balance," says Telrus. "I care for you *and* Miss Eldra, but I would trade you both if it meant saving this country. However, I would prefer all three surviving."

"I'll try not to disappoint," Delsar says, pushing Telrus' fingers off his chest.

Elidria walks over and interrupts their fairly heated talk. "They finished hooking up the horses."

"This is goodbye then." Delsar extends his hand.

Telrus takes it and adds a bow. "The best of luck to the both of you."

Elidria returns his bow, but Delsar settles for just the handshake.

"I didn't want to distract you earlier, but I do have news from your friends," says Telrus.

"Glade and Cade?" Elidria asks with excitement.

"Roki, too," he replies. "They were very shaken up, as you can imagine, but they wanted you to know that they are continuing the mission."

"I'm proud of them," says Elidria. "I hope for their success."

"They also wish you both the best of luck."

"Thank you, Telrus." Elidria grabs around him for a hug.

Telrus doesn't say anything. He just accepts it.

Even Delsar decides to let it linger.

Telrus finally lets out a sigh. "You're welcome, Eldra. Now, you two should get going if you want to make it to your staging point before dark."

"Right." Elidria releases Telrus and climbs into the cart, followed by Delsar.

"Take care of my horse."

"Which one is yours?" Elidria asks.

"The one on your left," Telrus replies. "Her name is Amber."

"And what about the other one?"

"I'm not sure. They didn't give a name when they brought him over."

"I like Gendief," says Elidria.

"Gendief?" Delsar questions.

"The razzmatazz," she says, smiling with glee.

"But he's bay."

"I don't know what that is, but he's named after a wizard my mom used to tell us stories about."

"Wizards are illegal, you know?" Telrus reminds her.

"It's just a name, Telrus. Don't pull a 'Delsar.'"

"Irrelevant," says Delsar, raising his voice. "We are leaving now." Delsar gives Telrus a salute. "Until we meet again."

"Hopefully sooner rather than later," Telrus responds.

Delsar snaps the reins and the horses start their ten-mile walk toward Bihnor.

Elidria turns around in her seat. "Bye, Telrus!" she yells, waving. "Thanks, again!"

Telrus removes his helmet and gives a courteous bow. "Don't fail, Delsar," he says, not loud enough to be heard. "Don't give them what they want."

CHAPTER 15

THE TRUTH

6 Years Ago...

"Please, Elly, come out," Aldameer pleads with his daughter.

"Go away!" Elidria screams while also throwing one of her books against the inside of her locked door.

"She wouldn't want this. Please, come say your goodbyes before it's too late."

"It's already too late! Saying goodbye to a dead person is stupid!"

"She's not just a person, Elly," Aldameer says much more sternly. "Come out now!"

Elidria rips open the door. Her face is a burning-red, and she looks up at her father with just her eyes. There is fiery anger in her eyes, but tears also drip off her chin. She opens her mouth to say something, but her lips begin to quiver. She instead turns her head from her father and huffs.

"Honey," Aldameer says, reaching over and trying to give her a hug.

"Don't touch me!" Elidria yells, pushing him back.

Aldameer throws his hands up and backs off.

"It's not fair!" she shouts at him. "We just got her back! Why was she taken from us again?"

"Some things are out of our hands," Aldameer says in a soothing tone.

"Well, this wasn't!" she snaps.

"What?"

"We never should have moved to this stupid place! This was your idea and now she's dead!"

"No, Elly, it was an accident. No one is to blame."

"Well, I blame you! I hate this stupid place and I hate you for making us come!" Elidria goes back into her room and slams the door.

Aldameer presses his hands and forehead against the door and is no longer able to keep back his tears. "I'm sorry, Elly. I truly am. This wasn't supposed to happen. I know that, but please, let me help you through this."

"You want to help me? Then go bring mom back!"

Aldameer drops to his knees and starts to weep. "You know I can't."

"Then we're done here. Leave me alone."

Aldameer wipes his face with his sleeve and climbs back to his feet. "If that's what you want. I know you'll forgive me so I won't ask for it again," he says more calmly. "We're about to bury her coffin, should you change your mind."

"I won't."

"I understand," he says, turning away from the door. "One day, Elly, I hope you'll understand." He leaves Elidria alone in her room.

Elidria buries her head in her hands. This is only the first day of healing for a wound that will likely never truly close.

"I'm so scared, Delsar," says Elidria, walking in circles around the small camp set up as their staging point. Her hands and chest shake uncontrollably as her nerves hammer her.

"Breathe," Delsar says, calmly. "You know the village better than anyone. Sneak in, make contact, sneak out. You'll do fine."

Elidria closes her eyes and starts to tear up.

"Elidria, you fought trolls, you escaped guard custody, you battled a tree, and you even survived an execution. You can handle a little sneaking."

"Those are just words, Delsar. Plus, I had you at each of those moments."

"I'll perch on the ridge. If things, for some reason, get hairy, I can cover you from there." Delsar places his hands firmly on her shoulders. She turns her head away so he gently places his hand under her chin.

"Listen," he says, turning her face toward him, "there is only one person in this world that I trust more than myself to do this."

"That's because I'm the only person you know from Bihnor," says Elidria.

"Elidria, this is your home. They don't even know you're coming."

Elidria takes a deep breath. Her heart pounds and she still shivers despite the warm night. "Shield," she somewhat whispers, "do I need it?"

"It's your call. If you take it, move even slower."

"But with it, I might be able to escape if they spot me."

"Yes, so it's *your* decision."

Elidria grumbles as she turns her head again. "What if my choice ends up being a mistake?"

"This is *your* mission. You need to be comfortable. Whatever makes you feel safer is what you need to choose. *Don't* overthink it."

Elidria clenches her eyes shut and scoffs. "Fine." It's a one-word response she got from Delsar. "Just slide it on my back."

"Are you sure that's what you want?"

"Delsar, please!" she exclaims. "I feel like you're maybe making this harder than it needs to be."

Delsar gives her a nod and grabs the shield from being used as a paperweight for the map. "Don't bump it against anything or back into any walls. The noise will—"

"I get it!" she snaps, extending her arms straight down and making two fists. "Just slide the stupid shield on my stupid back!"

Delsar doesn't move after her outburst. He grinds his teeth around in his mouth and clears his throat before swallowing.

Elidria looks over her shoulder, the moonlight reflects off her tearing eyes. "I'm sorry. Please just slide it on so I can get this over with."

"I can do it."

"No, Delsar. Even if I'm scared and don't believe in myself, you've always had my back and your judgment is incredible. It's something I trust more than I trust myself. You said I'm the best person for this so I'm going to do it. You just need to be patient with me. This is the scariest thing I've ever willingly walked into."

Delsar slides the shield on her back and gently whispers in her ear. "Then whenever you're ready."

Elidria lets out a tension-filled sigh. "If I think about it any longer, I'm going to lose it."

"Just start with the ridge. Clear it and wave to me. Nothing else."

Elidria nods and bites her lip. She doesn't say anything as she slowly begins her terrifying quest through the hilly terrain in the dark. She feels every pebble, twig, and tiny undulation through her boots with each step. It's something that she would normally pay no mind to, but tonight it starts to really bother her. Whenever she feels the pressure from one of these tiny obstacles through one of her boots, she purposely tries to step on another with her other boot.

Elidria tries to even off the pressure under her foot after stepping on a larger stone, but her opposite foot steps softly into sand. Something so simple fills her with frustration and getting her legs pricked by seagrass adds to it. She lets out an aggravated grunt but quickly realizes that this is where she's supposed to be. Her mind gave her something to be distracted by. Something to help her through the weight and fear she's feeling.

Elidria lets out a huge sigh and even giggles. She clamps her hands over her mouth and waits a few moments to make sure no one heard her. She wipes her hand across her sweaty face and pushes up the ridge, through the seagrass.

She scans the ridge for anyone or anything that doesn't belong. She appears to be alone but the movement of shadowy figures passing in front of Bihnor's street lamps frightens her. She ducks in the grass, thinking she's been seen, but quickly realizes they're only patrolling the village below. Elidria calms her breathing before waving to Delsar, though she can't see him.

A few moments go by before Delsar appears next to her. She spooks but only lets out a gasp.

Delsar brings a finger to his lips and begins whispering. "Why is there sand here?" he asks.

Elidria's upper lip begins to curl as her head jerks back. "I don't know," she says with an annoyed tone. "Why ask such a stupid question at a time like this?"

Delsar shakes his head and rolls his eyes. "It was just a thought."

"Since when do you ask irrelevant things?"

"Forget it," Delsar says, pointing down at the village. "I only spy two patrols. They are both circling the village clockwise. Wait for one to go by, then sneak to the bottom of the ridge and wait for the next patrol to pass before entering."

"Uh-huh, sure." Elidria's eyes close and her face winces.

"Is it your arm?" Delsar asks.

"No, and shut up. I'm just thinking."

"Sorry for asking."

Elidria's head tilts over her shoulder as she looks at Delsar with the corners of her eyes. "People don't change overnight so stop pretending you suddenly care."

"Hey," Delsar says, grabbing Elidria's shoulder. She pushes his hand off so he grabs her again and turns her around. "Look at me." He firmly grabs her other shoulder and looks into her eyes.

Elidria does her best not to return his look, but eventually gives in and lets a few tears drip as she does.

"Just breathe," he instructs.

"I have been."

"Then lie down."

"I'm not a dog, Delsar."

"I know, just do it."

Elidria's lips start to tremble as she breathes in through her mouth. She bites down on her bottom lip and begins to cry.

Delsar wraps his arms around her. "Shhh," he softly hushes.

Elidria's eyes widen and she returns his embrace, laying her head on his shoulder. "This is where I lost everyone," she says, sobbing in his ear. "Everyone I loved. I saw them do awful things to my friends and now I have to go back. I'm being asked to face something that I barely escaped. An evil that terrifies me and that I'm not equipped to stand against. I don't want to die tonight, Delsar."

"Elidria, I-I," he says, starting to stutter, "I don't know what you want m-me t-t-to say."

"Tell me you have my back. Promise you won't let anything happen to me and that you'll stand with me no matter what."

Delsar places his hand on her head and runs it down her hair. "You are under my guard, Elidria. Nothing will happen to you. I'll make sure of it."

Elidria lets out a long-winded sigh. "Okay, Delsar. Now I'll lie down." Delsar lets her go and she slowly lies flat in the sand on her shield and back. The high blood pressure from the stress relieves as her blood starts dispersing evenly throughout her body. Her eyes fade and jostle for a moment as she feels her heart rate slow considerably. She lets out another sigh and closes her eyes. "I'm ready," she says with a calmness she's been missing since arriving in Bihnor.

"You're going to have to wait for another rotation from the patrols, but remember, they have no reason to think anyone is here," Delsar reassures. "They're in twos so they'll likely be distracting each other."

"You mean talking?" Elidria asks, opening her eyes and sitting back up.

"People tend to do that." Delsar brings his finger to his lips again and points down the ridge as one of the patrols starts to walk by.

Elidria holds her breath as they pass, though they haven't noticed she and Delsar thus far, so breathing won't likely give them away. She looks at Delsar and he gives her a nod. She releases her breath and begins the short descent down the sandy ridge. At the bottom, she quickly locates the well and crouches in its shadow, waiting for the second patrol to pass. Again she holds her breath until they do.

"Now that I know how I want it, I thought I'd get another," she hears a voice say.

"You're obsessed," says another. "Why get another if the one you have now still works?"

"Shields are my passion. Imagine duel-wielding shields. Just blocking and bashing."

"Whatever, man. You do you."

The voices start to fade and Elidria sprints across the road and into the cluster of houses. She peers around a corner to see how far the patrol has gone before circling around one of the houses. Every step she takes sounds like an anvil dropping against a rock floor in her ears. With every move, she's sure someone will hear her. Despite her fears, she slowly shimmies along the wall of this first house.

The house has no lights and seems abandoned. Locking prisoners in a house at the edge of the village would just be contributing to an easy escape. Elidria figures as much and only takes a moment to glance through a window before moving on.

Next is the blacksmith, which tells the same story. Plus, it has no room to house prisoners. A quick peek and she continues.

Her house is next. It's one of the bigger ones and one she knows very well. She rounds the corner of the blacksmith and sees light beaming out the library window. Elidria has a quick debate in her mind about going between her house and the blacksmith shop but decides against it. The light may give her away.

"Elves do," comes a voice from behind.

Elidria's heart skips and she freezes in her tracks, trying to figure out where she needs to go to avoid detection. She places a hand over her mouth as she starts breathing heavily and spins in circles, looking for a good hiding spot.

"How would you know?" asks another voice, coming from the same direction.

Despite her previous decision, she realizes she has no choice but to hide between the buildings. Her hope will be that they don't look down this alley. She dashes in and drops flat on the ground, against the house, banking that the light from the window will shine above her.

"I've fought one before." This time the voice sounds like it's passing the alley she just barely escaped to.

"I doubt that."

"A few months ago. Remember that job I did up north, that you missed?" The voices pass to the other side and the conversation remains uninterrupted.

She takes a breath and stands back to her feet. Peering around the corner, she hears, "I don't remember because I wasn't there." She sighs and clasps her hand against her chest, closing her eyes and taking a moment. She peers the other way to make sure the other patrol isn't already circled back around and waits until she hears no more voices at all. As confident as she feels she'll ever be, she moves along the side of her house and peers through the lit window. A few candles are ablaze, but the wax is all heavily melted and the room seems vacant of all life.

Only a couple bookshelves her father often reads from and his favorite chair are present. She ducks under the light and scooches over to the kitchen window. This time she spies a man washing dishes.

Elidria clamps her hand over her mouth as thoughts of excitement and questions race through her mind. It's a man she recognizes from just seeing his back. She wastes no time sneaking around to the front but remembers to check if the road is clear before climbing the stairs to the door. The door is surprisingly unlocked when she turns the knob and it swings open without a sound. This first room is a room she's very familiar with and knows exactly which boards creak and which ones don't. Delsar's idea of sending just her is making much more sense to her now.

She quickly clears the dining room the way Delsar taught her and glances up the stairs that extend up from the right side of the room. With a satisfactory nod to herself, Elidria moves through the dining room, avoiding the table and chairs before peeking through the archway leading into the kitchen. She creeps in with nary a sound. She bites her lip and brings her hand to her chest. "Dad," she says, only loud enough for him to hear.

The man stops moving and even from behind he looks like he just heard a ghost, straightening up and freezing. He places a plate down and slowly turns around. "Elly?"

"Dad." Elidria runs to him and embraces him. "You're alive," she says, digging her head under his shoulder.

"How are you here?" he asks, still in shock.

"Arviakyss, Dad. I found him and we're going to save you."

Aldameer places his hand on Elidria's head and starts to laugh, tears forming in his eyes. "Thank you, Elly," he says with a smile. He feels her body shaking violently against his. "You're shivering. You must be freezing."

"This is... something different," she says, teeth clattering. "I'm relieved is all."

"As am I. You accomplished something I thought to be impossible."

"I wish finding him was the hard part."

Aldameer pushes Elidria's hair behind her ear and looks directly at her. "What do you mean?" he asks. "What's harder?"

"Today was scary, but I fear for tomorrow. That's when we're busting you out."

Aldameer gives his daughter a stern look. "No," he says bluntly.

"What's wrong with tomorrow?"

"I don't have a problem with tomorrow. I have a problem with you fighting."

"Arviakyss has a plan that should keep us from fighting. Besides, this was my choice. I asked him to teach me to fight and now we're doing it together."

"This is *his* job now. I won't let my daughter—"

"I'm twenty years old!" she exclaims, pushing away from him. "A woman can join the army at seventeen. I am *more* than capable, Dad. I'll have you know, I fought and defeated two guards on my way here."

"Why were you fighting guards?"

"It was just a misunderstanding. Please, Dad, just support me in this and trust me."

Aldameer bears his teeth and turns his head away from his daughter. "I do trust you, but I don't know Arviakyss."

"I trust him with my life. He said he won't let anything happen to me and I believe him. It's also my job to make sure nothing happens to him."

Aldameer looks down at his feet and back at Elidria. "So why are you here alone?"

"Recon. I need good, accurate intel."

"Then ask me anything. I know quite a bit about these guys."

Elidria gives her father a smirk. "Thanks, Dad."

Aldameer nods in return.

"How many bad guys?" she asks first.

"Exactly twenty. They usually hang out on their boat, but they come up a ramp they built pretty much every day. They have two patrols at night and usually just hang out during the day."

"I've encountered the patrols. They're pretty dumb."

"Don't underestimate anyone."

"Yeah, sure," she says, rolling her eyes. "*Golly*, you sound like Delsar."

"Delsar?"

"I mean Arviakyss."

"Oh, yeah."

"What about survivors? If you're here, where's everyone else?"

"There's only six of us left," Aldameer says, turning his head. "They usually just keep us on the boat with them, but tonight they had me prepare them a feast."

Tears run down Elidria's face and she bites her bottom lip thinking about how much has been lost. "Punks," she says, making a fist. "Raiding a boat is going to be hard, but that ramp you mentioned should help."

"Elly, they kill one of us every odd day and tomorrow is another one."

"Wait, at what time?"

"It's always at the crack of dawn. It will be early tomorrow."

Elidria takes a breath through her teeth. "Then we'll stop it. Thanks for—" She stops herself short hearing the front door slamming. She looks around and dashes into the library, hiding behind her father's chair.

"Aldameer!" shouts the man as he enters the kitchen. "Splendid feast as always."

"What do you want, Gorgan?"

"Can't a guy just stop by to say hello?"

"But you're not here to say hello."

"Eh, I guess not." Gorgan tosses Aldameer a bracelet. "I just wanted to give this to you."

"This is Raymar's," Aldameer says, inspecting the arm piece Galia made for her father so many years ago.

"It is, and he's fallen ill. We've decided that since tomorrow is another odd day, we'll be putting him out of his misery."

"You're a monster!" Aldameer yells, throwing a punch.

Gorgan catches the fist and twists Aldameer around, pinning the fist to his back. He leans to his ear. "You don't have many days left. That girl had better return with Arviakyss. I hope you didn't tell us not to shoot her just because you thought you could save her."

"She's coming back," Aldameer says amidst his crying, "and you're going to wish she hadn't."

Gorgan twists Aldameer's arm tighter. "Arviakyss will hardly be a match for me."

"Drop dead!"

"Tsk, tsk, tsk. After everything I've done for you?"

Aldameer pulls his arm away. "I'd rather you killed me."

"That can be arranged." Gorgan snaps his fingers. "I know what will lighten you up! Watching a game. I'll let you watch the fight between your very own Raymar and one of my soldiers. It should be a close match," he joshes. "Bets are allowed."

Aldameer picks up a plate and starts drying it, trying his best not to have another outburst. "Leave me so I can finish."

"Whatever, Aldameer. I'll grab you early-early so you can enjoy the show."

"I'll fight," Aldameer says.

"Ha! So there's a man in there after all. Trying to make up for your past mistake?"

"I don't know what you're talking about."

"It doesn't take a genius to put the pieces together," says Gorgan. "I know why we're here."

"Gorgan, please. Just leave me alone."

Gorgan starts to laugh. "Looks like I hit that one on the nose," he says. "Whatever, pal. I really just came to give you the bracelet. See you in the morning. Go Wanderers!" he shouts, pumping his fist in the air. He starts laughing again as he leaves the house.

Elidria processes everything she just heard and her heart sinks thinking about it. She leaves her hiding spot and gently places her hand on Aldameer's shoulder who turns around to reveal streams of tears dripping down his face. "Please tell me you had nothing to do with this."

"I'm so sorry," he says, completely breaking down and looking away in shame.

"Dad, look at me." She gently grabs his chin and turns his face toward her. "Why did they listen to you and let me go? What did you do?"

He starts shaking his head and weeping. "It's my fault," he says. "It was me."

"Dad, please," she says, starting to cry with him. "I need you to focus."

"You'll never forgive me," he says, burying his head in his hands.

"You know that's not true. I will *always* forgive you. Please, Dad. I *have* to know. Why are they here?"

Aldameer shakes his head. "I can't. Please don't make me."

Elidria reaches up and wipes his tears from his face. "Whatever it was, it's over and I forgive you, but I feel it's only fair that I know."

Aldameer bites his bottom lip and turns away from his daughter. "He said to just shoot the hole. He gave me a finger and said he'd get me another if I didn't. I didn't know."

"What? Dad, you're not making any sense. What hole and whose finger?"

Aldameer looks down at his feet. "It was your mother's finger."

"The bandage?" she exclaims.

Aldameer looks back at Elidria and nods. "Yeah. The King had her finger removed and ordered me to shoot a hole. If I didn't, he was going to remove another."

"Wait...," Elidria says, trying to wrap her head around what he just said. "Wait...," she says again, shaking her head in confusion. "I don't get it. What was behind the hole?"

"It was," Aldameer swallows hard and grinds his teeth, "the Queen. *I* killed the Queen."

The words hit Elidria like a jab in the stomach. It's a confession she could have never guessed. Her world begins spinning around her. The words he spoke can't be true, but the more she thinks about them, the more they make sense. The Queen died around the same time her mother returned with Aldameer. Telrus' theories. The mercenaries wanting Arviakyss. No one allowed past Lar. It's all a coverup. For the murder of the Queen. The murder her own father just admitted to. A chill shoots through her body and she pushes her father away. "How could you?"

"I'm sorry," is all he can say.

"It was you!" she snaps. "Mom didn't *accidentally* fall from the cliff. She jumped because, unlike you, she had a conscience and couldn't live with herself!"

"That's not true," Aldameer defends.

"It's thirty feet down to soft sand. She would have needed to jump headfirst. Of course she killed herself! And all these innocent lives.

They're dying for *your* mistake but you couldn't just stop there! Now you're sacrificing Arviakyss for something *you* should have died for."

"Elly, I'm—"

"No," she says, stopping him, "I've heard enough lies from you. I'm saving this village. The *whole* village. Unfortunately, that includes you."

"Elly, please."

"Please, what?" she exclaims before storming away from him and for the door. She then looks over her shoulder. "Arviakyss will never forgive you for this and I'm not sure I do either. You'd better *hope* I do because *I* decide your fate." She leaves the house and closes the door, ignoring anything else her father has to say.

Delsar is exactly where Elidria left him on the ridge. "We're clear," he tells her, letting her know that no one followed her. "That was fast."

"It was... too much," she says, shivering uncontrollably. "B-b-but I got what w-we need."

Delsar gives Elidria a funny look which she doesn't see as she feels too ashamed to look at Delsar directly. "Okay?" he questions, taking Elidria's reluctant hand and helping her down the ridge.

The walk back to the camp is emotionally grueling. Every step Elidria takes is one more step that the truth is held from Delsar. A truth she now has.

Delsar leads her safely back and flattens out the map from Lar. "Okay, what did you find?"

Elidria sniffles and wipes away her tears. "Right, um, there are twenty mercenaries, but I only encountered four on patrol. Another came to the house I was in. His name was Gorgan and he sounded like the leader. The other mercenaries are on their boat with five Bihnor survivors." One of Elidria's tears drips onto the map and Delsar notices.

"What happened down there?" he asks.

"Morning, Delsar," she says, brushing off his question. "We have to rescue everyone by morning. They plan to execute another prisoner then."

"We'll sleep for two hours tonight and leave three hours before the sun rises. Infiltrating the boat is going to be a real challenge though."

"There's a ramp down the cliff which should help."

Delsar looks at Elidria. "Anything else?"

Elidria closes her eyes. "Yes." She takes a moment before continuing. "The survivor I found was my father."

"That's good news."

She shakes her head and even more tears fall. "No, the mercenaries are here to silence you."

"I know that."

"And him, Delsar."

Elidria's words hit Delsar. He already knew they wanted him dead, but Elidria's father, too? Now it's all starting to make sense. Delsar starts to back away. "What are you saying?"

Elidria is overwhelmed with emotions. "I'm sorry," she says, "for everything he put you through."

"Your father—"

"Killed the Queen."

Delsar turns away from Elidria. The bubble of emotions and memories he shared with Elidria throughout the month pops and it gets replaced by the same hate he had when they first met. "No," he says, walking toward the horses.

"Delsar, where are you going?" Elidria asks in tears.

"I'm not doing this."

She knew it would be hard on him but his sudden reaction to just leave is not what she was expecting, though this whole night feels like it's moving too fast. It's surreal, a nightmare. She reaches out for Delsar's shoulder. "What he did hurts me as—" She gets cut off as Delsar flips her over onto her back.

"This is justice, Elidria!" Delsar yells, saliva flying into her face. "He deserves to watch as everything he created with his lies gets ripped from him!" Delsar straightens back up and composes himself. "There are two horses. If you wish to come, I'm leaving."

Elidria rolls over into her knees. "What's wrong with you? There are six innocent people down there."

Delsar just scoffs. "Six?" he asks over his shoulder.

"Don't you dare turn your back on them!"

Delsar whips around and points directly at her. "When they all turned their backs on me? They deserve nothing less."

"But I didn't."

Delsar jumps on Amber and ignores her.

"Delsar!" she yells again. "I've never turned my back on you! Don't you turn your back on me!"

"Gendief can get you anywhere you want to go."

"You're making a mistake," she pleads.

"My only mistake was giving my trust away."

"That was no mistake," she says, on the verge of breaking down. "Please, don't do this."

Delsar looks back at Elidria. "Goodbye, Elidria." He kicks his horse into a gallop.

"Delsar!" she cries after him. "Don't leave me! Delsar!" Elidria gets back on her feet and then slams them down. "Fine! I'll do it myself! Do you hear me, Delsar! I don't need you! I can—" Her words get interrupted by her own whimpering. "I-I can—" She collapses to her knees and drops her head. It's no use. He's gone and it is just her. No more words will come no matter how hard she tries, because tonight, she lost everyone. Just like when she first fled Bihnor, she is all alone.

CHAPTER 16

THE DARKNESS

6 Years Ago...

"Arviakyss and the Queen have returned, my Lord," Malgo says, bowing gracefully.

"Then bring in our guest of honor," the King instructs. "I think it's time he gets reunited."

"As you wish, my Lord." Malgo hustles to the throne room doors and pulls them open.

Two guards escort a confused Aldameer. "My King!" he exclaims and quickly bows.

"Leave us," the King commands the guards.

They both also bow before leaving and closing the doors.

"Arise, Aldameer, and come forward."

Aldameer gets to his feet and slowly approaches the King.

Malgo walks beside him and begins giving him instructions. "Do not touch his Highness or his throne. You do not need to bow again until you are leaving. He wishes to have a conversation with you so you are allowed to talk freely with him, but always be courteous and never interrupt him. He prefers 'King' when being spoken to by commoners. Got it?"

"I...I do."

Malgo stops with Aldameer before the King and bows one more time. "I present Aldameer of Bihnor, my Lord." He then looks over at Aldameer and gives him a nod.

"M-my King, you summoned me here and I know not why. Am I in trouble for something?"

"No, nothing like that. This is about your success at nearly *all* my archery competitions. You're a natural and I would very much like to use your skills."

"I've heard the offer from your Queen. I've already told her that I can't right now."

"This isn't the request from the Queen, nor will I be asking."

"Of course, my King. What do you need of me?"

The King grabs castle prints and an arrow from his stand and walks them over to Aldameer. "Do you recognize this arrow?" he asks.

"It looks like one of Arviakyss'."

"That's because it is. I need you to take this arrow and bring it to the top of this northern battlement," the King explains. "There is a tower directly west, about two hundred fifty feet, from it. This one," he says, pointing at the prints. He turns the paper over. "As you can see, this tower has small slits all along its eastern wall. I want you to shoot through the one that's sixth from the top with this arrow and that's it."

Aldameer shakes his head. "My King, I don't want anything to do with your dirty work. If there is an enemy in that tower, it might be best to use your guard."

"Aldameer!" says the King, raising his voice and standing straight. "I am not asking! You *will* take this arrow and you *will* shoot it through the vent."

"No!" Aldameer says back. "I'm not killing anyone."

"I never said you were."

"Then why have your guards leave unless you don't want them to know."

The King scowls at Aldameer before signaling to Malgo. Malgo approaches the King and the King whispers something into his ear.

"Yes, my Lord," he says before going into another room connected to this one.

"I understand your wife went missing a few weeks ago," says the King. "Actually, it was right after the Deadliest Draw, wasn't it?"

"What do you know of this?" asks Aldameer.

"I know it would be a shame if you were never to see her again."

"I still won't do it!" Aldameer exclaims. "And I don't need your help finding her."

"I never said anything about helping you find her, Aldameer."

A muffled scream emanates from the room Malgo just disappeared in. Aldameer recognizes it and immediately turns.

The King draws his sword and presses it against his neck. "I didn't dismiss you."

Malgo returns to the room with a small pouch in his hand, dripping a trail of blood behind.

"What did you do?" cries Aldameer.

"I have it, my Lord," says Malgo.

"Then show him."

Malgo opens the bag but Aldameer looks away. "I won't look," he says.

"Look in the bag, commoner," Malgo demands.

Aldameer shuts his eyes tight. "No."

"Malgo, he doesn't need to look. Instead, just go get another one," the King instructs.

"Of course, my Lord." Malgo turns back for the room.

"Wait!" yells Aldameer, grabbing Malgo by his arm.

"Unhand me!"

"It's fine, Malgo," says the King. "I assume you changed your mind."

Aldameer swallows hard and nods.

"Very well. Show him again."

Malgo holds the bag in front of Aldameer and opens it back up.

Aldameer only peeks for a moment and is immediately flooded with grief. "Oh, no," he says as tears streak down his face. "Why would you do this? My wife's done nothing wrong."

"You disobeyed me and she paid the price. It seems fair to me seeing how marriage makes you an equal in my country."

"As partners!" screams Aldameer, trembling. "Not like this! I disobeyed. Not her. Please, just let her go."

"Then take this arrow and shoot it through the vent."

"You'll just kill us after."

"Malgo, even things off."

"Yes, my Lord," he answers.

"No, stop!" Aldameer closes his eyes and starts taking quick breaths. "Just give me the arrow. I'll do it. I'll do your bidding. Please, just promise you'll let her go."

"You have my word as King of Ithendar. No more harm will come to her *should* you succeed. If you miss, I'm afraid I won't have a promise anymore."

"I won't miss," says Aldameer. "I'll hit the shot, just don't hurt her."

The King smiles and hands Aldameer the arrow. "Be sure not to touch the tip of that arrow. That could end your mission pretty quickly."

"You're a despicable monster." Aldameer snatches the arrow from him and turns to leave.

"Oh, Aldameer," says Malgo, backing away from the furious husband, "you must bow to his Highness before leaving."

Aldameer looks over his shoulder and spits on the ground before continuing.

"Collect your bow from the guards outside," says the King. "And Aldameer, if you tell anyone, I can assure you her death will be worse than you could possibly imagine," he warns.

Aldameer walks through the doors and doesn't look back.

The King waits until the doors close again before giving Malgo more instructions. "He'll figure out who he killed when he hears reports about it. Kill his wife and when he completes his job, kill him, too."

Malgo bows but stays in his lowered position. "Leaving no loose ends is very wise, but might I suggest something else?"

"Always."

Malgo straightens up. "His skills are extraordinary and killing him would be a waste. If he goes through with your orders, he'll prove he can be easily manipulated. We can use him again for other targets."

"Then what about his wife?"

"She's the key. As long as she's alive, he won't tell anyone."

The King considers for a moment. "Very well. We'll let them return to Bihnor together. We know where they live should we ever need their services again."

"Or should we ever need to silence them."

"A splendid call, Malgo. He will definitely be of use to us again."

He took everything from me! Delsar thinks to himself, playing back what Elidria told him in his head. *Yet, she wanted me to save him? It's not just me he took everything from, he took it all from Elidria, too.* Delsar pulls his horse to a stop and jumps off. He picks up a stick and hurls it as hard as he can. "Why?" he screams into the woods.

He drops to his knees and closes his eyes but now only images of Elidria fill his mind. One specifically from the gibbet. It's of her with her hand on his chest, smiling up at him. *"Everyone makes their own mistakes, big and small,"* she had said. *"You need to accept it, both theirs and yours. Once you realize your mistakes, it's much easier to help others with theirs instead of judging them and casting them aside."*

"This wasn't how it was supposed to be," Delsar says to himself. "Why did I care?"

"Forgiveness, Delsar."

"No!" Delsar yells, jumping back to his feet. "Forgiveness leads to betrayal."

In Delsar's mind, Elidria's face changes from crying to smiling to crying again. All the memories flood in, of him letting her down, betraying her. Failing her. *"I forgive you. I always have. I never turned my back on you."*

Delsar brings his hands to his face and then runs them up, through his hair. "Please smile," he says to his image of Elidria, but she doesn't. His last memory of her is of him leaving her in tears.

"Who's there?" comes a voice from the road.

Delsar pulls out his sword as the sounds of hooves and wheels rapidly approach. "Don't come any closer!" he warns.

One of the riders jumps off his horse and sparks a torch. "Mr. Delsar, is that you?" he asks.

"Telrus?" Delsar drops his guard for a moment but quickly raises his sword back up. "What are you doing here?"

"I should be asking you the same thing. Where's Miss Eldra?"

Delsar's face goes white and he grinds his teeth. "You first."

"Put your sword away, son." An older, gruff man dismounts his horse.

"M-m-master?" Delsar's eyes widen in disbelief.

Galius stands by his horse, an unsure smile lifting the corners of his mustache. Above his smile, his brow is furrowed with concern. He senses the emotional turmoil racking Delsar's heart.

During his darkest hour, Delsar always thought the unexpected arrival of his beloved mentor would fill him with the strength and light he needed to conquer any challenge. But now, he only feels shame. He knows he possesses many good memories with this man, but none come to mind. Guilt and confusion rise like shadows in his heart, blotting out the unconditional love and respect Galius has always shown. "I don't understand. Why are *you* here?" Delsar asks his master.

Telrus smiles. "Galius is my partner. He's the reason we started tracking you in the first place."

"Why keep this from me?"

"I wanted you to trust me for who I am. Not who I know."

"So *you* told him who I was," Delsar says to his master, looking betrayed.

"I told no one," answers Galius. "He figured that out on his own."

"It doesn't matter," Delsar says, his voice unsteady. "I told you not to come. Yet, here you are."

"You said not to leave my family," Galius explains, "so I didn't. They're in Lar until I'm done here. That's another reason why Telrus traveled so much faster than us on his own."

"You came to help?"

"Yes," Telrus cuts in. "Consider us reinforcements."

"Then you came for nothing." Delsar turns away. "They don't deserve to be saved." The darkness comes crashing down around Delsar. All these years, he had held close to the belief that caring about others only got you hurt. Elidria had almost changed his mind about that, almost broken down his walls. But she was wrong. *In the end, everyone betrays you.*

"Why do you say that? Mr. Delsar, where is Miss Eldra?"

"It was the King, Telrus. He had the Queen killed. I'm going to kill him myself."

"You didn't answer my question. Where is Miss Eldra?"

"Her father killed the Queen. They're getting what they deserve."

"So you left her?" exclaims Telrus.

"I did!" yells Delsar. "Her father took everything from me. I want nothing to do with him or his—" Delsar gets overwhelmed and shakes his head. "I don't know."

"You can't do that," says Telrus. "You had a job to do."

"That's enough, Telrus." Galius approaches Delsar. "Let's talk, just you and me."

"Just go away."

"She didn't choose her father," Galius says, getting closer still. "Just like you didn't choose yours. Things like that are out of our hands, but this choice to hate is your own. Don't cast her aside for something she had no control over."

"The world did it to me."

Galius quickly grabs Delsar's blade with his gloved hand and steps in with a palm strike, knocking Delsar down and taking his sword.

Delsar doesn't attempt to catch himself. He lands on his back, breath rushing from his lungs as he hits the forest floor limply.

Galius places the blade against Delsar's neck. "You could have stopped me from knocking you down and turning your own sword against you, but you didn't. You failed. Just like how you failed to save the Queen."

"I didn't kill her."

"But you were with her. She was under *your* guard."

Delsar looks away. "Her quarters were secured. How was I supposed to know there was a flaw?"

"That doesn't matter," says Galius. "You and Eldra are both failures."

"Eldra is not a failure!"

"She should have stopped her father from killing the Queen but she didn't. You both failed and now the Queen is dead."

"Don't you say that! She couldn't have known what he planned."

"And she didn't," Galius confirms. "Just like you didn't know about the room's flaw or that I was going to knock you down. The King and her father killed the Queen. Don't blame anyone else for that."

"Tell that to everyone else. I killed the Queen. That's what everyone believes."

"How can *everyone* believe it if *I* don't? People repeat things they've been told, that doesn't make them right. Don't let the lies told by others define you." Galius removes the blade from Delsar's neck and holds out his hand. "Everyone here believes in Delsar and Eldra. If that means getting court-martialed, then so be it."

Delsar stares at the proffered hand. "You shouldn't. Arviakyss is a failure."

"I said 'Delsar,' not Arviakyss."

"I don't get it."

"It was Arviakyss who failed and was betrayed," says Galius. "It was Delsar who was found and saved by the girl. You turned on her because of what happened to Arviakyss, not what happened to Delsar."

Delsar turns his head away from Galius. "She never turned her back on me," he says. "I did. Delsar *is* a failure."

"If you walk away you are, but that's what makes you different from Arviakyss. You're allowed to make mistakes and stumble. Getting up and rising, that is something someone viewed as perfect couldn't do, but someone imperfect, like Delsar, can."

Delsar only moves his eyes to look back at Galius.

"Follow us to Bihnor, please. If you decide to help, you'll already be there. If you decide not to, you can just abandon us again."

"I don't want her to see me after what I did to her."

"Then her last memory of you will be of your failure."

Delsar pictures her crying face again. His eyes shut and more tears form. "I don't want that," he says, whimpering.

Galius bends forward, letting his still-outstretched hand move closer to Delsar's. "Then rise."

Delsar stares at it. How many times would he have to fail before Galius gives up on him, he wonders bitterly. *How can he be so... forgiving?*

There was that word again. Elidria's voice rings in his ear. *"Then start here. Forgive yourself."*

Galius' outstretched hand comes into focus. His face comes into view, a glorious light chasing away the darkness of his despair and confusion.

I accept it, he thinks, a silent commitment. Blinking fiercely, he takes the hand.

Galius pulls him to his feet and immediately wraps his arms around Delsar. The two embrace for a long time. Delsar's shoulders shudder with silent tears. Galius stands and holds him, offering no further words, letting him release six years of guilt and frustration.

Finally, Delsar pulls away. Eyes red and puffy from his tears, he looks into Galius' face. His cheeks are marked with glistening, wet trails as well. "Thank you," Delsar says hoarsely.

Galius nods and holds Delsar's sword out.

As Delsar takes the weapon and returns it to its sheath, he feels a weight has lifted off his shoulders. A weight he had carried since the Queen's death but never realized could be dissolved. Delsar thinks of the Queen and feels none of his old bitterness. *Ah*, he thinks, amazed by the change. *This is what it must feel like to forgive oneself.* He turns to Galius, including Telrus in his gaze. "Okay. What now?"

Galius grins broadly. "Let me introduce you to the team."

Delsar nods.

"Good." He places his hand on Delsar's shoulder and gestures to Telrus. "That's Telrus. He's my very young partner." He then leads Delsar over to a very large wagon with two men sitting up front. "These are Castor and Allbus. You met them entering Lar."

"It's a pleasure to fight for Bihnor," says Castor.

"Sure," replies Delsar. "What's with the paddy wagon?"

Telrus takes his question. "For all the arrests, of course. You can't just cuff everyone and hope they follow."

Delsar brings his hand to his eyes. More tears roll down his cheeks. The arrests were Elidria's idea and even Telrus is trying to go through with it.

"There's one more on the team." Galius points to a man walking from the side of the carriage. "Once I learned your birth-name, I had Telrus do some digging."

"Hello, Delsar," says the man.

Delsar reaches into his bag and pulls out his knife. He grabs the man by his collar and slams him against the wagon.

Galius and Telrus are about to intervene, but the man holds up his hand. "No," he says to them.

Delsar lifts him to his toes and places his knife against his neck. "You left us!" he shouts, spitting in his face. "You left her and now she's dead!"

One of the patrolling mercenaries puts his arm out to stop his comrade. "Did you hear that?" he asks.

"It's just that fox again."

"Possibly. It came from the blacksmith. I'm going to check it out."

"May as well. It beats walking in circles for two hours."

The mercenaries approach the blacksmith shop and listen outside. "I don't hear anything anymore," one of them whispers.

"We should still check it out. We *are* expecting that Champion to show up at some point."

"It's gonna be pitch-black in there. Do you have a light?"

"I don't. Let me go grab the wick from the street lamp."

"And I'll watch the door to make sure it doesn't escape," he says, crouching down and readying his blade.

"All this for a fox."

"Just pretend it's not. It's more exciting that way."

"Yeah, yeah," the other mercenary says, on his way toward the lamp.

"You know, if we can catch it, maybe we can make it our pet or our mascot. That would be pretty neat." The light behind him disappears. "Sevv, you weren't supposed to put it out," says the mercenary watching the door. He turns around and is met with a sword through his shoulder. It pushes him back and pins him against the blacksmith door. A pain shoots through the man's body, but before he can scream, the edge of a shield bashes into his temple, knocking him out.

Elidria slides her blade out and lets the man drop to the ground, completely limp. "Two down," she says as she slides her shield over her back. She grabs a pair of cuffs from her belt and restrains the man before dragging him into the blacksmith shop.

She then grabs and cuffs the man who was retrieving the wick that she knocked out with a rock. Dragging him proves more difficult than the first one. "I know, exactly, how, you are—*Golly*," she says, completely out of breath, "why are you so heavy?" She starts again and slowly inches him into the shop, plopping him next to the other. "I know exactly how you're *both* going to feel when you wake up. Believe me."

"The lamp is out again," says a voice from outside, spooking Elidria. "The glass is open, too. The other patrol must already be on it."

"You know what might be funny?"

"What?"

"If we can get it relit before they come back. We'll keep the glass open, too."

"That's great! They'll be so confused."

"The blacksmith probably has some wicks."

"We won't be able to find anything in there without a light. Let's grab a torch."

"There's no time for that. I'm sure there are lights in the shop."

Elidria scans her surroundings for anything useful. It's no use. The shop really is pitch-black. *I can use the darkness,* she thinks to herself and moves away from the door, waiting.

The door opens and the silhouettes of two men appear. "Find his desk. The blacksmith likely kept a candle there."

One of them trips over one of the knocked out men as he enters. "Watch yourself," he warns. "There's stuff on the ground."

"Yeah, I'm not moving until my eyes have had time to adjust. I'm not tripping into something sharp."

Of course. I've been in here longer, Elidria realizes. She sneaks along the wall and closes the door.

"Why'd you close the door? Now it's even darker."

"I didn't close it."

There are only two patrols and I already dealt with one. That means I don't have to be quiet with these guys.

"It must have a spring or a weight that closes it." He walks over to open the door again, but when he extends his arm, Elidria drops her elbow against his hand. He cries out in both pain and shock before Elidria drives her palm up into his chin. He stumbles back and trips over the two unconscious bodies laid on the floor, landing on his back.

"You see what I mean? Just wait until your eyes adjust."

His eyes wobble around before coming back to his senses. "There's someone else in here," he says, keeping his dislocated jaw from moving. "I'm hurt bad, Rolend."

"Where are you?" demands Rolend, drawing his sword.

Elidria tosses a coin from her bag behind him.

277

He spins around with his sword swinging, only for it to get caught on the wall.

Elidria kicks the back of his leg, dropping him to a knee.

He swings back around, but this time his blade meets Elidria's shield which she braces with two hands. The sword slides down the shield and Elidria drops her shield's edge into the man's wrist, snapping it.

He drops his sword and cries, "Wait! Please don't kill us."

"No promises," she replies.

She doesn't notice the other mercenary grabbing his partner's sword. He swings from the ground with his hand that didn't get its fingers crushed and impacts one of Elidria's shinguards. The plate armor bends from the strike making the attack feel like someone bashed her shin with an iron rod.

She screams and pulls her leg up before smashing her foot down on the hand that holds the sword. There's more crunching under her foot before she brings her knee up into the face of the mercenary, knocking him on his back again. This time, out for good.

Rolend grabs Elidria's hair and she quickly drives her shield up, forcing him to let go. Rolend then kicks her unguarded stomach, moving her back. "I can see you know," he says.

"Good. Now you can tell your unconscious friends that you all got beat by a little girl." She switches her shield to one hand and draws her sword.

The mercenary throws up his hands, realizing he has no weapon of his own anymore. "I have to be alive to tell them," he says.

"Doesn't mean I won't kill you after. Put your hands behind your back and turn around." The man does just that and Elidria grabs another pair of restraints for him.

"That hurts!" he shouts. "You broke my wrist!"

"Oops. Let me help relieve your pain." She smacks the back of his head with her sword's counterweight, dropping him to the floor.

She cuffs the other mercenary with her penultimate pair of restraints and exits the shop's side door. The very one she used to trick the first patrol.

The lights are out in her house, which means her father is either in bed or not home. The second scenario would be a huge blow to her plan.

She enters the very familiar house and even with no lights, she easily locates and climbs the stairs. Her father's room is the one at the end of the hall. She draws her sword and slowly opens the door.

There he is, sitting in his chair by the window. Elidria sneaks in behind him and places her blade on his shoulder. "Aldameer," she says.

Aldameer starts to turn his head.

"Don't look at me!" she exclaims.

"Are you here to kill your father?" he asks.

"I would never kill anyone, even you. Besides, you're too important."

"Elly, I—"

"Don't *ever* call me that name."

"Elidria—"

"It's *Eldra*."

Aldameer sighs and nods. "Eldra, everything I did I did to protect you, your mother, and everything we worked so hard to create."

"Good job. Your protection led to the death of your wife, the destruction of your village, and risks the life of your daughter as she tries to pick up what's left. You're a horrible person."

"Eldra, I didn't know I was killing the Queen. I swear. The King chopped your mother's finger off and said he'd do more if I didn't shoot through a hole in the wall. I had no idea what was on the other side."

"But did you know there was a person on the other side?"

"I didn't know it was the Queen."

Elidria's nose crinkles as she grabs Aldameer by his collar. "But you knew you were killing someone, didn't you?" she quietly screams, pulling him from his chair and pinning him to the wall.

"What would you have me do? They had your mother. What if it was Galia they had? What would you have done?"

"What I'm doing now. Fighting back. They already took her from me but you don't see *me* giving up. You should have fought back or told someone. You could have even asked for help."

"He would have killed Arlayna."

"She's dead anyway! She's dead because of you! You let her kill herself!"

"That's not true! She didn't kill herself. I swear."

"Look around you! Maybe you did save her, but she's *all* you saved. You doomed this village, all its people, our friends, family, all of it because you didn't stand against what was wrong. You taught me time and time again to stand up to injustice. To speak up when something is wrong, yet when it was needed from you the most, you blew it."

"I'm working hard to fix this, Eldra. There's more going on than you know. That night I killed the Queen was the start of one rolling snowball out of many. Saving your mother was more important than you realize."

"Again, you failed. You saved her for nothing. On top of that, you took everything from Arviakyss. He has nothing. You even took me away from him. You've sacrificed him to save your village. You're evil! How can you say you're trying to fix things when you're doing what you can to make things worse?"

"I planned for him to win, not lose. He's the Queen's Champion. He can handle a group of mercenaries."

"You know that's not true. You told me not to fight and to let him handle it. You expect him to lose." Elidria closes her eyes. "You took his hope and meaning away. I did everything I could to give those back to him and I did. Then you took them from him again. Everything we worked for. And I hate you for that! I hate you for killing the Queen! I hate you for killing mom! I hate you for dooming Galia and everyone else! How dare you care for only yourself."

"That's not true, Elly."

"Don't say that name!"

"You don't understand and I need you to," he says.

"I understand enough. Turn around and put your hands behind your back," she commands, putting her sword away.

"What are you doing?"

"I'm doing things *my* way."

"What will this accomplish?"

"I'm turning you in to Lar. You'll admit what you did and explain what's happening here. Then, Lar will deploy its army and wipe these fools out. *That* is what I'm doing."

Aldameer looks over his shoulder as she restrains him. "Tell me, did you ever tell anyone about this attack."

"Everyone," she says.

"Then why would they believe me?"

"They just will so shut up! I know a guard there who already knows what's going on here. If I can get you to him, your testimony will prove Delsar's innocence and then they'll believe me."

Aldameer places his forehead against the wall. "I'm sorry for putting you through all this."

"You deserve no forgiveness. Only justice."

"What about Raymar? You won't be back in time to save him."

Elidria's plan shatters before her. Raymar being executed in the morning slipped her mind while making her plan. "I can't save him," she says, her voice filled with regret. "Not without the man you destroyed."

"You must mean Arviakyss," says a voice from the door. "That's a shame. Does that mean he's not coming?"

Elidria spins around and grabs for her sword but gets met with a shoulder that sends her toppling over Aldameer's bed. She scrambles to her feet and gets grabbed around her neck by a firm hand.

Gorgan lifts her off her feet with just one of his hands, his arm fully extended. He carries her back toward the center of the room.

The sudden realization of just how strong this man is sends a pulse of terror through Elidria. Fear is something she's used to, but she's almost always had Delsar to help her overcome such fears. She's on her own for this.

She smacks the hand with her fist, but that does nothing. She then reaches for her sword again, but another hand grabs her arm and starts twisting. She screams and swings her legs over the arm that holds her, pressing her feet against Gorgan's shoulder and chest. She pushes and slides from his grip, crashing hard against the floor.

She starts to get back to her feet but gets met by a fist, punching down into her face. She goes back to the ground but quickly retaliates with a kick to his knee. Gorgan's knee stands firm so she brings her other leg up and between his legs, bending him forward. His bent posture allows her to kick his face, stumbling him back. With the window she created, she finally climbs back to her feet.

Her face hurts like nothing else before, but broken bones are the least of her concern right now. *Avoid and counter,* she remembers. She throws her hands up, ready for the next strike. It comes in the form of another punch. She gracefully parries it away with her right arm and sends a roundhouse kick into his stomach.

The kick connects but Gorgan is not hurt or surprised by such a counter. He wraps his left arm around the leg in his stomach and raises his right elbow to snap her knee.

Elidria spins more to her right, allowing her leg to bend with the strike. On her hands and knees, she then sends the back of her left foot into his face, knocking him back.

She uses the time she thinks she has to get to her feet again but is met by another fist. This time she goes down and her body doesn't let her get back up. She lays there as Gorgan grabs her by her upper-left arm and he pulls her to her feet.

Elidria screams from the pain in her arm, which sends another rush of adrenaline through her body. She drops her bracer on the man's thumb, popping it from place and releasing its grip. Elidria then sets herself and jabs Gorgan's face. She follows it up with a cross and an ascending palm strike to his chin.

Gorgan stumbles back but she doesn't let up. She keeps her hands open as she repeatedly palms his face, even as his back hits the wall.

Elidria makes fists with her hands in hopes of finishing him off, but that is a mistake. She sends another jab with her left hand but Gorgan thrusts his head forward against her fist and the wrist gives. She screams but quickly retaliates with another right cross.

Gorgan sends his own fist into hers, driving straight through it. Her hand crunches from the impact and she steps back in more pain.

She tries again but Gorgan simply swats the attack away with his right hand, and then again when she tries with her left. Her right attacks but he easily avoids it and delivers his own strike to her ribs.

He follows it up with a kick to her other side but she catches his leg under her arm. This does not deter him in any way. He punches at her face, and even on one leg delivers enough force to drive Elidria's own fist into her face as his attack impacts her block.

She releases and stumbles back.

He raises his right fist again and she throws her hands up. His punch pushes through her arms and into her face, dropping her to a knee. He punches again through her defenses and his fist connects with her face for the fourth time.

She drops to all fours, blood dripping to the floor. Gorgan grabs her hair and lifts her up to face him. Her face is cracked and bruised, covered with blood. Her left eye is completely black and won't even open. Her other eye droops and only her right arm moves as she tries again for her sword. She gives her all trying to pull it from its sheath but her arm gives up. "Then get it over with," she says with what little energy she has left.

"With pleasure." Gorgan brings his right arm back for what will likely be a killing blow.

"Wait!" shouts Aldameer. "She knows where Arviakyss is. You need her."

"Is that so?" Gorgan brings her face closer to his. "Well, Little Missy, looks like we'll have to continue this later. You're going to help me kill Arviakyss."

She mumbles something, but it's inaudible.

"What was that? I couldn't hear you."

"Finding him will be your mistake," she repeats.

"Maybe so." Gorgan slings her over his shoulder, causing her shield to slide from her back and crash to the ground. "Grab that and come with me, Aldameer."

"But my hands are behind my back."

"Figure it out." Gorgan walks from the room. "You're a good fighter. Tough, too. I respect that. Your talent will be perfect for the ring."

"Mother loved you more than anything!" Delsar yells into his father's face. "She loved you even more than she loved me. How could you leave her?" Delsar's angry face changes to a sad and disappointed look.

"It's my biggest regret, Delsar," Ligrei responds. "I never would have left if I knew she was going to get sick."

"But you never came back. Even after she died. For three years you left me on my own. Then I met him," Delsar says, pointing at Galius. "He was a real father to me."

"I'm sorry I wasn't there for you. I'm here now, not to be your father, but to be a help. I know I've lost my right to call you my son."

"But that's just it. My life was molded around the year you left and mom died. It shaped me and I never would have met Elidria if you hadn't."

"What are you saying?"

Delsar tightens his grip around Ligrei's collar and presses his knife harder against his neck, drawing a drop of blood. "This is me hating you for letting mom die and abandoning us!" he snarls.

There's a fear on Ligrei's face as he turns his head and closes his eyes, waiting for the blade to pierce through his throat.

Delsar glares at his submissive father and watches the drop of blood slowly drip down the man's neck before disappearing into his tunic. He takes an exasperated breath through his teeth before grinding them.

Ligrei slowly opens his eyes up and looks back at Delsar. His breathing trembles.

Delsar quickly turns his own head away, digging his mouth into his own shoulder.

"Delsar—"

"Don't speak," Delsar says, stopping his father. He looks down at their feet and shakes his head. "Always," he says, under his breath. He looks back into his father's eyes. His adrenaline begins pumping through his blood and his face changes to red. His breathing hastens and his grip on Ligrei's collar tightens, lifting his body higher off the ground.

Delsar lets out a loud, frustrated growl, causing Ligrei to close his eyes again. He can sense the turmoil in his son and the pain he's in. The same pain and turmoil he felt when he left his son so many years ago. Ligrei holds in his breath and waits for the plunge. The plunge that in Delsar's mind is justice. A long-awaited justice. Ligrei opens his eyes, feeling the knife pulled from his neck and dropping by his foot. Before he can look down, two arms wrap firmly around him.

"And this is the forgiveness she shared with me," Delsar says, calming his breathing and placing his chin over his father's shoulder.

Ligrei's mouth hangs open. He doesn't know if he should just accept the forgiveness or hug his son back. "I don't understand," he says.

"I'm defeating the darkness," Delsar replies determinedly. "I'm supposed to be a hero now. That's something I forgot." Delsar releases his father.

Ligrei's eyes start to water up. "I didn't expect to be forgiven."

"Neither did I, but no matter what I did, she never gave up on me and *always* forgave. It's a grace I don't deserve." He looks back, sharing the subtlest of smiles with Galius. "She's who *I* want to be like. She's *my* inspiration."

"She sounds like an amazing person."

"Dad," says Delsar, grabbing Ligrei by his shoulders, "I need your help."

"What is it, Delsar?" Ligrei asks.

"I'm afraid I just made the same mistake you did so many years ago."

"How so?"

"I left her. I left Elidria."

"Then you get her back," says Ligrei. "You do whatever it takes."

A chill shoots through Delsar's body. His realization of what he just did with his father and the situation he left Elidria in hit him hard. He looks down at their feet and hides his tears. "I… I have to go."

"We'll be behind you."

Delsar wipes under his nose with his sleeve. "Telrus!" he shouts, whipping around.

"What is it?" Telrus asks, fondling with his horse's bridle.

"I need Amber."

"I just got her back," says Telrus, as the bridle slides off.

Delsar ignores the comment and deftly mounts her.

"All right, Delsar," says Telrus, sliding the bridle back on and handing the reins to Delsar. "She'll get you there."

"Do you have a plan?" Galius asks.

Delsar's horse spins on its hooves being amped up by its rider's sudden excitement. "A plan? Actually, I do."

"Wakie, wakie." Gorgan kicks Elidria in the stomach.

She sits on her knees with her hands bound by the very restraints she put on her father. Her arms are behind her back and wrapped around a post. She makes no sound and doesn't react to the kick.

"Get up!" Gorgan yells. He bends to Elidria's height and grabs under her jaw, forcing her to her feet. "Pathetic," he says, looking at her wincing face.

"Why don't you take these restraints off and we'll see just how pathetic I can be," she replies, faintly.

Gorgan smirks at her response.

Elidria returns his smirk with a stare from her drooping right eye.

One of Elidria's wrists feels the pressure of her restraint coming off. She attempts some form of resistance, but her arm doesn't move as it's grabbed by someone else who stands behind her. She hears and feels the restraint being strapped back on.

"Now come." Gorgan steps behind her and grabs the back shoulder of her top and pushes her along. "Time to kill another villager. I thought you'd enjoy the show."

Elidria says nothing and allows herself to be pushed along.

"We're missing four soldiers from last night. That wouldn't be your doing, would it?"

"You're thugs, not soldiers," she replies.

"I guess you're right," says Gorgan. "Not that I care. Being a thug pays more."

Elidria stomps on his foot and Gorgan yanks her back. "You're a terrible human being," she tells him.

"Oh my," he exclaims, sarcastically. "You've opened my mind. From now on I'll change my ways."

Gorgan brings her to the village center. Another eleven mercenaries gather and Aldameer is bound and held by one of them.

"Eldra!" he shouts to her.

Elidria looks away from him but Gorgan leads her directly next to him.

"Welcome, fellow Wanderers!" Grogan yells to the crowd, all men. "Today is yet another odd day of the month. This means another villager will have a chance to fight for his life in a battle to the death!"

The mercenaries begin cheering and smashing their weapons and shields together.

"Bring out the first competitor!"

Two mercenaries escort Raymar into the square. He blinks as the sunlight hits his face and Elidria can see a sheen of sweat coating his dark face. If not for the guards supporting him on either side, he looks as though he wouldn't be able to stand on his own.

"His opponent today will be..." Gorgan reaches into a helmet and pulls out a slip of paper, "Fulcus!"

The small crowd cheers even louder as a man enters the imaginary ring. He removes his belt and helmet before pumping his fist in the air and joining the cheer.

"The rules are quite simple," Gorgan explains. "Of course you all know them by now, but we have a new face in the crowd today!"

The crowd shouts and screams even more.

"Quiet down!" Gorgan's shouts. He waits until they stop before continuing. "The rules are simple. No weapons, armor, or shields. Other than that, fight to the death!"

The crowd explodes into louder cheering than ever and begins chanting Fulcus' name.

"You're all barbarians," Elidria says to Gorgan.

Gorgan looks down at her and that's when he sees something shiny sticking out of her arm's bandage. "What's this?" He grabs her arm and slides out a key. "You cheeky girl. How were you going to reach this with your arms behind your back."

"You can't figure that out?" she asks. "Barbaric *and* stupid."

"I'll show you barbaric." Gorgan holds up his hand and stops the chant again. "If I'm not mistaken, Raymar has a wife. Bring her here. I'm sure she will love to watch her husband beat up poor Fulcus."

The crowd starts laughing and two of them head off in the direction of the boat.

"You're all monsters!" Elidria cries, adrenaline surging. "I'll fight! Put me in! I'll fight for him!"

The crowd goes silent again.

"You want to fight?" Gorgan asks.

"Yes, and if I win, you let him go."

Gorgan brings his hand to his beard and begins stroking it. "So be it. Listen up, everyone! Little Missy, here, wants to fight! That means we get to watch two fights today!"

"What?" exclaims Elidria.

"The first will be Raymar versus Fulcus. The second will be Little Missy versus me! She apparently wants a rematch from last night."

"That's not what I said!" Elidria tries to break free but she fails to make it even one step as Gorgan grabs her as soon as she starts moving. "I'll fight you both!" she yells. "I'll fight Fulcus and win! Then I'll fight you!"

"You're in no condition to fight twice," says Gorgan. "You'll throw one punch and knock yourself out. You're just the dessert after the first fight.

"Oh yeah? Watch me!"

Fulcus screams out in pain and drops to the ground, squirming with an arrow through his back and poking out by his clavicle.

The crowd turns to see who is responsible.

Delsar stands with his bow in hand. His shield is mounted on his back, but he does not wear his cloak. Just the dark-green hunting outfit he got in Midori Trails. "I'll fight," he says while also nocking another arrow, "since, you know, he can't anymore."

Gorgan releases his grip on Elidria. "Finally," he says, grinning.

CHAPTER 17

THE RISE

7 Years Ago...

"Stay down!" Arviakyss commands, out of breath. He has his blade against the kneeling mercenary leader's neck.

"I know when I've lost," Gorgan replies, putting his hands up.

The Queen pushes past Lucas, Arviakyss' partner and their choice as her last line of defense. "You saved me, Corporal," she says to Arviakyss.

"I wouldn't come any closer, ma'am," Arviakyss warns.

"Please, you have him well-in-hand." She approaches Gorgan and begins to walk circles around him. "An attempt on my life is a very serious crime. The penalty is death. I'm sure you know that."

"I knew the price," Gorgan responds.

"Then your pay must have been substantial for you to risk so much. I might be able to cut you a deal. If you tell me who hired you, I'll waive your death sentence."

"It's a tempting offer, but I was never given a name."

"That's a shame. You do realize that I'm Queen, don't you? I can deem you guilty and have you executed this very instant."

"You definitely could, but I know that's not how you go about things," Gorgan says with a smug look.

"Hmm, maybe." The Queen waves over one of her guards. "Captain, please put together a court for me. Use the villagers as the jury and I'll be the judge."

"Yes, ma'am."

"Wait!" exclaims Gorgan. "That's not fair! They will be completely biased against me!"

"That's true, but it was them that you terrorized. It seems fair that they decide."

"You can't do that! The court system is supposed to be just!"

"You're guilty. Everyone here knows that. Be thankful I'm even giving you *this* chance."

Gorgan snarls at the Queen but doesn't say anything after that.

The Queen spins away from him, purposefully letting her cape whip against his face. "Tell me, Corporal," she says to Arviakyss, "how sharp is your sword?"

"Sharp enough to remove a boar's head in one swing, ma'am."

The Queen looks down at Gorgan. "His neck isn't *that* thick. Very good. Have yourself prepared for the guilty verdict. His justice will be swift."

"Wait!" Gorgan shouts. "I thought you were merciful."

"Mercy is not justice."

Gorgan glares, but his tone changes. "Maybe I do know something about who hired me."

The Queen's eyebrows go up. "Not quite ready to die?" She leans closer to the brute. "Neither was I, but that certainly didn't stop you from trying."

Gorgan starts to speak, but he says nothing, surrendering eye contact with the Queen.

The Queen smirks. "Very well. Captain, throw him and his friends in the carriage. I have questions for him later."

"Yes, ma'am." The Captain switches from assembling the jury to escorting the mercenaries into the carriage.

The Queen lets out a sigh of relief and sits on a stump, slouching forward. "Thank you for what you did, Corporal. That was truly a terrifying experience."

"It was my job, ma'am," says Arviakyss, giving her a bow. "I do have a question though. Why are you here in Boforest?"

The Queen sits up straight. "I'm visiting my family. I chose a small team to avoid detection. I guess that didn't work. What about you, Corporal? Why are you here?"

"Lucas and I are returning from a trip east of the border. We had some special training out there, ma'am."

"So I'm lucky you were passing through." She stands up from her resting place. "What is your name, soldier?"

"Arviakyss, ma'am."

"And how old are you?"

"I'm sixteen."

She blinks hard. "So young," she says. "I see you becoming something great. Escort me back to the palace. I'd very much like to have a talk with you and your partner."

"Yes, ma'am." Arviakyss gives her another bow before letting her get back to enjoying her time with her family.

"Take him!" Gorgan commands two of his men.

The two mercenaries, one from either side, charge Delsar. One carries a mace and shield while the other only wields a great sword.

Delsar's choice is simple. He launches an arrow into the swordsman's abdomen, stopping him in his tracks. Delsar then kicks both his feet against the man's chest and propels himself backward into the man with the mace. He crashes shield and back first, knocking the man down and landing hard on top of him. Delsar rolls back to his feet and sends an arrow into this man's shoulder, pinning him to the ground.

Delsar nocks another arrow and points it at Gorgan. "I'm here for the girl, her father, and whoever that guy is," Delsar says, referring to Raymar. "Then I'll be taking the rest of the villagers with me."

"You want this traitor?" Gorgan asks, pushing Elidria away and grabbing Aldameer by the collar. He places his knife against his throat and says, "Even after everything he's done?"

"No one's perfect. I'll turn him in if that makes you feel better."

"You think you can beat all of us?"

"You're already down three. Soon it will be three more."

As if on cue, two more mercenaries slowly approach Delsar. Delsar moves around them to place them between himself and Gorgan. He aims his bow at them but they throw their hands up. "We just want them," one of them says, pointing at two of the downed mercenaries.

"Take them and leave," orders Delsar. "Now."

"R-right. Come on." He gestures to his buddy and they begin helping the two injured men to their feet.

"If you leave, I will personally find and kill all four of you!" Gorgan bellows at his men. "And to make my point clear, Arviakyss, I'm going to show them just how willing to kill I am."

"Don't you do it!" Delsar yells, aiming his bow back at Gorgan.

"Well done, Aldameer," Gorgan says in Aldameer's ear. "You really did lure him here." Gorgan slides his knife through Aldameer's throat without a second thought.

"Dad!" Elidria screams.

Delsar sends his arrow at Gorgan but he steps out of the way and draws his own sword.

The other mercenaries begin scrambling around, drawing their own weapons and getting ready to take down the Champion.

One of the men helping his injured comrade also draws his sword and tries to catch Delsar off guard.

Delsar drops his bow and dives under the strike while pulling out his sword and slicing deep into the man's thigh. He then spins and stabs his sword up through the man's armpit. He slides it out and then immediately thrusts it into the other man's shoulder who is still helping his friend.

He cries out in pain and says, "I wasn't going to try anything!"

"I don't care." Delsar removes his blade and bashes the man's face with his elbow, knocking him to the ground. Delsar then grabs his shield from his back and prepares himself for the onslaught that is to come.

With the confusion, Elidria unlocks one side of her restraints with another key she hid under the bandage around her torso. She spins and smacks one of the mercenaries in the side of the head with her cuff before reaching for her blade that Gorgan wears around his waist as a trophy.

Gorgan feels the sword begin sliding from the sheath and swings for her arm.

She pulls the sword free and jumps back, barely avoiding Gorgan's strike. She turns away and dashes toward Delsar.

"Stop her!" yells Gorgan.

A couple mercenaries stop to see what Gorgan is yelling about, but one of them topples over as Elidria's blade is pulled from his leg.

At the same time, Delsar parries a sword strike and side-steps the long reach of a glaive.

"Behind you!" warns the man Elidria just took down.

The glaived man spins around and avoids Elidria's attack as she slides past him to meet with Delsar.

Delsar takes this advantage and parries another strike from a sword and then launches with a side kick to the glaived man's back.

The man screams and falls forward.

Elidria blocks another strike intended for Delsar with her sword. The man and Elidria both slide their blades across each other until both hilts clash.

The man pushes against Elidria and she doesn't try to resist. Instead, she drops to her knees and leans back. The man stumbles forward, expecting some sort of resistance, and Elidria slides her sword across his inner thigh as he passes over her.

Delsar steps out of the way as the man falls past him. Delsar gives a hard kick into the man's head before he has any chance to get back up.

Elidria sets herself directly next to Delsar. "You came back," she says.

"I shouldn't have left," Delsar replies.

"Never mind that. I only see four still standing," she reports.

"Then let's finish this."

Two of the mercenaries start backing away from Delsar and Elidria. Both of them are afraid for their lives after seeing Delsar take down six men and now he's joined by a girl, who despite her clear injuries, took down another two.

"Enough!" Gorgan holds the barely standing Raymar against his chest with a knife to the side of his neck. "Lay down your sword or I'll kill him!"

"If he dies, you die," Delsar counters.

Elidria looks up at Delsar. Concern fills her eyes for her best friend's father.

"Don't put your sword down," Delsar tells her. "Here's my proposition!" he then yells to Gorgan. "You regroup with your men since you clearly just lost your upper hand. Elidria and I will step back and give you room to gather your wounded."

"You're stalling," says Gorgan.

"You're scared," says Delsar as he walks closer toward Gorgan.

"Don't move!" Gorgan commands.

"I have the girl, now I want her father. You can have your men back and you can even take your hostage with you."

"Delsar!" Elidria interjects.

"He's more than willing to kill his hostages," he whispers. "While he has him, we can't do very much. Just trust me."

Elidria nods her head.

"So be it!" says Gorgan, stepping aside to let them pass. After, he puts himself between them and his injured men. "Grab whoever can't walk and bring them back to the cliff," he tells his three standing men.

"Check your father," Delsar tells Elidria as he stands guard above him.

"Dad!" Elidria drops to Aldameer's side and begins frantically shaking him. "Please, Dad, wake up," she says as tears roll down her cheeks. "I didn't mean any of it. I don't hate you and I do forgive you. I'm so sorry."

It doesn't matter what she says or does, Aldameer won't hear any of it. Gorgan's slash was lethal and Aldameer choked on his blood long before the fight was finished.

Delsar wants nothing more than to turn around and comfort Elidria, but dropping his guard with Gorgan still present would be a mistake. Instead, both men continue their glaring stares.

Elidria's crying grows louder, becoming more heartbreaking with its increasing volume. It's her regret-filled sobbing that hits Delsar hard. His own tears drip off his chin listening to Elidria's world shattering behind him.

"What have I done?" she says amidst her relentless sobbing. She grabs Aldameer's head and rests it on her thighs. "I'm sorry," she says again to him, closing his eyes. Her weeping doesn't get any better after that. Even with Delsar standing above, she is alone and no one will comfort her.

A good fifteen minutes go by before one of the mercenaries finally reports to Gorgan that the men are cleared.

"Such a shame," Gorgan starts, "that the bad man had to die. I don't think even *he* deserved to be hated so much by his daughter. I can't imagine the pain he felt after hearing you say it. I probably eased his suffering."

His words hit Elidria hard. Horror rolls over like a cold, all-encompassing wave. Abruptly, she leans to the side and vomits.

"Just leave!" Delsar demands.

"We'll continue this later, Little Missy." Gorgan backs away and disappears behind some buildings.

Delsar sheaths his sword drops to his knees, embracing Elidria. "I'm so sorry. I was too slow."

"You didn't kill him," she says in his ear, trembling and wiping her chin. "And it wasn't you who hated him. He'll never know that I still loved him."

Delsar releases her and grabs her by the shoulders. "Am I too late for forgiveness?" he asks.

"Never. I've always forgiven you," she replies.

"And I already knew that. Elidria, I've known you for less than a month and I *knew* you'd forgive me. He was your father and he's known you all your life. I know, without a doubt, that he knew you forgave him and that you still loved him."

"For one to murder, one must first hate," she says.

Delsar hugs her again. "Don't," he says. "Your regret is proof that you still truly loved him. He knows. I'm sure of it."

"But I won't. I won't ever know."

Delsar closes his eyes. It was only earlier that he was given the opportunity to forgive his father face to face. That's something she will never be able to do. Something that may haunt her for the rest of her life. "Eldra, I'll hear you. Whatever you need to say, I'll listen."

"Delsar," she says, looking up at him. Her one opened eye as red as the blood around Aldameer's neck. "Could you still call me Elidria?"

"Don't you prefer Eldra?"

"It's comforting when you call me Elidria," she says, resting her head on Delsar's chest. "It reminds me of where we started."

Delsar places his hand on Elidria's head. "That's fine," he says. "Elidria is a beautiful name."

It's a position they remain in for over an hour. Elidria's body went back into repair mode and the mix of her crying and Delsar's comforting hand put her right to sleep.

"Hey, Delsar," comes a voice on his right.

Delsar hears it but doesn't alert to it. He knows to whom it belongs. "Dad," he says, looking over at him, "I couldn't save him."

Ligrei lets out a sigh. "I'm sorry."

"Not to me." Delsar looks down at Elidria. "He was her father."

"Then share with her the good news."

Delsar lets out his own sigh of relief. "So your mission was a success?"

"We only found four villagers on the boat, but we got them all. We also captured four other mercenaries."

"The other villager was up here," Delsar says. "They got away with him." Delsar gently shakes Elidria. "Hey, Elidria."

"I heard," she says. "Thank you." She extends an invitation for Ligrei to join the hug. "You too, Mr.—?"

"Ligrei, but I'm not a hugger."

"Neither was Delsar, so get in here."

Ligrei gives a big grin. "All right." He's about to join the hug but notices a slip sticking out of Aldameer's inside pocket. "Hold up," he says as he procures it. "I think it's for you, my dear," he says after inspecting it.

Elidria grabs it from him and unfolds the paper. "Oh no," she says, bringing her hand to her mouth.

"What is it?" Delsar asks.

"It's my mother's suicide note," she replies as she digs her head back into Delsar's chest and begins crying again.

Delsar snatches the paper from her and decides to read it for himself:

Elidria, my dearest princess,

Our move from the capital was just the first step in our grand adventure. Since you are reading this, I must assume your father deemed you ready. That also means you likely know what he did. Please, don't hate him and try to be understanding. For everyone makes mistakes, big or small, we must always forgive each other.

With such an assassination being ordered by the King, it's clear that he isn't fit for his rule and while he held me captive, I felt great fear and hate coming from him. It gave me my own fear of our future. A future that lies in the palms of a power-hungry mad man. These are secrets that can't be shared lightly. A king willing to kill his partner will also be willing to silence the truth at any cost. It's because of this that I must find allies willing to hear me. The Ithendar he rules I will no longer call my home.

Your father agreed to stay behind to keep the King from looking for me. If we both left, he would surely hunt us. The borders of Ithendar are also wild and dangerous. This is why we decided to keep you with him, just until I can return. I don't know when that may ever be, but I do know this; no matter how long or how far apart we are, I will always love you and I never meant to hurt you.

I love you, sweetie.

-Mom

Delsar looks up from his read in complete awe. "Elidria," he says. "Did you read this?"

He feels her shake her head against his chest.

"You need to."

"Not now, Delsar. Please."

"Elidria, it's not a suicide note. Read it."

Elidria looks up at Delsar while biting her lip. "Don't do this to me," she says.

"Trust me. Read the note."

Elidria sniffles and yanks the note from Delsar. She reads it through and drops it. Her face says it all. She stares past Delsar at nothing in particular and her mouth gapes open. "I-I-I d-don't understand," she finally says. "Is she— Could she be alive?"

"That's the message I got."

She brings both her hands to her mouth and squeals. "Oh, Delsar!" She then hugs him again. "Mr. Ligrei, I think my mom is alive!"

Ligrei gives her a giant grin. "That's wonderful."

"What are your plans?" Delsar asks.

Elidria's sudden glee quickly disappears. "We save Raymar. *That's* priority." She stands up and looks down at her father. "We need to bury him, too, and I need to say my 'goodbyes.' We are taking that boat, Delsar."

Delsar smirks. "Then I'd like to introduce you to our team."

The King's dressing room...

"And now you look splendid, my Lord," says Malgo, admiring his own handiwork.

"I'm not one for dressing up," says the King. "I feel no greater like this than I would in my robes."

"Never mind that. You must look presentable at the ball tonight. Women like professionally-dressed men."

"I'm the King. They don't care how I dress, they just want to be queen. Speaking of that, I refuse to remarry if my future queen will be considered an equal. I need that law changed."

"And I have been looking for loopholes. The only way you'll be able to make it happen is if you can get four council members to agree with you."

"I'll need a good argument," says the King.

"I have been working on a couple solutions for you."

"I only need the rule changed *if* I remarry."

"All six members agreed to assign a new king if you don't."

"They can't really do that, can they?"

"Unfortunately, the people will likely side with the council seeing how the council represents them."

The King squeezes his hands into a tight fist, disregarding the pain of his royal rings digging into his fingers. "Except the capital," says the King. "The capital of Ithendar is strong enough to be its own country, let alone a district. They'll have to force me off my throne and I doubt the other districts will want to have a civil war."

"Maybe not, but for now, just focus on having a good time at the ball. Meet lots of pretty women. Maybe you'll actually become fond of one, and remember, I *am* working on your 'equal marriage' issue."

"Very well, Malgo. As always, you're on top of things. I will do my best to have fun tonight. I'll worry about *civil war* later."

"Merith!" Elidria runs through Delsar's camp and grabs both of Merith's hands with her own. "I'm so happy you're okay."

"Oh, Eldra, I'm grateful you made it out alive yourself."

"They killed Dad," Elidria tells her.

Merith gives Elidria a sorrowed look and puts one of her hands on Elidria's cheek. "I'm so sorry, hon."

"And they still have Raymar. We couldn't get him out."

Merith closes her eyes shut and nods her head up and down. "He's tough," she says. "He'll hang on."

"And so will we," Elidria says, pumping her fist.

"And we *will* get him back," Delsar cuts in. "Now we have me, Elidria, four guards, Ligrei, and the four survivors if you guys are interested in helping."

"Absolutely," says the enthusiastic Merith.

"No you're not," says Telrus, answering for the rest. "You four are witnesses. I'm getting you to Lar. There you will testify and hopefully bring an end to the stupid Bihnor restriction. You will *not* be staying here."

"Hi, Telrus." Elidria gives him a wave and then a subtle bow.

"Miss Eldra, you came back in one piece though you look like just barely."

"My dad actually—" Elidria lets out a sigh. "He stopped the man from killing me."

Telrus gives her a concerned look but then eyeballs the four individuals in restraints behind her. "And who are these fools?" he asks.

"Oh, right, um, I don't know their names, so I call them the Four Idiots. I beat them all up earlier," Elidria explains.

"It definitely wasn't you," says one of the imprisoned mercenaries.

"Oh, it was and I'll be more than happy to do it again," Elidria snaps back. "These big boys don't want to admit they all lost to a girl."

"And I assume they did *that* to your face?" Telrus asks.

"They *wish*," Elidria sasses. "No, this was from the boss. His name is Gorgan."

"I know of him," says Telrus. "Defeated by Arviakyss and sentenced to life by the Queen seven years ago. He escaped without so much as a fight two years ago with two other buddies."

"You say that like you don't believe it," says Delsar.

"If you ask me, I'd say someone *let* them escape. It was too clean."

"Oh, and another thing," Elidria starts to add, "Gorgan was really strong. Like, unnaturally strong."

"Explain," says the intrigued Delsar, hand on his chin.

"I know I'm not very heavy, but he managed to pick me up by my neck with one arm *and* it was fully extended."

"He is big."

"But not that big. Delsar, if they are connected to the troll attacks, then maybe they used some kind of magic or science on him like they did with the trolls."

"A superhuman," says Telrus. "This mission isn't worth the risk anymore."

"Now wait a minute!" exclaims Elidria, but Telrus continues.

"We saved four already. They are what's important. We get them back and let Lar handle this from here. If we go up against this guy, people will die. I'm not going to trade X amount of people on the off chance that we save just one."

"And now we've heard your concerns," says Delsar, "and we do appreciate it, but Elidria's the boss. It's her call."

"Well, it's an easy choice. I'm saving Raymar and putting all these sorry numbskulls behind bars. No one else has to help."

"As if I'd make the mistake of leaving again," says Delsar. "I'm standing with you, Elidria."

"I'm here now," starts Ligrei. "Fat chance you could convince me to leave."

"Whatever!" snaps Telrus, annoyed by their ignorance. "If the civies want to stay, they can."

"He's my husband!" shouts Merith. "I'm fighting, too."

"So will—"

Telrus stops the other survivors from getting their say. "No! Because he's your husband, fine, you can stay. You three, however, not happening. I'm taking you back to Lar immediately. Got it?"

Galius puts his hand on Telrus' shoulder. "Hey, partner?"

"What is it, Galius?"

"I'm staying and so are Allbus and Castor. We came to fight."

"You already did," Telrus reminds him. "That's why we now have eight of these goons including Elidria's four. You did your fighting and now it's time for our reports."

Galius smiles and shakes his head. "That's the Lieutenant's job."

"I could order you three to stand down."

"And I wouldn't listen, but I do want your support. We're partners. I don't want to do it if you say 'no.'"

"But you'll still do it, won't you?"

"Yup."

Telrus takes an exasperated breath. "Whatever. I'll get these three survivors to Lar and fill out a report. I'll also get these thugs out of here. Then, I guess I'll be coming back."

"Thanks, Telrus," says Elidria.

"But I still don't like it," Telrus adds. "If even one person dies—"

"Then they'll die fighting for someone in need," Allbus chimes in. "That's what we signed up for. To give our lives if needed. This is what's right."

"Then it's decided," Delsar looks over at Elidria. "We follow you."

Elidria's face goes white and she slowly shakes her head. "I don't know how to lead. I can't make strategies."

"But you've been leading this whole time," says Delsar. "You're the person that we *all* will be depend—"

Galius lets out his girthy laugh, interrupting Delsar's explanation. "What he means is where you fight, we'll follow," he tells Elidria. "Just keep being you," he says, giving her a slight but loyal nod. He turns to Delsar and whispers in his ear. "There's no need to put more pressure on her than she already has. Everyone here knows who we're fighting for."

"I'm scared to lead," Elidria says.

"You see?" Galius asks, still whispering to Delsar.

"I know you're talking about me." Elidria places her hands on her hips. "Perhaps you wish to share with the rest of us?"

"I've got your back, Elidria," says Delsar, "and so does everyone else. That's along the lines what Galius was whispering."

"Partners then," Elidria responds, holding out her hand, but for only a moment. She pulls her hand back and looks at it. "That's what we all need." Elidria turns to the others. "No one is ever alone, got it? That's how I keep getting hurt. Always have someone with you, no matter how small the task."

"Yes, ma'am," says Ligrei, unaware that she hates such titles.

"Then I'm taking Ligrei with me to deliver these survivors," starts Telrus, taking charge back. "Galius and Delsar can formulate a plan. Allbus and Castor, why don't the two of you show Merith a few moves? Elidria, go with Galius and Delsar. Ligrei and I will be back soon."

"That sounds like a good plan," says Elidria.

"Yup. Let's go, Ligrei."

"Coming."

"Bye, Mr. Ligrei. It was nice to meet you," says Elidria, giving him a wave.

"Likewise, Miss Eldra." He gets closer to her and whispers into her ear. "Thank you for everything you did for my son." He gives her a nod and joins Telrus with loading the mercenaries in the back of the paddy wagon.

Elidria approaches each of the survivors and gives them all their own hugs. "Bye, Faebella," she says squeezing her.

"Many thanks," she responds.

"Wyn and Fil, safe journeys."

"You've been a blessing, Eldra."

"Good luck."

"We'll do our best." Elidria waves as they load aboard the front, but her goodbye gets delayed and a bit awkward.

"Wait a sec," says Delsar. "Only take the four most injured mercenaries with you. I have a plan for the other four."

"I'm not even going to try anymore." Telrus hops around back and unloads four of the mercenaries he just finished loading. "If you need nothing else from my services, I'm leaving."

Elidria waves again to her neighbors. "Bye again!"

With a snap of the reins, Telrus leads them away.

"He's not a coward," Galius says to Delsar.

"I know," Delsar responds while helping tie the mercenaries to a tree. "He puts his country first. Sometimes you need someone like that to keep you realizing the big picture."

Elidria whips around to face Delsar and Galius. "So, what's your plan?"

"They have a hostage so I figured we should, too. A simple trade may be all we need."

"A trade is risky," says Galius. "Any kind of mistake or mishap and they might kill the hostage."

"Then we use our prisoners to apply pressure. As it stands, I'm not sure how we're getting on that boat."

"What kind of pressure do you have in mind, son?"

"Every day we turn another one over to Lar," Delsar explains. "They will likely be tried for treason, so they *will* face the death penalty."

"So we make demands," Galius realizes, bringing his hand to his chin.

"Exactly. They release Raymar and we'll stop turning mercenaries in. Once he is safely in Bihnor, we'll leave."

"We can't leave!" Elidria exclaims. "Justice, Delsar. Who will stop them when they do this somewhere else?"

"We won't actually leave. That's just what we'll tell them. We'll come back here for a day or so and wait for them to enter back into the village. When they do, we'll fight them on equal grounds."

"Excuse me?" Elidria is disgusted. "So we lie to win? Not happening."

Delsar winces. The whole lying thing completely slipped his mind. The plan made sense to him. "You're right. We'll find another way."

"Are you sure about that, Delsar?" Galius asks.

"We're heroes now, Galius," Elidria says. "We're keeping each other straight, just like you said."

Galius smiles and nods. "Then another way we shall find. Oh, my old age almost made me forget."

"A plan?" Elidria questions.

"Not a plan, but they will help." Galius grabs a pair of bracers and shinguards from near the fading campfire. "I found these on the boat. They look just like the ones you stole from me."

"Now wait a minute!" exclaims Elidria. "You gave them to me."

"Did I? I'll chalk that off as being old, too."

Delsar rolls his eyes. "He's kidding, Elidria."

"I figured that out, Delsar. I'm not *completely* oblivious, you know?"

"Then why play along?"

"Look at the man smiling. He's clearly enjoying himself."

Galius gives an even bigger grin. "It's true."

"But he's basically lying," Delsar points out.

"Lying is trying to make someone believe something that isn't true. Someone fooling around isn't lying if you know they're joking. It's like watching a play. You wouldn't call an actor a liar, would you?"

"Where do you get this stuff?" Delsar asks, not actually caring for an answer.

"That one was from Glade," she answers, which is likely the last person he wanted to hear that come from.

Delsar rolls his eyes again. "The bumbling idiot."

"Hey," snaps Elidria, "the word 'idiot' is reserved for you and the Four Idiots *I* beat up. You can't just throw it around willy-nilly."

"Don't make me roll my eyes again."

"Is that what they're doing? I thought you had some strange medical condition or something."

"Ha," yells Delsar, pointing his finger at her, "I think I just heard a lie come from you."

"If it was a lie, you would never have known. I literally just explained to you what a lie is. You really are an idiot."

"He's good at a lot of things, Eldra," says Galius. "Unfortunately, humor isn't one of them."

"Sarcasm isn't funny," says Delsar. "Besides, Telrus thinks I'm pretty funny."

"He's a boy. You could burp and he'll laugh."

"Would he actually?" Elidria asks, genuinely.

"Probably not," replies Galius. "That's actually me who would."

"Oh. Interesting."

"Gah!" exclaims Galius. "You've both distracted me. I have one more thing, Eldra." Galius runs and grabs Elidria's kite shield. "It's the same style as Delsar's but smaller so I figured it must be yours."

"Or maybe you just found it with the rest of her stuff."

"Shut up, Delsar," Elidria says through her teeth. "Thank you so much, Galius. This tool has worked wonders." She lowers her voice. "Between you and me, it's had my back more than Delsar."

"You'd drop me," says Delsar.

"If you could fit on my back, I'd drop you on purpose because you're annoying."

"I think Delsar is rubbing off on you a bit," says Galius.

"More like rubbing against me. He's like that little bit of sand that gets under your bracer that you just can't get out, no matter how many times you slide your finger underneath."

"I know that feeling all too well."

"Imagine not having *my* 'padded' armor. Then it would feel like Glade," says Delsar.

"Rude. He's not even here to defend himself."

"It's Glade. He wouldn't be able to even if he *was* here."

Elidria rolls her eye.

"I saw that!" Delsar says with his finger pointed at her again.

She can't help herself from giggling. "I guess you win then," she says, shaking her head. She lets out a relieving sigh. "Thanks, guys, both of you, for everything. For coming all this way and supporting me both physically and mentally. I really mean that."

"I'm getting paid," says Delsar

Elidria laughs and rolls her eye again.

"That's two!" Delsar exclaims. "You're slipping."

"Shut *up*, Delsar. I'm trying to have a moment," she says, still grinning ear-to-ear.

Galius places his hand on Delsar's shoulder. "When a woman says 'shut up,' even if she's smiling, you'd best shut up."

"You called me a woman. Delsar usually calls me a girl."

"And what would you prefer?" Galius asks.

Elidria shrugs. "Woman makes me sound mature, but girl makes me sound cute. It's a toss-up, really."

"Or we just call you by your name," Delsar says, rolling his eyes.

"Looks like I'm back on top," Elidria says, flexing her small, right bicep.

"You're going to make me rolling my eyes a game?"

"It wouldn't be much of a game seeing how easy you are."

"What's easy?"

Elidria puts her hands behind her back and smiles. "Oh..., nothing."

Delsar starts to roll his eyes again but catches himself. "Don't even. I already know. Just grab something to eat."

"Yes, everyone here has already eaten except for you and Delsar. We have eggs and toast over in that pan," Galius informs.

"Oh, thank you. Who's the chef?" she asks.

"You're looking at him." Galius puffs his chest out.

"Then I'm sure I'll love them."

Galius gives her a smile. "When you're done, go find Merith and the other guards. I'd like you both to find a *real* bed to sleep in. Take today and tonight off. Your body needs it."

"I will and I appreciate it."

"That will give Gaius and I ample time to come up with some sort of plan, too," Delsar adds.

"Then I will leave you both to it."

"Oh, and Elidria," says Delsar, turning her back around to listen, "when you head back to the village, take something from camp with you. I'd like to start setting up base there."

"Sure thing." She turns away to eat and lets her tears fall again. Her momentary laughter with Delsar and Galius really was just a temporary distraction from the reality she just faced. The traumas and horrors she experienced earlier return to her front-most consciousness as she begins chowing down on Galius' delicious breakfast.

"What's our status?" asks the very stressed Gorgan.

"Not good," Onus replies. "The prisoners are gone and so are the men we had posted here."

"Don't tell me things I already know. Who can still fight?"

Onus gives Gorgan a worried look before giving him the tally. "Fulcus, Hastios, and Vinali won't be fighting anytime soon. Everyone else who took hits may take anywhere between a day to a couple weeks before they're up again."

"So we are potentially down to nine."

"No, sir," says Onus. "It's Pozon."

"What happened?"

"Arviakyss nicked an artery in his armpit," Onus explains. "He's bleeding out as we speak."

Gorgan pushes Onus aside and races to the boat's infirmary. "Pozon!" he shouts while running to his friend's motionless body. "How can I make this right?" he asks.

Pozon's extremely white face starts to stir as he does his best to open his eyes for the last time. "Gorgan," he says very weakly, "make him pay." Pozon struggles to swallow and then continues. "Take from him what he took from you."

"The girl then?" Gorgan asks.

"Make him watch as she suffers." Pozon's eyes start to roll back.

"Stay with me," Gorgan says as he shakes him.

"Then you kill them both." Pozon takes a heavy breath. "Don't let me die in vain. Avenge me and finish this job. Arviakyss must die." Pozon gives his all to grab Gorgan by his collar and looks him in the eyes. "No survivors."

Gorgan grabs his friend's hand and head as they go limp. He gently lays them down on the cot and bares his teeth. "I'll make him pay," he snarls. "I'll beat her in front of him. I'll break her bones and crush her skull. Whatever it takes, I *will* make him suffer."

CHAPTER 18

THE ENCOUNTERS

6 Years Ago...

"It was a beautiful funeral, Aldameer," Arlayna says to her husband. "I only wish our daughter attended."

"It couldn't be helped," Aldameer responds. "This is a lot for her to deal with. I hope we're doing the right thing."

"The less she knows about me and what happened that night, the safer she'll be." Arlayna pulls a note from her pocket. "Here, give this to her when she's in as much danger knowing as not knowing."

"You think that day will come?"

"I hope it's later rather than sooner."

Aldameer gives his wife a concerned look and wipes a tear from her face. "I'm sorry I did this to you," he says.

Arlayna grabs his hand from her face and clutches it against her chest. "The King was always going to kill his Queen. It may feel like a curse, but it was actually a blessing that he pulled us into it. Now we know and we can do something about it."

"Are you sure your friends will help?"

Arlayna gives a light snort and smiles. "I've known them longer than he's been king and I also know that they've been waiting for an opportunity like this."

"I know murdering the Queen was wrong, but perhaps we are going too far," says Aldameer, giving his concern.

"We both know he didn't kill her just because he didn't like her. He needed her gone for something. Something sinister. We have to prepare."

Aldameer lowers his head and subtly nods it. "You are the best person for this," he says and then sighs. "That doesn't change how much I'm going to miss you."

"Oh, sweetie, we'll see each other again. This will ensure it's under good circumstances."

"I know that, it's just...." Aldameer sighs again. "Here's your bag. I triple-checked it."

Arlayna reaches for it, but instead grabs around Aldameer's head and pulls him in for a lingering kiss.

Aldameer brings his own arms around her and embraces her for what he believes to be their last physical contact for a long time.

Arlayna finally pulls her head away before resting her chin on his shoulder. "Keep her safe," she whispers in his ear.

"I'll do whatever it takes," he answers.

"I know you will." Arlayna slides her hand down Aldameer's arm and procures the bag from him. "I love you," she says before giving him another quick kiss on his cheek and turning for the door.

"Arlayna," Aldameer says before she can leave, "keep yourself safe, too."

Arlayna tilts her head and gives her husband a tear-filled smile. "I will be. I promise."

Aldameer nods and says, "Then so long."

Arlayna's lips begin to quiver as she turns away to leave. Saying anything else will just make things harder.

Aldameer sees her bring her sleeve to her face to wipe her tears as she exits the house. He sniffles and looks out his window to watch her for as long as he can. She disappears over the ridge before Aldameer says to himself, "And so it starts."

"I was kind of hoping we'd be doing more than just guarding," says Castor, hurling a rock into the water below.

"We *are* guards," Allbus reminds him while throwing his own rock over the cliff.

"Duh. After seeing them all interact with each other, I feel like we're just the extras."

"I get that," Allbus says, rummaging for another stone.

"And who is this Delsar? I get the girl because this is her home, but what makes Delsar so special?"

"Maybe they're betrothed?"

"That doesn't explain why he's in charge."

"I guess not." Allbus tosses Castor his near-perfect rock he just found. "I don't know the answers, Castor, but if both the Lieutenant and Sergeant trust him, then so do I."

"But since when does the King abandon one of his villages and then keeps everything hush?" Caster questions. "I just want to know who we're fighting for. What if the villagers are enemies of the kingdom and the King hired the mercenaries to take them out discreetly?"

Allbus chuckles. "You're thinking too hard. Lieutenant Telrus said this attack is related to the attacks against both Boforest *and* Orange Peak. Why would the King attack there, too?"

"I guess I forgot those details," grumbles Castor. "I was just hoping for more adventure and less of this special operation stuff. Just good old fashioned slice-and-dice." Castor chucks his rock, but instead of splashing in the water, the rock crashes against the dock and makes a loud crack before harmlessly bouncing into the ocean.

Moments later, two mercenaries emerge from their boat and begin the one hundred yard travel across the long dock.

"Now you've done it," says Allbus.

"Shut up and go grab the Lieutenant," Castor instructs.

"Right!" Allbus takes off in a sprint toward the village. Metal and wood clatter as both his sheathed sword and his hipped crossbow rattle against his armor plates. He grabs both items to keep them still as he runs.

"Hey, Castor!" says Elidria as Allbus runs toward her and Merith.

"I'm Allbus," he says as a matter of fact and doesn't stop, "and I gotta go!"

"Okay," she responds without trying to further the conversation. "He's a man on a mission," she says to Merith.

Allbus strides up the ridge and sprints for the hill that hides the encampment.

Delsar and Galius are still discussing different ideas with the map stretched out.

"Sergeant, where's the Lieutenant?" Allbus asks, interrupting the two from their theory-crafting.

Galius turns his head but keeps his hands on the crate they use as their table. "He hasn't returned from Lar yet. What do you need?"

Allbus takes a quick moment to catch his breath before quickly explaining. "Two men are approaching the ramp from their boat."

Delsar grabs his shield and slides it on his back. "They may want to negotiate. We need to get over there."

"I doubt that," says Galius. "They probably just want intel. With the survivors escaping and more of their men missing, they know it's not just you and Eldra."

"Galius, you're with me," Delsar instructs. "Allbus, stay here and watch the prisoners."

"And who are—" Allbus stops himself. "Never mind. Roger that."

Delsar and Galius take off on their own sprint. The heavier and older Galius surprises Allbus as he manages to keep up with Delsar.

We're not extras, Allbus thinks to himself. *We're going to make a difference, even if it is just guarding.*

"Don't put even one foot on this ramp!" Castor commands, with his crossbow aimed.

Delsar runs to Castor's side and peers down the cliff. "What's the situation?" he asks.

"Two men from the boat are here," he explains without taking his eyes off the mercenaries. "They say they just want to talk and that shouting up and down the cliff won't do."

"Thanks for keeping them down," says Delsar. He changes his focus to the two men in the knee-deep water at the bottom of the ramp. "Gorgon," he mutters to himself before yelling, "Why'd you build it in the water?"

"Because the tide wasn't this far up when we did," responds the mercenary next to Gorgon.

"The dock extends out from the bottom of the cliff. It's pretty obvious that's how far the water reaches. You should have built it on top of the dock."

"It's—" starts the other mercenary before receiving an elbow to his ribs from Gorgon.

"We aren't here to talk about the ramp," yells Gorgon.

"It's just that your boots are all wet now."

"We would like—"

"If you had to run you'd not only be slower, but you might run right out of those boots."

"We would like to peacefully discuss both our situations."

"Peacefully? I could hear you a mile away with that water sloshing away with every footfall."

"You have my men. I have your villager."

"And you want to come up and see how many of us there are," Delsar states.

"Now tell him he can't come up with his muddy boots," Galius whispers to Delsar, out of view from Gorgan.

Delsar holds his hand open behind his back, signaling to his master to stop feeding him lines.

Gorgan's silence and subsequent glare not only confirms Delsar's accusation but projects his annoyance.

"Here's the deal, Gorgan. We *do* have your men, actually, now only four of them, and every day we will be sending another one to Lar until you release Raymar. You and I both know what waits for them in Lar."

"If you do that, I'll kill my hostage!"

"Then maybe we shoot you where you stand," says Delsar. "As I recall, only four of you remained this morning. We take you two out and the boat will be ours."

"He's right," says Onus, whispering in Gorgan's ear. "We have to keep our hostage alive until we can grow our strength."

"Arviakyss," shouts Gorgan, causing Castor to flinch before looking over at Delsar, "I will not be releasing my prisoner until you return every last one of my men! You got that?"

"Then bring him out," Delsar counters.

Gorgan says nothing, and in a rage turns to leave with Onus on his heels.

"Wipe your feet," yells Delsar as he watches them until they climb back onto the dock, toward the boat. "They're not coming back with him," he says. "You were right, Galius. All they wanted was intel."

"That means they're looking to fight," responds Galius, his face beaming as he holds back his laughter.

"We can't take that boat and they can't climb this ramp," says Delsar. "Perhaps we can lure them to the beach and fight there. Then we'll at least be on a level playing field."

"We have plenty of time to wait. We shouldn't give up the high ground so easily."

"Raymar didn't look like he had much time left," Delsar informs. "Saving him was Elidria's priority. Plus, we can't give them too much time to recover."

"Eldra also needs a few days to recover," says Galius. "We shouldn't do anything drastic until she's ready."

"We have Castor and Allbus. She can sit this out if need be."

"She won't and you know that."

Delsar can't help himself from smirking. "That's completely true, and with her will, she'll likely tell us she's ready to go by morning."

"That's a dangerous game."

"But it's needed when you're fighting for your life."

"It's not hers she's fighting for," says Galius.

"What are your thoughts, Castor?" Delsar turns only to be met with a crossbow aimed at his chest.

"I've figured it all out," says the guard. "This is all a conspiracy against the King."

"What are you talking about?" asks the now aggravated Delsar.

"Easy, son," says Galius, trying to defuse the situation.

"You killed the Queen and the people of this village are your cohorts," Castor explains. "The army can't make strikes against its own citizens and we guards are supposed to serve and protect. That's why the King hired the mercenaries. They're here to clean up the filth and that includes you, Arviakyss."

"That would be a good theory *if* I killed the Queen," says Delsar.

313

"You did and I have 'Kill on Sight' orders."

"Wait a minute!" Delsar exclaims, realizing it's too late to talk reason into Castor. He reaches for his shield but isn't fast enough to get it around to his front.

Galius jumps in front of Delsar as the crossbow's string releases from its locked position, sending a bolt at a blistering speed, intended to kill. The bolt splinters against Galius' breastplate before spinning over the cliff.

Delsar pulls Galius out of the way and strikes Castor's crossbow with his sword. The string snaps and Delsar sends his foot into the guard's chest, knocking him down. He then presses his sword against Castor's neck. "We don't have time for this! Are you all right, Galius."

Galius checks where his armor was struck and with assurance says, "I'm okay."

"Take care of your man," Delsar commands, storming away.

"Where are you going?" Galius asks.

"I'm grabbing Allbus and bringing him here," he says. "We keep them both restrained until Telrus returns. Then he can explain the entire situation to them. As it stands, Castor, your theory wasn't that far off."

"You both are traitors!" Castor screams from the ground where he lay.

Delsar pays no mind and continues on his way.

Galius grabs Castor's sword from his sheath before resting on one knee in front of him. "Let's talk, shall we?"

"How did it go?" Navarre asks, giving Onus and Gorgan a helping hand into the boat.

"They gave us nothing," Onus replies.

"On the contrary," Gorgan contradicts. "They gave quite a bit away."

"What did you hear that I didn't?" Onus asks.

"If Arviakyss is operating like a normal guard, he'll have everyone up there in pairs," Gorgan begins to explain. "We saw one guard and he likely had a partner who went to fetch Arviakyss. Arviakyss also mentioned only having half of the men he captured left. That means another pair is likely delivering them to Lar. Then there's Arviakyss and the girl. Now we know there's at least six of them."

"When you put it like that, you make me wonder how I didn't notice," says Onus.

"Who's going to be ready to fight tomorrow?" Gorgan asks Navarre.

"Kharis only got his leg nicked by the girl and Arviakyss stabbed Iolrath in his off-shoulder. They can both fight if necessary."

"And Zaos was only kicked," Onus adds.

"That's good. I have a plan for the six of you."

"Just like that?" questions Onus.

"Indeed." Gorgan examines the coastline before explaining. "Arviakyss' second team couldn't have used the ramp to free our prisoners. That means there's another way up." Gorgan looks south at Widow's Peninsula that juts out with giant, rocky cliffs. Likely impossible to climb. "Hmm, it's likely north," he decides. "Navarre, that's what you're going to find out tonight. Take one of the dinghies and search north at nightfall. Then, infiltrate the village and find where they keep our men. Don't engage, just return when you have the info."

"Sounds like a plan," Navarre confirms.

"Cast on our starboard side. I don't want them seeing you dropping the boat."

"They'll never have a clue."

"You said the six of us, Gorgan. What are *we* doing?" Onus asks.

"If they're delivering one of our men to Lar each day, there will be a time they are down two men of their own. More specifically, there will be a time when those two men are alone," Gorgan explains. "The six of you who can fight will lie in wait at the road and ambush the transport, killing whoever is there. Except for our guy, of course. Then there will be seven of you and the village should be easy. Start your attack and I'll sneak up the old stairs and free the rest of our men. Not only will they be pincered, but we'll also have them outnumbered."

Both Onus and Navarre can't keep themselves from grinning and Navarre says, "This plan is giving me goosebumps."

"Arviakyss will still be an issue," says Onus. "He took down six of our men in mere seconds this morning."

"Fulcus was a cheap shot," says Navarre. "I wouldn't count that one."

"Five is still scary-impressive."

"I'll handle Arviakyss," says Gorgan. "Kill everyone else and leave him to me."

"The strength you've been given won't save you from an arrow or a blade," Onus warns. "Don't forget your body is still human."

"This super-strength I possess enhances my speed, too. I'll make sure to get in close and engage in sword combat."

"I suggest a brawl," says Onus. "It will only take one good strike from him to kill you with a sword. At least in a brawl, you can afford to take a few hits. He won't be as privileged."

"That's what one would think," says Gorgan. "It took four blows to take the girl down. Even with normal strength, four should have been more than enough. These people have strong resolve. I believe in my skills with a blade and my speed. He won't be a match."

"Whatever you're more comfortable with. Just don't be afraid to ask for help."

"Yeah, yeah."

"Gorgan!" yells Sandro, running from the infirmary.

"What is it now?" asks the now annoyed Gorgan, expecting something bad.

"It's Zaos. We thought he'd be one of the faster ones to recover seeing how he only got kicked, but I'm afraid that's not the case."

"Well? Spit it out."

"It's his back. It's broken."

"How did that go unnoticed? He practically walked back here himself," Gorgan states.

"It happened when he was getting out of his cot a few minutes ago," says Sandro. "His back shifted and he collapsed. The break is clearly visible now. I'm not sure he's ever going to fully recover. It's really bad."

Gorgan kicks a bucket full of water that flies over the boat's guardrail. "I'm going to break Arviakyss' back and make him watch as we kill his friends! I'll even keep the girl alive and snap her in two right in front of him!" Gorgan furiously turns to face Navarre. "What do you need to get you on your way."

"I need the sun to go down," he replies.

Gorgan takes a deep breath to calm himself down. "Onus, prepare everyone's gear. If someone has armor, they wear it."

"Got it," Onus copies.

"This job has cost us more than we've made. It's about time we share that cost."

"Will that room hold them?" Delsar asks Allbus.

"As far as rooms designed for living go, this one's not that bad and I don't see them getting out anytime soon," he replies.

"Good, now put these on." Delsar tosses Allbus a pair of restraints which he effortlessly catches.

"On what, Delsar?"

"Your wrists. That's what they're designed for."

"On myself?" asks the visibly confused Allbus.

"Either you can put them on or I will put them on for you," Delsar says, walking from the building.

"Uh, why?"

Delsar spins around. "Fine, just give them to me and I'll put them on *for* you."

Allbus throws his hands up, still not sure what's going on. "Wait, wait, wait. You're being serious?"

"Always. Put them on," Delsar says, walking back toward Galius.

Allbus jogs next to Delsar and spies Galius and Castor sitting on a bench overlooking the beach. "Hang on," he says to Delsar. "Galius, what's going on?" he shouts over.

Both Galius and Castor look over and Castor's red face says it all. He holds up his own restrained arms to show to Allbus.

"What is the meaning of this?" Allbus asks with much concern.

"You'd best just put them on, son," says Galius.

"You aren't trading us for the hostage, are you?"

"Tempting," says Delsar, "but, no. Your partner just tried to murder me and you both are unknowns. Neither of you are even supposed to be here."

"Hold on, Castor would never try to kill someone unless he had a good reason," Allbus defends.

"Delsar is Arviakyss, Allbus," says Castor. "He killed the Queen!" Castor tries to stand up, but Galius holds him down.

"You're afraid I'm going to try to kill you since that's our duty?" Allbus asks.

"Yeah, so put them on." Delsar gives him a stern look and places his hand on his sword.

"You're not doing a very great job convincing me," says Allbus. "Why would I leave myself defenseless in the presence of an enemy?"

"Let me be blunt," says Delsar. "I didn't kill the Queen and these mercenaries are here to make sure that truth never surfaces. Put the restraints on."

Allbus clicks one on but pauses for the second. "I'm not putting the other on until I get a confirmation from my Sergeant," he says.

"Son, I assure you that Delsar is the good guy. Once Telrus gets back, he'll explain everything." Galius gives Allbus a nod. "Now put them on, Corporal."

Allbus follows his orders and clamps on the other cuff.

"I don't give a care about Telrus' explanation," Delsar says. "I'm sending you both back to Lar in the morning. Trust isn't something I like giving freely."

"But I'm here to help," says Allbus.

"No one here knows you!" yells the aggravated Delsar. "If *I* was with Telrus and Galius, I would *never* have let you join." Delsar removes Allbus' sword and crossbow.

"Delsar," says Galius.

"What?" exclaims Delsar, showing no respect to his former master.

Galius pays his exclamation no mind and says, "They've been a huge help already and we may need the extra hands. Plus, like us, they are both guards so we *can* depend on them in the coming combat."

"I'm no guard."

"That doesn't change the fact," says Galius.

"You're not the one they want dead," Delsar says, crossing his arms. "Let me say it again; trust is not something I like giving."

"But you have come a long way since you visited me in Dukla."

"The people I trust have earned it. The three of *you* have never tried to kill me."

"And your father?" Galius asks.

"I'm still deciding."

Galius looks at the two guards and asks, "Are either of you going to try to kill Delsar again?"

Allbus shakes his head, but it's Castor who has something to say. "That depends on what the Lieutenant has to say and whether I believe him or not."

Delsar scowls and grinds his teeth with his mouth closed. "He'd better have a pretty convincing story for me, too. As it stands, I have no intention of letting either of you stay," he says before storming off.

"Delsar, where are you going?" Galius asks.

"Someone has to figure a way to save Raymar with just the six of us." He disappears into the house that they decided will be their headquarters.

"The map is still at camp," Allbus says.

"He's blowing off steam first," Galius says before letting out a sigh. "I hate to say it, but he's right. I doubt he'll change his mind."

"I hope he does, Sergeant," Allbus responds. "I hate not finishing things I've started."

"What about you, Castor?" Galius asks.

Castor says nothing. He merely glares at the door Delsar disappeared through. Fire in his eyes.

Telrus weaves the paddy wagon through the houses and buildings before bringing it to a stop at the village center, the very place the mercenaries held their fights. He and Ligrei jump down from the carriage and are quickly greeted by Delsar, though not quite the greeting either of them are expecting.

"It's ten miles there and ten miles back!" Delsar yells. "How did you manage to take fourteen hours being pulled at three miles an hour?"

"It's good to see you, too," Telrus responds.

"There was a lot of paperwork and reports we had to fill out," Ligrei explains. "Telrus also had a three-hour debriefing thing they had him attend."

"Today was going to be long already," says Telrus, "but we still needed to place the survivors in protective care. That was a pain. I assure you that my trips back and forth will be only a few hours now. I only need to sign a couple things when I drop the next mercenaries off."

Delsar crosses his arms. "Your day isn't over yet."

"Oh? Well, that's too bad." Telrus takes an exasperated sigh. "Unfortunately, your life just got harder, too."

"Fine, I'll hear yours first, then I'll tell you what I need," says Delsar.

"Yeah, yeah." Telrus straightens his breastplate before giving Delsar his news. "Apparently, you had a tussle with a couple guards, about a month ago, in Eskor."

"I remember."

"Well, the guards interviewed the people in the bar and pretty easily put the pieces together. Everyone in the kingdom now knows that Delsar is Arviakyss. Sorry about that."

Delsar rolls his eyes. "Whatever. Everyone in the kingdom aren't the only people who know."

"What happened?" Telrus asks, raising an eyebrow and crossing his arms.

"Those extra guards you brought found out who I am and tried to kill me," Delsar explains while pressing his finger into Telrus' breastplate.

"That's quite the event, Mr. Delsar."

"You didn't tell them much when you brought them, did you?" Delsar asks.

"Just the bare minimum," Telrus says, pushing Delsar's hand away. "They already wanted to help, so I only told them about the mercenaries and possible hostages."

"I put them both under house arrest. I want you to tell them *everything*. Even after you do, I'm not sure I'll be ready to trust them."

"Yeah, I can do that." Telrus hears more people approaching and turns around to see Merith and Elidria coming his way. He gives an over-the-top courteous bow and says, "Good evening Mrs. Merith and Miss Eldra."

Merith gives her own simple bow, but Elidria doesn't so much as slow down. "I swear it's in one ear and out the other with you," she says, walking past him.

Telrus straightens back up and adjusts his breastplate again. "This is quite a welcoming group of individuals," he says. "'Good job, Telrus.

Thanks for handling all the paperwork none of us know anything about, Telrus.' Instead, I immediately get berated by both of you!"

Merith can't help herself from chuckling as she walks by him to join with Delsar, Ligrei, and Elidria.

"Yeah, my apologies for being *polite*," Telrus says.

"Politeness only gets you so far in life," says Ligrei.

"And yet, here I am." Telrus places the tips of his fingers on his chest. "I'm higher ranking than any guard here and I'm only nineteen."

"Topping out at nineteen," says Merith. "That's rough, bud."

"And Arviakyss became a Captain at seventeen," Ligrei adds. "I think that's a bit more impressive."

"Biased much?" says Telrus.

"Arviakyss wasn't even seventeen. He lied about his age so he could graduate two months earlier," Delsar adds.

Telrus scoffs. "You realize he was Captain of a team that consisted of just himself and the Queen? He wasn't even an officer. It was just a complimentary title the Queen gave him. Even if he *was* called Captain of the Queen's Guard, he was still only a Corporal."

"Well done, Telrus," says Elidria, grinning ear-to-ear, "you one-upped a murderer... *and apparently a liar*," she finishes, under her breath.

"As if!" Telrus exclaims. "If all you *amazing* people will excuse me, I have guards that require my attention." Telrus turns from the group and begins to walk off.

"Telrus," Delsar says to stop him.

"What wisdom do you wish to beseech upon me now, Mr. Delsar?" he asks, whipping back around.

"The house isn't that way." Delsar points the other way with his thumb. "It's the one next to the blacksmith shop. Aldameer's house. Galius is inside with them and will let you in."

"Then excuse me again." Instead of going around, Telrus pushes straight through the four individuals and continues on his way.

"I just got Newville vibes," says Elidria.

"How so?" Delsar asks.

"This whole exchange with Telrus. It was like with you trying to buy the carriage."

"Perhaps, but that makes you the common instigator."

"And I'll keep instigating until he stops calling me *Miss*," she says.

"Interesting," is Delsar's response.

"Interesting, yeah," Elidria says as she fades into thought. "Oh, yeah! What, um, what's going on with Castor and Allbus? You locked them up or something?"

"I did," says Delsar. "Castor tried to kill me because I'm Arviakyss. He has some crazy theory that the people of Bihnor are my cohorts and that the King hired the mercenaries to eliminate enemies of the kingdom, like us."

"Hmm," responds Merith, taking it all in.

"What about Allbus?" Elidria asks. "What did he do?"

"Nothing yet."

"So you punish him, too?"

"They're partners, Elidria. If I can't trust one of them, I can't trust either of them," Delsar says.

"Well, that seems stupid. They're both different people."

"Different people that have been trained to trust each other without hesitation," Delsar explains. "They're supposed to believe each other and follow each other everywhere. Where one falls, so does the other."

Ligrei cuts into what sounds like an almost, or soon to be, heated debate. "Whatever you decide to do with them, you'll have our support."

"Speaking of blindly following," Elidria says while scrunching her nose, but only for a moment as her very bruised face doesn't agree with the movement. "I guess my own face doesn't want me to be mad at you."

"Why are you mad at me?" asks Delsar.

"I'm not," she replies. "But if I was, I wouldn't be."

Delsar shakes his head, confused by what she said. "I don't have time for this. Don't you three have someplace to be, like sleeping?"

"It *has* been a long day," says Ligrei. "I think sleep is exactly what I need."

"I agree," Merith confirms. "The bit of training I did, albeit, by myself, because of certain events, really exhausted me. I'll sleep like a not-so-newborn baby tonight." Merith and Ligrei part ways and enter into their houses. Merith to her own and Ligrei to a vacant one next door.

"And what about you, Elidria?"

Elidria tilts her head and stares back at Delsar.

"I'm starting to think concussion," says Delsar.

"Obviously," she replies.

"Do you need me to wake you in a couple hours or something?"

"I've been sleeping since early this morning," she says. "If you think I'm going to be able to fall asleep again tonight, you are very mistaken. If anyone needs sleep, it's you." She presses her finger against Delsar's chest.

"I'm not sleeping tonight," says Delsar. "Just come guard the ramp with me tonight."

"That's fine." She follows him to the bench that overlooks the beach. "I used to sit here with Galia to watch the sunset and stare at the moon. Mom would join us all the time."

They both sit down and Delsar watches the crescent moon disappear and reappear behind a cloud, illuminating the boat that carries the mercenaries.

"We would sit here and wait for Dad to return from his many trips to the capital," she says, continuing her reminiscing with Delsar. "During the winter, we could see the Diamond Rays light up the water as they escape the cold from the north. One of my favorite memories is one of my father trying to fish from up here. He would cast his line thirty feet below during high tide and wait for hours. He never caught anything. We would taunt him all the time." Elidria feels something rest against her shoulder. She looks down at Delsar who is fast asleep, resting against her.

You don't need sleep, huh? she thinks, giving a warm smile. "Don't worry, Delsar. I'll make sure those big, scary guards don't hurt you tonight." Elidria looks back over the horizon. She takes a deep breath, admiring the starry sky and the beams of moonlight as the clouds move across the sky. A few tears begin to swell as she thinks of all that has been lost and will never be again.

"Please, reconsider."

"Get in the carriage, Allbus," Delsar orders.

"I just want to help," he pleads. "I have no quarrel with you."

Delsar looks in the carriage and at Castor. "Is that true, Castor? Do you have no quarrel with me?"

Castor gives no response.

"Forget it," says Delsar. "Just get in." Delsar forcefully pushes Allbus in with his partner.

Allbus turns around. "Can I at least get these off?" he asks, extending his restrained wrists.

Delsar tosses him a key. "Don't try anything stupid," he says.

Galius slides a sack with two shields, two swords, two crossbows, one of which is broken, and two quivers with crossbow bolts. "Here's your stuff," he says. "Unlock yourselves and acquire your gear. Once you have, we'll send in the prisoner."

Allbus unlocks himself and then helps Castor out of his cuffs. "Do you want your key back?" he asks Delsar.

"I doubt it," Telrus says, answering the question for Delsar. "I grabbed two dozen pairs of restraints and each one came with two keys. The man could start a key business."

"In that case, we'll hold on to these restraints, too," says Allbus.

"I don't care," Delsar responds. He grabs the mercenary prisoner by his shoulder. "Your turn, pal." He pushes the man in so only his top-half makes it through the door. Delsar then grabs the man's legs and hoists him the rest of the way in. "Enjoy your time in Lar."

"Delsar—" starts Allbus.

Delsar slams the door shut. "Get them out of here."

"Right," says Telrus. "Let's go, Ligrei."

"You're taking my father again?" Delsar questions.

"Do you have a problem with me?" Ligrei asks.

"Not at the moment. It's just, if Galius was *my* partner, I'd take him everywhere," says Delsar.

"The people of Lar are already familiar with Ligrei," Telrus explains. "He also knows what to do after yesterday's long escapade. Galius also needs to teach Merith a few things. Ligrei is the most logical choice."

"I didn't need your explanation."

"But you got it anyway."

Delsar rolls his eyes. "Get back quickly and be safe."

"Be safe?" Telrus asks. "I was thinking about taking risks and getting hurt, but you've changed my mind."

Delsar rolls his eyes again and starts to walk away.

"We'll see you in a few hours!" Telrus shouts to Delsar.

Delsar throws his hand up, only showing the back of it as his wave.

"Bye, son," says Ligrei.

"Yup," Delsar responds and the paddy wagon begins its journey.

Galius follows after Delsar. "He seems like a reasonable man," he says. "He also seems like he's come a long way from when he wronged you. I'm sure he'll stop calling you 'son' if you ask."

"It's fine," says Delsar. "I *am* his son."

"Then I'll stop calling you 'son' if that's what you need."

"You don't need to baby my feelings. I really don't care. Besides, you call everyone 'son.' You wouldn't be you if you stopped."

"I suppose," says Galius. "It was different for you, though."

Delsar grinds his teeth before giving Galius an order. "Go feed the prisoners and then find Merith. I'm going to meet back up with Elidria at the bench."

"Copy that, Delsar," says Galius.

Delsar looks at his former master with the corner of his eyes. "I told you I don't care."

Galius smiles. "Yeah, sure. You two have fun now."

Delsar watches Galius walk away and waits for him to get out of earshot before shaking his head and saying, "'Son' is fine." Delsar sighs and approaches Elidria who is standing with her arms crossed, facing the ocean. The wind blows her hair and ruffles her skirt. Delsar stands to her side and gazes out with her. "Anything new?" he asks.

"Nothing," she says, "and that's what scares me." She looks over at Delsar. "They lost and could have easily left and yet they stay."

"We'll beat them, Elidria," Delsar assures. "Whatever they throw at us, we can overcome it."

"I'm not afraid of losing," she replies. "I'm afraid of what we *will* lose." She looks back over the ocean. "Telrus, Galius, Ligrei, Merith, Raymar," she says, tearing up. "So much has already been lost. I can't bear to lose anyone else."

"The cost of freedom and justice is high. Not for those who live, but for those who *choose* to live."

"Maybe it's my head, but I don't know what you just said," says Elidria.

"My time as Arviakyss helped me realize that most people live their lives without a clue in the world. They don't know what was paid for the easy lives they live. Pain, death, suffering, mistakes, betrayals, sacrifices. All of that is needed for freedom. When you got attacked two months ago, you were given three choices. The first and easy one was to just give up and die. All your suffering would be over and you wouldn't have experienced everything else. Another choice was to live and forget about it. Leave and go somewhere no one would look for you or hurt you. Those aren't the choices you made. Instead, you chose to make a difference and live. You chose life so now comes the burden of such. You see? The only people in this world are those who live and those who *choose* to live."

"I wish everyone had the choice to live." Elidria drops her head. "I've been thinking," she says, "specifically about the inevitable battle. People will likely die. I may have to kill to survive and stop injustice." She pauses for a moment, but Delsar doesn't try to get a word in. "I thought even more after that realization." She starts to shake her head. "I won't do it. I won't take someone's choice to live from them." She looks directly at Delsar. "If I'm strong enough to kill someone, then I must also be strong enough to save him."

A part of Delsar wants to tell her she's being foolish, but the other part of him can't help but agree. "Sometimes I hate your logic," he finally says.

"Because you don't agree?"

"No, it's because I do." He finally returns her look. "Every time you have some sort of realization, you make me realize just how wrong I've been, but in this case, I will do what I must. I *will* choose our lives over theirs. I believe they forfeited their choice when they chose their path."

"You said you agreed, but that didn't sound like you were agreeing."

"I agree that your convictions are who you are. You don't want to kill? Fine. But even so, your words always leave me with feelings of regret and disappointment in myself."

"Regret and self-disappointment seems a bit redundant."

"Perhaps."

"I don't mean to have that effect, Delsar. I apologize," she tells him.

"Don't," he says. "Don't ever apologize for being right. People need to hear the truth, even if it offends them. Unfortunately, so many people ignore what offends them, even though it's right. That won't be me anymore."

"Were you offended by the truth before?" Elidria asks.

"Not really. I just shut people out so I never got the chance to hear it. Not until you."

"Like how you're sitting Allbus and Castor out," she says.

"Say the word and I'll catch the carriage to stop them."

"No," she says, looking down, "it's not worth the risk. You can't change someone's outlook on life in just a day. Believe me, I've tried."

"So I was a project to you?" Delsar has a tinge of disappointment in his voice.

"The Outcast wasn't going to save my village. I don't even think Arviakyss could." She looks at his chest, where his cloak used to tie. "Delsar can." She looks up at his face and smiles.

"Not alone," he replies.

"Good thing you're not." Elidria and Delsar look past the idling boat. "Do you think we should tell them?" she asks.

"Why so vague? I'm not psychic."

"The mercenaries. Perhaps we should tell them we just shipped another one of their Idiots to Lar. You know, to keep the pressure on them."

"I suppose. Maybe we can get some good intel while talking to them. My main concern would be them trying to kill us while we're down there."

"I doubt that. That would risk compromising any plans they are formulating. They would have to take us down without a hitch."

"I guess that's true," agrees Delsar. "Your grasp of combat strategy impresses me."

"It makes sense," she explains, swinging her sword through the air. "If there are only four of them left and we take out two of them trying to take us out, suddenly they only have two themselves. They likely still don't know how many of us there are, so I'm sure they'll use this opportunity to try and get more info for themselves."

"Right again," he says. "You have the ability to make what should be obvious, *very* obvious. However, assuming someone is smarter than they are can get you killed."

"That's why I'm taking you with me." Elidria gestures down the ramp. "After you."

"Does Delsar know?" Telrus asks Ligrei, sitting next to him.

"Not yet," he replies. "You know how he is. It's not relevant information at the moment. I also don't want to add anything to his plate."

"He's an interesting character. Nothing like the stories."

"He was younger and successful back then. Much like you are now."

"That's somewhat creepy, Mr. Ligrei. It sounds like you kept a secret eye on your son."

Ligrei leans back in his carriage seat, watching the trees as they go by. "I was… ashamed. Not because of what I did, but because of how I *knew* he felt. I wonder, now, if I was wrong."

"Maybe."

Ligrei smirks, looking back at his driver. "You're not very insightful."

"I'm nineteen and have no regrets. What did you expect?"

Ligrei chuckles, smacking his hand against Telrus' pauldron. "Valid point. Then I'll have to run my story past you again when you're a father."

"Maybe."

"Again?"

"Yup. Maybe."

Ligrei shakes his head, keeping a smile on his face. "You were much more lively during yesterday's transport."

"I was."

Ligrei sighs and looks back at the passing trees. "I'm sure there's a lot—" He stops short, seeing something reflect from the treeline. "Hey, do you see that?" he asks, pointing right.

"Ambush!" shouts Telrus as a reactionary response. He snaps the reins to make the horses pick up their speeds, but it's no use. The mercenaries are already caught up and two begin climbing the front.

Telrus reaches for his sword, but Ligrei grabs his arm and pulls him off the carriage with him, sending them both tumbling to the ground. Telrus' armor cushioned much of the fall, but Ligrei isn't wearing any. The impact for sure caused him some damage. Telrus struggles to his feet with all his gear, but looking over, Ligrei is already up and moving.

One of the mercenaries, who wasn't fast enough to catch the carriage, is first to Telrus and Ligrei. He swings his axe at Ligrei who steps back to avoid it. Ligrei steps back again to avoid the second strike. The mercenary raises his axe above his head and Ligrei dashes in, jabbing both hands into his chest before catching the axe's handle and sending his knee into the man's stomach.

The mercenary sends his helmeted-head toward Ligrei who quickly switches his grip from the axe's handle to his assailant's right wrist. As he does, he steps to the side to avoid the headbutt and pulls the arm around, tucking the man's arm into his own back.

He grunts from the pain and drops the axe allowing Ligrei to kick him away. Turning back around, the mercenary gets met by his own axe to his helmet. A blunt pain and bright lights flash for just a moment before everything goes dark. The mercenary plops to the ground. It doesn't matter how good his helmet is. A blow like that will knock anyone out.

The cart stops ahead of them and three of the mercenaries who caught up to it begin charging Telrus and Ligrei, while another starts dealing with the locked door.

Telrus reaches for his sword again but quickly realizes that he never picked it up after dropping it when Ligrei pulled him from the carriage. He steps back and raises his fists. *Can we run?* he thinks to himself. *Can we make it back to the village to warn Delsar?* Telrus remembers who else they carry in the carriage and leaving Allbus and Cator to die isn't something he's willing to do. The time to decide is over. The three mercenaries are right on top of them and they all wield swords.

Telrus makes an "X" with his bracers and catches the first strike above his head, but is immediately struck in his sideplate by another. The strike winds him but doesn't take him down. Telrus grabs the blade by his side with his gloved hand and sends a backfist into whomever just struck his side. His strike misses but the sword he grabbed stays in his hand. Telrus catches himself on his back foot, completely thrown off by the move. A fist returns from that direction and meets Telrus in the face, knocking him on his back.

The sword he had in his hand drops to the ground. Telrus knows he has to get back up and he has to do it now. He tries to sit up, but his body refuses to move. He tries again, but only produces heavy breathing. He closes his eyes tight and that's when he feels it. A blade slides from between his breastplate and abdominal plate, dripping his own blood.

Two mercenaries loom above him. The one that stabbed him snarls before joining his friend versus Ligrei.

The other mercenary reaches for his sword that lies beside Telrus. Telrus grabs his leg but the man simply shakes it off before joining the two versus one.

"No," Telrus says, giving his all to roll over. He pushes up on his hands and manages to get on all fours. His head droops and his blood pours from his wound because of his position. He gets dizzy and lightheaded in an instant before tumbling down, again on his back. Everything spins and starts to fade, but before it all goes to black, Telrus sees Ligrei take a strike to the leg and drop to his knee. "Ligrei," he says, weakly. Then everything disappears.

"Come on, Elidria," Delsar says, annoyed that Elidria stopped on the ramp and didn't follow him into the high tide.

"Give me a minute," she says, unstrapping one of her shinguards. "I'm not getting my boots and socks wet. I'll be uncomfortable for the rest of the day if I do."

Delsar looks down at his own boots that are now drenched by the knee-deep water. *That's not a bad idea*, he thinks. *Too late now.* "Whatever. Take your time, I guess." Delsar trudges through the water and hoists himself on top of the dock. From there, the boat is almost three hundred feet from him.

"That's one," she says, tucking the contents of her left foot under her arm. "What if we catch them by surprise?"

"What do you mean?"

"What if they're all gone and we can just waltz aboard and grab Raymar?"

"I highly doubt that will be the case," says Delsar.

"But imagine it is. We show up and no one's on deck, so we board and *still* no one stops us. It could happen."

"That would be insanely risky. For us *and* Raymar. If we don't encounter anyone on deck, we leave," he informs. "Something like that would be too suspicious. They could be lying in wait."

Elidria switches her footwear to both arms and holds it in front of her. "I suppose," she says as she begins her march through the water.

Delsar watches the boat intently. An ambush would put a dampener on his spirit.

GLUG!

Delsar turns to face Elidria. "Did you just drop one of your items in the water?"

Elidria looks down and spins around. "I don't think so."

Delsar looks up and spots Gorgon, in full armor, halfway up the treacherous staircase. "Get to me, now!" he shouts, startling Elidria. A smaller rock plops into the water.

Gorgon, knowing he's been spotted, jumps into the water.

Delsar draws his bow but Gorgan hides behind the ramp. "Run, Elidria!" Delsar yells.

Elidria gives up on her items and drops them all in the water. She begins pushing through the water as quickly as she can.

Gorgan jumps out from behind his cover and chases after her, positioning himself so Elidria provides cover from Delsar. Delsar traverses the dock to find a shot but Gorgan continues to readjust every time he tries. Gorgan's strength allows him to push through the water with ease, closing his distance on Elidria rapidly.

"Draw your sword!" Delsar commands while placing his bow down and drawing his own sword.

Elidria whips out her sword and turns around. Gorgan's strike is powerful, but she is able to maintain the grip on her weapon. Gorgan's attacks, however, are quick and relentless. Elidria has no opportunity to avoid or retaliate. She is completely on the defensive as Gorgan continues to push her back with his strikes. Elidria loses her footing and tumbles over a rock. She falls backward and wholly submerges underwater.

She relocates the rock with her feet and pushes off, propelling herself through the water before slowing down and standing back up.

The saltwater drips from her hair and burns her tattered face and eyes. The world is a blur. She can barely see Gorgan approach, but she can make out him swinging and she raises her sword to parry.

The sword clashes with something big and heavy. "Get to the dock!" Delsar shouts, shield-in-hand. Another loud impact is heard, followed by the clash of swords.

Elidria isn't going for the dock without Delsar. She wipes her eyes as best she can with her top and blinks a few times. The world starts to become clear again, but she doesn't like what she sees.

Gorgan rips Delsar's shield from his arm, pulling him off balance toward Gorgan.

Instead of trying to fight against this man's superhuman strength, Delsar decided to let himself be pulled to use his momentum against the man. Delsar follows in, but the back of his shield bashes hard against his face. His head is knocked back and he flops into the water.

Gorgan steps on top of him, pinning him under the water.

"Delsar!" Elidria cries as she starts pushing through the water, back toward Gorgan.

"Looks like you're getting that rematch, after all, Little Missy." Gorgan tosses Delsar's shield away but keeps his leg on top of him.

"Get off of him!" she demands.

"Make me."

CHAPTER 19

THE SCORCH

"Ambush!" Castor and Allbus both hear Telrus' warning cry.

"They're after him," Allbus says, pointing at the captured mercenary.

Castor jumps on the man before he has an opportunity to shout a warning to his comrades. The mercenary stands no chance against Castor's chokehold, not with both his arms bound behind his back. He struggles and kicks, but Castor hangs on his neck, reinforcing his chokehold with his other arm.

Allbus hears men climbing on the outside of the carriage and armor crashing to the ground. He draws his crossbow in anticipation as the carriage comes to a stop. A fight ensues outside, but there's nothing he can do about it from inside.

The lock on the door begins to jostle.

Castor squeezes with all his might and the mercenary finally falls limp.

The door opens a crack and Allbus immediately kicks it out, putting all his weight into his strike. The door jams the rescuer's fingers and its edge crashes into his face, knocking him to the ground. Allbus jumps out and launches his bolt aimed at the back of a mercenary withdrawing a blade in Ligrei's shoulder. The projectile easily pierces the assailant's studded leather and exits out the front, killing the mercenary in an instant.

The man bashed by the door starts to come to his senses and scrambles to his feet. Before he's able to do anything more, Castor stabs his blade up and under the man's breastplate. He screams and collapses.

The two standing mercenaries turn to face the threat that none of them were expecting. Allbus and Castor are already charging them. The momentum has shifted and they know it. The mercenaries turn and flee from the heavier guards, giving Allbus and Castor no chance of catching up.

"Crossbow!" yells Allbus.

"It's broken!" Castor replies, still in chase.

"Then hold!" Allbus stops and pulls a bolt from his quiver, readying another shot. He pulls the string back until it locks into place and then places the bolt upon its track. He aims at the nearest target, but both mercenaries have already dashed into the woods. He fires anyway, narrowly missing as the bolt lodges itself deep into a tree. He doesn't bother with a second shot. "Ligrei and Telrus!" he shouts, turning back toward the carriage.

Ligrei is already at Telrus' side. Blood seeps from his Ligrei's leg and shoulder.

"Are you okay?" Castor asks, trying to aid Ligrei.

"I'm doing better than Telrus," he answers. "He's not responding and bleeding a lot."

"Move," commands Castor. He forcefully pushes Ligrei aside and drops to his knees. "Allbus, help me," he says as he starts unstrapping Telrus' two body plates. Blood continues to drain from the guard and his face is a ghostly white. "Grab me something to stop the bleeding!"

Allbus cuts a shirt from a mercenary and hands it to Castor.

Castor presses down on the wound, but the pool of blood continues to grow. "He's been stabbed through-and-through," he reports as he turns him on his side. Castor tears the shirt in two and presses on both sides of Telrus's body.

"We have to get him to Lar!" says Allbus, in a panic.

"He won't make it that far," Castor deducts.

"But we don't have what we need in Bihnor."

"I know that." Castor closes his eyes shut, trying to keep himself composed. "Grab his legs."

"Right." Allbus and Castor pick him up and race him to the back of the carriage.

"Drive!" Castor orders.

Allbus jumps around to the front as Ligrei hobbles his way in the back. The carriage begins moving, but turning around becomes a pain on the narrow road. It takes a precious minute from Telrus' life just getting the horses in the right direction.

At a walk, it took eight minutes to get where they are now. With the horses galloping, it should take less than three.

Telrus wakes up in a start as the carriage jostles around on the road. He begins to breathe heavily and he can feel his heart fluttering. He looks up at the man applying pressure to both his back and his stomach. "Castor?" he asks in a daze.

"You've been stabbed, Lieutenant," Castor replies. "Do me a favor and don't stop breathing."

"Roger... that."

Even with the rapid shaking of the carriage, Castor can feel the Lieutenant shivering from his wounds. The fact that Telrus is showing no signs of pain tells him that his body is in shock. Massive blood loss and shock isn't a good combination.

The carriage clatters a few more times before coming to a stop. "Galius!" Allbus shouts, hopping from the front. "Help us!" He runs for the small clearing Galius is using to train Merith.

"Castor," Telrus says, faintly.

"Lieutenant?"

"Please. You must trust Arviakyss. Help him."

Castor looks away. "You're asking me to go against everything I've been told."

Telrus places his bloodied-hand on Castor's breastplate. "Allbus believes in him. Believe in your partner."

Castor looks back at Telrus and hangs his mouth open.

"Telrus!" Galius exclaims, running to the back of the carriage. His tears are already forming. "My medpack is in the house," he says, turning to go fetch it. He stops when Telrus' hand reaches through the door and grabs his arm.

"Wait," says Telrus in a pant. "Please."

Galius nods as a tear drips through his beard. "What is it, son?"

"Get them out," he answers.

Castor and Ligrei look at each other. Merith looks anxiously over Allbus' shoulders.

"Get out!" Telrus cries with what strength he has left.

Ligrei and Castor climb out, allowing Galius room for himself. He looks out the back and mouths, "Thank you," before closing the door behind him.

The four back away from the carriage, giving the space and respect Telrus deserves, allowing him to say what he needs to say to his partner.

Minutes go by before the door opens back up. Galius slowly emerges. He has a blank look and his lips quiver. He stands, scanning Castor, Allbus, Ligrei, and Merith with no attempt to hide his tears.

The four stare back and none of them know what to say.

Merith breaks and starts to cry.

Galius lowers his head and lets out a quick weep, but that's it. He's over it in a moment and looks to his party. Tears and determination fill his eyes. "Prepare for combat."

3 Years Ago...

"I thought I made it clear that I was done apprenticing," Galius says, examining the "Assigned Partner" slip.

"He's no apprentice," the Major states, "though I assume you're just saying that because of his age."

"I'm nearly four-times his age, sir. I don't want to have to baby anyone anymore."

"I completely understand that, but I did personally observe his trials and I can assure you that he's the real deal. He scored higher than anyone on the written in the last fifteen years."

Galius frowns and hands back the piece of paper. "Intelligence doesn't translate to maturity."

"Listen, Galius," the Major starts, placing his hand on his shoulder, "you've done more than enough for your country and, frankly, could have retired twenty years ago, but I'd like you to give this kid a go. You have no partner and he specifically asked for you. If you don't like him, reach out to me and I'll transfer him myself."

Galius lets out an exasperated sigh. "I'm not fond of working with officers, sir. No offense. Now not only will I be working with one, but you're asking me to take him as my partner."

"Just try him, Galius. His whole ride here he was no-nonsense. Straight to business, just like you," the Major says, giving Galius a quick pat on the pauldron.

"Is that an order, sir?"

"No, but as a friend, it's a recommendation. Every guard needs a partner. You've been pushing this off for far too long."

"I don't need one here in Dukla."

The Major gives Galius a reassuring smile.

Galius shakes his head and holds out an open hand. "Give me the slip."

The Major produces a huge grin handing Galius back the paper. "You won't regret your decision. My boy has prepared long and hard to be a stellar guard."

Galius signs the slip and hands it back to the Major. "I'm not going to treat him any different just because he's your son."

"I wouldn't think of it."

"And I'm not going to be treating him like an apprentice either. If he can't pull his weight or needs reminding of the basics, you're going to be hearing from me sooner rather than later."

"Of course. Thank you, Galius."

"Uh-huh."

"Well, I'm sure you're just dying to meet him," the Major says, urging him on toward the door.

"Not really."

The Major opens the door. "I hope you both have a fine partnership." The Major practically pushes Galius through the door before saying, "Thank you," again and closing the door.

A young guard with an officer's kama and Lieutenant stripes stands up from his seat.

Galius snaps to attention and salutes.

The Lieutenant returns the salute and speaks first. "That's the only time I want to see you saluting me. We're partners now, Sergeant," he says.

Galius drops his hand. "Saluting an officer is professional."

"It wastes time."

"I'm not going to salute when we're downfield."

"We're guards, Sergeant. We're always downfield."

Galius can't help but smirk. "Okay, sir, no more saluting."

"Please, if anything, your experience overshadows my rank. Call me Telrus."

"I appreciate your clear lack of concern for regulation," Galius says, facetiously, "but I'd prefer if you still call me Sergeant."

Telrus shrugs. "We'll work on that."

"Tell me, *Telrus*, what's with your father?" Galius asks, folding his arms across his broad chest.

Telrus shakes his head and smiles. "The old fool is a bit too proud of me. I mean, I do get it, but he needs to let *me* handle things. I wanted to personally talk to you about being my partner, but he insisted on doing it himself. If you're not happy with who I am, I'll be more than happy to fill out a transfer form."

Galius gestures with his hand without moving his arm. "Not yet, but I do have one more question."

"Shoot."

"Why did you want *me* as a partner?"

Telrus drops his smile and straightens his breastplate. "As partners, I hope I'm allowed to speak freely with you and with an open mind."

"You mean, you hope I don't tell anyone what you're about to say?"

"Yeah, that."

Galius thinks it over for a moment before deciding. "If it can go both ways."

"Absolutely."

"Then proceed, Telrus."

"Uh, well, you see, I don't want to be a guard," he says, putting his hand on the back of his neck, "or at least, I didn't. It was forced on me by my father. All the extra training I did as a kid and getting into army school early were his doings. It wasn't until the rise of Arviakyss that I really wanted to be a guard. I really wanted to be like him. To save people and bring hope wherever I go." Telrus fades off and smiles.

"Arviakyss was a unique person," says Galius.

"Oh, I know that," Telrus quickly defends. "I learned early that I can never live up to him. However, I do think I can save him."

Galius tilts his head. "What are you saying?"

"The reason I chose you, Sergeant, is because I believe Arviakyss could be innocent. I wish to clear his name and I figured you of all people know his character better than anyone. If you think he could be innocent, then I *know* I can clear his name."

Galius starts to chuckle.

"What's so funny, Sergeant?"

"All right, Telrus. It's a deal." Galius extends his hand.

"Huh? I didn't make a deal."

"You want to spend your time in boring-old Dukla trying to clear my apprentice's name and I want to help. Arviakyss didn't kill the Queen. I guarantee that."

Telrus grins ear-to-ear and takes Galius' hand. "That means a lot coming from you. I feel actual hope now. Thank you, Sergeant."

Galius lets out his girthy laugh. "Please, go ahead and call me Galius. This is a partnership I know I'll enjoy to the end."

"You got it, Galius. Let's make a difference together."

I can't—water! Delsar's brain scrambles from the heavy blow he took from Gorgan swinging his own shield against him. He squirms around under the water, but the pressure from the foot on his chest prevents him from surfacing. Delsar reaches for the knife in his bag, but he left his bag on the beach. He grabs an arrow instead and jams it against Gorgan's shinguard. The arrow tip merely slides against the armor with his stab. Delsar grabs the leg with his other hand and begins feeling around for his exposed calf.

Gorgan quickly realizes what Delsar is trying to do and raises his leg before slamming his foot back down on Delsar. The blow is powerful, even with the water as a cushion.

Delsar loses much of his precious air as a result and even drops his arrow. His body instinctively tries to breathe, but his same instincts reject the water, making him cough out even more air.

The boot on his chest shifts and rotates, causing pulling and burning sensations on his skin. The pain he feels is much duller than it would be if his nerves weren't so deprived of oxygen.

Thoughts fade and feelings begin to disappear. Delsar grabs the foot as another shot of adrenaline shoots through his body, giving him one last chance to survive. The foot's weight lessens until it comes off completely. Delsar sits up and gasps for air. Oxygen surges through his body and the pains to his chest and head come back in full force.

Someone says something but he can't make it out with waving water and his ears readjusting. It speaks out again. "Get up, Delsar!" it commands.

Get up? Delsar's eyes begin to refocus but his head is still jumbled.

"Get up and fight!" it commands again.

A chill shoots through Delsar's body as he remembers where he is and what's happening. He spins over and stands to his feet much too fast. His eyes roll and everything swirls around him. He stumbles around and something crashes into him, knocking him back down. The same force grabs under his arm, helping him back to his feet.

CRACK! A sword smashes into Elidria's shield that she keeps attached to her back. She spins back around to face Gorgan after tackling Delsar to avoid his strike. "Find your sword!" she orders Delsar. She pushes him again as Gorgan swings for both of them. She ducks under and slides her blade against Gorgan's protected thigh, doing no damage to the man.

Delsar stumbles back but catches his footing. His eyes clear in time for him to block a strike by raising his leg and catching the blade with his shinguard.

Gorgan's blade slides off the plate and swings back to the other side, parrying a strike from Elidria.

"Get your sword," she says again, swinging from side to side and keeping Gorgan on the defensive.

Gorgan gets pushed back by the flurry of strikes. He throws a kick in hopes of knocking the girl back, but she swiftly avoids and continues her unrelenting attack. Elidria's sword clashes with the left side of Gorgan's breastplate. He drops his arm around the blade and grabs her hilt, pulling her in.

She throws her other hand up, but it's no use. Gorgan's fist drives through her block and impacts her already bruised face. She lets out a cry as she drops to her knees. Her hand grasping her sword is the only thing keeping her upright.

Gorgan shakes the blade to get her off, but she holds on. He uses his backhand and bashes her face, knocking her from her sword and into the water. He flips the sword in his hand and grabs it by its handle. A glistening light catches his eye and he shifts just enough to keep Delsar's blade from connecting between his pauldron and arm plate. Instead, it glances off the top of his pauldron and knicks his face, leaving a non-lethal gash by his right ear.

Delsar doesn't wait around for a surrender. He swings again, but this time he aims for Gorgan's neck.

Gorgan blocks the strike with his own blade and follows up with an attack from Elidria's, completely throwing off Delsar's offensive.

Delsar blocks the oncoming strike with his bracer and then stops the next strike by parrying it up and over his head, making both of Gorgan's arms end up together. Delsar chops down, aiming for both of Gorgan's hands, but his opponent's reactions are too fast.

Gorgan pulls his hands away and waits for Delsar's strike to swing past before delivering a kick to his chest, sending Delsar flying backward.

Delsar crashes into the water unharmed and gets right back up. Gorgan is already closing the distance, giving Delsar no time to breathe.

The edge of a shield bashes into the monster of a man's head, knocking him sideways.

Elidria is back on her feet, about ten yards from where the shield struck. It was a near-perfect throw. A hard one, too, considering it's a kite shield.

"The dock, Elidria!" Delsar shouts.

Elidria grabs her shield as she runs past Gorgan's staggering body. Delsar grabs Elidria's hand and helps pull her through the water. Her battle-skirt is not ideal for pushing through the water very quickly.

"Come on!" Delsar says, looking over his shoulder and seeing Gorgan on their heels. He gives Elidria a boost up the dock. She rolls to her knees and extends her hand. Delsar reaches out but gets grabbed from behind. He drops his sword as he is tossed through the air.

Gorgan stampedes through the water after Delsar, but his sword he left in the water behind. He hides his daze well, but it's clear Elidria's blow to his head is messing with his judgment. Regardless, with Delsar's sword also in the water, Gorgon's hand-to-hand advantage becomes even greater.

Delsar throws his hands up, but even with his bracers, every punch from Gorgan makes his arms feel like they are cracking more and more.

Gorgan throws a punch into Delsar's stomach, dropping his arms down. He then jabs Delsar in the face, staggering him back, and he finishes with a spin-hook kick into Delsar's cheekbone, knocking him into the water.

A blade cracks against Gorgan's side and he turns, only to get pummeled by multiple strikes from Elidria using Delsar's sword. He tries to punch and kick Elidria to stop the annoying stings to his armor plates, but she avoids each of his retaliations. The sword catches a leather strap on Gorgan's side and slices through, dropping his abdominal plate a few inches from his breastplate.

"Delsar," Elidria yells, "grab your bow!"

Delsar adjusts himself and turns for the dock where he left it.

"I dropped it next to you!" she says, still hacking away.

Delsar snatches the bow and quickly nocks an arrow.

Gorgan sees what's about to happen. He ignores the pain from Elidria's bludgeoning strikes and pushes straight through them.

She slashes at his arms but inflicts no damage. He grabs at her, but she steps back.

He doesn't stop coming.

He grabs her wrist and yanks her in, spinning her around. She struggles, but he easily overpowers her and uses her to cover his exposed abdomen which keeps losing more protection as the plate droops even lower.

Elidria reaches back with her other arm and yanks on Gorgan's beard. She then drops her weight and frees her other hand by pushing it against his thumb and sliding it out. She reaches up now with both hands and takes a hold of his beard. Pulling down with all her weight, she drops his head down while she flips herself up and over his head, landing on his backside.

Delsar releases his arrow, letting it cut through the air.

Gorgan tries to react, but a split-second is all it takes for the arrow to hit its mark. It drives itself deep near his left kidney. Gorgan drops to his knees.

Delsar nocks another arrow and points it at his head. "Don't you move!" he commands.

Gorgan pants and places his hand around where the arrow entered his body. He says nothing and lowers his head.

"Gather your gear," Delsar tells Elidria.

Elidria backs away from the mercenary and takes a couple recovering breaths. She gives Delsar an exhausted nod and leaves Gorgan at Delsar's mercy. She quickly locates her sword and shield under the water and Delsar's shield, too. She walks back to Delsar, her eyes wide open, and places his sword in his sheath. She then slides his shield on his back and grabs him under his arms, embracing him, laying her head on his shoulder as she whimpers.

"We're not done," he says. "Go grab some restraints and bring Galius and Merith back with you. We are taking that boat now!"

"R-right," she says, turning to leave. She starts up the ramp but hears some kind of crackling. She looks at Delsar to ask him if he hears it, too, but as soon as she does a bright light flashes and the air around Delsar explodes.

Delsar flies through the air and crashes into the water. His armor plates hissing and steaming as the water touches them. Even his bow is just a charred twig now.

"Delsar!" Elidria cries. She grabs her shield and runs over to him, covering him with the shield as she crouches next to him. There's another crackling sound, followed by the loudest noise she's ever heard. Whatever it is engulfs her shield in flames and fire explodes in all directions off it. Heat wraps around her but quickly dissipates. "Help!" she yells as loudly as possible. Another explosion crashes against her shield, fear fuels her screaming. Her eyes fill with tears. She can see no escape.

Gorgan stands back to his feet and smirks at Elidria who is completely distraught.

"Hey!" someone shouts from the cliff.

Gorgan looks up and is met by a bolt, hitting him almost in the same location as Delsar's arrow and dropping him back to his knees.

Galius and Castor run down the ramp with their shields at the ready. "Protect us, Eldra!" shouts Galius as he and Castor both grab Delsar and start dragging him through the water.

She stands to her feet and closely follows them to the ramp. This time she sees the streak of light as another fireball crackles through the air and crashes against her shield. Her ears start to ring and her exposed skin feels burned and tight.

Allbus sends another bolt aimed for Gorgan. This one bounces off his armor but it deters the mercenary from following. "Let's go!" Allbus shouts, readying up another shot.

Another fireball shoots through the air, but it's not aimed at Elidria. It crashes into the cliff under Allbus's feet, sending rocky debris everywhere and knocking Allbus back.

Galius and Castor pull Delsar to the top of the ramp and continue to drag him away from the danger zone.

Elidria climbs to the top and looks for the attacker. There, at the end of the dock and by the mercenaries' boat is a single man in red robes. He doesn't seem to be shooting anymore, but Elidria doesn't risk looking any longer. She turns and disappears over the cliff with the others.

"He's burnt pretty bad," Allbus says, running over to help carry Delsar but finding no room to squeeze in.

"Just hold the door for us," Galius instructs.

"There was a man down there!" Elidria exclaims. "Who was that?"

"Bad news," Galius responds.

Allbus pushes open a door to one of the houses, surprising Merith who is wrapping Ligrei's wounds. "What's going on?" she asks, sensing the urgency.

"We just need that table," Allbus replies, not expecting her to quit what she's doing. Allbus hustles over to the table and pushes everything on it to the ground.

Castor and Galius follow in with Delsar, blood dripping from his ears, and hoist him on top of Allbus' clearing.

Elidria is close behind them and secures the door. "Is he—" she starts.

"Alive," says Galius. "He's just knocked out." He unstraps Delsar's charred bracers, warped from the sudden heat of the fireball and rapid cooling after his fall into the water. The extra padding added to them are likely the only reason they didn't fuse with his skin.

"His ears are bleeding," Elidria states, sounding concerned for her employee.

"So are yours," Galius says as a matter of fact and not taking his eyes off Delsar.

Elidria dabs her finger in the blood running down her jaw, confirming Galius' statement. "What does the blood mean?" she asks.

"Your eardrums are perforated."

"Is that bad?"

"It just means we'll have to speak louder," he replies quickly, hoping to concentrate on Delsar.

"What does he need?" she then asks, switching back to worrying about Delsar.

"He's just burned," Galius explains. "He was lucky he fell into the water. His bracers are done, but he'll be okay. Right now we can't do anything for him except make him comfortable." Galius looks over at Elidria. "You look pretty burnt yourself."

"It's nothing," she says. She looks around the room and scans twice before asking, "Where's Telrus?"

"Why are you here?" Gorgan asks the newcomer while being lowered onto his boat's deck by a troll.

"I would think a 'thank you' is in order." The man walks over to Gorgan and rips the two projectiles from his abdomen.

Gorgan bellows as his blood starts to gush out.

"You're lucky these aren't barbed," the man says, inspecting the arrow tips.

"I'm bleeding out," Gorgan remarks. "Are you gonna help me?"

"You're nothing without us, aren't you?" the man asks while also placing his hand over Gorgan's wounds.

"What are you doing?"

The man smirks and says something that Gorgan can't understand.

Suddenly, Gorgan feels an intense burning on his stomach and he can't hold in another howl.

"There," says the man, removing his hand, "nothing to it."

Gorgan looks down at his abdomen. A tough, but tender patch of skin sits completely sealed where his wound was. "I hate magic," he states.

"You hate something that keeps saving your life? How strange."

Gorgan scowls at the man in red and stands up. "I'll ask again, why are *you* here?"

"Isn't it obvious?" the man asks, opening his arms up. "I'm here to finish the job *you* have yet to complete."

"My men are finishing the job as we speak. We don't need you."

"Your men are finishing the job? Then who are those people on that boat over there?" The man points to a small craft returning from where Gorgan left his mercenaries.

Gorgan lets out an exasperated grunt knowing that their attack must have failed. On top of that, he only sees three men aboard and one of them is drooped over. "This is a nightmare!" he exclaims. "You ill-prepared us for Arviakyss! He was supposed to be alone!"

"You're the one who fought him before," the man states. "You told us you could handle him."

"And we can. Arviakyss is down now, thanks to you. The others will fall."

"You had your chance." The man points toward Bihnor, and the troll that carried Gorgan jumps down from the boat and begins running full speed toward the ramp. Five other trolls hop off a different boat and follow after it. "They will clean up your mess."

"Eldra," says Galius, "it looks like your bandage fell off. Allbus, go grab her a fresh one."

"Don't," Elidria says, stopping Allbus. "You're avoiding my question, Galius. Why isn't Telrus with you?"

Galius' composure fades for a moment as he places a wet rag over Delsar's raw shoulder. A single tear trickles down his face and through his beard.

That's all Elidria needs to see to figure out the answer. She steps back, her dread overtaking her confusion. "Oh, please no," she says, bringing her hands to her mouth and tearing up. "This was my fault, wasn't it?"

Galius looks over at her and shakes his head. "It wasn't anyone's fault. People die in combat. It's oftentimes unavoidable."

"Galius, this *was* avoidable," she states, realizing what she believes to be her mistake. "Telrus was the one who said our job was done. He was the one who said continuing wasn't worth the risk. I pushed him and everyone else to keep going and now he's dead. It *was* me." Elidria's eyes glisten in the darker room and her teeth begin to clatter from her shivering. "I'm so sorry," she says to Galius.

Galius lowers his head and clenches his eyes shut, stopping them from tearing. "No," he says, "everyone is here by choice. The people responsible for this are from that boat."

Despite what anyone may tell her, that's not what she feels. Saving Bihnor is her burden. Going after Raymar was her call. Someone innocent and having nothing to do with the matter just died and she feels in her heart that it was her fault. "Galius, I—"

Castor interrupts her with loud shushing noise. He points out the window as six trolls trudge up the ramp.

"Everyone down," Galius whispers.

Castor drops under the window and Merith helps Ligrei from his chair before joining the rest on the floor.

"Their Achilles, throat, and eyes," Elidria whispers before the trolls get too close.

No one else makes another sound as the trolls begin roaming the village, looking into one window at a time.

The ground begins to shake and something scrapes against the house. A massive shadow looms through the window and moves on. Another shadow follows but stops at the window.

Elidria clasps her hands over her mouth, making sure she doesn't let out any kind of squeak like she did during her first encounter.

Moisture begins building up on the window, indicating the troll is looking in. They all hold their breaths and no one dares even swallow.

The first troll wanders around the house and peeks through the other window. Spying Delsar on the table, the troll leans through the window, shattering glass all over Castor. It slowly looks around the room and then straight down, making eye contact with the motionless guard.

Castor reacts first and plunges his blade through the troll's eye. The creature starts to fall in through the window, but Castor quickly slides his blade back out and rolls out of the way. He jumps to his feet and shouts, "I'll lead them away!" He climbs over the dead troll and out the window.

"Wait, Castor!" Allbus clambers to his feet and follows.

Elidria takes her hands off her mouth to speak, but Galius grabs her and shakes his head.

The other troll runs from the window and another passes the house right after.

Galius removes his hand from Elidria and whispers, "Now speak."

"They can't outpace those trolls," she says. "They're going to get overrun and killed."

Galius is already pulling his sword from his sheath. "Probably. Will you be joining?"

Elidria's emotions flip flop and she gives Galius a nod. "I've got your back."

Galius tosses Merith one of the mercenaries' many swords that they procured after Elidria's and Delsar's fight with them. "Keep an eye on Delsar," he says, "and both of you stay quiet."

Merith and Ligrei both nod.

"For Telrus," Elidria says, raising her sword up.

"For Ithendar," Galius responds. He puts a hefty kick into the door, swinging it open, and runs out.

Elidria races after him.

The King's mess hall...

"You're up earlier than usual, my Lord," Malgo says, seeing the King sitting at his table. "Breakfast won't be ready for about an hour."

"What was that, Malgo?" the King asks, his mind elsewhere.

"That woman from the ball is on your mind, isn't she?"

"I can't help it," the King confirms. "Her crimson hair was so enchanting. I'm going to marry her."

Malgo almost exclaims in disbelief, but catches himself and calmly says, "But, my Lord, you only just met her. The council has given you three months to pick a bride. Besides," Malgo switches to a hushed tone, "we haven't sorted out your 'Equal Marriage' problem."

"To be equal to her...," the King says, fading out and resting his chin on his hands.

"Look at you!" Malgo exclaims this time. "You're head-over-heels for this woman you've only met once. For all you know, she could be playing you. As your head-advisor, I highly advise against making such rash decisions so quickly. Please, my Lord, really get to know her first."

The King frowns at Malgo. "You're nearly right about everything and I hate it. This time, I believe *I'm* right. I'm King after all. Why shouldn't I be allowed to indulge myself for once in a while?"

"You speak as if she is just a prize to you. She's a woman who will have feelings, needs, wants, and even mood swings. This isn't a weekend thing, either. You will share the rest of your life with her."

"I've thought of all these things, Malgo. Sharing the rest of my life sounds absolutely incredible."

"That's what you said about your first wife," Malgo reminds the King. "You remember how that turned out."

"She chose to betray this country. Unfortunately, it was my job to put the kingdom first."

"That's my point, my Lord. You knew Taharial for over thirty-five years and she still stole your trust. This maid you've only known for one night. Don't you think you're too intoxicated by her charm to make a rational decision?"

"You question my judgment?" the King asks, standing up abruptly.

"She might be perfect, my Lord. I'm not saying she's not, but please allow some of your spies to do some investigating first. After which, you will have my full blessing."

The King crosses his arms. "I don't need your blessing."

"You're right, my Lord, you need nothing from me. I am merely here to provide a different angle on your various matters. What you do with my words is up to you." Malgo gives the King a bow.

The King sighs and brings his hand to his face. "Fine. Have someone look into her private life, and please do it discreetly. Stalking isn't very romantic."

"Would you like me to set you up with a date, my Lord? Perhaps you could get to know her and ask her questions of your own."

"A date isn't very kingly."

"But it is very human."

"So be it. I'd very much like to see her again. Can it be tonight?"

Malgo lets out a small laugh at his King's eagerness to see the woman again. "Yes, my Lord. It can be tonight."

Bihnor...

The troll swings its club straight down.

Elidria sidesteps the strike and dashes to the left of the troll, slashing at its heel. The sword cuts into a thick, leathery strip around the troll's Achilles, but does no damage to the troll itself.

Galius follows her in from the other side and also slashes at its opposite heel. Again, the blade only cuts into the new armor the trolls are wearing around their Achilles and their necks.

The troll slowly turns around to face them. It doesn't appear to have even noticed the attempted takedown as it looks no angrier.

"This is bad," says Elidria. "Those are some of its only weak spots."

"We'll figure something out," Galius replies. "Heads up. We have another behind us."

"This way!" Elidria shouts before dashing between two houses.

Galius follows as well as he can, and so do the trolls. They knock down support beams and fences, crumble stairs, and plow through a shed as they chase the duo.

"Watch ahead," Elidria warns as she runs between two more buildings. She jumps a safety rail and makes an immediate ninety-degree right turn. Galius huffs over after her and she grabs him, pulling him around the corner with her.

The first troll tries to stop, but the second one runs into it, sending it through the rail and over the cliff.

Galius and Elidria make a complete circle around the building and charge the standing troll. Elidria slides under its massive body and delivers a slash to its calf instead of its Achilles. The blade barely leaves a scratch, but it's enough to steal the troll's attention from Galius.

The troll turns its side to Galius, who slams into its hip with his shield. The troll spreads its legs to catch itself, but the edge of the cliff starts to crumble as its weight comes down. It drops to its hands and knees. Its left leg starts to slide off the cliff.

Elidria runs by the troll again and tries her luck with its throat. The blade leaves a small split in the leather and causes no harm to the beast.

The troll grabs at Elidria but never reaches her.

Galius plunges his sword into the troll's eye and quickly slides it back out before the troll falls backward over the cliff.

They both peer over the cliff to see what became of the trolls. The one Galius stabbed lies motionless in the shallow water. The other, however, is already back at the ramp.

"At least we got one of them," Elidria says.

"We have a few moments of breathing room," Galius reports. "Let's try to meet up with Castor and Allbus."

"Right!" Elidria takes off in a sprint again.

Galius takes a deep breath and follows. "The neck won't work," he says as he chases.

"I figured that."

"The eye works well."

"It definitely does." Elidria spots two trolls who both look mad at something. "There!" she declares.

The trolls are too fixated on Allbus and Castor to notice Galius and Elidria running up behind them.

"Watch out!" cries Allbus as he blocks a club strike with his shield. Parts of his shield splinter and he gets grabbed by Castor as his partner moves him away from the other troll's strike.

Delsar told Elidria that stabbing the trolls will put her dangerously close to them. However, since slashing won't work, stabbing seems like the most logical course of action to her. She runs up behind the nearest troll and drives her sword into its hough behind the knee. The troll's knee starts to bend, pulling the sword away from Elidria as it does. She quickly yanks her blade out before it gets ripped from her hands.

The troll drops and spins on its knee to face Elidria. She circles around it so it never gets a glimpse of her. It instead sees Galius still approaching and assumes it was him.

Elidria slices through the straps that hold the leather guard around the troll's neck and the armor drops to the ground. She spins around to its front and strikes horizontally at its throat.

The toll catches her blade with its hand. She tries to pull it free but the troll holds tight. The blade digs deeper into its hand, but the beast doesn't seem to care.

She pulls with all her strength, but the troll pulls back. She gets drawn closer until the counterweight of her weapon jabs into her stomach when the troll suddenly thrusts the sword toward her. She drops the sword and falls to the ground with her arms out beside her. The edge of her shield hits the ground first, causing it to pop off her back.

Galius tries to get his own strike in, taking advantage of the troll's preoccupation with Elidria, but the troll suddenly notices him and swings Elidria's sword like a club. The hilt digs deep into Galius' wooden shield. The troll tries to swing again, but its arc is much slower, as it whips Galius around, the hilt still buried in his shield. Galius slides his arm out of its straps and crashes against the ground.

The troll grabs the shield and rips it from the sword's hilt. Then, perhaps by a stroke of intelligence or dumb luck, the troll grabs the sword by its handle. It looks back at Elidria who sits a few feet from it and thrusts the point of the blade in her direction.

Elidria grabs her shield and brings it to her front, bracing it with both arms. The blade pierces straight through and doesn't stop until it connects with her sternum. She grimaces as she is pushed back.

The troll stands to its feet and begins pushing harder.

Elidria raises a leg and presses it against her shield, pushing it up until it locks with the hilt. Despite her best efforts, she still feels the blade start to push its way through her skin and dig into her chest. An uncomfortable trickle of blood starts to streak down both her sides. She presses her other leg against the shield and clasps the flat sides of her blade with her hands. "Help!" she cries, knowing that at any moment, her legs will give and the blade will stab through her heart.

A bolt hits the troll in the very wound Elidria gave it when she stabbed its leg. The troll's knee crashes to the ground next to Elidria and a bit of weight is lifted as it catches itself with one of its hands. The weight shifts for only a moment. The troll uses the sword, partially in Elidria's chest, to stand itself back up.

Elidria screams as her legs feel like they're going to snap under the pressure and the sword digs even deeper into her bone.

Galius puts his crossbow away and pulls his sword back out. He starts running in Elidria's direction but gets intercepted by the troll that fell off the cliff earlier. Galius doesn't see it until it crashes into him, sending them both tumbling to the ground.

Still pushing against her shield, Elidria looks over at Castor and Allbus in hopes that they might come to her rescue. Right as she locates them, Castor gets tossed like a ragdoll into a nearby house. He hits hard against the wall and falls to the ground. He rolls over slowly, his grimace and wincing in full view of Elidria

The two trolls he was fighting with Allbus now close in on his partner. Allbus swings his sword around wildly, trying to keep them back, but they are not fazed by the little pokes and pricks whenever the sword hits. One of them swats the sword and grabs Allbus by the neck, lifting him from the ground.

Elidria's attention snaps back to her situation as she cries out in pain with what feels like her sternum starting to split. She grinds her teeth and tears pour from her eyes as she puts every last bit of strength into her legs. Her knees ache and bend, letting the blade slide even deeper. She lets out another scream, but anything she does now will be futile. No one is strong enough to fight against a troll with strength alone. *Delsar, please,* she thinks to herself. *I need you.*

"So Nikarat," starts Gorgan, "can any of them fight?"

The red-robed man exits the infirmary, wiping his hands on a rag. "I'm not a healer," he states. "None of them are bleeding anymore, but their conditions haven't changed."

"Some sorcerer you are," Gorgan says, jeering a little.

"Do not scoff the Dark Arts. My talents are perfect for what I need them for."

"Whatever, pal." Gorgan walks from the cabin, back to the deck.

"Your strength comes from magic, you know," Nikarat sneers.

"Renon said it was a result of science."

"Science is repeatable and his success with you he has not been able to duplicate."

"Are you trying to get on my nerves?" Gorgan growls.

"I'm just stating facts."

"Well, don't."

"Then remain an imbecile!" Nikarat snaps.

"Hey, boss!" shouts a voice from the water.

Gorgan peers over the guardrail to see the dinghy with his three men finally arriving. "What happened?" he asks.

"The ambush failed and they killed Iolrath and Navarre," Onus reports, "but that's not all. Look!" he exclaims, pointing south.

Gorgan looks over at the small craft approaching and gets met by an arrow clanging off his armor. Gorgan stumbles back. The startle from the arrow doesn't slow him down. He runs back to the rail and leans over it. "Get up here, now!" he orders, extending his arm to help his men up.

"I'll handle this," Nikarat says, holding up his staff. He begins uttering indecipherable words and a bright orb appears at the end of his staff. Before he can finish, another arrow strikes him high in the chest. He screams and falls to his back, sending the fireball shooting straight up. Nikarat struggles back to his feet and takes cover. "More unexpected variables, I see," he calmly says, despite having an arrow in his chest.

"Just conjure up another one of your fireballs and blast them into oblivion!" Gorgan commands, pulling up the last of his minions. "We'll keep whoever it is looking at us."

"Simply put, but agreed." Nikarat comes out of cover to cast. As soon as he starts uttering, another arrow whizzes through the air and nicks his shoulder. Nikarat spins around and hides back in cover. "Not happening," he says.

"Then we'll just have to wait and fight them here," Gorgan decides.

"Oh, don't worry," says Nikarat. "I've got that part covered."

CHAPTER 20

THE FORGOTTEN

7 Years Ago…

"It's an arrow with yellow feathers. So what?" asks Lucas, examining the arrow his partner just handed him.

"But this is *my* arrow," Arviakyss responds. "The Queen wants me to be a symbol of hope so I thought I'd make my arrows symbols themselves."

Lucas tosses Arviakyss back his arrow. "And how do yellow feathers do that?"

"Standard-issue arrows have red feathers. Mine are unique and stand out. Yellow also represents both hope and fear. When someone in trouble sees one, I want them to be filled with hope knowing that I'm there. When an enemy sees one, I want them to feel the same fear they spread knowing that I'm there to stop them."

Lucas can't keep himself from chuckling. "You're taking this whole 'Queen's Champion' thing very seriously. It almost sounds like it's going to your head."

"That's not my intention, Luke," says Arviakyss. "I'm only human and can easily be killed like anyone else. The Queen wants a symbol so I'm playing it up. People will know about Arviakyss, even the bad guys. If my name deters even one bad thing from happening, then this extra work will be worth it."

Lucas thinks about his partner's explanation for a moment. "I guess I can see that. If I suddenly decided to be a *bad guy*, as you put it, just seeing that arrow would definitely scare me. And that's before you've played yourself up."

"That's because you *do* know me. I need everyone to know me for this to work. Just seeing a yellow arrow won't mean a thing if I can't spread my name."

"That's all fine and dandy, but what about me? You're planning on becoming some hotshot, but I'm just a guard."

"Association, Luke. You'll be known just by being my partner." Arviakyss taps Lucas' chest with the fletching. "Besides, the Queen asked me to represent *her*, so I feel like I need to work extra hard."

"How am *I* supposed to excel if I'm always following in your shadow?" Lucas shakes his head. "This won't work."

"I think it will. Just having the Queen's influence will be huge."

"I don't mean you being some superhero everyone loves and adores, Arv. I'm talking about us."

Arviakyss is taken aback by his partner's statement. "You were laughing literally just a moment ago. You're not being serious, right?"

"This program was designed for you. I see that and you *are* perfect for it." Lucas places his hand on Arviakyss' shoulder. "I'm not like you. I'm nothing special. It *should* just be you."

"The Queen said we'd both be a part of her team," Arviakyss reminds him.

"Arviakyss, I mean it. You're in a whole different league than me or anyone else. Having me on that team would be the same as having any other guard on it. I would destroy some of that symbol you and the Queen are trying so hard to create just by being there."

"You think we shouldn't do this then?" Arviakyss asks.

"No, I think *I* shouldn't."

"Then I won't either."

"Don't be ridiculous," Lucas snaps. He then calms himself and takes a breath. "This is good. You'll be that symbol and I'll finally be able to grow since I won't be chasing after you all the time."

Arviakyss closes his eyes knowing that his friend is right. It's times like this he wishes logical things didn't always make sense to him. Then maybe he'd put up an argument with Lucas and convince him otherwise, but everything he's said is true. It was Arviakyss the Queen wanted. Not his partner. Having a random guard will make the team less than what's planned. Lucas has never been able to keep up, but that's never been a problem and Arviakyss never held it against him. "You've clearly made up your mind," Arviakyss says.

"Yup."

"I wish you talked to me about this first."

"This is me talking to you about it."

Arviakyss looks up. "More like 'telling.'"

"I want to shine, too. You're an incredible person and even *I* want to be like you. This is your calling to move on and become something more. Now I'll have the chance to continue what you've started here and maybe become great myself."

"How long?" Arviakyss asks.

"Two weeks," Lucas replies, knowing exactly what his partner means.

"Then I'll put off joining the Queen's Guard until then," Arviakyss says extending his hand. "Shall we have one last adventure together?"

Lucas smirks and takes his hand. "It'll be an honor, Mr. Queen's Champion."

The troll has an intelligent thought as it grabs the sword through Elidria's shield with both hands.

Elidria screams feeling the added pressure against her legs. With her hands, she desperately tries to slide the blade off her chest, but it's too deep to move. Any deeper and her sternum will likely split, allowing the blade to slice through her heart. Elidria throws her head back and clenches her eyes shut. Even with her adrenaline careening throughout her body, she can feel her nerves crying out, telling her that something is very wrong. "Delsar!" she cries, but he is not coming to save her. Her mouth gapes open as she feels the pain from trying to breathe. Her cry for Delsar only makes things worse. Taking a breath will push her own chest through the weapon. Her right arm squirms and then grasps onto the grass beside her as her body tries to force her into taking that breath.

Finally, her body has enough. She inhales, wincing as she does, waiting for a splitting sensation followed by a shroud of darkness engulfing her, but it doesn't. None of it does. She feels the weight pull from her chest, the sword and shield jut up, falling to the side. Her legs splay onto the ground, numb from the ordeal.

Elidria gasps and rolls to her hands and knees. She begins wobbling as she stands to her feet, the feeling in her legs coming back slowly. She grabs her sword, expecting a fight, but struggles to wield it with the shield lodged at the blade's base.

The troll she was fighting hobbles away on its bad leg and the other three that were fighting Allbus, Castor, and Galius are ahead of it. All of them running toward the ramp.

Elidria hears Allbus gasping for air. "Allbus!" she shouts before curling over in pain.

"I'm fine," he says, out of breath. "Are you okay?" he then asks, running to her side.

Tears drip off the tip of her nose and chin. "It hurts to breathe," she says, "but I've felt worse." She uses her sword to lean on and straightens up as best she can. "Help Castor."

"You first," Allbus declares.

"I've got her," Galius says, slowly getting to his feet.

"Galius, how are you—" Elidria starts, but never finishes as she clenches her chest in pain.

"Padded armor," he replies. "Maybe you should lie down." Galius gestures to a patch of grass.

"No!" she snaps. "I'm still standing so that's how I'll remain."

"Then what's next?" Galius asks.

"How's Castor?" Elidria turns to see Allbus hunched over the downed guard.

"Conscious, but he's done," Allbus informs.

"I'm sorry," Castor says with what strength he has left.

"Fine," Elidria says, stabbing her sword into the ground. She begins to struggle trying to pull her sword from her shield. "Take him to Merith and then join us—" Elidria's sword doesn't budge. "Galius, if you would?"

"Sure." Galius takes her place and forcefully disconnects her blade from her shield and hands them both to her.

"Thank you." She looks at the hole in the shield for a moment before trying to slide it on her back. As she stretches her arms back, her sternum screams in pain, causing her to drop her shield.

"I'll get it." Galius grabs the shield and slides it on for her.

She nods this time instead of saying 'Thank you.' "Listen," she starts, "we have to see where the trolls are going. Allbus, take Castor to safety and then meet us at the ramp. They wouldn't just leave unless they had a good reason. If we can, we take the boat. Got it?"

"Just the three of you?" Castor asks in disbelief.

"I said, 'if.'"

"You got it, Eldra," Allbus confirms. "Let's go, buddy," he says, helping Castor to his feet.

Elidria looks up at Galius, her eyes still watering. "Tell me I'm wrong and we'll leave before we lose more than we have."

Galius places his hand on her shoulder and smiles. "You and your village have lost more than anyone here. Telrus isn't coming back, but that's not true for Raymar. I'm willing to lose a little more if it means giving Bihnor something back. I'm ready to finish this with you."

Elidria closes her eyes and lets out a quick weep before nodding. She wipes her tears with her sleeve and says, "You guys are incredible. Thank you."

"There are three boats now," Galius reports, standing at the ramp before Elidria.

Elidria peers past Galius's point. "That's Bekka's Fury!" she exclaims, regretting the shout as pain shoots from her chest.

"You know that boat."

"They're friends," she says while wincing. "Wait, Telrus knew them. Roki, Glade, and Cade."

"I remember them. Those are loyal friends."

"They won't stand a chance versus the mercenaries *and* the trolls," Elidria states.

"Then we let Allbus catch up," Galius says, starting down the ramp. "Come on. We can catch the troll you wounded," he says, referring to the troll that is still making its way through the water while the other three are already sprinting across the dock.

"Then keep up," she says, dashing down the ramp past him.

"The impossible is not possible," he shouts after her. Galius grits his teeth and puts all he can into his speed.

The wounded troll begins climbing onto the dock, bringing its knee up first. Elidria strikes the unexpecting troll across the bottom of its foot. It shrieks and falls backward into the water. Elidria stabs her sword straight down through its unprotected throat and into the sand underneath. The troll makes no attempt to move after that. Likely because the blade passed clean through its vertebrae.

Elidria slides her blade out and dips it in the water, cleaning off the grey blood. She climbs up the dock and turns to face Galius who is slowly pulling himself up the dock. "Shoot one of the trolls," she orders. "Get the attention of one so we don't have to fight three of them at once."

"Good call." Galius sheaths his sword and grabs his crossbow. He aims quickly, but carefully. The bolt launches mere moments later before striking and lodging into one of the troll's backs. The troll doesn't slow down. It has someplace to be and distractions will be ignored.

"So be it," Elidria says. "They look like they're returning to help fight Bekka's Fury. That means they may not pay any attention to us. I think we can take out another troll before we get noticed and then we can take the boat. Once we have the mercenaries' attention, our friends on Bekka's Fury can return our help."

"I'm good to try." Galius points up the ramp at the guard running down. "Allbus is coming."

"We don't have time to wait." Elidria takes off in a sprint.

"Catch up, kid!" Galius shouts to Allbus before running after Elidria.

"Onus," shouts Gorgan from his cover, "get to the helm and start shooting back at these guys!"

"The trolls are back," Nikarat informs. "Wait for the archer to start shooting them before sending your man."

"You heard him," says Gorgan.

"Sure thing, boss."

Gorgan looks back at the trolls climbing into the boat. "How many did you summon," he asks.

"They sensed I was in trouble so they all should be returning to me," Nikarat answers, holding a rag by the arrow in his chest.

"Only three came back."

"Then the other three died killing Arviakyss. Nikarat ducks slightly as arrows start peppering the trolls' armor. "Send your man."

"Go, Onus!"

Onus crouches as he runs to the stairs and up to the helm. He pulls open a crate and acquires a bow and arrows from it. "I'm all set!" he shouts down.

"Then start shooting!" Gorgan screams.

Onus opens fire and the arrows from Bekka's Fury slow before shooting back.

"Now get to blasting them out of the water!" Gorgan shouts, grabbing Nikarat by his robes.

"Unhand me, barbarian," Nikarat says, shaking himself free. "One cannot simply touch a sorcerer's attire."

"Just fireball them!"

"Look who needs magic again," Nikarat says, leaving his cover and beginning his spell.

Gorgan growls before facing his other men. "Kharis and Sandro, we are going back to the village and making sure those trolls did their job."

"That's going to be an issue," Sandro responds, pointing at Elidria and Galius coming up their ramp and boarding their boat.

"Deal with them!" Gorgan orders. He taps Nikarat on his back, interrupting his casting.

"What do you want, fool?" the magic-user asks, very annoyed.

"Your trolls didn't finish their job," Gorgan tells him.

Nikarat looks at the intruders and sighs. "Handle this little incursion yourself."

"What are you doing?"

"I'm going into your cabin. I have an arrow in my chest and don't feel like fighting."

"Coward!" Gorgan shouts as Nikarat escapes through the door. One of the trolls follows him and unnaturally fits through the door. "Magic," Gorgan says in near-disbelief.

Onus notices Galius and Elidria and fires an arrow at them instead of the boat.

Galius stops the arrow with his shield. "Sniper first," he says.

"Copy," Elidria responds.

Galius makes it to the stairs first and Elidria climbs behind him.

On the other side, Karis mirrors them climbing the opposite stairs.

Galius makes it to the top, but before Elidria can, someone grabs her bare foot and drags her down before sliding her across the deck as Sandro runs by, chasing Galius up the stairs. Elidria jumps back to her feet and points her sword at the man responsible. "Round three?" she asks Gorgan.

"Our previous fight was hardly fair," he replies, holding his wound he received from Delsar's arrow. "I think I'll return the favor. Kill her," Gorgan says before backing off.

Elidria turns to face two huge trolls looming above her. Elidria's teeth clatter as she instantly slips into fear. Her whole body shakes as she steps back and sets herself.

"I'll handle this one," comes a voice from behind the trolls. A sword slashes against the one to Elidria's left and it turns around to face Allbus.

"Kill it and help Galius," she says to him. "He's fighting three men by himself."

"I'll do what I can," he responds.

The troll swings horizontally at Elidria. Despite all her training and Allbus' arrival, her body is still filled with fear and she panics. She wonders if she should step back to avoid or duck in and counter. Her time quickly disappears and she finds herself completely dropping to the ground and on her side. She lets out a horrified scream as the club passes over her head. She scrambles back to her feet and jumps to the side, letting the next attack splinter against the wooden deck.

Elidria's training and experience fighting these trolls kicks in as she calms herself enough to refocus. She dashes in after her dodge and slashes across the troll's thigh, breaking only the skin. The troll spins and retaliates, but Elidria is ready. She ducks in and lunges for the same location, digging even deeper into the thigh.

The troll roars in anger, but Elidria doesn't move. She lets the beast attack again. It swings straight down again. The trolls only seem to have two attacks. Horizontal and vertical.

Elidria slides through the troll's legs. She grimaces feeling the skin on her bare foot and knee burn and rub away from the friction. It hurts, but it's not a disabling pain. She does her best to not let it hinder her. She stands up quickly and slides her sword into the troll's hough. She doesn't stick it in far before sliding it out and stepping back into Allbus.

"Watch yourself," he says before grabbing her and pulling her down to the ground with him. His troll's strike misses overhead. He then rolls with her to avoid the strike from Elidria's troll. He pushes her off and both stand back up. "Let's spread out so that doesn't happen again."

"Right," she says, a bit dazed by that whole exchange. She dashes wide around her troll and pulls it away from Allbus while running closer to the helm stairs.

The bolt from Galius' crossbow pierces deep into Onus' shoulder. His eyes widen from the hit, but he only lets out a small gasp from the shock. The man drops his bow and pulls out his sword with his offhand.

Galius senses the other mercenary climbing the stairs behind him and wastes no time lunging for the one he just wounded. Onus' sword moves first which Galius bashes away with the edge of his shield, leaving Onus wide open. Galius follows in by putting his sword through the mercenary's chest.

Onus seizes up and drops to the floor when Galius kicks him off his blade.

Sandro and Karis may have been too late to help Onus, but now they have Galius between both of them, outnumbering and surrounding the grizzled veteran.

Galius spins himself back and forth, trying to keep an eye on both mercenaries while also trying to figure out who to go after first. Both mercenaries take a step toward Galius and he acts. He faints toward Sandro but immediately whips back around, catching Karis mid-lunge. He drives into him with his shield first. Both men crash to the ground with Galius on top. Galius rolls over to his feet and stands with his leg atop Karis' arm.

Karis tries to knock Galius away with his other arm that holds his sword, but Galius is easily able to block the strike by intercepting it with his shinguard.

Galius spins back around, barely in time as Sandro's strike swings for his head. Galius instinctively throws his right arm up to protect his face. The blade clashes with his bracer and Galius follows it up with a back fist. His hilt connects with Sandro's face, knocking him back and allowing Galius to finish with Karis.

Galius steps off of Karis' arm to avoid another strike, but jumps right back on top of him, slamming both feet on the mercenary's chest.

Karis' neck arches as air rapidly escapes his mouth and nose from Galius' weight. Before he has any time to do anything about it, Galius slams his boot against Karis' forehead, knocking the back of his head against the floor.

Sandro is back and stabs at Galius, who turns and bashes it away with his shield, just like he did with the archer. However, this is exactly what Sandro anticipated. He allows Galius' defensive shield bash to spin him around as he ducks down, swinging for Galius' open thigh.

Galius raises his leg and blocks the strike with his shin.

Sandro spins around again and both blades clash, digging into each other.

Galius starts pushing Sandro back, hoping to trip the mercenary over his downed comrade. He tries to distract Sandro by using his shield to trap the swords together, but the sly mercenary has his own plan.

Sandro sneakily pulls out a knife with his offhand and stabs for the small gap between Galius' breastplate and abdominal plate.

Galius sees the play and crunches his stomach, closing the gap. The knife scrapes against his armor and Galius slams his shield against the attacker's hand. The knife drops and Sandro bends over. Galius pushes the lowered man's sword away and he starts to spin around him.

Sandro's blade chases Galius, but only meets metal as it clangs against the guard's back. Everything starts to blur for the mercenary. He looks down and sees Galius' sword through his side. "You—" he starts to shout, but gets stopped short when Galius' shield edge bashes against the bridge of his nose.

Galius grabs the knife from the floor and whips it at Karis, who was somehow only dazed when his head slammed against the deck. The knife sticks into his chest, not deep enough to cause any real damage, but enough to startle him. He stumbles back and almost catches himself from going over the stairs; however, something crashes into the boat and rocks him off his balance. The knife clatters down the stairs with him before they both end up at the bottom. Karis doesn't move this time.

Galius runs over to the starboard guardrail to see what just hit the boat. Leaning over he sees Bekka's Fury scraping against the side with Glade at the helm.

"Hey there, guard!" someone shouts up from below.

"Roki?" exclaims Galius.

"Oh, hey! Galius, right?"

"Yeah."

"Good. Tie this rope." Roki tosses an end of a rope that is already tied to Bekka's Fury's mast to Galius.

Galius catches it and ties it to the guardrail. "What are you guys doing here?" he asks.

"We're here to finish the mission," Glade responds. "Though I've been instructed to stay with the boat and I plan to listen to my instructions this time."

"Uh-huh," Galius doesn't understand what Glade might be referring to, but he does reach out his hand to help Roki climb the rope. "Your help is appreciated," he says to Roki as he climbs over the guardrail.

"What's the situation?" Roki asks, drawing a near-identical sword as Galius'.

"Three trolls, a wizard, and a superhuman," he quickly says. "Allbus and Eldra are fighting them below. Come on!" Galius turns to lead Roki with him down the stairs, but before either of them make it, the floor in front of them explodes.

Wood and splinters plaster against Galius' armor while some of the smaller pieces pierce the skin of his face. He looks over at Roki who went down during the blast. The shrapnel tore cuts and holes throughout his clothes, with scrapes and blood under each of them. Galius reaches out to help him back up, but two figures catch his eye through the smoke.

The obstruction begins to clear and a man in red robes stands with a fist that appears to be on fire. Next to him is a troll nearly twice his height.

"Kill them," says the man.

The troll squeals in delight.

The troll swings furiously at Elidria. She jumps one way and dodges another. Her chest burns with every breath. Not just from nearly getting impaled, but also from her adrenaline ripping through her body and her lungs screaming for more oxygen. The feeling reminds her of Orange Peak, right before she passed out. She has to finish this now if she's going to have any fight left for the other trolls and Gorgan.

Elidria dashes in at the troll, without waiting for another attack. She's taking her fight to the troll and on her terms. The troll swings for her but she's already in. With added strength from her adrenaline, she drives her sword deeper into the troll than ever.

The troll shrieks and begins to topple over on the same leg. It lands hard on the ground, nearly crushing Elidria, but she nimbly twists out of the way.

Elidria jumps on the downed troll's back and plunges her sword straight down. It doesn't penetrate very deep and the troll shakes her off, standing back up. Elidria trips coming off the troll and rolls to the ground. Her shield slides off her shoulders as she comes to a stop on her back. She spins over to her hands and knees and searches frantically for her sword but quickly realizes she never heard it fall.

The troll gets back to its feet and turns back around. As it does, Elidria spies her sword still lodged in the troll's back.

No sword and currently no shield. The three simple armor strips on these trolls are making fighting even just one harder than fighting a town full of normal ones.

Elidria makes a disgusted face as an idea hits her. Her thoughts of disgust disappear as the troll swings down at her with its typical tried and not-so-true strike. She rolls left and scrambles to her feet. She ducks under the next strike and lunges in. Jumping up, she digs her bare toes into the gash she took several attempts to create. The slimy warmth curdles her stomach as she pushes off and grabs her sword's handle.

The troll flails its arms around, dumbfounded by the strange attack and screeches in pain at the same time. It whips around to find Elidria, but she's not there. It spins around again, knowing she's somewhere behind it, but still can't find her. The pain in its back jars and pulls. It starts spinning on its feet, trying to grab whatever is back there, but it can't reach.

Elidria hangs on dearly as she gets whipped back and forth. She screams and shuts her eyes tight when the troll's hand comes uncomfortably close to grabbing her.

"Don't let go," says Allbus, seeing her predicament and slipping away from his own troll for a moment.

"The leg!" she shouts. "Its wound!"

Allbus sees the gash and fully expects the troll to be wary of him; however, it pays him no mind and only cares about the intrusion on its back. Allbus swings his sword like an axeman splitting wood, using gravity and sheer strength to cause maximum damage. The sword cuts deep and strikes bone.

The troll cries out in pain and falls forward. Elidria hangs on to her sword and shifts herself so the handle rests under her arm with the hilt pressed against her peck and bicep. The troll hits the ground and Elidria's momentum plunges the sword deep into the troll's back. The impact also knocks the wind from her. She rolls off its back and onto the deck, gasping for air.

"I've had enough of these mindless beasts!" exclaims Gorgan's booming voice.

The other troll stops in its tracks and watches as Allbus strikes at Gorgan.

Gorgan blocks the attack with his bracer and with a quick movement, slams his bracers in opposite directions, snapping the blade in two.

Allbus is stunned by Gorgan's strength and pays for it. Gorgan's backfist smashes against his breastplate, sending him flying into the wall of the cabin.

Gorgan clenches his fist and winces before turning for Elidria.

Elidria jumps to her feet and frantically pulls at the blade in the troll's back as Gorgan walks closer. She's had no luck removing her blade from its many snares and this is no different. She looks back at Gorgan and realizes he left his sword back at the beach. Giving up on removing her sword, she hops off the troll and puts her arms up, readying for a fight.

"I'm going to snap you!" Gorgan yells.

Elidria bites her lip and tries not to close her eyes from such a strange comment, letting out a quick snort. "You know, I woke up this morning never thinking I would ever hear someone saying that to me," she says with a grin.

Gorgan growls. "You pretend to be all jokes."

"I'm also sugar and spice and other things nice, but I appreciate you noticing," she replies.

"I know who you really are. How you really feel. There were no smiles when you told your father how much you really hated him."

"I actually loved my father and he knew it, despite what I may have said. You, however, I'm having a difficult time loving, so I figure I may as well just punch you." She eyeballs Gorgan's hands and for the first time, notices that they're gloved and not armored.

"Big talk for a small girl."

"Small talk for a big man," Elidria says, lowering her stance.

"Do you have something for everything I say?"

"Only when you make it so easy." She gives Gorgan a smirk.

"Like you were when I beat your face in front of your father."

Elidria snorts again and grins from ear-to-ear. "I guess I have to give you that one."

Gorgan snarls at her unbreakable spirit. He pulls back his fist and throws a simple straight punch with the same hand he walloped poor Allbus with. He completely expects her to dodge and counter, but she doesn't.

Elidria points her elbow toward the attack and braces her arm against her chest. Gorgan's fist meets her bony elbow and bones crunch as she gets knocked back. She extends her arm back out, fully expecting her elbow to scream out in pain. She winces for just a moment and realizes it's not broken. She gives a nervous smile, completely surprised that her idea worked.

Gorgan doesn't throw a subsequent strike after that one. He instead steps back and clutches his wrist. He looks like he's holding back a scream.

"You have very strong muscles," she says, raising her arms back into a defensive position.

"So what?" Gorgan snaps, clearly in agony.

"Oh, nothing," she says, keeping a smirk on her battered face.

"You perceptive little snot!" Gorgan makes a fist with his broken hand to show her that the pain he feels means nothing to him. "My hands and my arms may break hitting you, but I wonder what will become of that pretty little face of yours."

"You think so?" Elidria asks, placing her hand on her cheek. "I don't know if the black and blue bruising is for me. I like my more natural looks."

"Shut up!" yells Gorgan.

"Make me."

"One punch is all I'll need."

"Yet here I stand," she replies, waving her elbow around.

Gorgan lets out an exasperated growl and his eyes fill with rage. He swings hard at her face, but she simply ducks and switches positions with him without retaliating. His entire body is nearly completely covered with iron armor and hitting metal doesn't sound like a pleasant experience to her. Not after breaking her hand after simply punching a guy in the mouth.

Gorgan punches again, but without as much grit and he doesn't step in. He's certain she just analyzed his previous punch and decides to take this one slow to figure out what she has planned.

The speed doesn't matter. Elidria doesn't move her feet either. She simply leans to her left and uses her right arm to help guide his strike past her head. She then grabs his wrist and pulls at the same time, sending her foot onto the same location Delsar shot him. Gorgan starts to bend over and Elidria's knee is there to meet him. She feels his nose squish from the impact and then a liquid drips down her leg as the man trips backward over the troll.

Elidria jumps on top of him and begins using her palms to repeatedly bash his face. This is very short-lived. Gorgan grabs her by her collar and throws her off. She crashes hard into the ground and Gorgan stands up. He pulls Elidria's sword from the troll, blood oozing from his face, and storms toward Elidria.

"You're nothing," he says, "and your people are nothing. You exist in this world just to be culled."

Elidria grabs a crate that sits against the cabin wall and uses it to pull herself up. "Everyone has a right to live," she retorts.

"You're a simple inconvenience that I have a right to destroy!" Gorgan swings down with his full strength.

Still trying to get her footing, she has no way of avoiding this catastrophic attack. She raises her arms above her head and creates an "X" with her bracers. The sword connects and she fully expects the blade to split her skull in two, but it doesn't. It's the handle that splits in two. The strain in between Gorgan's grips and the sudden impact with Elidria's bracers is what breaks it.

Gorgan loses any leverage with the break being between his hands, and the blade almost goes into his face as he stumbles forward.

Elidria moves out of the way and pushes him to help him along. He immediately sets himself and she feels like she's pushing against a tree.

Gorgan drops both sword pieces and grabs at her. She ducks down, but her hair doesn't drop fast enough with her. He grabs a chunk of her hair and laughs as she screams from the pulling. "Your luck has finally run out," he tells her.

"Let go!" she yells, smacking her fists against his grip. When that doesn't work, she presses her hands against Gorgan's chest and tries to push herself away from his grasp despite the pain her brain is translating from such an action. What is the point? He has superhuman strength. How can a one hundred pound girl overpower him?

"I don't think I'll kill you yet," Gorgan tells her. "I want Arviakyss to watch as I rip you limb-from-limb."

Elidria stomps on his foot, but Gorgan doesn't flinch. He then returns her stomp with his own booted foot on her very bare foot. She screams and drops, but she doesn't hit the ground as Gorgan is holding her up by the hair.

"Pathetic," he says.

"Hey, you!" shouts an incoming voice. Gorgan raises his arm to block the incoming strike, but that's exactly what Allbus was hoping he'd do. The small nub of a blade Allbus has left slices through the tuft of hair Gorgan clutches.

Elidria drops to the ground and rolls out of the way.

Allbus sets himself between both of them. "Thanks for softening him up for me," Allbus says with a glint in his eye. "I'll handle him from here."

"Have you ever fought one of these?" Galius asks Roki while standing in front of him, allowing Roki to get back to his feet.

"Just one," Roki replies, wiping blood from his chin, "but it destroyed my arm and I'm not healed yet."

"You a lefty?"

"Nope."

"Then this might get interesting. Mind the gap," Galius tells Roki as he makes his way toward the troll.

In a standing leap, the troll clears the massive hole in the floor created by Nikarat's blast. It lands next to Roki, giving Galius no time to turn back around to help his new injured friend.

Roki swings his blade against the troll's side with no ill effect against the beast.

With no club like its compatriots, the troll swings both arms around, trying to bash and crush Roki.

Galius doesn't turn around to help Roki with the troll. Instead, he goes straight for the sorcerer. A bright light flashes from Nikarat's hand and Galius blocks the blast with his shield, igniting his defensive weapon ablaze. Galius spins around and hurls his flaming shield like a disk.

Nikarat catches in against his gut, setting his robes on fire, but for only a moment. He snaps his fingers and the fire goes out, but that was all the time Galius needed to close the distance.

Galius swings with both hands at the man, but Nikarat effortlessly dodges while holding his own hands behind his back. Galius swings again and again, but the man seems to be toying with him. Galius swings low and Nikarat jumps over the sword and kicks the guard in the face, knocking him back. Galius fixes his crooked helmet, but Nikarat is now on the offensive.

Galius tries to hit the charging man, but Nikarat ducks past the strike and places his hand against Galius' breastplate. The guard tries to slash him away, but Nikarat uses his other hand to catch Galius' hands and, with a simple pinch, the sword drops to the floor.

Galius can feel his chest heating up, a slow burn rising, but the grip Nikarat has on his hand is preventing him from moving. He drops to his knees, unable to resist the supernatural power.

"This is the power your country rightfully fears," Nikarat says.

Galius tries to respond, but even his mouth won't move. Nikarat's hand melts through the iron breastplate and rests directly on Galius' chest. The pain is unbearable, but he's not able to emit even a reflexive scream.

The troll cries out, stealing Nikarat's attention from Galius over to his pet, but his spells stay active.

Roki chuckles as he wobbles around with no troll in sight. "Structural integrity," he says, looking through the floorboards. "That's what happens when you blast a hole in the floor." Roki sheaths his sword and pulls out his bow.

Nikarat removes his hand from Galius's chest and places it around his throat. "I'll kill this guard!" he exclaims.

"And then I'll kill you," Roki says, aiming an arrow at Nikarat. "I wonder what's faster, whatever it is you're doing or my arrow."

Nikarat snarls and his fiery hand starts to burn brighter. "This situation is irrelevant," he says, letting go of Galius' hand and reaching into his robe.

Galius' freedom comes back and he grabs his sword off the ground, swinging at the sorcerer.

Roki releases his arrow at the same time, but neither attack hits anything.

The ground around Galius singes and Nikarat disappears in front of him. A small, blue rock hits the floor where he stood as Galius falls back, coughing and grimacing.

Roki runs over to Galius and drops to a knee beside him. "Are you all right?" he asks.

Galius lightly dabs his burnt neck with his fingers and with a groggy voice says, "Never worse."

The troll lets out a squeal, making Roki look back over his shoulder as it starts pulling itself out of the hole it fell in.

"Please tell me you can still fight," Roki inquires, grabbing around Galius' arm and helping him up.

"Yeah," he simply responds, but even just saying that causes him to wince.

"Just leave the talking to me then." Roki places his bow away and pulls his sword back out. "Hopefully this will be easier now."

Galius nods his head and grabs his blackened shield from off the ground.

"Then let's get this done."

Gorgan laughs at Allbus. "You think you can stop me?"

"I wouldn't be here if I didn't," responds Allbus.

Gorgan's smile disappears. "Foolish."

Allbus swings what he has left for a sword which Gorgon easily blocks with his bracer before punching Allbus' shield.

Gorgan winces for a moment but doesn't let the pain stop him. He kicks into Allbus, knocking him back. Without letting Allbus ready himself, he steps straight back in. He grabs Allbus' hand with the sword and crushes it with a quick squeeze.

Allbus shows only his teeth from the pain and tries to bash the mercenary with his shielded right hand. Gorgan spins and smashes his shield into pieces with an armored elbow. A hand reaches out and grabs around Allbus' neck, lifting him completely off the ground.

"Trying to beat me with just your strength," says Gorgan, shaking his head. "*Very* foolish."

Elidria gets back on her feet and tries to sneak up on Gorgan.

"Don't," he says, still aware of her presence. "Any closer and a squeeze is all I need to crush his neck."

Elidria has no choice but to stop. "Let him go!" she demands.

"Or what?"

Elidria bears her teeth at Gorgan with no answer to his question.

"It's over," says Gorgan. "You've lost. These men you brought will die for nothing. You've led them all to their dooms, and for what?"

A tear drips from Elidria's chin and lands on her purpled foot. "Battles may be won by those who live, but they are remembered because of those who died. I promise that your name will be forgotten."

"Cute proverb. Did you make that up?"

"Maybe."

Gorgan smiles with an evil grin.

"It wasn't supposed to be funny," Elidria says, but she quickly notices he's looking past her. Elidria follows his gaze.

"I'm here," Delsar points his blade at Gorgan, "and we haven't lost."

"Nikarat, why are *you* here?" Renon asks, puzzling over his comrades' sudden arrival in his laboratory.

Nikarat shakes his robes, letting sparks and little bits of burnt cloth fall to the ground. "It got too hairy for my liking," he explains, making a face as he inspects parts of his robe. "I used one of the stones."

"I can fix your robes," Renon says, "and never mind the stone. We have plenty. Are the pieces in place?"

"Bihnor is ripe for the taking," Nikarat tells him.

"That's good. Malgo says the King has a new girlfriend."

"She wouldn't happen to have scarlet hair, would she?"

Renon smirks. "How on earth could you have figured that out?"

Nikarat smiles, too. "I guess that means these mercenaries are no longer needed."

"It's about time," Renon says, full of exasperation. "Jugack is killing me with all his stupid inspections."

"The Wanderer's liaison?"

"That's him."

"Where is he now?"

"He's actually inspecting more of my trolls as we speak."

Nikarat chuckles and shakes his head. "The poor fool."

"Phase three?"

Nikarat nods. "Phase three."

"That's a shame," Renon states. "As annoying and stupid as Jugack was, I really enjoyed watching him pretend to be smart."

A scream emanates from beyond Renon's laboratory.

"He never stood a chance," Renon says with a sigh.

"None of them do." Nikarat picks up one of Renon's notebooks. "When will the ones with thicker necks and heels be done?"

"Maybe four months. Just add the armor I made on the ones we have now."

"Novinri will be pleased. I'll go inform him of our progress."

Renon grabs a sparkling blue stone from a small chest and tosses it to Nikarat. "Just in case," he says.

Nikarat places the notebook down. "I'll try not to use it this time."

"Oh, one more thing," starts Renon. "On your way out, have my maids clean up the mess the trolls have likely made."

"Very well. Goodbye, Renon. Excellent work as always."

"Likewise, Nikarat. The Five Fingers of the Forgotten *will* be remembered," Renon says, holding his hand up and opened.

Nikarat copies the gesture. "Ithendar will be free once more."

CHAPTER 21

THE UNBROKEN

The resonating crack from Allbus' back slamming against Gorgan's knee leaves Elidria with knots in her stomach. Her heart feels like someone has their hand in her chest and is squeezing the life out of her. Her mouth gapes open from witnessing such a horrible display of brutality from the big mercenary, an event that furthers her realization of just how little that man cares about the lives of others.

Delsar dashes past Elidria, his sights on Gorgan, forcing the giant to drop Allbus to the floor.

Allbus screams out in pain, but that's all he can do. He hits the ground, motionless, and his agonizing cries of pain don't stop.

A huge presence turns Elidria around. The troll ignores her and runs straight at Delsar who is already swinging away at Gorgan. "Look out!" she cries.

Delsar's blade catches Gorgan's side, but Elidria's warning prevents him from pressing his weaponed advantage. He glances back at the troll and rolls out of the way.

The troll's feet screech to a halt, stopping itself from running into Gorgan. It faces Delsar and follows after him with a relentless fury of attacks, keeping Delsar from getting back to a fighting position.

"Eldra!" he shouts for help, still rolling and dodging the mindless beast.

"I don't have a weapon," she replies.

Delsar avoids another strike and rolls through the legs of the troll. "Then take care of Gorgan," he says, putting a slash into the back of the troll's calf and getting back to his feet.

"Yeah, 'cause *that's* easier."

Delsar ignores her comment and teases the troll away from Gorgan and Elidria.

Elidria throws her hands up, readying for the final bout. Her mouth quivers and her hands tremble. The memories of Telrus losing his life and seeing Allbus in agony at Gorgan's feet only add stress to her burden of needing to beat this man. The thought of getting bashed, bruised, and maybe even crushed doesn't help in any way. Sweat and tears mix as they drip from her face. Her body shivers as chills shoot through her. Seeing Gorgan's all-too-pleased smirk makes her heart beat even faster.

"Your time's up," Gorgan says to her.

She drops her stance lower. Not because she's purposely letting Gorgan make the first move, but because her feet refuse to move. Her body is getting overwhelmed with fear and it feels like the world around her is getting colder and colder. The pain from her various injuries all begin hitting her at once.

Gorgan's smirk turns into a grin. "The people of this village looked just like you do now when I slaughtered them. The only difference is that many of them were screaming for their lives. That's a difference that I will soon change. You're going to—" Gorgan gets distracted by a pull on his foot as he tries to take a step toward Elidria.

"I'm not finished with you," grumbles Allbus, face down and hands clasped around Gorgan's ankle.

"But I am," Gorgan responds, lifting his other leg to crush the guard's head.

"No!" Elidria cries. Her feet leave the floor as she jumps at Gorgan, despite the incredible pain she's in.

Gorgan throws his arms up, but Elidria's small fist weaves through his defense and splits his lip against his teeth.

She's been careful not to hit hard surfaces with her fists since her fight with the thugs in Grandell, but now the small bones in her hand are the least of her concern. Her other hand connects with Gorgan's nose, knocking him back. He trips over Allbus and falls to the deck. Elidria jumps over Allbus to continue her attack.

Gorgan sticks his leg straight out, impacting Elidria's stomach. Spit flies from her mouth. Gorgon follows with a roundhouse kick with his other foot that bashes against the side of her face.

She releases a squeak as she gets sent sideways across the deck, crashing hard against the guardrail. The world begins to spin around Elidria and an all-too-familiar nauseous feeling overwhelms her. Her head splits with pain and her arms and legs feel like they each weigh a ton.

Gorgan is back on his feet before Elidria's brain even has enough time to unscramble. Allbus reaches for Gorgan again, but Gorgan kicks him in the side of the head as he walks past.

Elidria grabs the guardrail above her. Before she can pull herself up, Gorgan's powerful hand grabs her around the neck and lifts her off the ground. She tells her body to move, to fight back, but it does nothing. She dangles from Gorgan's grasp completely defenseless.

"You were right," says Gorgan, pulling her face in close to his own, "that was easier. I do hope Arviakyss wins his fight against the troll. Then he can watch me pull you apart with my bare hands."

Elidria cringes from her pain and the threat. Her adrenaline spikes and she feels a slight surge of energy.

Gorgan feels her start to stir and latches onto her face with his other hand.

She instinctively grabs at his hand, trying to free her face, but her efforts are futile. Her surge of energy dissipates and her arms go limp.

"Now we can watch the show," he says, turning her around in his grasp. "Either way, one of you *will* watch the other die."

Delsar spins around the troll and slides his blade through the armor strip around its ankle. As the troll twists around to find Delsar, he pulls down on his sword like a lever and severs the leather from the ankle.

The troll swings at Delsar's head, but Delsar ducks under. He spins counterclockwise and slashes the troll's Achilles. It drops to its knee but immediately tries to locate its adversary.

Delsar stays low, beneath the troll's vision, allowing the beast to turn. As soon as the troll's head comes around, Delsar drives his sword up, into its jaw. The blade passes easily through the jaw, but Delsar's heart skips a beat when it stops against the mouth's roof.

The troll howls and grabs the blade, ripping it from its jaw before trying to yank it away from Delsar.

Delsar holds on and gets pulled off the ground. He releases his sword and grabs one of the troll's ears, using it to pull himself up and around the troll. He snatches his dagger from his satchel and drives it into the troll's neck, just above its armor strip.

The troll shrieks and swats at him like he's a pesky bug. Delsar avoids the strike by swinging over the troll's other shoulder. The troll's hand impacts the knife, driving it deeper into its neck.

Delsar reaches for the troll's gaping mouth and grabs hold of its teeth. He presses his feet against its chest and yanks against its jaw.

The troll can't stand the pain and its body follows.

Delsar releases and avoids the troll as it comes crashing down. He picks up his sword from off the ground.

The troll gets to its hands and knees but cries out again as Delsar stabs his sword through the back of its hand. It tries to pull its hand away, but the blade pierced even a few inches of the wood beneath it, keeping it from escaping. With its other hand, it reaches for the sword, but the knife getting pulled from its neck distracts it.

Delsar nimbly avoids the troll swatting at its neck again as blood starts to gush from its wound. He circles it and uses the heel of his boot to stomp against the troll's stuck hand.

The troll shrieks and instinctively pulls its hand away, causing the blade to slice through the rest of the hand. Even with its hand split in two and bleeding as bad as its neck, the troll struggles to its feet.

Delsar pulls his sword from the wood and readies himself for the troll's next attack.

The troll raises its arms above its head, splattering the gray blood everywhere, and lets out its infamous battle cry. It takes a step toward Delsar but begins to waver. Its next step crosses over its last and its eyes roll back. It begins moaning before falling over sideways.

Delsar runs over to the fallen beast. Without hesitation, he stabs his sword through its eye, confirming its fate. Delsar slides his blade out and flicks it through the air, ridding most of it from the thick blood.

"Bravo," says a voice from behind, spinning him around in an instant. "You looked like a small monkey climbing its favorite tree," Gorgan continues.

"Put her down!" Delsar commands, eyeing Elidria's helpless body being clutched by Gorgan's tight grip. Her face is full of fear and her mouth hangs slightly open.

"Funny," says Gorgan. "I think you've been in this situation before. Twice. The first was with Aldameer, who I killed in front of you, and the second was that guard, who probably wishes he was dead."

Delsar takes a step and Gorgan squeezes Elidria's neck even harder. Her mouth gapes completely open and she closes her eyes. A long, agonizing moan squeaks from her mouth as she tries to grab at the hand crushing her neck. Her pulling at the thumb and flailing of her legs do nothing to relieve the pressure.

"Stop!" Delsar cries.

"I don't think I will."

Delsar drops his sword and throws his hand up. "It's me you want, not her," he says, his eyes filling with tears. "Please, leave her and kill me."

Gorgan grins and points at the ground. "Kneel," he commands.

Delsar slowly gets down on his knees but keeps his hands up.

"Do you see what his compassion gets you, Little Missy? It gets you a front-row seat to the agonizing death of the Queen's Champion. You may live, but your fate will be worse than his. With so many of my men missing or dead, I'll need a way to fill those numbers." He squeezes her neck even tighter, but she's already given up. "You'll fit that role just fine."

Delsar snarls at Gorgan. "You're dead!"

Gorgan shakes his head. "Tsk, tsk. I've heard Arviakyss get called a 'hero' before. That must have been a lie."

"If killing monsters is considered heroic, then maybe I am."

"You're going to kill me from your knees? How does that work?"

Delsar starts to get back up, but Gorgan shakes Elidria's body with his wrist. She winces, dropping Delsar back to his knees.

"Wow. Being a hero looks so annoying. I can't imagine being helpless because of someone else's helplessness. Sure, she would die, but I have no weapon. You probably could have beaten me with your sword. You could have killed me and found that precious *justice* everyone is always looking for. Instead, you sit on your knees, beneath the man who was once beneath you. You're a nobody without your Queen."

"Why do you talk so much?" Elidria faintly grumbles. "Your voice doesn't even sound pretty."

"She's a funny girl," Gorgan remarks. "I'll enjoy having her around."

Delsar growls and stands to his feet.

"I didn't say you could move," says Gorgan.

"You can't have her," Delsar says, pointing his finger at Gorgan. "I know she would rather die than be used by a thug like you."

"It's true," Elidria gurgles. Gorgan squeezes her neck tightly, rendering her completely motionless.

"Enough!" he yells. "I can break her neck faster than you can blink. I think the hero is supposed to *save* the girl, not get her killed."

"Fair enough." Delsar slides his foot under his sword and kicks it up to himself. "Our terms have changed," he says, pointing the blade at Gorgan. "Let her go or die."

Gorgan's smug look washes into concern. The sure victory in his mind disappears as he realizes that Delsar plans to stop him despite the cost. "Take her from me yourself," he says as he uses his other hand to grab her by the belt. He raises her limp body while lowering his stance, readying her as his own shield.

Delsar begins circling around him, and Gorgan keeps Elidria between himself and Delsar.

Delsar stops circling as a sight behind Gorgan leaves him dismayed.

Gorgan sees Delsar's eye change but controls himself from taking his own eyes off of him.

An older man yells behind Gorgan as Galius and the troll he was fighting fall from the helm's banister. They crash to the ground with the troll on top. The troll is slow getting back to its feet and Galius lies motionless. His armor is slightly caved from the impact.

Gorgan takes a couple steps back, putting enough distance between himself and Delsar to safely look over his shoulder. He looks back at Delsar with the same smug smirk he had earlier. "That's the last of your reinforcements, Arviakyss. With this troll at my side and the girl out of commission, you have no hope." Gorgan tosses Elidria to the side. Skin scrapes off her face and hands as her near-unconscious body crashes to the wooden floor.

"You shouldn't have done that," Delsar snarls.

"You didn't stop me." Gorgan points at Delsar. "Kill him," he commands the troll.

The troll walks up behind Gorgan and stops.

"Kill Arviakyss, you nit," he commands again.

The troll tilts its head before reaching out its massive hand and grabbing Gorgan around his neck.

Gorgan grimaces but is able to grab the troll's thumb and forcefully pry it from his throat.

The troll looks terrified at Gorgon's show of strength.

Delsar thinks about using the troll's distraction to finish the job, but Gorgan punches the troll in the jugular, making it stagger back. Its feet come dangerously close to Elidria's body. Delsar dashes in and nimbly avoids the two fighting monsters. He grabs Elidria by her collar. "I've got you," he says as he pulls her away, just as a massive foot slams down where she was.

Elidria's bare heels drag against the splintering deck, leaving two trails of blood as Delsar pulls her away.

"How badly are you hurt?" he asks, as he sits her against the ship's mast. Her eyes are rolled back.

"I can't see you," she says as her head droops to her chest.

Delsar lifts her chin up and moves the hair from her face. "Hey, Elidria, you need to stay with me."

Tears and blood run down Elidria's face. "I'm scared, Delsar," she says. "There's a feeling of dread inside me. Like a shadow is creeping through my body."

Delsar clenches his eyes shut. His own tears begin their brief run down his face. He grabs Elidria and embraces her. "You can't let it," he tells her. "Please, hold on for me. I don't know what I'll do without you."

Elidria places her hand on his chest. Delsar places his own hand on hers. She pulls her hand free and grabs his. "It doesn't matter what you do," she says. "I will never leave you. I won't let go." Elidria reaches into her pocket and pulls out the deformed, wet, and tattered contract from Orange Peak. She places it in his hand. "Finish the job," she says softly. "Be a hero."

Delsar gently squeezes her hand and caresses her cheek with his other. "Okay, boss," he says with a sniffle. His diaphragm compresses, forcing him to almost whimper, but he lets the reaction pass him by. "Hang tight," he says with a subtle smile. "I'll finish what you started."

Gorgan kicks the troll's knee in, snapping it and dropping the beast to its other. He then blocks a strike from the troll with his arms that makes him wince, but only for a moment. He pushes the troll's arms away and grabs its forehead and chin. With a quick twist, a loud crack echoes back from the cliff walls and the troll drops to the floor.

Gorgan cries out in rage, just like the trolls do. He turns around and faces Delsar with his fiery eyes. "You're next!" he exclaims, pointing his purpled-finger at Delsar who is wearing Elidria's shield on his arm, his own shield on his back, and his sword in his right hand.

Delsar clinks the sword and shield together before readying them. "I don't think so."

Gorgan growls at Delsar and snatches Galius' sword from the ground. "I want you to know that when I remove your head from your body, I'll be doing the same to everyone on this ship. Even that Raymar guy. Then you'll all have died for nothing."

"Except Elidria," Delsar corrects. "I think you said you had other plans for her."

"You'll be dead. You won't care *what* I do with her."

"Exactly," says Delsar. "I won't care if I'm dead and I've never cared while I'm alive. Today is different. Today I care and I plan on caring more often. Dying will make that difficult. I will make this impossible for you."

Gorgan grabs the bridge of his nose and scoffs. "Corny speech, Champion. Or do you call yourself a hero now?"

"Not yet."

Gorgan scoffs again and clutches the sword with both hands. "Then you can die the failure you are!" he screams, charging at Delsar.

"I'm forgiven," Delsar says under his breath, preparing his shield for the rage-fueled onslaught that is on its way, "not a failure."

Roki's ears ring and his head throbs as his eyes start to clear. He winces from pain and lets out a grunt, feeling the sharp pains in his right arm. It was just over two weeks ago that it snapped like a twig versus another troll. Overusing it today with the bow and fighting the troll is now haunting him. He bites on his inner cheek, trying to distract his brain from the crippling pain it's feeling, but it's the comprehension of the situation he's in, filling his consciousness, that relieves him temporarily of his agony.

"Galius?" he says as he rolls onto his left arm. He grimaces as another sharp pain from his arm shoots through his body from the position change. "Galius?" he says again, but even louder. He tucks his right arm tightly against his chest and slowly crawls on his other arm and legs across the helm. He peers through the guardrails, overlooking the main deck, and sees the carnage below him. His downed friends, the dead trolls, and Gorgan and Delsar about to face off.

Roki scans the ground behind him for his sword. The only thing he seems to have left behind is a trail of blood, but he doesn't recall taking a blow that would leave so much of the red fluid. He scans his body and rears back his head, letting out a stifled scream. He instinctively bites on his left hand as tears quickly fill his eyes. He's not sure how he didn't feel the sword through his leg until now. It wasn't until he saw it that his brain told him something was wrong.

The boat jostles, causing Roki more discomfort as a gust of wind taps both boats together. Roki looks over at the tied rope he used to board the ship and begins his tormenting crawl toward it.

"...and that was how I met your mother," comes a voice from below.

"Yeah, Dad, I've heard that one already."

"Glade!" Roki shouts down to the father and son manning Bekka's Fury.

"Oh, hey there, Roki," Glade says, giving him a wave.

"How long is this rope?" Roki asks, pointing at the one securing the two boats together.

"I think it's two hundred feet or so," Glade replies.

"Good," Roki says as he begins untying it with his one good arm.

"I'll untie our end and pass it up to you," Glade says, trying to help.

"No. Just make sure your end is secured."

"What are you planning?"

"I need to sail your boat," Roki answers.

"Where?"

"Wherever the wind is blowing. Just go!"

"Right!" Glade shouts with a salute. "Cade, get that anchor back up and set those sails!"

"On it," Cade confirms as he starts cranking the anchor to its return.

"Good luck," Glade says to Roki as he gets behind the wheel.

"I hope so." Roki removes the rope from the banister and ties a loop in his end with his hand and teeth. It looks somewhat like a noose. "This is all I can come up with."

Their blades only meet for a moment at a time. After every impact, Gorgan is swinging again with the intent to kill. Delsar uses every bit of knowledge, every reflex, every technique he knows to keep pace with the mercenary's flurry of strikes.

A heavy blow to Elidria's shield spins Delsar around and another immediately strikes the shield he wears on his back. He gets knocked away and turns around, only to have his sword almost get jarred from his hand. Gorgon's strength and energy are unwavering, every block sapping Delsar's own, every effort draining him. He reinforces his grip with his other hand and stays on the defensive.

Delsar's back hits the starboard guardrail, and with a quick duck and lunge, he avoids a vertical strike that effortlessly cleaves through the rail. Delsar skirts past Gorgan and along the way, slides his blade against Gorgan's side. The same spot where Elidria removed his armor plate.

Gorgan cries out and clutches his side. Blood seeps through his clothes and fingers. It was a strike that would slow most men, but it only seems to fire Gorgan up. He swings at Delsar with more power than ever.

Delsar raises his sword above his head and the edges of both blades dig deep into each other. A bloodied hand reaches out and grabs Delsar's hair. Delsar slams the top of Elidria's shield into the wrist, but it hangs on. A low swing comes from Delsar's left and he brings his leg up to block it. The sword connects with his shinguard, but the force of the blow swings both his legs out from under him.

Gorgan slams Delsar, face first, onto the deck. He kicks him over and places one foot on his chest. He steps on the shield with the other and stabs at Delsar's head.

Delsar instinctively uses his arm's bracer to guide the strike away from his head and into the wood, but he forgot he isn't wearing his bracers. He screams in agony as the blade slices through his skin and grinds against his bone. Blood drips from his arm into his face, but the blade did miss his head. It was a mistake, forgetting the bracer, but one he won't repeat. If he survives.

Gorgan grabs Delsar's arm and digs his fingers into the gash.

Delsar screams again. He slides his arm from the restrained shield and tries to pry the hand from his arm. The blade next to his head starts to come loose from the wood. He releases his grip from Gorgan's hand and grabs the hilt of the sword instead.

Gorgan pulls but Delsar's persistence prevents it from coming loose. He lets Delsar's arm go and punches his head.

Delsar's hand drops from Gorgan's hilt as his brain rattles in his head.

Gorgan pulls his sword free and tries again for Delsar's head.

Delsar places both hands on his handle and pushes the strike away with his sword. He follows it up with an upward slash, aimed between Gorgan's legs.

Gorgan spins away, keeping his left leg pressed against Delsar's chest as he rotates around, avoiding the strike.

Delsar brings his legs up and squirms himself out of the shield mounted on his back, allowing him to slide out from under Gorgan as he twists around.

Gorgan rolls his ankle and tumbles over.

Delsar scampers away on his hands to the stairs before getting back to his feet. Both men pant, so exhausted they no longer exchange words. Surrender is not an option for either man. They stare at each other as Gorgan gets back on his feet and Delsar catches his breath.

"Delsar!" shouts a voice from the top of the stairs.

Delsar looks up and Roki tosses him the end of a rope. A knot already added.

"Tie that around him," Roki instructs. "Trust me."

"What?" Delsar asks in between breaths.

"And do it fast."

Delsar rolls his eyes. "Yeah, sure."

"You're going to tie me up?" Gorgan asks, approaching him on the stairs. "*That's* your plan?"

"It's not mine, but I guess it's something." Delsar takes his sword in his left hand and the rope in his right.

Gorgan scoffs and resumes his attack.

Delsar narrowly avoids the sword as part of his trouser gets sliced on his way past Gorgan. He positions himself closer to the middle of the deck, allowing him more room to maneuver.

Now it's just sword-on-sword. There are no shields for Delsar to use and it's only a matter of time until one of them hits their mark.

Delsar ducks under a strike and Gorgan nimbly jumps over Delsar's counter. The swords clash on one side and then clash on the other. Delsar throws in a kick against Gorgan's knee, but the knee holds strong.

Gorgan adds his own spin-hook kick which Delsar avoids and slashes at as it goes by. The blade scrapes off Gorgan's metal plates and neither man is struck.

Delsar gets another good hit against Gorgan's arm, but Gorgan hardly shows any pain and proceeds to backhand Delsar across the face.

Delsar staggers back and Gorgan gives him no breathing room. He sends a massive front kick into Delsar's chest, sending him flying back and through a crate against the guardrail. Arrows spill out all over Delsar and his head hangs over his chest.

"Finally," Gorgan says with a grin. "You were a tough adversary, Arviakyss. Your title suited you. However, now that you've lost, that title

no longer belongs to you. Now I'm the champion and you're the failure."
He points back at Elidria who still sits against the mast a few feet from
where he stands. "The girl will go with me and I will be rewarded."

Delsar subtly moves his head and looks at Gorgan with the top of
his eyes. He gives him a smirk and exclaims, "Gotcha!"

Gorgan looks down at his foot and sees the rope around his ankle.
"Really?" he questions. "Getting a rope around my leg is a victory
to you?"

Delsar rolls his tongue around in his mouth before letting out a
chuckle. "You're part troll, aren't you?"

"So what if I am?"

Delsar scoffs and looks down the rope. "I hear trolls sink."

Gorgan's pompous face is quickly replaced with fear as he watches
a boat sailing away that's attached to the other end of the rope. He
raises his sword to cut the rope, but Delsar masterfully flings an arrow
that sticks into his hand. The sword drops and clatters to the ground.
Gorgan's foot starts to pull as the rope tightens. He desperately leaps
toward Elidria, his leg pulling out from under him. He slams against
the wooden floor and begins sliding toward the ocean.

Elidria screams as she begins getting dragged with him. Her ankle
clutched by Gorgan.

They begin sliding past Delsar and he jumps to his feet before diving
for Elidria. He grabs her hand and also begins getting dragged across
the floor.

Gorgan yells out as his body gets pulled through the guardrail he
sliced through earlier. His body hangs over the ocean.

Elidria slides through and Delsar maneuvers himself over to part
of the rail that's intact. He slides to his feet and lets his torso hang over
as his thighs hold him in place.

Elidria screams even louder. It feels like her arm is going to get
ripped off. She looks up at Delsar and shakes her head, tears filling her
eyes. "Please, don't let go," she pleads.

"I won't," he replies, reinforcing his grip with his other hand.

"Arviakyss!" Gorgan shouts. "Tell them to cut the rope or she dies
with me!"

"Don't!" Elidria says.

"You have to kick him off," Delsar desperately tells her.

"I can't," she replies. "He'll drown with all that armor on."

"He dies anyway. Elidria, kick him off."

She shakes her head again.

"Elidria, I am *not* letting you go. We will *all* die if you don't kick him off."

"I'm not killing anyone!" she cries.

The guardrail starts to give and the sudden posture change almost causes Delsar to lose his grip. "Elidria, please. I put the rope on him. I'm the one who put him in this situation. Kick him off!"

"You'll be a murderer!" Gorgan yells to Elidria.

"No, you won't," Delsar assures her. "Look at me."

She looks at his tearing face and his quivering lips. His face looks kind and yet afraid. A subtle smile creeps across his face. He just nods his head up and down. She can't stop herself from crying, seeing him like this.

"Elidria, I'll forgive you," he says.

His words feel so real. They mean more to her than anything anyone has ever said. The youth and innocence in his eyes that she's never noticed before only adds more emotion to his words. Elidria closes her eyes shut and nods. "I'm sorry," she says before pulling her leg back.

"You brat!" Gorgan screams.

Elidria doesn't respond to the insults and names Gorgan throws at her. She slams her heel against his broken hand, again and again, eliciting unknown profanities from the beast.

The grip begins to slide down her foot until it hangs at the very end. Elidria looks past her skirt and directly at Gorgan. "If I don't hate you," she says, stunning him, rendering him silent, "how can I hate my father?" She kicks her foot against his hand and her other foot slides from his grip.

He falls into the water and begins sinking as the boat drags him out to sea.

Elidria slams against the side of the boat and her face scrapes against the wood as Delsar pulls her up.

Delsar falls over backward and she lands on top of him. He throws his arms around her and begins to cry.

"I need to save him," Elidria says weakly, with her head against his chest. "If I'm strong enough to kill him...,"

"But you weren't," Delsar states. "None of us were. It took *all* of us."

"I need—" Elidria's breathing starts to get heavy. "I need to try," she says before her eyes roll back and lids droop.

"Elidria, stay with me," Delsar says while shaking her. "Elidria—"

That's all she hears before Delsar's voice vanishes. Before his touch fades. Before all the pain disappears. The world around her dims. Her consciousness dissipates. Everything becomes black.

13 Years Ago...

Delsar sprints through the halls of the hospital in Thya. "Sorry!" he exclaims to a group of nurses as he pushes through them. *Room 109. Where is it?* He passes room 127 which means he entered from the wrong side of the building. Counting down is going to take longer than if he actually thought things through and entered the main entrance.

"Slow down!" someone shouts as Delsar knocks over a tower of clean bedsheets.

"Sorry!" he shouts back without slowing down.

He makes a sharp left turn and almost crashes against the wall with his momentum. He slides against the wall and takes off again down the new hall. He looks up at the room numbers and sees 'Room 107' fly past him. He was just here yesterday, but all the rooms still look the same. He skids to a stop and almost wipes out, but manages to regain his footing.

He starts to back up and passes 107 again before stopping at the previous room. *Room 109.* Delsar starts to shiver as he reaches out to open the door. He doesn't so much as knock and just lets himself in.

A doctor stands at the foot of a bed by the window. He looks over at Delsar and gives him a gentle nod. Delsar slowly walks over to the bed as the doctor makes his way out. He places his hand on Delsar's shoulder as he goes by and gives him a sympathetic smile. "You have a wonderful mother," he tells him. "I'll leave you both alone."

Delsar watches the man leave before whipping around and grappling the foot of the bed. "Mom!" he shouts as he pushes along the bed to her side.

Her eyes start to open and seeing her even try to move her white and sickly head shows just how much agony she's in. "Delsar," she says, giving him a warm smile, despite what she's going through. "Come here." She painfully moves her arms to give him room to snuggle.

Delsar lets her wrap her cold arms around him and he digs his head into her cheek. "I don't understand," he says. "You were almost better."

"You being here makes me feel better than I ever have," she tells him, weaker than even her previous words.

Delsar shakes his head against her face. "Please," he says, lifting his head and teary eyes to look at her, "why do you have to leave me now?"

"Oh, sweetie," Sariah remarks, stroking his hair, "I'm not leaving you."

"But you are, just like Daddy did."

Sariah's smile disappears as she puts her hands on Delsar's cheeks. "Then what are you going to do about it?" she asks, sternly.

"What do you mean?"

"Things will always go wrong, whether on purpose or by chance, things will never be perfect," she explains. "For every wrong in the world, there are a dozen new opportunities to make it right. How are you going to make this right?"

"What can *I* do? I don't know how to save you."

"Let me see you smile."

Delsar is taken aback by her solution. A smile is just a smile. "How will that fix anything?"

"My favorite thing is to see you smile." Sariah coughs as she struggles to continue. "I can't be saved from being sick, but you *can* save me from the darkness."

"The darkness?"

"Shine, Delsar. For me."

Delsar starts to shake his head but gives in. He gives her a forced smile that speaks no emotion.

Sariah returns his smile with her own pleased smile.

Seeing his mother truly happy is enough to warp Delsar's smile into a real one. "I'll save others, mom. So this doesn't happen to anyone else."

Sariah's eyes close, sending tears down her cheeks. "Then save them."

"Mom!" Delsar exclaims, thinking she wouldn't open them ever again.

"There's one more thing I wish of you," she says, putting what she has left into her words and looking at her son.

Delsar closes his eyes and tries to swallow the knot in his throat. His mouth trembles as he looks back at his mother. "Anything," he tells her. "Whatever you ask of me, I'll do my very best."

Sariah's head sinks into its pillow as she starts to go limp. Despite being out of energy, she keeps her eyes open and even smiles as she delivers her final words to her son. "There are people in this world that don't know how to truly smile. Promise me you will help them as you have helped me."

Present...

The strong smell of freshly baked bread and smoking ham wafts through the window before hitting Elidria's nose. She starts to stir and gets blinded by a bright light as she opens her eyes. She throws her hand up to block the sun and then notices the clean, white gown she wears. The sounds of birds and kids playing emanate from outside. Elidria looks around this luxurious room that she doesn't recognize and spies someone she knows very well sleeping in a chair. "Delsar?" she asks, waking the man.

Delsar wakes up calmly and looks over at Elidria. His face is blank, giving no reading.

"Did you die, too?" she asks.

Delsar chuckles and shakes his head before embracing her.

"Ouch!" she exclaims. "I guess I'm not dead. Be careful."

"It's good to see you awake," he says, gently releasing her.

"Bihnor?" she questions with sincerity in her voice.

Delsar nods. "Bad guy free." Delsar notices her looking at the bandages around her hands and feet. "You have multiple fractures in your hands and your right foot. You scraped almost all the skin from the bottom of your feet as well. You also broke your face in multiple places, two of your ribs, and nearly split your sternum. None of those are *too* serious and will heal. It was the multiple concussions we were all worried about, but you waking up means you're going to be just fine."

Elidria smiles and Delsar and slowly looks at all her different bandages. Tears start to form from all the weight being lifted from her shoulders. She grabs Delsar's sleeve and begins sobbing in his arms.

Delsar places his hand on her head and lets her get it all out.

"What about everyone else?" she finally asks, looking up at Delsar full of concern.

"Most of them are downstairs. I can go get them."

"No," she says. "Take me down there."

"You need to remain in bed."

"You said I'll heal so take me to see my friends."

Delsar rolls his eyes and Elidria notices, but it makes her smile instead. "Come on," he says, wrapping his arm under her arm and around her back. He hoists her up and grabs a crutch that was laid by the bed. "Here," he says, giving it to her to use on her right side.

"Thanks, Delsar."

"Um-hm."

"Hey, Delsar?"

"What is it?"

"Thank you, for everything."

Delsar takes a deep breath and nods. "You're welcome."

"One more thing."

"Anything."

"Where are we?"

Delsar lets out a surprised scoff. "A recovery facility in Lar," he tells her. "They're helping patch us up and resupplying us."

Elidria tilts her head. "Resupplying us for what?"

Delsar smirks. "Let's get you downstairs before I explain."

Elidria lets out a grunt in acknowledgment. She slowly hobbles down the stairs leaning against Delsar. He holds nearly all her weight and opens the door at the bottom to let her through.

Seven pairs of eyes are filled with glee seeing her walk through the door. Many of them shout, "Eldra!" upon her appearance.

Elidria blushes and looks down at her feet. "Hey everyone," she says with a huge grin.

"We're not in the floor," Glade points out.

Elidria looks at Glade and rolls her eyes. "Hi, Glade." She scans the room twice after thinking she may have miscounted. "Delsar, where's Allbus?"

Castor stands up from his chair to take this one. "He's hurt pretty bad," he bluntly states, a sniffle swelling in his nose. "He's going to take a while to recover."

Elidria lowers her head again. "I'm sorry."

"He knew the risks."

Elidria nods and looks over her shoulder at Delsar. "What about Gorgan?" she whispers.

"He was dead before Glade could return with the boat," Delsar informs her. He feels her heart start to race and senses her mood change. "You didn't kill him," he assures her. "You need to remember that."

Elidria shakes her head. "What you say may be true, but it will still take me a while to convince myself that."

Delsar wipes a tear from her face. "I understand."

Elidria's tone completely jumps as she locates Roki. "What about you, Roki?"

Roki's white teeth contrast brightly against his face as he gives her a grin. "My arm is back to square one and I've got a crutch, just like you." He taps the crutch with the mug he holds in the same hand.

"Anyone else hurt?" she asks the room.

Delsar pipes up. "I likely broke my right arm blocking one of Gorgan's strikes," he says.

"Likely?"

"I didn't actually have it checked. I'm keeping my presence here in Lar a secret seeing how everyone now knows I'm Arviakyss."

A spew of morning brew ejects from Roki's mouth before he is able to swallow it. "What?" he exclaims with a cough, bringing his sleeve to his mouth. "*You?*"

Galius lets out a huge girthy laugh and smacks Roki on his back.

Roki coughs again as he's jerked forward, spilling the rest of his brew at his feet.

"Clearly not everyone," Elidria states, one eyebrow raised and a grin across her face.

"I guess it pays to be on time," says Glade, sitting the wrong way in his chair.

"Cade's Log: 2 Days since his perilous rescue – The girl, beat to a pulp and looking like a preschooler's art project, finally emerges from her convalescing slumber. With her, she brings our mystifying Captain who recently relieved himself of such a role. He carries a veracity of knowledge that he dropped on his oblivious crew of indomitable warriors. One is so aghast by such a development that he has lost all proper and instinctual function to his pharynx. A truly unexpected and crippling situation to find oneself in. Without nourishment or liquids, he will likely not last the week."

"Cade!" Delsar yells, about to storm over to the boy.

Elidria grabs onto Delsar's sleeve to stop him. "It's funny," she says. "And I get to learn new words listening to him."

"Words that no one will *ever* use."

Elidria tilts her head and closes her mouth, but her smile remains. "He used them so that makes your point void."

Delsar rolls his eyes and scoffs. "He only does it out loud because he *knows* it annoys me."

"You make it too easy, Delsar. You really need to lighten up."

Delsar scoffs again and turns his head away.

Elidria sees his ears turn red and she starts to giggle.

"Ham's done!" Raymar exclaims, pushing through the front door. "Though, I will say, the quality of these 'city' pigs aren't up—" The pan he holds crashes to the ground seeing Elidria in the room. "Eldra," he says in dismay.

"Come here." Elidria's teeth glisten and her arms open wide.

Raymar runs through the room with tons of joy and excitement plastered all over his face. The amount of energy he's giving off scares Elidria for a moment.

"Gently, please," she says, squeezing one eye shut and preparing for the pain. The embrace is soft and she feels his lips peck her forehead.

"Thank you, Eldra. Thank you for not giving up on me."

Merith approaches them and takes her husband's hand. "What you did for us is more than anyone deserves," she adds.

Elidria blushes again. "*Golly.* What about everyone else who helped."

"We thanked them already," says Raymar.

Elidria takes in a huge breath and then sighs. "Then, you're welcome."

Raymar pats her on the head and straightens up. "I've got to go clean the food. We'll have a nice talk when we're all eating around the table." Raymar leaves, but Merith stays.

"What is it?" Elidria asks.

Merith looks at Delsar and smiles.

Elidria follows her look as Delsar pulls paper from his pocket. "This is our contract," he says.

"Payment!" she exclaims.

"Don't worry about that. We found your treasury in the mercenaries' ship. I'm paid."

"So, are we done?" Elidria asks.

"We are. The contract is complete."

Elidria lowers her head. "Oh."

"But," Merith starts to add, "I have a new job offer that everyone here has already agreed to. That is except for you and Delsar."

Elidria tilts her head with intrigue. "Oh?"

Merith's face beams with excitement as she begins to explain. "While Raymar was being held captive, the sorcerer started talking about the prisoners he grabbed from this village and Orange Peak. Raymar said one of the descriptions sounded exactly like Galia. Eldra, I think my daughter might still be alive!"

Elidria's jaw drops and her face shines as bright as Merith's. "I can't believe that!"

"So, that's the job. Find and rescue Galia and any of the other prisoners they may have taken."

"I'm in," Elidria says without hesitation. "Do we have any leads?"

"Just one," Galius chimes in. He pulls out a blue rock. "The sorcerer used this to vanish. If we can find out where these come from, we can probably find *him*."

"That's a start," Elidria replies. She turns and places her arms against Delsar's chest and looks up at him. "So Delsar, are you in?"

Delsar turns his head away and starts to stutter. "Y-you're t-t-too close."

"You've hugged me before."

"I h-h-hate hugs and only d-do s-s-so when ap-p-propriate."

Elidria tilts her head and grits her teeth, stepping back from Delsar.

Delsar's eyes glare past her and his breathing is heavy. His whole body does a quick shake and he clears his throat. "You want to know if I'd be willing to risk my life to try and find someone I don't know, who may or may not be dead?"

Elidria doesn't answer and watches him walk to the center of the room.

He stands between everyone and scans all the faces staring back at him. His father gives him a nod and Delsar looks back at Elidria. "You've asked me to go on an adventure with *people*?"

Elidria's smile fades. "Are you not coming?"

"I won't do something like this with random people," he says.

Elidria's mouth opens slightly, trying to understand why he would say no to something so noble.

"But," he continues, "I will with my companions."

Elidria brings her hands to her mouth and that smile that just disappeared returns immediately.

Delsar walks up to Elidria and holds out his hand. "I will never let go," he says.

"I'll stand with you," she responds, taking his hand.

"Then I'll go with not only my companions," Delsar gives her a huge grin, showing her his white teeth for the first time, "but also my partner."

Elidria can't help but hug him again. "'Friends' is a good word, too," she says, burying her head.

"Then with my friends," he replies, returning her hug and resting his head on hers. His grin replaced with a calm, gentle smile.

Elidria's excited tears race down her cheeks, crying with joy. *I can't believe it*, she says in her head while playing back all the tribulations she's been through with him. *He's smiling. He's truly smiling.*

The End

CHARACTERS

(In order of mention)

Sariah - (sar **iy** ah) | Female | Age 36 at death | 5' 4" 134 lbs | The mother of Delsar and inspiration for Arviakyss.

Delsar - (**del** sahr) | Male | Age 22 | 6' 0" 185 lbs | The Outcast from the eastern borders of Ithendar.

Lloyd - (loyd) | Male | Age 9 | A child saved by Arviakyss at a young age.

Arviakyss - (ar **viy** ah kihs) | Male | Age 16 | 5' 10" 170 lbs | The Queen's Champion, formally known as Delsar.

Hemway - (**hem** way) | Male | Age 48 | The mayor of Newville.

Pailess - (**piy** les) | Male | Age 33 | Barkeeper at *Rina's Food and Inn.*

Mungie - (mun gee) | Female | Age 28 | The head chef at *Rina's Food and Inn.*

Brianna - (bree **ah** nah) | Female | Age 55 | Waitress at *Rina's Food and Inn.*

Elidria - (ehl **lee** dree ah) | Female | Age 19 | 5' 5" 105 lbs | Snail farmer from Bihnor and Delsar's employer.

Galia - (**gal** ee ah) | Female | Age 21 | 5' 7" 138 lbs | Snail farmer from Bihnor and Elidria's best friend.

Aldameer - (**al** dah meer) | Male | Age 45 | 5' 11" 190 lbs | Bihnor's elder and master marksman. He is also Elidria's father.

Arlayna - (ar **lay** nah) | Female | Age - | 5' 4" 115 lbs | From Bihnor and mother of Elidria.

Galius - (**gal** ee us) | Male | Age 63 | 5' 10" 220 lbs | A royal guard from Dukla and master to Arviakyss.

Yera - (**yehr** ah) | Male | Age 54 | A turnip farmer and seller in Dukla.

Gypsy - (**jihp** see) | Male | Age 4 | 15 hands 1,050 lbs | A horse procured from Newville.

Pattermen - (**pah** ter men) | Male | Age 40 | The sheriff of Dukla and personal friend of Galius.

Raymar - (**ray** mahr) | Male | Age 46 | 5' 10" 189 lbs | Aldameer's best friend and Galia's father.

Merith - (**mar** ith) | Female | Age 46 | 5' 9" 155 lbs | Raymar's wife and Galia's mother.

Lucas - (**luke** us) | Male | Age 23 at time of Queen's death | 6' 0" 200 lbs | A royal guard and Arviakyss' partner.

Abi - (**a** bee) | Male | Age 4 | 15 hands 1,050 lbs | A name for Gypsy used to annoy Delsar.

Club - (club) | Male | Age Unknown | 5' 7" 230 lbs | The shorter of two thugs who assault women in Grandell's capital.

Dagger - (**dah** gehr) | Male | Age Unknown | 6' 5" 170 lbs | The taller of two thugs who assault women in Grandell's capital.

Yera - (**yer** ah) | Female | Age 44 | Morning shift dockmaster at Gandell's main port.

Roki - (**roh** kee) | Male | Age 43 | 6' 2" 205 lbs | A cook from Grandell's *Salty Crustacean* and ex-hunter.

Hirro - (hih lroh) | Male | Age 27 at death | Roki's best friend.

Glade - (glayd) | Male | Age 45 | 5' 9" 183 lbs | Survivor of Orange Peak and the only one able to escape to find help.

Wanda - (**wahn** dah) | Female | Age 69 | An elderly woman from Orange Peak that many consider the heart of the town.

The Shifter/Renon - (reh **non**) | Male | Age Unknown | 5' 5" 135 lbs | A snobby magic-user and scientist who can manipulate light and sound.

Thoms - (toms) | Male | Age 31 | A survivor of Orange Peak tasked with carrying Elidria.

Nikarat - (nee kah lrat) | Male | Age Unknown | A magic-user who can manipulate temperatures.

Cade - (cayd) | Male | Age 13 | 5' 0" 100 lbs | The son of Glade and Roki's rescuer.

Jaysahn - (jay **sahn**) | Male | Age 51 | The owner and barkeeper of Grandell's *Salty Crustacean*.

Jina - (**jee** nah) | Female | Age 38 | Grandell Library's librarian.

Nomar - (**noh** mahr) | Male | Age 25 | 5' 10" 190 lbs | Self-taught fisherman and navigator from Orange Peak.

Bekka - (**behk** ah) | Female | Age 39 | 5' 3" 121 lbs | Glade's wife and the only adult to go missing after the Orange Peak attack.

Treye - (tray) | Male | Age 54 | One of the first villagers from Bihnor to get shot and killed by mercenaries.

Raielyn - (**ray** lihn) | Female | Age 33 | One of the first villagers from Bihnor to get shot and killed by mercenaries.

Holder - (**huhl** dehr) | Male | Age 51 | Owner and operator of *Bellrock Voyage and Supplies.*

Soren - (**sor** ihn) | Male | Age 60 at death | 5' 10" 185 lbs | Single-father to Nomar and self-taught fisherman from Orange Peak.

Freya - (**fray** ah) | Female | Age 61 at death | Nomar's aunt and the older sister to Taiana.

Taiana - (tee **ah** nah) | Female | Age 33 at disappearance | Nomar's blood-mother who ran away after being defiled.

Jed - (jed) | Male | Age 49 | 5' 6" 210 lbs | Dockmaster who runs "Dock G" in Fairview.

Millicent - (**mihl** lih sent) | Female | Age 27 | 6' 2" 210 lbs | A surprisingly masculine woman who is easily agitated by any kind of disturbance.

Captain Jahvess - (**jah** vez) | Male | Age Unknown | 5' 5" 135 lbs | An alter-ego used by Renon.

Halamar - (**hal** ah mahr) | Male | Age 63 | 5' 11" 220 lbs | The crowned-king of Ithendar and husband to Queen Taharial.

Malgo - (**mahl** goh) | Male | Age Unknown | 6' 1" 199 lbs | The king's favorite advisor.

Phillious - (**fihl** lee us) | Male | Age 44 | 6' 1" 182 lbs | A divorced tailor from Midori Trails.

Margret - (**mahr** gret) | Female | Age 62 | Midori Trails' village caretaker.

Caalson - (**cahl** son) | Male | Age 38 | The sheriff of Midori Trails.

Taharial - (tah **hah** ree el) | Female | Age 54 at death | 5' 5" 130 lbs | The married-queen of Ithendar and sponsor of both Bihnor and the Queen's Champion.

Conah - (**coh** nah) | Male | Age 68 at death | Aldameer's father.

Lindsia - (**lind** see ah) | Female | Age 71 | 5' 4" 135 lbs | A retired wife who travels between her homes in Fairview and Stalton with her husband.

Ellis - (**el** lis) | Male | Age 70 | 5' 7" 169 lbs | A retired husband who travels back-and-forth between his homes in Fairview and Stalton with his wife.

Gareth - (**gar** ith) | Male | Age 23 | A royal guard who assisted with the capture of Delsar and Elidria outside of Stalton.

Wulner - (**wuhl** ner) | Male | Age 50 | 6' 2" 230 lbs | The mayor of Stalton.

Telrus - (**tehl** rihs) | Male | Age 19 | 5' 8" 158 lbs | A royal guard determined to clear Arviakyss' name and partner to Galius.

Bart - (bart) | Male | Age 30 | The royal guard assigned by Stalton's mayor to fetch Delsar's and Elidria's gear.

Juunsun - (**juhn** sun) | Male | Age 24 | The guard that Telrus assigned with finding the governor of Fairview.

Karrahn - (kah **rahn)** | Female | Age 40 | The governor of Lar's secretary and representative.

Amber - (**am** behr) | Female | Age 7 | 16.4 hands 1,380 lbs | Telrus' trusty steed.

Gendief the Razzmatazz (**gehn** deef - **rahz** mah tahz) | Male | Age 11 | 16.6 hands 1,400 lbs | A random horse that had no name when assigned to Delsar and Elidria.

Gorgan - (**gor** gahn) | Male | Age 42 | 6' 3" 240 lbs | The leader of the Darkened Wanderers and the man responsible for the ruthless killings in Bihnor.

Allbus - (**al** bus) | Male | Age 30 | 5' 11" 190 lbs | A royal guard assigned to the borders of Lar with his partner.

Castor - (**cast** or) | Male | Age 37 | 5' 9" 201 lbs | A royal guard assigned to the borders of Lar with his partner.

Ligrei - (**lee** gray) | Male | Age 42 | 6' 0" 180 lbs | Father to Delsar, he left his family right before his wife became ill.

Sevv - (sev) | Male | Age Unknown | A mercenary tasked with patrolling Bihnor.

Rolend - (**rol** nd) | Male | Age Unknown | A mercenary who faced-off versus Elidria in a blacksmith shop.

Fulcus - (**ful** cus) | Male | Age Unknown | A mercenary ready to fight Raymar to the death.

Faebella - (**fay** ah **bel** lah) | Female | Age 55 | One of the last remaining villagers in Bihnor.

Wyn - (wihn) | Male | Age 49 | One of the last remaining villagers in Bihnor.

Fil - (fihl) | Male | Age 56 | One of the last remaining villagers in Bihnor.

Onus - (**oh** nus) | Male | Age 38 | 6' 1" 200 lbs | One of three original members of the Darkened Wanderers. He served with Gorgan in the army before they left to become mercenaries.

Hastios - (**hay** stee ohs) | Male | Age Unknown | A member of the Darkened Wanderers.

Vinali - (**vihn** ah lee) | Male | Age Unknown | A member of the Darkened Wanderers.

Pozon - (**poh** zahn) | Male | Age 37 | 6' 0" 205 lbs | One of three original members of the Darkened Wanderers. He served with Gorgan in the army before they left to become mercenaries.

Navarre - (na **vahr**) | Male | Age Unknown | A member of the Darkened Wanderers.

Kharis - (**kahr** is) | Male | Age Unknown | A member of the Darkened Wanderers.

Iolrath - (**iy** ohl rath) | Male | Age Unknown | A member of the Darkened Wanderers.

Zaos - (**zay** ohs) | Male | Age Unknown | A member of the Darkened Wanderers.

Sandro - (**sahn** droh) | Male | Age Unknown | A member of the Darkened Wanderers.

Paris - (**payr** is) | Male | Age 54 | 6' 1" 205 lbs | Major in the royal guard, friend of Galius, and father to Telrus.

Jugack - (jue **gak**) | Male | Age Unknown | A member of the Darkened Wanderers and troll-keeper.

Novinri - (**nah** vin ree) | Male | Age Unknown | An unknown individual who was only mentioned.